An Unproductive Woman

Khaalidah Muhammad-Ali

An Unproductive Woman

*****

O ye who believe! seek help with patient perseverance and prayer: for Allah is with those who patiently persevere.

Qur'an 2:153 Surah Al-Baqarah (The Heifer)

Had it not been the will of Allah, I would not be here and I would not be able. Alhamdu Lillahi.

For my husband Muhammad. Thank you.
For my son Ali, my oldest critic and my newest inspiration. Thank you.
For my daughters Hadizah and Habibah, my girls and my strength, I thank Allah for you both. Thank you.
For Ibtisam who listened to each and every word. You have always been a friend. Thank you.
For Ade who read and critiqued and encouraged a Sister. Thank you.
To the rest of my family and those who always believed that I could. Thank you.

ONE

Today Fatima will arrive. She will be the new wife, the one who will give Adam the son that Asabe had not.

Asabe was in the kitchen, preparing food for the *walimah*. She privately prayed the new wife would not arrive. Already Fatima was quite late, two hours. Perhaps Asabe's prayers would be answered, and she would be left alone with Adam. Perhaps not.

Adam's agenda, though, was quite the opposite of Asabe's.

Adam stood beneath the cool winter sun at the end of the walk near the wire fence that surrounded his property. Adam shielded his eyes as he stared down the road for signs of an approaching vehicle in a billow of sepia colored dust.

Adam had never seen the woman who was to be his bride. However, he had in his possession one of her photographs, taken five years earlier when she was only nine years old. The photo revealed a thin girl, the color of sweet cinnamon with eyes large enough to drink up the world. She was awkward looking then; but now, Adam reasoned, she'd be a ripe young flower on the very threshold of her bloom. A woman. His bride. Adam was eager to compare the real face of his bride with the face he'd held in his heart for months. His eyes never wavered from the road in the distance.

Adam had never intended to take a second wife; he'd promised Asabe. That was before he knew that she would not give him a son. No children at all.

Even a whining girl would have been better than nothing.

"I've found the girl I intend to marry," Adam announced two months prior. "I know that you do not want me to marry again, but I must. If it disturbs you, if you find it too painful, I will divorce you if you like; but I know of no other man who would want an unproductive woman."

It was that simple. Adam had never been any good at mincing his words to sweeten the bitter. He had no time for that. But when he saw Asabe's face crumble in utter despair, he then wished he'd taken the time to stir in a little honey with the bitter inevitability he'd so tastelessly served her.

He owed her at the very least a bit of tact; after all, she had been a good wife. She'd been silent, not a nagging insect like other men's wives. She'd been obedient even when he knew she should have defied him. Even when she knew that his commands where merely his way of testing the depth of his power over her. A stroking of his tentative male ego. Yes, she had been a pleasant companion, so much so that in afterthought, Adam wished to take the words back and exchange them for softer words. Words that might cushion her bruised heart.

Nothing he said would have mattered. If he made his words of less effect, Asabe would have seen it as a wavering of his determination. She would have exploited the perceived weakness to convince him to abandon his plans. She would have begged him, undignified, on her knees. And then, her heart would be crushed over and over again when he told her the truth. That yes, his desire for a son was far greater than his love for her. He would readily sacrifice her.

Asabe knew from the outset that any argument would be futile. She knew not to give ultimatums because the answers were evident.

In the two months since Asabe had known, she recovered quite nicely, it seemed to Adam. She even agreed to cook for the walimah. Of all the things Adam loved about Asabe, it was her cooking that he loved best. Too bad for Asabe, her cooking wasn't good enough to keep him from turning to another woman.

Adam heard the determined grumble of an engine struggling its way down the unpaved road long before his eyes ever caught sight of it.

Could this be her?

It seemed like forever had passed before the car finally ambled its way to him. His heart was pounding in his chest. His stomach was uneasy.

"You'd think I was myself a virgin about to take my first bride." He chuckled to himself. How silly, how juvenile, how desperately he could not help himself. How unlikely it was for a man of his age and stature to be standing on the tips of his toes, happily grinning and squinting his failing eyes to get the first peek of his bride.

Disappointment prevailed as the third tardy hour came and went. It was not her, but the ragged '82 Honda Civic of his neighbor and best friend, Jabar. Adam waved, but Jabar seemed not to notice his anxious friend. He idled by in his beaten auto, not once glancing in Adam's direction.

Just as Adam was about to call out to his friend, he heard in the distance the faint grind of another engine. This engine sounded smooth and oily from care. It moved with purpose.

Impressive clouds of red dust floated above the road, a calling card, a promise to Adam of better and more to come. This coming would be the fulfillment of his dreams and the reality of Asabe's nightmares all wrapped up in a small brown girl.

This was one of few times that Adam could recall in all his fifty-two years that his expectations were not only met but also exceeded. He did not see the real Fatima who stepped haltingly from the back door of the grimy taxi. He saw only the vision his hungry imagination had dreamed. He failed to notice that she had not yet approached her season of bloom, that the girl who stood ducking behind her father, refusing to meet his eyes, was scarcely different from the wide-eyed wonder that stared back at him from the worn photograph he kept in his breast pocket.

Adam embraced the father of the bride, a friend from his days at university in the States, and led them both inside. Greetings were exchanged, stories of their years apart were told, lamented over, concern was expressed regarding their own personal difficulties.

We all have them, thank Allah.

Truly Adam wanted to reminisce with this friend of his, but he was terribly anxious, as though a few minutes more mattered at all. Adam reasoned to himself, though, that at his age, each minute was definitely of consequence. Already he'd wasted so many of his years exploring life's trivialities, tasting vice, dissecting sin, a life that he was too ashamed to admit even to himself. His conscience couldn't survive it.

This made him wonder why his longtime friend. Yahya knew the worst of Adam's secrets; still, he was giving the hand of his callow daughter to Adam. It was as if he'd never known him. Yet it was Yahya who proposed the startling match.

"There are eight children, and their mother is now dead. I cannot afford to feed them all, so the mature must go. Besides, the eldest are girls. They cannot be allowed to attain full maturity while I sit and look on. It would be a shame for me."

Yahya would have begged Adam, if need be, to take Fatima in marriage; but this was not necessary. Of course Adam played the game, as if he was only obliging an old friend, for mercy's sake. Too much interest would have been vulgar. But interested he was, and Yahya knew it to be so. They both went on in a haze of semideception, respecting each other's pretense.

Asabe offered tea and biscuits to the worn travelers, but the small man graciously refused, requesting only a kettle of clear water for ablution and a rug for prayer.

"I regret I cannot stay. I must be leaving within the next hour if I am to take the next train back to Mali." He offered a smile full of yellowed and missing teeth.

In the name of Allah, Adam thought to himself, *time has not been kind to him. Is this the proud braggart I knew so many years ago?*

Fatima remained silent, neither accepting nor declining Asabe's offer. Her wonderful eyes did not leave the lone brown suitcase she clutched on her lap.

Once Adam had seen to his friend's departure, he set out in search of Asabe. He found her in the kitchen, diligently preparing the feast for the walimah scheduled for that evening. The odor consumed the room and rose in puffs of thick steam from well-used pots. The scent, an intoxicating amalgamation of sweet spices, fiery peppers, and bitter herbs, caused Adam's mouth to water like a rabid dog's.

"Have you seen her?" he asked like an excited child. "She's very pretty, isn't she?"

Asabe said nothing to this.

"She will have many children, she will fill my house with sons," he bragged.

"If Allah wills," said Asabe. She stirred the stew boiling in the stockpot atop the stove.

"Let me taste," he said, leaning forward.

Asabe let a few oily drops fall into the palm of his hand.

"Needs salt." Adam poured a few granules of salt into the bubbling concoction. "That should do just fine." He was smiling a hideous grin.

"Now," he said, rubbing his palms together, "I want you to go show Fatima to her room. Talk to her awhile. Make her feel at home."

"I cannot leave the kitchen. I must attend to the food." It was the best excuse Asabe could summon.

"You can leave the kitchen, and you will," he insisted, "and the food had better be right." The grin reappeared. "Go now, and welcome your sister."

"My sister, and your granddaughter," Asabe mumbled into the pot of stew.

"What did you say?" he asked.

They both knew that Adam heard her just fine.

"I said that I would be glad to."

"Wonderful." Grinning, grinning. "Do you think there is enough salt in the stew?"

"Don't concern yourself, Adam. I will take care of every detail. Have confidence in me." Asabe tried to match his grin. "The food will be memorable to all who eat it. Believe me."

SO MANY VOLUMPTUOUS WOMEN, hovering, smiling, probing the bride with giddy questioning eyes. *How old is she?* they wanted to inquire but dared not. They watched the little woman, stealing glances from over plates of unfinished food, shattering conversations with glances held too long. They could not help themselves. She was a sight, and obviously of meager means.

The food was salty enough to make a sane man drink his own blood.

Asabe must not be herself.

None of the ladies complained. If their husbands had dared ask them to cook for his wedding to another woman, they too would have sabotaged the food or at least given it serious consideration. So they politely accepted small helpings of the food and paid the chef the highest compliment there is.

You must give me the recipe.

Some of the men quietly led Adam aside to warn him of the fury of women done wrong. "Discipline her now, and harshly, brother, or she will think this behavior acceptable. Women are a trial. Sometimes you have to treat them as children."

Fatima cared not about the flavor of the food. She abandoned her utensils and spooned the brackish food into her mouth using her fingers. She was starved and undernourished, anyone could tell. She had gaunt cheeks, limp wrists, and a thin little back humped over in order to cradle her concave belly. It wasn't until the food, piled high, was placed before her that she seemed revived from her listless trance.

"Eat, young bride!" cheered the women around her.

And she did, diving in like a woman trying to save her drowning child. For dear life.

Once Fatima had filled her shrunken gut until it hurt, she was able to fully comprehend all that was happening around her. The women crowded around her were dressed in their most treasured attire. They assembled for her sake, to welcome and congratulate her on her marriage.

They seemed genuine. The glittering impractical gifts they'd given her were proof of their generosity. Fatima could detect no hidden agenda in their faces. They looked upon her with tender eyes; Fatima always looked to the eyes. Strangers though they were, Fatima felt a certain buffered comfort among them and dreaded the approaching hour when they would inevitably depart for their own homes.

Then, she'd be left alone and unprotected in the house with the bitter, sorrowful first wife and the husband who lurks in dark corners, watching, watching, trying to swallow her with his eyes.

Adam was nothing that Fatima hoped and everything she feared, a hoary old man with a hungry face. The moment she glimpsed him through the taxi window, her heart sank.

Clutched in her damp hand had been the photo her father had given her of her husband-to-be. She hadn't really believed Baba when he told her the photo was recent. It was considerably yellowed, and the young man with slick black skin pictured within wore antiquated Western-style clothing. She did not expect to see the man in the photo, not the same exact man. But at least some semblance of him. Perhaps he would be a bit broader around the shoulders, or perhaps he had developed a bit of a paunch. Fatima expected some of the youthful shine would have worn away. Some of it, but not all.

The sly smiling man who was her new husband was far more than a little heavier. Adam had grown more than a paunch. He had a head full of knotty white hairs that framed a face ample with folds and lines, especially around his eyes. His eyes, behind spectacles in bad need of wiping. His eyes that kept probing her, even then as he knelt in the shadows behind the curtained archway that led into the dining room beyond.

The male guests could be heard in the distance. They were in the garden, laughing and speaking among themselves. Adam had abandoned them all in preference of creeping in the shadows to steal glances at a helpless girl.

And then Fatima knew the most terrific anger. Had it not been for her fear of Allah, she would without remorse quit the house of the man who was her husband and flee to anyplace else. Anyplace.

To Fatima, it felt almost incestuous that Adam, who very closely resembled her recently deceased grandfather, was eyeing her with ravenous eyes. Already, she hated him and his home, a prison far from the only home she ever knew, and her seven brothers and sisters. More than anything, Fatima was sure of her hatred for Baba.

Baba barely allowed three months to pass after her mother's death to marry Fatima off. It did not matter to him that she did not want the marriage or that for two months she cried herself to sleep because of it. Baba didn't care that her mother had always wanted Fatima to finish high school before being married. Nothing mattered, except getting her married, getting her out.

Fatima eventually resigned herself to Baba's verdict and prayed to Allah to make her future husband a young man from one of the better-known families in her quarter. Even a poor man would have been acceptable, as long as she wasn't far from home. Fatima prayed with more sincerity than she ever devoted to any prayer that Baba would be merciful in the decision he made concerning her life, and she became confident that he would be. Fatima simply would not allow herself to entertain any other thought, for if she had, she would have gone mad.

This is why Fatima half believed Baba when he said, "Oh no, this photo is only two years old."

She half believed even when he avoided looking into her face. She half believed even when he said that she would be moving five hundred miles away.

She half believed even when Baba said it would be best because she had to believe that her father would never place his first child in harm's way.

Fatima had to believe, even now when every promise was proved a lie.

"YOU'RE BEHAVING LIKE AN INFANT, Asabe. You have a house full of guests, and all you can do is sit in your room sulking and pouting."

Asabe's mother stood before the dresser mirror, tugging at her blouse.

"Definitely gaining weight," she mumbled to herself. She retied the scarf on her head.

Asabe watched her mother with growing disinterest. She valued her mother's advice and was often afraid to contradict her mother's suggestions. In the past, her wisdom had been invaluable. This time, however, Asabe didn't care to hear what her mother thought she should do. Asabe didn't care to even see her mother.

"Let the new bride tend to her own guests. I've already done enough." Asabe could taste the bitter words in her mouth.

"Your presence will assure her that she is welcomed in this home by all. She will know that there are no hard feelings."

Asabe could barely unclench her throat to speak. Her voice was guttural and strained. "Good, because I don't welcome her, and the feelings are hard."

"She hasn't done anything to cause you harm, Asabe."

"She's here, isn't she?"

"Yes, she is, but have you seen her? She is even younger than you were when you married Adam. She is an innocent little girl. Have mercy on her. Besides, from the look on her dour face, I suspect she has no desire to be here. I'll bet that she's even afraid. I know that I would be."

"I don't care," lied Asabe.

Even then Asabe was struggling to contain the tears stinging at the back of her eyes. Asabe cared more than her pride would allow her to express. The very reality that her new cowife was a mere child was difficult for Asabe to reconcile herself with. Not only had Adam sought another woman to bear his children, but also the woman she'd now compete with for her husband's affections was no woman at all, but a child. A child who probably hadn't seen her first blood.

Asabe wished she was the cold, brash type. She wished she had the nerve to say all the things she'd been practicing in her mirror for two months.

I am Adam's wife. You are just the vehicle through which he will have his son and nothing more. So don't go getting any grand ideas about running this household because I am the wife. I am my husband's confidant, and you are of no consequence. You are nothing, you hear? Nothing, nothing, nothing at all.

Asabe could never say those things; it would be the worst lie she would ever have the indignity to tell. Even if she had ever been so disillusioned as to believe her words, Adam had effectively crashed down those misconceptions the moment she saw him set his eyes upon the beautiful brown woman-child.

Adam was proud of his new bride. His back was straight, his chest full. It had been a long time since Asabe had seen him this way. During the walimah, he asked for silence while he said a prayer of thanks.

"Thank you, Allah, for my health, peace, and this abiding happiness. Thank you for bringing these people here to share in my joy. And lastly, thank you for my new wife, young and beautiful Fatima." Then he cheered, "May she have many sons." It wasn't until someone in the crowded room called out, "And your first wife?" that Adam added, "Oh yes, and Asabe, my kind, intelligent wife."

Already, she was virtually forgotten.

Asabe crumbled in her seat. The words were flat and hollow. Forced. Worthless. Not enough to keep her from running from the room like a meek child tripping up the stairs. All her grace and intelligence had evaporated like a shallow puddle on a scorching day.

Asabe resembled her mother, with skin the color of a black plum, lucid oil-pool eyes, and fleshy lips. She was confident of her beauty until she saw the passion with which Adam gazed upon his new bride's face and the way the other men's mouths curled with envy. Then she realized that perhaps she had never been beautiful. No one, not even her own husband, had ever gazed at her with such unmasked longing.

The inadequacy was enough for Asabe to struggle with. How many women would be overjoyed at the prospect of sharing her husband with another woman? Asabe did not expect her mother's defense of the young interloper.

"Have you abandoned me too?" said Asabe. "Have you forgotten that I am your daughter? Not her. I should be the one you defend. I am the one with the broken heart." This time the tears fell.

"I was once in the very same position as Fatima," her mother began. "I was your father's fourth wife. Have you forgotten that I didn't have a friend in that house? Not even your father, my husband, would defend me against the plots of his other wives." Asabe could see the relived pain on her mother's face.

"Do you recall the way those women abused you, leaving lumps and knots all over your tiny head, simply because you were my child?" Hannah trembled with years of delayed fury. Asabe could not summon the words, not the slightest sound in reply.

"No, Asabe. I have not forgotten whose mother I am. How could I forget you, my only child in the world? But I wouldn't wish on Satan himself what was unleashed upon me by those vengeful, jealous women."

Hannah sat next to her daughter on the bed. With her arm cradled around Asabe's shoulders, she said, "I know that your heart aches, believe me I do, but that girl is alone with not a real friend in sight. She is not the source of your pain, it is your pride that ails you. It was Adam's decision to marry again, and it was also his right before Allah himself. There is nothing you can do but accept the way of things. Make yourself available to her. Be an ally. In Fatima, you may find the best friend you'll ever have."

Asabe sobbed into the crook of her mother's neck. Asabe took solace in the words her mother whispered in her ear while she cried. "All things happen by the command of Allah, be they good or bad. Be assured that this situation will turn out for the better, *Insha Allah.*"

TWO

The clothes were more beautiful than any Fatima had ever owned or even dreamed of owning in all her young life. She was captivated by the silks that cascaded like the waves of a waterfall through her fingers. She could barely comprehend the varied hues she never knew were possible anywhere but in nature. The blinding saffrons, the burning vermilions, the royal emeralds and blues—she wished to wear them all at one and the same time.

Often she did, piling one blouse atop the other, a wrapper skirt over an intricately embroidered caftan, just to feel the cool slickness of the fabrics against her skin, skin grown used to the coarseness of handwoven hemp, cheap cotton, and beggar's cloth.

If Fatima had been able, she would have even worn two pairs of shoes at once for no other reason than to hear the tick ticking of the short heels against the kitchen tile or the concrete outside. Her feet had never felt the inside of a shoe, only the flat resoluteness of secondhand thongs. It took some time to become accustomed to the feel of leather encasing and binding her entire foot, but she terribly fancied the absence of sand on the soles of her feet.

No one knew that sometimes Fatima would wear her new shoes to bed, not even her husband. She locked her bedroom door at night, and for good measure, she'd push an old bureau in its way. Fatima did this in the instance that she fell asleep, which she rarely did. When she did not have the strength to keep her eyelids from falling, Fatima would use her fingers to hold her eyes open by the very lashes themselves, or she would pinch the tender flesh on the inside of her upper arm until it was black and blue.

Fatima was afraid of Adam. He kept smiling at her with his eyes. It did not matter to Fatima that it was because of Adam that she gained nearly ten pounds in the month that she was in his home. It did not matter to her that because of him, gaudy gold trinkets dangled from her stressed earlobes and from around her delicate neck like ropes.

Donning neither her robe nor her slippers, Asabe entered the hallway. Fatima stood in the doorway of her bedroom. Not one tear stained her perfect cocoa-dusted face, only the ugliness of terror and disgust. But still Fatima continued to holler.

Asabe led Fatima, her cowife, the child, into the unkempt bedroom and sat her on the bed. Asabe sat next to her, intending to wrap her arms around the girl and whisper a few agreeable words into her ear. But before she could, Fatima plunged her thin frame into the curve of Asabe's own. She nuzzled her soft angular face into Asabe's neck. Asabe could feel Fatima draw in her scent.

Asabe removed Fatima's scarf. Her smallish head wore an ocean of wavy blackness. Now she seemed even smaller, even younger than before.

Asabe stroked her hair. They rocked together, back and forth until Fatima was purring like a feline. Through this one act of empathy, they became like mother and child. Between them was sealed a trust that would not end until death returned one of them to the realm of the one god.

"WHAT ARE YOU TELLING ME FOR?" asked Jabar. "I told you not to marry that infant in the first place. I told you, but you did not listen."

"She isn't an infant, she's a young woman. My wife. What is so wrong with me that she'd vomit and scream when I come to her? You'd think I was an ogre."

"To her, you probably are." Jabar grinned and leaning forward on the sofa. "Did she really vomit?"

"Yes," confirmed Adam, trying to hide a smile. He couldn't, and they both burst into several minutes of uncontrollable stress-relieving laughter. With their sides sore and spasmodic, Adam grew serious. "Do you really think that I've made a mistake?"

"Brother Adam, it's still too soon to know. Wasn't Asabe around the same age when you married her?"

"Yes, but she loved me from the start. She never locked her door to me, even when she was angry. She's never looked at me in disgust, never uttered a harsh word." Adam threw up his hands. "But this girl has told me straight out, 'I hate you.'"

"What do you expect? She's been dragged far from her home and family. This might as well be another world. And look at you. You aren't just an older man, but a man who is old."

"You're older than I am."

"Perhaps I am, but I haven't married a child either. What you've done is unsound. There are so many ways for it to go wrong, her being so young."

"Prophet Muhammad married Aisha when she was only nine, and he was fifty-four."

"But you are no prophet. You, my old friend, have not been a man of virtue all of your life. In fact, it wasn't until you married Asabe that you became respectable." Jabar pointed a thick finger at Adam. "If you recall, I stopped speaking to you for two months after you married Asabe. You never knew why, did you?"

Adam squinted his eyes in an effort to conjure up the ten-year-old memory. "No, I never knew why."

"I was angry with you for marrying Asabe. She was fifteen and positively innocent. She was my daughter's classmate. She used to come to my home to visit. When I looked at Asabe, all I could see was my own daughter, and I knew that I would never have given my daughter in marriage to a man such as yourself."

"How could you insult me? Aren't we friends?"

"Friend or not, I speak the truth, and the truth is that you were once a drinking man. You fornicated. When that weighed too heavily on your conscience, you married an unbeliever. As it turns out, that too was a farce. You only married that woman to get a green card so that you could remain in the States. What you didn't count on was that she would give up everything to be with you. You never expected her to submit to you or Islam. Then you deserted her and the child you made together.

"You weren't qualified to marry someone like Asabe. Like my daughter. And now, you've done it again. I feel no sympathy for your situation. If it is pity that you were hoping for, you've come to the wrong house."

Adam knew when he walked across the field between their homes that he would get no coddling. Fortunately, Adam was not in search of coddling.

Jabar and Adam were as close as brothers, had been since childhood; and despite the twenty years and a massive ocean that had once separated them, they'd managed to maintain a comfortable rapport, if not mutual respect. Jabar was as just and honest a man as Adam knew. Just the sort of man to go to with his sort of problem.

"I've been thinking that perhaps I should send her back to her family. Maybe I have made a mistake."

"Could be, but it's already done. Send her back now and you'll prove that you are no more than a selfish man. Stupid too."

"How so?"

"A divorced woman will never be able to raise herself to the esteem as that of a virgin regardless of how young or beautiful she is. You will have cursed her value in the eyes of others. Her future prospects for marriage will be no better than you, old men who already have wives. No young man will want to marry her."

"But she's not happy, that is obvious. Any woman who vomits because her husband wants to touch her obviously doesn't care one bit about him. Staying with me may be just as much a curse as letting her go."

"I wouldn't worry about that." Jabar waved his hand in dismissal. "She's in your home, and thus far, you've only been kind to her. Be patient. Love takes longer for some than others. If you send her back, how will you get the son you've been praying for?"

Adam stood before the grand bay window in Jabar's living room. The view, a field of dry grass three feet tall, looked like an ocean that waved and tumbled even when the wind stood silent.

The yellow stars winked at him, so it seemed, in an eternal joke. The clouds that half hid the full moon resembled hands over the mouth of a pie-faced joker, trying its best to suppress laughter.

Was the entire world laughing at him?

Not the grass or the moon or the laughing pitch sky interested Adam as much as what lay beyond. His home stood in the distance, cloaked by the waving grass and darkness.

Two hours earlier, Adam fled from his own home in an effort escape the horrible screams of his wife. Fatima's voice had sent icy bolts down his spine. She, an exquisite beauty, had turned into a fearsome creature, with her mouth stretched open. A sliver of saliva vibrated with each exhalation, and her fingers bent into frozen claws attacked the air. And him.

Had it not been for Jabar's harsh words, Adam would have been content to remain at Jabar's home, a frightened refugee seeking asylum from a child he was too ashamed to face.

"Get out and go home, you fool." With a sturdy hand on his elbow, Jabar led Adam to the door. "Unless you're afraid."

Adam was afraid; but with his courage, conviction, and manhood challenged all at once, he had to pretend.

"Afraid? No, not me," Adam said. "What have I to fear?"

"Exactly," agreed Jabar. "Now, get going. As-salaam alaikum."

Jabar shoved Adam out of the door and closed it before Adam could respond. The last thing Adam heard was the click of the latch. He had no choice at all except to conquer his own fears and walk into his home the man he'd failed to leave as.

Adam smelled the morning coming in, a damp expectancy that clung to the chilled air. The sun-dried grass moved around his hips as he walked through the field toward his home. Like a frightened rabbit, Adam's ears were piqued to catch the faintest sound. Anything would be reason enough to send him heading back to Jabar's house.

Above the sounds of cackling roosters and the songs of birds awakening, Adam heard the soulful voice of a muezzin in the minaret of a mosque in the distance, calling men to prayer.

"Allahu Akbar, Allahu Akbar."

A cleansing breeze moved through the field and pushed Adam along, closer to home than he wished, faster than he wished.

"Allahu Akbar, Allahu Akbar."

The wind swirled around his head, lifting his loose camise away from his body, whispering, whistling in his ear.

"Ash hadu anla ilaha illa lah. Ash hadu anla ilaha illa lah."

This would be the first day he'd missed dawn prayers in the mosque in over eight years. The last time had been due to an illness that had fevered him into delirium. This time, he was ashamed to admit, was because he'd lost count of the time . . .

"Ash hadu anna Muhammadar Rasooluhu. Ash hadu anna Muhammadar Rasooluhu."

Because he'd run away from home . . .

"Hai Allah salah. Hai Allah salah."

Because he'd fled from the bedroom of his own wife. She should have been begging *him*. As suddenly as the winds changed direction was his uncertainty replaced by anger. On the road to his right, Jabar's car sputtered and sped down the road past him. Jabar had no problems. He would be in the mosque for dawn prayers.

"Hai Allah falah. Hai Allah falah."

But Adam would miss dawn prayers in the mosque this morning, shoulder to shoulder, foot to foot, with men of faith and all because of a screaming wench. Never again, he decided, stomping off toward the house.

"Allahu Akbar, Allahu Akbar."

She'd either submit her whole self to him or leave on the next bus to her hometown a divorced woman and as poor and sickly as the day that she arrived.

"La ilaha illa lah!"

Through the door, roughly, wishing to unhinge it, Adam strode sure footed and alive with resolve. He stopped in the front corridor. The darkness enveloped him like a blanket. Adam moved through the darkness toward the sound of their voices, through the living room and down the hallway toward the kitchen. The bright light in the kitchen beyond poured from the seams of the door like a halo.

Fatima was in the kitchen, and Adam was prepared to lay down the law. *Submit or leave* hung from his tongue like a heavy bead of water about to drip from a leaking faucet.

Submit or leave.

Adam burst through the door, offering no greeting, only an ironhard face and his rehearsed words as ready to be fired as the bullets in an automatic weapon. Both women were present. Adam had startled them, though not enough to scare the smiles from their beaming faces or extinguish their laughter.

Asabe and Fatima were sitting together at the kitchen table, bowls of half-finished porridge still steaming before them. The teapot screeched a streak of cinnamon- and clove-scented steam. They all stared at one another.

The words he'd planned to use melted away. The sight of their faces, glowing with smiles he'd not thought possible from two such solemn creatures, robbed him of his breath just as if someone had landed a powerful kick to his chest.

Adam never imagined he would see Asabe smile again as long as Fatima was there. It was an assumption he'd grown comfortable with that he'd almost begun to welcome. Now, there was laughter and broad smiles between the two of them, virtual strangers just the previous day. They now leaned tenderly across the table toward each other. They were caught sharing a secret, a laugh, a bit of self.

The anger returned. Sweat beaded on his nose and forehead. Adam was prepared to joyfully release upon his women the very rage that threatened to burn him up. How dare they display any joy or contentment while he was seething with anger and confusion. Adam's fury was fully renewed.

"There is going to be a change in this house," he announced, "and it will begin with the newest member of our household. Fatima." Adam pointed an accusing finger in her direction. His mouth watered. He was just getting started. Just.

Adam would gain no satisfaction in this encounter; he would not reaffirm his manhood and would not be afforded the pleasure of such a venomous release of emotion.

"You are right, husband," said Fatima, rising from the table. She approached Adam dolefully and knelt before him on one knee. "If my mother were alive, she would have caned me for my insolence. Allah must be angry with me." Fatima gingerly closed his large hand in her two.

Adam half expected her to kiss his hand.

"If I have caused you pain or anger in any way, please forgive me. I've been a dreadful wife I know, but if you'll give me a chance, I will prove to you that I am worth the trouble."

Fatima gazed up into Adam's face. There was no reaction. He was speechless.

"Please?" she added.

Adam reluctantly conceded, nodding his head.

She stoops to conquer.

Adam got what he wanted—submission—though the victory wasn't so sweet as he'd hoped.

"Oh, thank you," yelped Fatima like an excited puppy. Fatima glanced over her shoulder, in the direction of the whistling kettle. "Let me get you a cup of tea," she offered, "before you make your prayers."

Did I see her skipping to the stove? Adam asked himself.

Asabe. Adam had almost forgotten her. She sat at the table, grinning impudently at his confusion.

Adam wasn't foolish enough to believe that it was his own charms that altered his new bride's mind. Only eight hours earlier, she vomited at the sight of him, and now, she was kneeling at his feet and begging his forgiveness. Of her own free will. Adam knew that it was because of Asabe that Fatima would deign to cast a glance in his direction, let alone submit to his will.

Adam had even less control over the affairs of his household and his women than he realized.

Asabe never wanted Adam's marriage to Fatima. Still, Adam reneged on his word never to take another wife, abandoning her because of her inability to produce. It wasn't Asabe's fault that she could not give him a son. Yet Asabe gave to Adam his second chance with the young bride with whom he was infatuated from the first moment he laid eyes on her.

Adam knew he owed Asabe a debt of gratitude he might never be able to repay.

THREE

The air was as hot and torpid as the inside of a vacuum, the violent sun refusing to let go its grip of the land. On occasion, drifts of scalding air would blow, lifting handfuls of sand, swirling and lifting them into tiny spiraling tornadoes no higher than a foot, but just as impressive in form. This was the extent of the relief.

Men retreated to the soft earth beneath mango trees to take advantage of the shade. Women deserted their kitchens for their bedrooms where modesty could be lax and clothes could be cast off for comfort's sake.

The house was still. Adam, in the torrid onslaught, had become scarce. Fatima soaked her plumping limbs in a cold-water bath upstairs. Asabe sat in a dark corner of the prayer room amid a mass of thick pillows. She was alone, but for Kasuar, who sat purring beneath her knowing hands on her lap. Tiny rivulets of perspiration ran from her brow to her chin.

Asabe lay in wait.

Asabe sat beneath a window and had a full view of the long dusty road that entered their property from town. She was expecting a guest, though unwelcome.

Asabe closed her eyes, about to sink into a heat-induced sleep, when she heard the crunch of gravel outside. She rose from the bed of pillows, nearly toppling the dozing cat, and straightened her garment. She ran to the front of the house.

From the front door, Asabe watched the Mercedes come to a halt in front of the house. Asabe headed outside, a lone greeting party.

A tiny elder man exited the driver's side and scurried around to the rear left door murmuring, "Coming, madam. Coming."

Asabe was disgusted that a man of his age would be running to and fro, undignified like a juvenile, for the pleasure of such a person.

Asabe felt a cool blast of air escape when the driver opened the door. Then there she stood, all six feet two inches of her. She was the most fiercely black woman Asabe had ever known in her life. It was Attiyah, Adam's eldest living sister.

"As-salaam alaikum," greeted Asabe. "Welcome. It is so good to see you again." Asabe leaned forward and embraced the giant woman. Attiyah was as stiff as the trunk of a tree. Any sort of physical display was beneath her sister-in-law, but for the satisfaction of causing Attiyah discomfort, Asabe was willing.

"Yes, well," Attiyah said, looking down her nose, "it is also a pleasure to see you again, though I'm surprised that you haven't left."

"Why would I leave, sister? This is my home."

"Yes, but you have been replaced, haven't you?"

Asabe's mouth was suddenly as dry as parchment paper.

Touché.

Attiyah smiled, pleased to know the power she held over Asabe. Her ability to disturb Asabe had not waned.

"My, my, it is hot out here isn't it? May we go inside out of this violence, or am I not welcomed anymore?" She was still grinning winningly.

It was a vicious game that Attiyah played with Asabe, well aware that there was nothing Asabe could do to put her out of the house. Attiyah had given the home to Adam and could take it back. It was partly because of Attiyah that their lives had been such an easy road.

"Of course, please come inside."

"It is good to know that you still have manners, if nothing else."

Attiyah headed for the house. Once inside, Attiyah unfolded a pair of ancient-looking wire-rimmed spectacles and placed them on the end of her ample nose. She began an intense scrutiny of the surroundings, remaining silent except for the occasional *humph*.

Her lips were crimped into a frown so natural to her masculine face that it was almost attractive. Her disapproval was obvious and expected.

"My brother, where is he?"

"I'm not sure. I haven't seen him for hours."

"Of course you don't know where he is, I mean, I suspect these days he doesn't tell you much of anything. Oh well," she said, waving her hand in dismissal, "that's the way life is sometimes." Attiyah snorted with satisfaction. "Perhaps the new wife, Fatima, will know where he is. Where is she?"

"Upstairs. I'll go fetch her."

"No need," she said, placing a wrinkled hand on Asabe's shoulder. "I'll go up and introduce myself. Meanwhile, why don't you make yourself useful and bring us up a pot of tea and some of those coconut biscuits you're so good at making. Oh yes," she called out from the top of the stairs, "give my driver something to drink. He's not a young man, you know."

This was not the first time that Asabe was forced to delve inward for the strength to restrain herself from lunging at the old woman with her hands primed for the throat. She had to remind herself, time and again, of Attiyah's age and the fact that she was family.

Asabe found Rashid wiping dust from the hood of the midnight blue Mercedes, his balding head beaded with sweat. "Father," she called to him in respect, "please come in where it is cooler."

She handed him a glass of cool water, which he emptied before replying. Out of breath he said, "Your kindness is appreciated, but I must complete my work, or the madam will not be pleased."

"You are probably old enough to be the madam's father. Surely, she won't mind if you rest a few minutes."

"Oh," he said, laughing, "you don't know how she can be when her orders aren't heeded."

"As a matter of fact I do, but if I were you, I am not sure that I would care."

"She pays me well for my services, young one. For that, I care."

"Is it enough to tolerate the indignity?"

"She's not so bad. She has suffered far more than she could ever inflict. Believe an old man when he says so. You are aware of the ugliness of her life. She could be worse."

"Her experience is exactly the reason that she should have learned to be merciful. There is no acceptable excuse for her behavior.

The old man said nothing.

Asabe accepted the empty glass and headed back toward the house. When she turned back, she saw that the old man had gone back to his work.

"When you are ready to come in, you may use the back door. The first room on the right is the coolest in the house. The second door on the right is the restroom."

"Insha Allah" He never looked up, continuing to scrub the gleaming hood.

FOR DAYS, ADAM wrote and rewrote the letter. Dozens of times he'd began, My Dearest Son, My Only Son, My Beloved Son, Son, only to tear the otherwise blank sheet of paper from the pad and send it in a wadded ball to the trash basket. He'd sit at his desk, full of purpose and concentration, with balls of papers surrounding him; but the right words never came.

Adam awoke from a nap one afternoon to find Asabe moving silently around his room, scooping up handfuls of wadded papers. She was opening them, smoothing out the coarse creases with the palm of her hand.

"Such a waste," she whispered to herself.

Like a gunshot, Adam leaped from the bed and confiscated the wrinkled beginnings. Thank Allah she hadn't read any of them. He would not have been able to explain the numbered salutations including the word *son*. There would have been no fitting explanation, none that would have washed away the lie on his face.

Hiding things from Asabe had never been a problem, but telling an outright lie was near impossible. Adam was simply no good at the game of deception, and Asabe could smell a lie before it ever passed from his lips. Fortunately, Adam's skills as a liar were not put to the test. She did not inquire that day.

She would never understand and would quite possibly never forgive him. Adam had spent years giving Asabe the cold shoulder because her blood would come every month without fail, because she had not given him a son.

And all along, he already had a son.

She would never understand the emptiness that flooded his heart at the loss of his only son. She would only see the lies he'd told her. She would realize that he was using her to recreate a past that she had no knowledge of. It wasn't fair to deceive her and then blame her for not measuring up to an imperfect past.

But he so much wanted to have a son, to have his son back, to leave an imprint on the world greater than the sins he'd committed in his life. Adam had been a failure at faith, admittedly so, always fluctuating wildly between devotion and depravity. It was his hope to at least leave upon the face of the earth one living soul that he could teach to be better than himself, to have a greater fear of Allah, whose propensity was not toward daring the benevolence of Allah such as he had done all his life.

Adam wished for a living redeemer, a righteous intercessor between him and Allah on Judgment Day. A good son.

Adam had named his son Mu'min, "guardian of faith." Twelve years had passed since he had last seen his son. The first time Adam held the burgeoning life of Mu'min in his arms, there was pride. But now, his very pride was a secret.

Adam knew that he had never deserved such a virtuous wife as Asabe, kind and purely innocent in all respects. He had not deserved to have a woman as sweet as she, wholly unencumbered by a past of shame. This he did not allow to stop him. He lied and prayed upon the ignorance and naiveté of Asabe and her family so that he could have her. She was the prize he had not acquired by fair play.

Yes, he was an approaching middle-aged man, but he possessed the virtue of a man half his age.

Lie.

Yes, he had spent sixteen years living in the West; but no, he had not indulged in its corruption and decadence.

Lie.

He had just been waiting to come home to marry one of his own. Allah as a witness, he would have kept himself into decrepit old age before he would ever wed a Westerner. They were not his cultural and religious equals. They were beneath him.

Lies, lies, all lies. Lies so ingrained in him that time had nearly transformed them into reality.

It was a sad irony, for despite her barren womb, despite the coolness Adam had showed her in the past, despite the young new future he'd recently wed, Asabe was his best friend in life. She was the only human being outside of Jabar that he trusted with his vulnerabilities and his secrets. Now in the depth of his most terrible heartache, he was forced to let the secret lie. He could not seek his consort or her soothing words.

Adam hardly noticed the people moving around him. He did not attempt to hide the tears slipping from his eyes. He let them fall freely onto the completed letter he held in his trembling hands. For two weeks he'd been conjuring the letter, unsuccessfully, until then. In the midst of the busy post office on a torn scrap of yellow paper, he penned the letter, without once pausing to think of just the right phrase or to scratch out a word. He wrote and wrote with aching fingers and burning heart until both the lead of his pencil and his words were exhausted.

My Beloved Son,

It has been twelve years since we have seen one another. With each passing day the pain of that loss grows. After all of this time, I would not be at all surprised if you do not remember me. But I remember you.

No doubt you are a man now as I write to you on this your twentieth birthday. Hopefully with your manhood you have gained maturity and independence of thought.

I say this son, because I know that your mother's justifiable criticism of me may have influenced you to stay away from me for so long. Please allow me to redeem myself, if that is at all possible.

There is so much that you do not understand, so much that you do not know. I say that the past is irrelevant. I beg you to allow me to become a part of your life, as no one will ever be able to replace you, and no action I have ever taken has erased you from my memory.

Whatever your mother has told you about me is probably true, especially the bad. The good was probably an attempt on her part to ease the situation in her merciful way. I was a horrible man, I'm ashamed even to recall those unfortunate years. But I have changed, I swear before Allah.

Please know my beloved Mu'min, that I love you, and always have. My life will never be complete without you in my life.

Sincerely,

Your Baba, Adam

Copying the letter on more suitable paper was inconceivable because undoubtedly he'd find some flaw within or altogether lose his nerve. He'd have to send it now. Or never.

Adam rose from the hard leather couch on which he'd been reclining, lamenting, and sobbing for close to two hours and took his place in the long line that snaked mercilessly through the crowded post office.

A pocket full of lint and change, an address scrawled in smudged ink on a red-and-blue-striped airmail envelope, a few more salty tears that no one took notice of, and the letter was off, with no more hope for a reply than the last eleven times he'd sent letters to his son.

ASABE COULDN'T BEAR to remain in the same room with Attiyah, the chameleon.

It nauseated Asabe to see the way Attiyah's bulbous eyes caressed Fatima with enchanted envy and a strange sort of lusty longing. It was the look of an old woman savoring the last vestiges of her youth.

When the conversation that conveniently excluded Asabe took a sugary turn, Asabe felt compelled to leave the room.

"I was once as beautiful as you," Attiyah had said. It was a tremendous lie, and Asabe desperately wanted to say so. There was no beauty in the woman, in or out. Asabe kept the truth to herself and quietly exited the room. Attiyah didn't notice and would not have cared. Fatima, so mesmerized by the praise and flowery words, did not notice either.

The strain of entertaining Attiyah could be tolerated only in brief spurts. Stepping into the hallway was like stepping outside on a crisp night. The fog of pretention was left behind. Asabe inhaled deeply, releasing tension, and turned left down the hall.

At first, she searched the eggplant-colored carpet for scraps of paper and lint, but there was none. Then she peeked her head into the restroom on the left, looking for something to occupy her time, an excuse for why she'd so rudely deserted her guest.

Fatima had left nothing out of place. Still, Asabe made a job of refolding each towel that hung in the bathroom as well as half of them in the linen closet for good measure. She cleaned the sink with a powdery cleanser that sent her into a fit of sneezing. She then scrubbed the mirror until each spot had retreated into nothingness. Asabe ignited an incense from the linen closet. She placed the incense in its holder along with the spent match and turned off the light.

In the hallway, she could hear Fatima's tittering voice rise from behind her bedroom door and then Attiyah's roar.

"She is charming, that girl," Asabe said to herself, "the same way she did me when I was so new and young to her brother. It took an empty womb for me to see her true face."

Asabe dried her damp hands on the back of her wrapper and continued down the hallway, running her fingers along picture frames in search of dust, checking mirrors for smudges and spots. There were none, of course. She probed the soil of potted plants with her finger to gauge the moisture. She was wasting her time. Asabe was meticulous, one of the qualities that Adam had once loved about her.

Next was her bedroom, to the right, all in white and immaculate. She only looked in briefly.

"Wonder if Adam has returned."

Adam's room was also to the right, at the head of the stairs. The door was ajar. There'd be plenty to do in his room.

Asabe halted in front of his door, hesitant about entering. She considered the possible consequences. His behavior had been strange the past few weeks. He had taken to brooding in the quietness of his room and had refused to confide in her. Adam was secretive and had even gone so far as hiding his trash. Asabe hadn't known whether she should fear him as he seemed lately to be hovering either on the edge of madness or racking depression.

Asabe had seen him sobbing that very morning, in the darkness of predawn. Quietly into his large hands he sniffled like a small child. He didn't know that she had been standing in the shadows watching him. She felt almost ashamed that she had. She wished she hadn't. It disgusted Asabe to see any grown man shedding tears, but to see her own husband was worse. The tears somehow emasculated him. She viewed him with different eyes; her desire for him temporarily disappeared into the desperate realm of pity. The memory lingered, but not as much as her curiosity about what had caused Adam such grief.

Asabe eased the door open, still unsure if she should venture into his bedroom. As of late, she had not been a welcome visitor; and considering his recent moods, he might accuse her of snooping. She couldn't understand him; she almost couldn't recognize him as of late.

Asabe had prayed that Allah might reveal to her her husband's grievance. His mood scared her. It was unlike him to stop confiding in her. Even when anger had built a barrier between them, still he would turn to her. Even when he knew his words might shred her heart to ribbons, he confided in her. Even when by speaking his mind he would inevitably lower the esteem in which she held him, he had to spit it out. But lately he only spoke to himself and Allah.

She had overheard Adam conversing with himself in the bathroom while he showered or in his bedroom while sitting at his desk hunched over crumpled papers, a pen clenched in his fist. The words were never clear enough to decipher. And when Asabe asked, he was a silent stranger.

Asabe looked around the room and was pleased to see that Adam had left her an abundance of tiny chores to occupy her time. She began first by sorting through the pile of clothes he'd cast off into the reclining chair next to his bed. Asabe checked the pockets for loose change or papers and then put each garment in its place, either on a hanger in the closet or in the hamper.

Asabe smoothed out the wrinkles in the comforter on his bed. She held his pillows to her nose before she fluffed them and inhaled until her lungs could hold no more air. Until his scent was all used up. Her mouth watered at the deeply intimate scent that was his. It carried her back into the blessed memories of a time when their life was uncomplicated and when there was no doubt about love or allegiance. She remembered in that moment just how much she loved him. She fluffed his pillows, the way he always liked, in a mound at the head of his bed.

Next, she directed her attention to his desk, which sat in the nook of an alcove beneath a sparse window. Crumpled papers lay scattered across his desk; there was a pencil broken clean in half and a pen pulverized and bleeding ink onto a pile of clean writing paper.

It was her urge to flatten out the only partially used sheets of crumpled paper; however, the last time she'd done so, he'd become irrational and irate. So she simply discarded the misused papers into the overflowing wastepaper basket beside his desk. The pencil and ruined pen followed.

Asabe used the hem of her blouse to message fingerprints and dust from the glass touch lamp on his desk. The light startled her. She had not realized that she had been moving almost in darkness. She had hardly noticed the marvelous absence of sound; she'd been able to hear herself think without the grating intrusion of Attiyah's voice down the hall.

In the sudden light, Asabe realized how large was the puddle of black ink in the center of the ink blotter. It was cheap and made of paperboard. Afraid the ink would soak through to the wood beneath, she lifted it to check for damage and to prevent a stain. Fortunately, there was an assortment of papers, mostly receipts and envelopes, that created a protective buffer between the blotter and the desk. She removed them and folded a few tissues in their place.

Most of the papers had escaped serious damage, with only a spot or two of quickly drying ink on them. Except one. An envelope yellowed from age, tattered, and dog eared was completely covered on one side with ink. In the top right-hand drawer, Asabe found a new envelope in which to place the contents of the destroyed envelope.

Inside the envelope, she found what appeared to be a letter, severely spotted with ink and folded over two photographs. Asabe removed the two photographs from between the folds of the letter. The first was a photograph of a honey-colored infant, around eighteen months old, so beautiful, so thoroughly plump, with curls so abundant and wild, the gender wasn't wholly discernible. The second photo was of a white woman with skin the color of bleached ivory and hair the color of butter. She was cradling the honey-colored infant in her thin arms. They both looked content, broad smiles on their blissful faces.

Behind the happy mother and child stood . . .

Asabe never heard Adam coming.

Adam had never struck Asabe before; even in the midst of his worst anger, he'd never even eluded to violence.

Until this day.

The blow would have sent a grown man to the floor in a heap and probably without his senses, but somehow Asabe remained standing against his sudden violence. The blow so stunned her that she soiled herself in the very spot in which she stood. Even after she'd emptied her bladder, she was still blinking the bright pinpoints clouding her eyes.

"You have no right," he hissed.

Asabe could find no words with which to reply. He snatched the photographs from her hands and stuffed them into the breast pocket of his camise.

"What are you doing in here?"

She blubbered, "I was only cleaning. I-I-I didn't mean to do anything." Asabe's hand went to her face, hot and still stinging. Anger and fear rose up together.

"You were spying on me!"

"No, no, I have not. I would not do that. You know—"

"No, I don't know. You can't be trusted! I'm not sure I know you anymore. You are a thief and a spy." His eyes burned through her, and when the flame within him flickered, she saw fear, she sensed deception.

"I have never stolen a thing in my life."

"Until today." Saliva was caked in the corners of his sneering mouth. He was trembling.

"I swear before Allah that I would never. I am innocent of what you have accused me."

"You shut your lying face or I'll shut it for you." Hot droplets of spittle flew from his mouth.

Asabe believed he was sincere in his threat. She ran from the room, dripping in urine and frigid with shock.

Asabe nearly ran over Attiyah in her escape. She had been peeking around the corner of the doorway for a better look at the commotion. How she loved controversy. She towered in Asabe's way, refusing to allow her to pass. A grimace darkened her black face.

"Finally put in your place," said Attiyah through a hail of laughter.

ADAM THREW HIS WEIGHT IN FRONT OF THE DOOR, and regardless how loudly Asabe screamed, he would not move.

"You cannot leave. I will not allow you to go."

"Why should I stay?" She struggled to budge his body from the doorway.

"I am still your husband no matter what wrong I may have done . . ."

"You haven't seen my face, have you? Do you see this?" she said, pointing to her blackened cheek.

"And I have not given you permission to leave this house. You will stay here, and we will solve this matter between the two of us. Now please sit down," he said, pointing to the sofa across the room.

"Brother, if I were you," began Attiyah coolly, "I wouldn't beg her to stay. Not in a million years. She isn't worth your time." Attiyah was reclining on the sofa Adam had intended Asabe to sit. Her lengthy legs outstretched so as to leave room for no other person.

The horn of an impatient taxi wailed outside.

"That's the taxi. I don't want to keep him waiting."

Feeling the weight of his sister's eyes upon him, and the rush of pride in his veins, Adam stepped aside. All sense of reasoning had left him and was replaced by arrogance.

"I won't beg you to stay, but you know as well as I do that if you leave your husband's home without his permission, all of Allah's creations and the heavens themselves will curse you." He glared into her eyes. "Already, you are an unproductive woman. Now you want to become a disobedient one? If you leave, I'll divorce you." His chest inflated.

"I may not be a productive woman, but I have always been a good wife. You had better remember that when you pray to Allah and ask his forgiveness for striking me."

Asabe became giddy from the strength that she felt growing inside her, rushing in her blood. Asabe saw the questioning fear in Adam's eyes, and she liked it.

"Pronounce my divorce, right here, right now. Then I can walk out of here a free woman."

"Well," he said, "I just might do that."

"Please do," she said, throwing her shoulders back.

"Listen to her, she's daring you." Attiyah's nose flared. "Adam, I will lose total respect for you as a man if you allow her to belittle you in such a way. Put her in her place."

Asabe swung around. "The same way your husband puts you in your place? Are you suggesting he breaks my nose or perhaps an arm if he doesn't get his way? Perhaps pushing me down a flight of steps would be a more fitting punishment for being angry because my husband slaps me for no reason at all." Spittle flew from Asabe's mouth, her full lips curled into a thin stitch. "You are an embarrassment to all women. Considering your experience, you should be the first person to rush to my defense. You should stand in the forefront to condemn what he has done to me.

"You might accept that type of treatment, but I will not. Unlike your husband, Adam hasn't enough money and prestige to make me stay. My personal safety, my quality of life, cannot be bought. I've tolerated much from your precious brother, but the minute I fear him, I know that it is time that I leave." By then, Attiyah rose from the sofa.

"What are you suggesting? Are you saying that I married my husband for his money?" But before Asabe could answer, she said, "I'll have you know that I have been married to my husband for forty-one years, and my parents agreed to the marriage only begrudgingly because he was a poor man."

"I didn't say that you married your husband for the money, but had he not become a man of wealth, you would have long since gone. He may be generous with his wealth, but I know that at best, he is a very physical husband. And I am not talking about love."

Attiyah looked to Adam. "How can you stand there and allow her to talk to me that way?"

"He'd be a hypocrite if he said a word. Who do you think told me?" Asabe laughed out loud to see Attiyah flustered. She enjoyed the pure rush of adrenaline that she was experiencing.

She turned back to Adam. " Now, I am waiting to be divorced."

Adam remained silent.

"You're not in such a rush now, are you?" Asabe picked up the old Samsonite that sat at her feet and opened the door. "Well, there's no rush. Write a letter of divorce and send it to me. You know where I'll be." Asabe closed the door behind her.

Waiting outside in the shadows of the porch was Fatima. "I was afraid you'd leave."

She startled Asabe.

"I don't feel I have a choice."

"It's not fair for you to leave me here alone with him." Tears formed in Fatima's eyes.

"He is your husband, and he loves you very much. You will have the pleasure of getting to know the best parts of him."

Asabe abandoned the suitcase and wrapped her arms around the woman-child, more child than woman.

"You will be just fine here, believe me."

"Yes, he loves me, but I do not love him. He needs you for that."

The first rays of regret slipped into Asabe's resolve. Adam had been her life. She'd be a liar if she said the love was gone. She doubted it would ever go away.

"Nothing will make me stay here, Fatima. Not even my love for him because it is useless if the love is not returned."

"Do you think he no longer cares about you? He speaks of you all of the time. One would think that you were a saint."

"Have you seen my face?" Asabe's hand went to the left side of her face; she could feel the warm throbbing beneath. She fought back the tears. "Have you ever seen me do anything that would deserve this?"

"No," Fatima whispered, ashamed to look.

"Do you think so little of me that you would want to see me living with a man I fear?"

"No, I think highly of you." Fatima let her head fall. "My reasons for wanting you to stay are purely selfish. I'm ashamed to say it, but it's true. I want you to stay for me."

Asabe picked up the heavy suitcase and headed down the driveway toward the waiting taxi. Fatima followed.

"We have become good friends, haven't we?"

Fatima nodded in the affirmative.

"But, Fatima, Adam is the reason you are here, not me. I am just your sister by marriage, but he is your husband. You need him far more than you need me."

Asabe handed the suitcase to the driver, huffy at her tardiness. "You can call me at my mother's, but I don't see any purpose in my staying. I don't want to leave. I love this house, and our neighbors and friends, even Adam. I can tolerate almost anything, but violence is out of the question because I am a good wife. I don't deserve it."

Fatima's eyes and nose were leaking. "Is there anything I can say to convince you to stay?"

"Nothing."

The driver opened the back door of the taxi, and Asabe sat down inside.

"Adam should be the one asking me to stay, not you." Just then, Asabe saw something in Fatima's face; it had grown dark and strained, like the face of a person bearing a great burden. The feeling settled heavily on Asabe's heart.

"I suppose this means you'll never be back. If there is one thing that I have learned about our husband, it's that he is a proud man. I don't think that he will be able to tame his pride enough to ask you back."

"Ready, madam?" called the driver from the front seat.

"Ready." To Fatima, Asabe said, "As-salaam alaikum, little sister. Call me." The taxi backed slowly out of the driveway. In Asabe's heart, there was an uneasiness. It wasn't Adam about whom she was concerned, but it was Fatima. Something had been left unsaid, and already, it had begun to gnaw at her conscience.

"Allah, what is the matter?" Asabe asked out aloud.

"What was that, madam?" asked the driver from the front seat.

"Would you please stop the taxi? I think I may have forgotten something."

"Yes, madam." Asabe could tell that he wasn't pleased. Before she could step from the vehicle, Fatima had reached the door.

"What haven't you told me, little sister? What is the matter?" She took Fatima's hands in hers.

"I'm pregnant."

FOUR

So much left with Asabe, including the parched countenance of the dry season. Within hours of her departure, the sky wrung from its lofty clouds a flood of cold water. Even the sky wept for her.

In the mornings, when Adam awoke to make prayers in the mosque, he expected each time to see her standing at the stove, preparing breakfast for his return. He expected to see her standing with her back to him, wearing the worn caftan she loved so well that had once been red but had faded to pink.

Adam would smile when he remembered how he tried to convince her to throw it away. Asabe mended it too many times to count. Still, she refused, saying that it was the first gift he'd ever given her and that she'd never part with it. That is how Adam knew she wasn't ever coming back.

The first night of Asabe's absence was the most difficult one for Adam. Guilt took hold of his neck like a noose. He lay in his bed until the digital clock on his nightstand read 3:43 a.m., and then as if being controlled by an invisible puppeteer, Adam donned a *jalabiyah* and walked down the hall to her room. Her scent burst from the room the moment he opened the door, a sweet enveloping musk. Adam was not a glutton for punishment, but there he stood in the black light. Smelling her, feeling her, wanting her, only reconfirmed his pain. Perhaps it was a way of proving to his lower self, the self that couldn't believe she would ever leave, that she was gone.

Asabe's bedroom was as always, as if no one had ever slept in the bed, as if no one had ever stepped foot on the carpet with its perfectly straight vacuum lines. Her room was like a model meant only for show. Not one item was out of place.

Adam noticed a dark mound in the trash can by the closet. Asabe would have never left a full trash can overnight. It would have haunted her. Adam decided to empty the trash can, his one final act of respecting the person she was to him.

He realized before he reached it, even in the darkness, that it was not trash. It was her favorite caftan, the one that had made her remember him, the one with which she would never part. Like their marriage, Asabe once said, "It may become tattered and old, but it will endure." That was a lie. Adam made sure of that.

Adam cradled the caftan in his arms as if she were still in it, filling it out at the shoulders, her thin leg showing through the tear in the left seam.

Adam slept with the caftan on his pillow that night, drifting in what was left of her. When he awoke after an hour of fitful sleep, he found his tears had dampened the soft faded cloth, leaving salty stains.

Fatima did not speak Asabe's name aloud, knowing that Adam would crumble. She didn't want to see him fall to pieces, determined not to feel the slightest bit of sympathy. Fatima had her own problems to be concerned with. Adam sent Asabe away when she needed her most. For that, Fatima planned to hold a grudge.

Adam was unaware that Fatima spoke with Asabe by phone several times daily. He did not know that she used every ploy imaginable to convince Asabe to come home.

"Please come home and help me. I would need a friend in my pregnancy since I have no mother." Fatima would strum away at Asabe's heartstrings.

"How do you think I would feel in that house now that you are pregnant? Do you really think I'm happy to know you are bearing the children I never could?"

"Yes, I do," said Fatima matter-of-factly. "You aren't so selfish as you're trying to sound. You wouldn't hold this child against me. Would you?"

"I suppose I wouldn't," said Asabe, but she wasn't as sure as Fatima.

Most of their conversations ended in much the same way, with Fatima begging her to return and Asabe emphatically refusing. Fatima began to lose hope that Asabe would ever agree to return. Little did she know Asabe would. Asabe had wanted to return since the day she walked away from Adam's home.

However, Asabe couldn't return of her own accord and keep her dignity intact as well. Each time her heart would soften, each time she began to question her motives, if her tenacity was fueled by some deep-seated pride, she had only to look in the mirror. For three weeks, there had been a sore and swollen black-and-blue reminder of the misunderstood violence her husband had perpetrated upon her. No amount of pleading from Fatima would change the events that had come to pass.

Asabe would go home, but only if Adam was willing to concede his guilt. This renewed in Asabe an entirely new set of fears because she knew Adam was a man too proud to number his own faults.

ASABE SAT IN HER MOTHER'S GARDEN beneath a rickety old bamboo trellis covered by vines of climbing roses. She wanted to enjoy the evening air before the rains returned for the night. It was altogether by accident that Asabe saw her sister in marriage, for Fatima had been standing in the shadows of an old tree for several minutes, unsure of how to entrance.

The glass from which Asabe had been sipping tea slipped from her damp and unmindful fingers, landing with a splash upon the thick cushion of grass at her bare feet. When she knelt to retrieve the glass, out of the corner of her eye, she detected a presence.

At first, Asabe did not recognize the woman who stood in the entrance of her mother's garden. It was Fatima, glowing in the exquisite pink of pregnancy. Asabe was temporarily silenced by her new friend's loveliness. The look on Asabe's face spoke the volumes she could not utter aloud.

Fatima came cautiously out of the shadows. She knew that her presence, in its altered state, would cause some degree of reaction; so she stayed back to gauge the situation.

"Why are you standing so far away, little sister? Come greet me properly," Asabe said this through a fog of shock. "Come, let me look at you."

Fatima headed straight for the arms of her dearest friend.

Asabe behaved toward Fatima like a mother would toward a long-lost daughter, embracing her, then standing back to gaze into her face as if she'd never known her in life. Asabe shamelessly made orbits around the woman-child, pulling and tugging at her clothes here and there and then giggling in vicarious delight of her obvious blossom. Months before, Asabe would have had to combat her own jealousy. There was no denying how terribly handsome the girl had grown in the three weeks of Asabe's absence. Pregnancy suited her well. The child in Fatima was quickly disappearing in a haze of womanhood. The girl that Asabe met only five months prior was lost forever. Her innocence was a mere memory.

"You have changed so, and I have missed you," said Asabe. They both laughed at this, as if some secret joke had been shared between the two of them.

"Not so much. Only my heart has changed. It is sad because you are not home, where you belong."

Fatima surveyed the surroundings. Hannah's garden was like an oasis in the desert, solitary and separate from the rest of the world.

"Your mother's home is beautiful. Are you happy here?"

"Truthfully?"

Fatima nodded.

"I do miss home. I mean, Adam's home."

"So why not come back? You know that you're welcome." Seriousness washed away the pleasantries. Asabe couldn't speak of going home and remain cheerful at the same time.

"You must have forgotten the circumstances by which I left, eh?" Asabe knew that Fatima had forgotten nothing.

Initially Fatima felt too ashamed to answer; it hurt her to recall the events of that day as well. To see her confidant cast away for no redeemable reason was traumatic for her. She hurt too. Surely, Asabe and Adam had far too much past to let a slap completely suspend relations. At least Asabe owed him the chance to explain.

Asabe refilled the glass from the pitcher on top of the garden table. She offered the drink to Fatima, who declined. Asabe too was uninterested, so she put the glass down. Her eyes were dark with conviction.

"I wasn't much older than you when I became Adam's wife. But I wasn't repulsed by him as you were. I wanted to be with him. From the moment that I stepped foot into that house, it was mine." Asabe smiled. "I made my husband happy. My job was to keep our home clean and beautiful and, of course, to fill it with babies." Asabe's eyes grew glassy as she gazed off into the past. "We were desperate for children, especially Adam. It was as if he had a mission. Allah did not see fit to give us children. Not one child. Not a miscarriage. Not a glimmer of hope. I was hurt when Adam announced that he would marry you, but how could I keep the man I love from getting the one thing he wants most in the world? Wouldn't it be selfish of me to try?"

Fatima remained silent.

"I convinced myself that nothing between us would change after you came. Even when he grew silent and moody, I made excuses for him. Then he gave me concrete proof that I no longer had any value to him."

Asabe's hand went without thought to the slightly dark aftermath on the left side of her face.

"It's been three weeks, and my face still carries a reminder of Adam's enduring love for me. I suppose it's not so bad." Asabe could not mask the sarcasm in her voice. "My face will heal."

"Why haven't you said these things to him? Perhaps he didn't realize how much pain he caused you."

"He knows."

"How can you be so sure?"

"I know my husband, Fatima. I've known him when your chin was still wet from your mother's milk. Our husband may be prideful; but when it comes to facing his own mistakes, when it comes to confronting them, he is a coward. If he was unmindful of the gravity of his actions, he would have called or come to me by now." Asabe gave a sour laugh. "Attiyah's presence doesn't help matters either. He's got to keep up the manly act for her too, you know."

"Attiyah left less than an hour after you did."

Fatima spent the next ten minutes explaining in strict detail the circumstances by which Attiyah's visit was cut short. She told how Attiyah rampaged, saying every ugly thing her mind could evoke to disgrace Asabe and convince Adam to render a divorce on the spot. Fatima recited word for word Adam's refusal to act so hastily.

When Adam made his position known, that he would not write a divorce unless Asabe requested it again, Attiyah became entirely irate. She called him a coward, a half man, a weakling, and a disgrace.

Adam did not respond to his senior sister. However, when Attiyah cursed him for telling Asabe lies about her own marital situation, Adam spoke up. It was the truth, he'd told her, and he would speak the truth even if it meant his life. Angry, Attiyah promised to cut Adam off financially and left, cutting her usual monthlong visit to four and a half hours.

Asabe stared at Fatima while biting her lower lip, enraptured by the incredible tale her co-wife spun. In all her years with Adam, Asabe never knew him to even defy his senior sister. Courtesy and respect were employed with a fierceness that had often angered Asabe. Knowing how Attiyah hated her for never giving Adam the son he wanted, Asabe feared at times that at Attiyah's provocation, Adam would divorce her. Perhaps she had been wrong about Adam all along.

Asabe found it difficult to restrain a satisfied grin. "Attiyah may be gone, but it does not prove that Adam wants me back. He hasn't told me so. In fact, he hasn't seen fit to telephone me. I deserve an apology, if nothing else."

"You are the one who said he was afraid to face his own mistakes. Perhaps this is one of those times." Cunning shaded Fatima's face.

Asabe shook her head like a defiant child, knowing she would not like what came next.

"Perhaps you should go to him." Fatima flinched as if expecting to be slapped.

"You mean apologize to him?"

Fatima nodded.

"Imagine me going back to that house and asking his forgiveness. As much as I long for my own bed, to prepare meals in my own kitchen, there isn't a thing in this world that will get me back there unless or until he comes to me first." Asabe clenched her teeth to restrain the boiling just beneath the surface. It wasn't Asabe's desire to make Fatima's visit with her unpleasant, so she forced a smile to her lips. She hoped that Fatima was unable to see her struggle for composure.

"Going back to Adam's home is out of the question. I want to go home, but not at the cost of my dignity. He must come to me. No other way is acceptable."

"What if I told you that you don't have to go to him, that he will come to you?" The look of cunning was still on Fatima's face.

"That would be the only way."

"Well," began Fatima, grinning shyly, "Adam is here. He's inside with your mother."

ASABE FOUND ADAM with her mother in the sitting room. He was kneeling at her feet.

Humility is a garment he should wear more often, thought Asabe.

Asabe stood in the far end of the corridor leading to the sitting room. She could see and hear everything while they were unaware of her presence.

Hannah's lower lip jutted outward in stubborn determination; she seemed unwilling to submit to Adam's coaxing. She rolled her eyes and sucked her teeth between sips of tea. Adam didn't have a cup of tea; evidently Hannah had offered him none.

Adam was dressed in a garment Asabe had never seen before, milk white and ornately embroidered in gold. A new watch adorned his thick wrist; he rarely wore one in the past. Its band was of a rich-looking chestnut leather with a glittering gold face. He'd wanted to look his best; that much was evident. He wore a fuchsia turban; the tail was wrapped around his neck and hung down his back.

Tucked under Adam's arm was a modest package wrapped in plain brown paper and tied with fraying twine. The package was shapeless and nondescript, but he cradled it there as if it were gold. Asabe hoped it was perchance a gift of reconciliation.

Whatever Adam said to Hannah before Asabe stumbled upon the inquisition had sent her mother into a hysteric of ticks and amazements. She was angry with Adam, and it was obvious he was backpedaling his way to safety as best as he could.

"Yes, Mother, you are correct. I was wrong to strike her. It is not the character of a good man." Adam shook his head vigorously as if to show disgust at the mere suggestion of such an atrocious act of violence.

"Yet it still took you three weeks to come forth and show your face. You owed *me* an explanation, if no one else."

Hannah raised a clenched fist into the air as if she meant to strike Adam. He flinched.

"I trusted you with my only daughter, and you repaid me by sending her home a broken woman, and I say this literally. You were not privy to the physical harm that you caused her, let alone the emotional harm. It was I who smoothed ointment into the wound you left upon her face. I heard her crying in the night, and I was helpless to soothe her pain. I never want to see her in that type of pain again."

Asabe's face warmed. She never wanted to give Adam the satisfaction of knowing how terribly he'd hurt her.

"Yes, Mother," he cooed, "if you will just give me one more chance, I swear before Allah that I will never allow Asabe to return to you again under such shameful circumstances. It was my fault. She is blameless."

Hannah placed her cup of tea on the mahogany table to her right. The tea was still hot enough to send drifts of steam into the air. She sighed heavily and then said, "I believe that you are sincere, really I do, but I will not be the one who will make the decision. If you want Asabe to come home, then you will have to seek her forgiveness. The choice is hers. Violence has no excuse. It is not the way of a good Muslim man. It was not the way of our *Rasoolulah.*"

Asabe came forward, prompted by the finality of her mother's words. Adam must have sensed her nearing because before she emerged from the shadows of the corridor, he'd turned in her direction. He offered a nervous smile.

Asabe was pleased to see her husband. She could not help herself.

Hannah rose stiffly from the sofa and left the room without saying a word. An attenuated silence hung in the air like smoke. Adam didn't move from the kneeling position he'd taken with Hannah. Asabe stood at the entrance of the sitting room. Adam had forgotten what a comfort she was to his eyes.

Asabe spoke first. "I wondered if you would ever come," she said. "I thought that you forgot me."

"Never," said Adam. His voice was thick and raspy. He motioned for her to sit.

Asabe approached tentatively, as a young maiden would her prospect for marriage, and sat before him in silence.

"I'm afraid that I don't know where to begin. I know that I owe you an apology, and I am very sorry." Adam lowered his head so that his chin grazed his chest. His shoulders shuddered, and for a moment, Asabe thought that he might be weeping.

"Will you forgive me?" he asked, raising his hand to touch the remains of her injury.

Suddenly it came to her, in a hideous vision, the details she had forgotten in the haste of anger and pain. Asabe saw, in a razor-sharp flash, a misty reenactment. Adam's hand lowering itself in slow motion, until it crashed down upon the meat of her cheek. The flesh jiggling. Her eye stinging. Then she saw the same massive hand swipe from her fingertips two photographs, the beautiful honey-colored baby and the European woman with silky yellowish curls. The look on his face was not the fury he pretended that day three weeks ago, but simple fear.

For the first time since that day, Asabe's mind allowed her to rehearse the facts. All of them. More than an act of violence occurred that day; the look of guilt on Adam's face as he begged her forgiveness was proof of that fact.

Asabe attempted to collect herself even as her heart was thumping wildly in her chest. She didn't know how to interpret what she recalled of that day. It had never been important to Asabe to ascertain why Adam had done violence to her. What had been of consequence is that he hit her at all. Suddenly, Asabe viewed her situation with different eyes, more objective eyes.

"Is there something wrong?" Adam sensed a coolness that was not there when Asabe first entered the room.

Asabe shook her head. "Forgiveness, Adam, is without question. If I cannot forgive you, then how can I expect Allah to ever forgive my sins?"

Adam sighed, his shoulders sinking.

"I haven't been able to admit it to myself, but I forgave you weeks ago. I've wanted to go back to you since the day I left, but I don't think I can now."

Adam stood quickly as if someone had set fire beneath him. Shock stiffened his entire body. Asabe flinched, but Adam barely noticed.

"But you said that you forgave me."

"I do, but I will not return unless you tell me why. What brought such ugliness out of you?"

Adam turned his back to Asabe and crossed the room toward the window.

He was hiding something, Asabe could tell. He said barely above a whisper, "It was nothing you did."

"That is good to know, but it doesn't answer my question." Asabe began to recite the events of that day, but Adam interrupted, unwilling to hear his own trespasses.

"I know what happened, you need not remind me. It's just important that you know I will never do it again. I give you my word before Allah."

"Haven't you already broken your word?"

"Asabe, I have never given you my word that I would not hit you."

"I didn't know you had to. Perhaps it was too much for me to assume that my consort, my protector, would not put me in harm's way." Asabe caught herself as her voice was rising. The venom of anger was in her blood.

"It will never happen again, Asabe." Adam turned to face her; this time, his face was streaked with tears.

A wave of disgust caused the hairs on Asabe's arms to rise as if hit by an arctic blast.

"Please, I am begging you. Is that what you want, for me to beg? All right then"—Adam fell to his knees—"I am begging you to please come home." Adam stumbled across the room on his knees.

Asabe had always found it difficult to deny Adam anything, but a determination she never knew rose up in her chest. "Not until you tell me why."

Still begging, Adam began to spew off explanations: he'd been hot, he'd been ill, he'd been temporarily insane, he'd thought she was someone else, he'd tripped and his hand fell into her face.

"Lies, Adam. Lies! Tell me why you hurt me. You tell me what about that letter and those photographs was so threatening to you that I ended up nursing a most embarrassing lump on my face for nearly three weeks."

"I cannot," was all he could say. He stood up and wiped his face with a kerchief he pulled from his camise pocket. "I cannot."

"If you cannot say what provoked you, then how can I believe that it will never happen again? If you will not speak the truth now, how do I know that your word is true?" Asabe pleaded with Adam to give her a reason to return. Any reason. She could taste the desperation in her mouth.

"I don't know how to answer that."

Asabe trembled; she wanted so badly to return with him to their home. Her bones ached with the desire, but she was afraid of the secret that Adam was keeping from her. She was afraid that it would one day rear its ugly influence again and that she'd relive the past three weeks a second time.

"I don't think that I can return to you. I don't see how." Those words caused Asabe a world of pain. Her stomach churned.

Adam shrugged his shoulders. He knew not what else to say other than the truth.

Adam held out the slightly crumpled package that he was toting under his arm. Asabe accepted the package, without allowing her hands to brush against Adam's. Asabe came too far to give in for something as simple as a touch. Though she eventually acceded for far less.

"If you change your mind, I'll be waiting."

Asabe watched her husband exit through the same corridor she'd previously been standing in. She heard him calling for Fatima in the garden, and five minutes later, she heard the engine of his car purr into extinction. He was gone. She was alone. All hopes of going home, dashed with only a few words.

Asabe wanted—needed—to know why Adam refused to confide in her. It was so unlike him that she could not help wrestling with apprehension. An Adam who would lie to her was not an Adam she knew. Or so she thought.

For several minutes, Asabe combed through the details of her encounter with Adam, trying to grasp onto anything that would explain what had taken place. None of it made sense; it all seemed so ridiculously insane.

She wondered if she might be making more of it than was wise. Maybe Adam was correct, that she should simply accept that he would not hit her again. Still, Asabe could not rid herself the feeling that there was something more, something obvious lying just beneath the surface. She wanted to know. Had to know.

In the distance, Asabe heard the muezzin calling the *azan*. It was time for evening prayers. Asabe rose to prepare herself for prostration to Allah. The package Adam gave her fell off her lap to the floor. She'd almost forgotten about it.

Asabe resumed her seat and unwrapped the package. The stiff brown paper fell open. She was surprised to find the caftan she discarded in jaded anger when she left three weeks prior.

There was a small note as well, folded in half. The note read,

My Dearest Asabe,

Never forget what you once said to me of our marriage.

It may become tattered and old, but it will endure.

Adam

The decision was made. Asabe would go home.

FIVE

Khadijah was just sitting down to her second cup of coffee when she heard the hinges of the mail slot squeak. The mail slapped against the hardwood floor.

At first, feeling a bit lazy, Khadijah decided to leave the mail on the floor; but she liked mail. She liked to receive letters from friends; it made her feel important and loved.

Khadijah carried the five envelopes into the kitchen and laid them in a neat pile next to her cup of coffee. On a rack on the counter, a homemade pound cake cooled. It was still warm, but she was going to slice herself a hefty piece anyway.

She leaned back into the chair and sipped the steaming brew, savoring the perfect hint of cinnamon. The buttery pound cake dissolved like sugar on her tongue.

Of the few things she enjoyed these days, there was her comfort food. There was also the rainbow of flowers she grew in her small garden. There was flavored coffee, vanilla and cinnamon being her favorites. There was the feel of the sun warming her pale face. But mostly there was Mu'min. It sounded cliché and even a bit pretentious, but Mu'min was to her the best son a mother could ever have.

The first envelope, blue and white, was a bill from the electric company. Fifty-three dollars. Not bad; however, the bill was sure to more than double as the summer wore on. August would be the worst, so unbearably hot the air-conditioning would have to run incessantly. Would, if Allah saw fit for her to live until August.

The second envelope was a letter from Zainab, her best friend and business partner, who was visiting relatives in upstate New York. "Be home soon," she promised. "Miss you much. Pray you are doing well." At this, Khadijah smiled deeply. The letter, with its clipped sentences and light phrases, was no different from Zainab's actual language. Zainab was a massive woman with the energy and agility of a ten-year-old.

By the time she finished reading the letter, only crumbs remained of the pound cake. Khadijah debated about whether or not to slice herself another piece but decided against it. The piece she ate was large enough to satisfy two people.

Khadijah drained the coffee from her cup, catching the last of the sweet cinnamon mud on her tongue, and set the cup in the center of the empty plate.

The third letter was international; she could tell by the stamps. A blue-and-red-fringed envelope. By airmail. Par avion. It was addressed to Mu'min Abdulkadir.

Khadijah's heart hammered in the hollow of her chest. She knew why, but it seemed fatuous and belated. Her hand went to the place just above her heart, as if by doing so she could stop the quickening.

"No reason to get upset," she whispered to herself. "No need." It wasn't as if it was the first letter. It wasn't as if it was completely unexpected. In two days, their son would be twenty years old. Twenty. Such a big boy. Handsome. Broad. Strong. Solid. Loyal. So like his father in many ways. Hardworking and honest.

Each year at the same time, a similar such envelope would arrive, addressed as usual to Mu'min, written in the same nervous script.

"After all of this time," she said, still clutching her chest, "and you still haven't forgotten. It's been twelve years, Adam," she said as if he were sitting just across the table from her. She smiled at the naked chair opposite from her.

"He is a big boy now. A man. If he didn't look so much like you, I'd say you would hardly recognize him. But that's not true, unless of course you wouldn't recognize your own face in the mirror."

She laughed out loud, and the sudden fierceness of her voice startled her. This made her laugh even more. It had been a very long time since she had laughed.

Only ten months earlier, traumatic surgery had taken both breasts from her. Two lumps of diseased flesh removed and discarded like the trash, leaving her with the body of a twelve-year-old boy. Unlike other women, she was eager to be rid of them. They were no longer of any use to her or her only child.

Counselors and nurses had come to her, with fancy boxes and bags full of prosthetic breasts. They were shapely sacks of jelly or mounds of plastic meant to resemble a breast. They wanted her to wear them in her bra. "This will make you feel more like a woman," they assured her. Khadijah never had doubts in that regard.

When she told them that she wouldn't wear the prosthetics, that she wouldn't perpetrate a fraud of that magnitude, they wanted to analyze her. Surely, she must have gone mad.

Then there was six and a half months of chemotherapy. The hateful sickness of it robbed her of nearly thirty pounds, a head full of blonde hair that had just begun to grow back silver, and all the smiles and cheeriness once so familiar to her countenance.

Six and a half detestable months of treatment, only to learn that it had been all for nothing. When she expected to be celebrating her cure, the doctors told her that the reason she had gained no weight, the reason she had felt no relief, the reason her breathing had often become so difficult she simply wanted to stop, was because the cancer, had been growing like the tenacious fingers of ivy on her lungs and her brain.

With the hopelessness, the knowing that the suffering was not yet over, Khadijah learned to appreciate many things that before she took for granted.

Standing in a rainstorm until soaked to the skin.

Baths with lots and lots of bubbles.

The laughter of dirty-faced children in the street.

The scent of moist black earth.

The serenity of dawn prayer while the birds are just awaking from a night of silence to drink dew from the grass.

And Mu'min. There was always Mu'min. It only made sense that her laughter would be about him. It was precisely because of him that each day, she told herself how absolutely merciful Allah had been to her.

The laughter turned into choked sobs, for the past still hurt. The past was still able to touch that part of her heart that at all other times remained buried.

"You hurt me so badly that I simply couldn't tell him that you still cared and that you still wanted him. Once the hurt was gone, it was just too late. After six years of saying, 'No, I don't know where your father is. No, he hasn't called or written.' Of making him believe that you were a deserter and nothing better. Of urging him to forget you. Of making him believe that all of the good memories that he had of you were false. How then do I say that you really loved him without calling myself a liar and the most selfish woman alive? There is no way. Since I had to live with him, I opted to make you the villain instead of myself."

Khadijah turned the letter over in her hands. She even held it to her nose in hopes of catching a whiff of the contents, as if words of endearment and sorrow could be smelled.

The letter along with eleven others would remain unopened and would eventually finds its place in the cedar box with the hand-painted flowers on the top shelf in her closet.

It was a box that was filled up with the only lie she ever told Mu'min. A lie she told over and over again. The worst kind of lie.

From the front of the house, Khadijah heard his keys jingling in the lock. Then came his voice as deep and urbane as music calling to her. "Mommy?"

Mu'min came into the kitchen in his stockinged feet. His work clothes were as clean as if they had just been washed and pressed. He kissed the crown of his mother's head.

Mu'min didn't see her stuff the envelope into the pocket of her faded housedress.

"As-salaam alaikum. Feels like you're growing some peach fuzz on top. It's about time."

"Walaikum as salaam." She touched the prickly new growth and said, "Allah does things in his own time. Never before, never after."

Mu'min sliced himself a piece of the pound cake and ate it hastily over the sink.

With a mouthful of cake, he said, "What did the doctor say? There hasn't been a reoccurrence, has there?"

Khadijah ignored his question. "Sit down to eat that cake. It is bad for your digestion to eat while standing."

Mu'min sat in the chair that only moments earlier had been occupied by the ghost of his father. Khadijah squeezed her eyes shut against the memory so that Mu'min would not see it on her face, so that he would not sense the deception she was just thinking.

"How was work?"

"Got laid off," he said, gobbling down another mouthful.

"Already? You just started working there."

He shook his head. "That's the way it is with construction. Sometimes there is work, sometimes there isn't work. It happened this morning, less than an hour after I clocked in."

"What took you so long to come home?" Khadijah glanced at the clock on the wall above the stove. It read 2:10 p.m.

"I applied for another job at the new grocery store they are building on Orem."

"What happened?"

Mu'min beamed knowingly, a hint of arrogance in the way he cocked his head.

"You see what I mean?" she declared. "Allah is merciful. When you remember him, he will remember you."

"Any mail for me?" He grabbed the stack of envelopes from the table in front of Khadijah.

"No, nothing."

The second lie she ever told Mu'min.

"Yes, there is." His face fell serious. So serious. For a fleeting moment, Khadijah was positive that he saw the lie on her face. That he read it in her mind. That somehow he knew her secrets.

Mu'min held up the envelope, his name typed neatly on the front. In the far left corner in green print, it read, Texas University.

"My grades," he announced as he ripped the envelope open. His dark eyes grazed the page. Khadijah watched in suspense.

Mu'min had always been an exceptional student, but he held himself to a standard far more elevated than the one she held him to. Khadijah hoped for his sake that he had done well. He was good at punishing himself.

Again, her heart was thudding wildly in her chest, and she was unsure why. Was it the grades that Mu'min was frowning over or perhaps the fear that Mu'min knew about the letter she was hiding from him?

So much excitement over words scribbled on paper. That is all they were. Words.

"Well, how did you do?"

"One A. Two B pluses. One C plus. Not bad, I guess."

"Not bad at all."

"I'll do better next year." After some thought, he added, "Insha Allah."

Khadijah smiled, that he would speak the name of Allah in reference to his pursuits. It had not been easy raising him to be God conscious in a society where God and religion are fickle concepts. Mu'min wandered in his late teens in an effort to conform, wanting nothing to do with his own religion. He had refused to make his prayers, refused to attend the mosque, refused even to speak the name of his god.

Then one day, as if a light switch had been flipped, he changed. Khadijah was sure it was the cancer, the way it ravaged her. When it seemed no treatment was effective, all he had left was prayer and submission. There was no other support he could offer his beloved mother other than his prayers and wishes.

That she had to court death in order to convince her son to turn back to Allah was to Khadijah a fair trade.

"What'd the doctor say about your weight loss? The cancer hasn't reoccurred, has it?" His usually animated face grew solemn. Dark.

"I'll be fine, Insha Allah. Don't worry about me."

"That is like telling me not to eat. It's impossible." Mu'min sliced himself another piece of cake and returned to the table. This piece he ate with feigned interest.

Mu'min watched his mother intently. Her skin was chalky, and her cheekbones protruded severely through her skin. She had wasted away so completely there was a time when he only waited for her to die. There was a time Mu'min almost dared to wish his mother dead if only to stop her suffering and sickness. But the thought did not last very long. It was the thinking of unbelievers is what his mother would have said had she known how he felt. He could not honor her by wishing for her anything akin to the desires of unbelievers. He would not dare.

"You always say that you are *fine*. I want to know what the doctor said."

"Doctors aren't God, you know."

"I know, but tell me anyway. Has the cancer returned?"

"No."

"No, what?"

"No, the cancer has not returned." Khadijah rolled her eyes in mock frustration. "Like I told you before, I will be just fine."

The third lie she ever told Mu'min.

SIX

The house called to Asabe in silent testimony from every dusty, disheveled corner. The well-oiled machine of a household she left three weeks prior was now stricken with crippling rust.

Asabe inspected each room and was more and more appalled with each step she ventured. A generous coat of dust disguised the shine of the black lacquer tables in the living room. The cushions on the sofa were twisted and out of place. The floors were gritty, the walls were spotted, the rugs were in bad need of beating, and the oppressive odor of forgotten garbage lingered in the air.

The kitchen was the worst of all. The stove, usually gleaming and white, was now heavily stained with thick rings of cooked-on grease around the burners. Dishes and cups half full with unfinished food and drink lay out in the open. Some of the plates and bowls were so entirely dry and crusted that the food was no longer recognizable.

There were sticky spots on the floor, in various colors, the remnants of some sugary concoction carelessly spilled and then disregarded. In the sink lay a formidable mountain of Asabe's treasured pots and pans of which the bottoms were burned and blackened.

The garden had also gone unattended. Vicious weeds had begun to overrun Asabe's pampered herbs and tomatoes. It was fortunate that she'd returned in time before the weeds choked the life from her garden. With the recent rains, it was a very real danger.

Adam and Fatima stood at attention in a cloak of nervous silence, unsure of Asabe's reaction at the work that lay ahead. They were hopelessly ashamed of their neglect. However, both felt they had good reason to so allow their lives and their home to become so disorganized.

Asabe's absence had inspired in them a depression that had effectively engulfed the entire home. They were unable to help themselves. This was the excuse they'd planned to use.

Asabe spoke little about the condition of the house and was actually pleased to have the extra work, a project to occupy her mind and her time. A release from the prison of reality.

Forgetting the events that led to her departure three weeks prior would not be easy. However, Asabe had returned of her own volition, based on the trust she once had in Adam and with the desire that history would not revisit her when she least expected it.

Cleaning had always served as soothing therapy, and she planned to use this time as an anesthetic to dull away the lingering pain of disappointment and uncertainty. The passage of time and a bit of hard work, she hoped, would make it all disappear. However, none of those remedies would work. Not one.

"Are you the one responsible for burning my pots and pans?" Asabe asked.

"I am," admitted Fatima. "But I didn't mean to burn your pots."

"Of course not. No one ever means to burn pots, Fatima. But right now you are going to go in that kitchen and scrub them clean of that soot." Asabe was smiling, but Fatima had no doubt as to her seriousness.

"All right!" said Fatima with the veracity of a drill sergeant. She was happy to have Asabe home. Fatima marched off toward the kitchen; all the mature countenance she adopted in Asabe's absence disappeared in a few lively steps. She was a child again. Almost.

Asabe lifted her Samsonite and headed for the staircase, leaving Adam to hover alone in the foyer.

"Allow me to carry that for you," he offered. He would not meet her eyes, though she tried. There was unfamiliarity between them where there had once been none.

Adam motioned for her to go up ahead of him.

Asabe could feel Adam's warm gaze on her back. The air was stiff. Fear silenced him. Mistrust silenced her.

Adam opened her bedroom door, the consummate gentleman, and let her pass in. He set the Samsonite down just inside the door and remained in the hallway. Adam shoved his damp fists into his pants pockets. He watched her go in and sit on the bed.

In Asabe's absence, Adam did not disturb anything belonging solely to her, in particular, her bedroom. When she had said she would return, he asked Fatima to dust the desk and the dresser. Fatima also polished the mirror, and she vacuumed the carpet.

Adam stood in the hallway and waited, for absolution. A pleased glance, a flip of the hand, a smile would have sufficed; but Asabe offered none. She was home, yes; and she meant wholeheartedly to forgive him, if not for his sake, then at the very least for her. Forgetting was another matter altogether. Forgetting would be a welcomed release from the fear instilled in her by Adam. Asabe was determined that as long as the memory haunted her, it would haunt him as well. It was only fair.

Adam finally broke the silence. "Did you know that I finally got that giant red electric sign that I ordered two months ago?"

"No, I had no idea."

One of Adam's goals upon opening his printing business only a year prior was to have a neon sign. When he saw his competition's sign, he decided to try to outdo him. When enough money had been saved, Adam ordered an old-fashioned lightbulb sign. It was so large that it took up every inch of the roof ledge. Asabe thought it was superfluous and that it would consume too much electricity, but Adam was adamant.

"You finally got what you wanted."

"Yes, I have what I want. That includes you. You can't know how pleased I am to have you back in my home." Asabe said nothing to this. "Are you happy to be back home?"

Asabe made Adam suffer in prolonged silence as she contemplated her answer. With so many conflicting emotions, she was not wholly aware of how she felt about being home.

Asabe studied her husband's face and was suddenly struck by the sheepish grin that played on his lips, how that grin disguised the old man forming beneath the veneer. It was then that she realized with a fierceness she'd long since forgotten that she loved her husband and that there was no other place for her than by his side.

"How could I not be happy to be home. I love this house, and our marriage, what it once was. I'm not sure there is any place in this world for me other than by your side. I would have nothing to do with changing that. The burden of keeping this marriage a reality lies on your shoulders." Asabe cocked her head and offered Adam a thin smile and said, "Are you up to the task?"

Adam returned the smile.

WHILE FATIMA BUSIED HERSELF in the kitchen with the dishes, Asabe went into the garden to free her vegetables from the grip of deadly weeds. Asabe crouched on her haunches with her bare feet in the cool, moist soil. She heard the free spattering of running water, the clanging of pots and pans, the clink of silverware, and the inspired little ditty Fatima sang to herself while she thought no one could hear. Something about a long-lost friend coming home with the aid of Allah, and wishes come true. Asabe smiled to herself as she raked the black soil with her poised fingers.

She began first by tearing away the dead and browning leaves, then she used a spade to dig the weeds up from their very roots. Once Asabe cleared away the weeds and debris, she trotted through the rows, still on her haunches, with her wrapper dragging in the soil. She picked the most ripe and robust tomatoes and placed them in a woven basket with the gentility of one handling eggs. She also removed a huge head of lush green cabbage and a few carrots. She had the taste for something spicy and decadent. Perhaps *riz yollof*, vegetables cooked in oil and tomatoes, or *domodah*, groundnut sauce mixed with vegetables and palm oil over rice.

The garden was Asabe's favorite place. It lay in the shadow of the house and was cool even on the most torrid days. The garden was sparse but functional. It calmed her soul. It was almost as if the soil, so moist and black, was able to draw tension and anxiety from her body right through her feet. This is the reason she discarded her shoes each time she entered the fragrant tiny sanctum.

Asabe had been sitting cross-legged in the soil with her eyes closed for close to five minutes when Maryam's voice hurdled itself at her.

"Have you heard?" she asked.

"Huh?" Asabe glanced up.

Maryam was Jabar's wife, a most mismatched pair in Asabe's estimation. Where he was tall and fluid, Maryam was squat and as solid as a cinder block. Where Jabar was quiet and honest, Maryam was bold and reckless with the truth. Where Jabar was decent, Maryam was tactless. She was a human tornado, dangerous.

Asabe always made it a point not to associate herself too freely with Maryam; she was a contagious gossip, and no one was safe from her scrutiny. Any slip of information was bound to find itself on Maryam's lips being recited to the wrong person. It was her specialty.

Asabe and Maryam weren't good friends, Maryam understood in some unspoken way that Asabe had meant to keep her distance, so she rarely trekked across the field for even a neighborly visit unless she had something to tell that she felt was directly related to Asabe.

"Have you heard?" she asked again. Maryam smiled insidiously. Gossiping and tattling gave her a high.

"As-salaam alaikum to you too." Asabe did not attempt to hide the sarcasm in her voice. "How is your husband?" It was the only thing Asabe could think to say that would divert Maryam's attention from the story she wanted to tell. Asabe didn't want to hear the latest gossip and was sure it had to do with the fact that she left Adam. Such events are the fodder for gossip.

"Jabar? Oh, he is fine, *Alhamdulillahi.*" Her face grew placid, for the moment as she thought of Jabar. Maryam adored her husband. She offered a weak smile and said, "I am sometimes so rude, forgive me please. It's just that I've been wanting to talk to you for a while now, but of course you haven't been home."

Maryam paused briefly to allow Asabe to elaborate, to fill in the blanks of her absence. The silence grew dense with nothingness. "Anyway, there is something that you must know, and I would not be a good friend to you if I failed to pass this information along."

"Well, Maryam, it certainly has been good to see you again, but as you can see," said Asabe, holding the vegetable-filled basket up for viewing, "I was just on my way inside. I've got some cooking to do." Asabe headed for the edge of the garden in search of her sandals, hoping to escape with her mind uncluttered with Maryam's useless gossip. It wasn't a matter of not liking Maryam; it was instead the matter of her mouth. It talked too much.

Maryam, blind to subtle pleasantries, plowed ahead with her calumny. "You went to school with Ladidi, didn't you?"

Asabe stopped short. Ladidi had been her best friend since the age of five until she married and moved to the States with her husband. They had been closer than any two sisters could be. "Yes." Asabe spun around. "Has something happened to her?"

Maryam smiled triumphantly. "Not that I know of." She waited for Asabe to bite again. She enjoyed stringing people along.

"Then why mention her?"

"You do remember her junior sister Sauda, don't you?"

Asabe nodded, losing interest. A picture developed in her mind of the girl she remembered Sauda to be. She was a plump spoiled girl who annoyed Asabe and Ladidi to distraction. She would whine to get her way. Being the youngest and a girl, she usually did. Asabe imagined she was probably not the same child she knew so many years ago.

"Have you heard that she is now divorced?" Maryam didn't wait for an answer. "It's a shame really, I mean, she is only eighteen years old, and already she's been divorced. Looks bad not only for her but for her family as well."

"What has this to do with me?" Asabe slipped into her sandals, readying for a quick exit.

"Oh! It has everything to do with you. You just don't know it yet."

Asabe leaned impatiently on one hip, bouncing up and down. "I don't mean to be impolite, Maryam, but if this is of any importance to me, I'd be grateful if you'd come to your point. I have other things to do, as I've already said."

"Well," said Maryam, taking her time, "it seems that Sauda is looking for a new husband. Her *iddat* was final two weeks ago. And . . ."

"And what?"

"It seems she has her heart set on marrying *your* Adam. And her father—you know how wealthy he is—is willing to do good things for the man who will take her off of his hands." Asabe wanted to wipe the satisfaction from Maryam's face.

Asabe thought on Maryam's words for a couple of brief seconds. Hesitation would show itself as worry and flustered fear in Maryam's eyes, providing more fuel for her idle chitchat.

Asabe was confident that Adam was on the verge of marrying no other woman; he'd only married Fatima so that he might have children. The matter of money was also questionable. Adam had access to any moneys he could possibly desire with his own printing shop in the central market. There was also Attiyah and her wealthy husband. Asabe had no doubt that there was no validity to Maryam's story. She was unwilling to give Maryam the satisfaction of an answer one way or the other.

"Well, isn't that nice," Asabe said as if speaking to a child. Then she smiled winningly as if Maryam had just told her she'd live forever. "I'll be going now, unless you have something else to report."

"You mean to say that you don't care that your husband may marry yet another woman? Already, you have one cowife." She leaned forward, speaking in guarded tones. "Isn't she the reason you've been gone for so long? I mean, if one cowife is a problem for you, then I know that two women would be a thorn in your side and in your relationship with Adam. You and Adam used to be so wonderful together—"

"We are still wonderful together." Asabe was losing patience with Maryam. She was only ever polite because she was the wife of Jabar, Adam's best friend.

"Do you ever grow tired of getting in other folk's business? Of trying to run their lives into the ground? What is this business about being my friend and wanting to help me? Nonsense. If you were really my friend, you'd keep your mouth shut and your nose out of my business. You couldn't care one bit about me or my family problems. The more turmoil in my life, the happier you would be."

Maryam placed a hand on her chest as if being seized by a heart attack. "You know that this is not true. I can't believe you would suggest something so vile."

"Stop with the hurt act. You are a human newspaper, and any little bit of controversy is fodder for your treachery. The worse my life is, the better your day. There are women like you in hell, hanging by their tongues with the fire licking at their heels." Asabe headed for the house.

"But there is more," Maryam said, following behind Asabe.

"Not interested."

"Oh, but I think you will be."

"Don't think so." Asabe climbed the porch steps.

"Just listen to me for a couple seconds more, you won't regret it. I swear."

"I already regret it." Asabe opened the door.

"All right," she said, finally giving in. "But you'll wish you gave me a fair hearing one of these days."

"Doubt it." Asabe joined Fatima in the kitchen and closed the door behind her. In Maryam's face.

The day would come when Asabe would wish she had listened to Maryam.

SEVEN

Fatima stood before her mirror; chill bumps raised the fine hairs on her arms. She shook the invisible icicles from herself. It was not cold, but as torrid a day as could be imagined. What had affected Fatima was the sight of herself. The jagged bones that once jutted grotesquely from beneath her skin were now gone, buried beneath mounds of soft, curvy flesh. Fatima saw before her a woman she scarcely recognized, beautiful and strong and full of life.

Full of life.

Full of life. Thank Allah.

Fatima ran her hand lovingly, tenderly, over the smooth skin of her stomach, naval protruding, and tumbling, tumbling with two pairs of arms and two pairs of legs and many tiny feet and hands. Two small heads, with lots of black hair, she imagined. Her babies that she never imagined she would welcome with a man she never thought she could care for even the slightest bit.

Instead of the racing hormones of pregnancy sending her into frenzied tirades and tantrums, Allah had made it so the confusion and uncertainty in her head was cooled, so that her heart might be warmed. Fatima had a husband she could imagine a life with, a friend she wouldn't trade for all the gold on earth, and a womb ripe with not one but two lives.

It was fear that sent Fatima to see Dr. Jamila Bilal earlier that day. Umms, the old midwife, had kept telling her that she was progressing normally; but she was still afraid.

So many people had commented that Fatima was large for one only six months into pregnancy. There were stories of friends, aunts, and sisters that had been large early on, who had given birth to babies with heads as large as their own bodies or to twisted clumps of flesh and hair.

Horror stories, most of which were greatly exaggerated, none meant to alarm the first-time mother. But they did.

Against the wishes of Umms, Fatima badgered Adam until he agreed to make an appointment for her in the modern new medical center in the heart of downtown Diourbel.

Asabe escorted Fatima, held her trembling hand, and cooed to her the way a mother would a distraught infant.

"Come now, Allah's will is best. Insha Allah, you will be fine." Fatima would have been convinced had she not glimpsed a bit of apprehension in Asabe's eyes that had grown as big and shiny as glass marbles.

It was the cool fluorescent bars of light above them, the chalk-white walls sparsely decorated with formal pictures of flowery gardens. It was the brief remarks of the receptionist who otherwise pretended that they did not exist. It was the white tile floor, the cold of which crept up through the soles of their shoes to their nervous feet. It was the overpowering stench of antiseptic. It was everything, everything her home was not when Umms would arrive with her weathered face the color of creamy milk chocolate and her warm hands that caressed and massaged the mass of life tumbling, tumbling inside the hollow of her belly.

Just when the frosty unwelcoming office had gotten the best of her, when she was convinced she could remain not a second longer, a door she hadn't noticed before opened to her left.

A woman with skin like red clay and the bright gray eyes of a cat came forward and called her name. Fatima looked to Asabe for assurance. Hand in hand, they followed the clay-colored woman into a maze of corridors until they found themselves in a closet-sized room with a narrow examination table as well as a myriad of important-looking devices.

The doctor introduced herself to them and then listened with rapt interest to each word Fatima spoke to explain her condition, her fears, and her worries. Often Asabe would contribute a bit of information coupled with her own ideas about the progress of the pregnancy. They went on that way for some time, speaking in unison as if she and Fatima shared a single mind.

Dr. Jamila Bilal began first by fingering Fatima's blossoming belly, never averting her gaze or showing any sign of alarm. Donning a stethoscope, the doctor pressed here then there, listening with closed eyes as if to some exquisite tune; and then she smiled, showing each perfectly straight tooth in her head.

"Ooo," she said. Then, "Uh-huh, mmm." Asabe and Fatima looked at each other and then at the doctor.

Within minutes, Fatima's stomach was slick with clear gel the doctor used to cut friction while rolling an odd instrument over Fatima's stomach. Fatima watched in awe as the doctor pointed to a fuzzy black-and-white image on the screen of a strange-looking television. The doctor called it a sonogram.

"There"—she pointed out with pleasure—"is why you are so large. Inside of you there are two."

Fatima could see the thin curved spines. Two. And the flurry of limbs. So many. And the empty-looking eye sockets. And the pulsing black hollows that were their hearts. Two. Two.

"Twins," said Fatima, over and over and over again—from the office to the elevator, to the car waiting in the parking lot to carry them home, to the front porch, through the door, in the kitchen, in the bathroom, in the hallway, to the cat that purred around her ankles, in her bedroom, to herself in the mirror as she watched her reflection.

"Twins."

ADAM WATCHED FATIMA in awesome fascination from her doorway. She could not see him standing in the shadows, and he took this advantage to see her in the way he decided he loved best. In full bloom, with his children in her belly.

Upon hearing the good news of twins, Adam had rushed home to congratulate his young wife and to celebrate. He'd brought with him five pounds of barbecued lamb and six sweet ears of roasted corn for dinner. He'd also brought Fatima's favorite, baklava, sticky and sweet with clover honey.

She was not the same innocent girl as when she arrived, but this was just fine with Adam. With her shift in disposition and the healthy weight of pregnancy, she was an even lovelier creation than when she first arrived.

Fatima stood facing the body-length mirror mounted on her wall, her enormous eyes moist with pride. A yellowish hue washed over her cheeks, making them seem as bright and glowing as stars, and then pride overtook Adam as well. She was his, a gift. The mother of his sons. Sons. Sons that were privy to the red warmth of her abdomen.

Adam tried to imagine how she'd look cooing to them or humming a soothing tune to put them to sleep or rocking one of them on her shoulder to quiet his tears, and he could not see it. It worried Adam that he could not see in his mind's eye Fatima with her children.

Adam pictured a child, or children even, but with Asabe as the mother and Fatima simply looking on.

Instead of entering Fatima's room to congratulate her on the twins, Adam turned back and headed for Asabe's room. It was habit that sent him there without a second thought. Whenever any mystery eluded him, even the mysteries of his own heart and soul, Adam had always sought Asabe. She could soothe his uncertainty into silence.

Asabe's door was closed. She never closed her door when she was present, and he knew that she was. Adam opened the door without knocking. The familiar hush of the door against the carpet welcomed Adam but went unnoticed by Asabe, for she offered him no greeting but continued to weep at her reflection in the mirror.

Knowing that he'd just tread into unwelcome territory, Adam kept his presence to himself and left the same way he came.

FLAT. FLAT AND SMOOTH, the beginning of no life. Asabe watched her own reflection.

Asabe could not shake the image of the smooth brown orb from her mind. Fatima. In the doctor's office, Asabe looked away, but her eyes were drawn back. Finally, she allowed herself to see what had been evident for months, that Fatima was indeed pregnant. It had been no more than an idea or a concept until reality broadened Fatima's nose, plumped her lips, left a glossy sheen in her jet-black hair, made the creamy palms of her hands and the soles of her feet pink and moist. Until her child's body simply became . . .

In the mirror, Asabe superimposed the memory of her cowife onto the slim woman that looked back at her. The image, though, would not assert itself. They would not become one, not in reality, not even in her imagination. Either she saw Fatima, the woman-child who carried not one but two children in her swollen belly, or there she was, a woman. Alone.

Asabe rubbed her abdomen, shifting from one angle to the next, until she realized how futile, how incredibly she was causing herself pain. Asabe could not damn the first jealous tears she'd shed since Fatima's arrival.

Adam was not the only one with desires to have children. His desires had been hers, and her desires had been his, until . . .

Now, there would be children, but this had nothing to do with Asabe. Nothing. In frustration, she grabbed at the front of her dress, crumpling the thin fabric where her belly would be, if she had one, like Fatima. She desired to tear the garment from her body, somehow to vent her rage, but control came easily to Asabe, and she simply lowered herself to the edge of her bed where she sat until the urge passed.

On the headboard of Asabe's bed, the clock read 4:30 p.m. The time for late afternoon prayers was still valid although the azan had been called almost twenty minutes earlier. Asabe rose, leaving her despondency in her room on the edge of her bed.

She left the sin of questioning Allah's will in the drops of cool water that fell away from her face and hands and arms and feet when she performed ablution.

Asabe abandoned the vicious, biting jealousy that curdled her inner soul on the masala on which she prayed. She released the issue so that Allah might solve her problem.

Soon enough, he did, in a way she dared not wish for.

ASABE HOVERED OVER the bonnet peppers the longest, pressing the waxy flesh of them against her nose to judge their potency. If the pepper caused a dry tickle in her throat, she would promptly deposit it in a clear plastic bag. She left the others on top of the pile.

The peppers were the most important ingredient in the stew she would prepare tonight. Young lamb, onions, green peppers, curry, four Maggi cubes, salt, red palm oil, and five bonnet peppers. Three of the peppers would be diced to oblivion, and two would be left whole with the stems still on. It would taste like sweet liquid fire, good for the mother and budding child-to-be.

Asabe brought her choice to be weighed by the merchant, a dusty old woman shooing flies away from the rest of her produce, a collection of black spotted yams, overly ripe plantain, and tomatoes in the first stages of shriveling. The peppers were the old woman's only real revenue, she knew it, but she still tried in vain to sell the others.

The peppers barely weighed one-eighth pound, they being so small and hollow, so Asabe had only to count out her small change to pay for them. She added a little extra to make up for the old woman's rotting produce.

It crossed Asabe's mind that perhaps this was the very reason the old woman insisted on displaying those fruits and vegetables untouched by all but annoying flies—to play on the uneasy strings of pity in the hearts of her customers.

The old woman offered a distracted but grateful smile that slipped away with simple ease with the approach of her next customer.

Asabe placed her peppers in the mesh shopping bag on her shoulder and then followed her nose in the direction of the meat. The meat was easy enough to locate in an open-air market where the air smelled and felt just as closed off as any housed shopping center could be.

The fresh slab of meat lustily dripping blood carried a heavy odor that collapsed in one's nostrils and found a home there, but it barely masked the rancid odor of meat from days gone by. It hung in the air with as much presence as a painting on a wall.

There was a group of people who formed a loose uneven line before the meat merchant. His appearance was vulgar, his apron smeared with blood and bits of flesh. His hair was as matted as a scouring pad. His hands were black with blood. The flies seemed to love him, and he seemed not to mind them buzzing in relentless circles around him. They landed with unmoving confidence on his face and on his apron, and strangely they seemed most attracted to his hair. Asabe imagined he must stink with the residue of his job.

Asabe took her place at the end of the line behind eight women and one man, reconciling herself to wait.

From behind, Asabe heard, "Well, if it isn't Asabe. How long has it been?" Asabe turned with a smile, but she did not recognize the person standing in front of her. The woman was young, her silky complexion and bright, clear eyes spoke to this. She was of average beauty; however, it was obvious from her wide-legged stance with her hefty bosom way out front and her shoulders back that she thought of herself as much more than average.

Asabe embraced the stranger and then stood back to search the young woman's face for any familiarity. Just when Asabe felt sure she would grasp the woman's identity, it eluded her. Asabe had to admit her ignorance. "As-salaam alaikum. Sister, do I know you?"

The woman let out a thunderous laugh of satisfaction. "I knew that you would not recognize me, Asabe, and I don't blame you one bit." The woman threw a heavy arm around Asabe's shoulder and laughed again. To Asabe, there seemed little joy in that laugh. It sounded pretentious.

This big woman did not instill in Asabe the feeling of friendship or kindness.

The woman laughed on, with added gusto at the confused look on Asabe's face. Passersby threw annoyed stares in the woman's direction that she would be so immodest as to carry on so loudly.

Asabe's face grew warm.

"The moment I saw you, I said to myself, 'I know that woman. It's Asabe.' You haven't changed one bit. Yes," she said, eyeing Asabe from head to toe, "you are still the same old Asabe, so tall and thin that you look half starved."

"Well, that certainly isn't the case with you," Asabe complimented. Still she did not know who the young woman was.

"That is the truth, isn't it?" The woman glanced downward at her ample body as if to confirm it was still there. "If there is one thing my husband was good for, it was providing food. He made sure that I never had want of anything in the way of food. Partly because he owns two groundnut plantations and more cattle than he could count and," she said with hysterical tears in her eyes, "because I believe he likes fat women." More laughter.

"Who is your husband?" Asabe asked, fishing for clues.

"Oh, you probably wouldn't know him. He isn't from here." The line inched forward, and they both followed. "He's from Kano, Nigeria.

He is Hausa," she said proudly. The woman smiled as she imagined she could almost hear the wheels turning in Asabe's head, raking over the names of every Nigerian she'd ever known or had heard tell of.

"How do you like living in Nigeria? Are the Hausa as wealthy as I've heard?"

"Yes, yes, it is very nice there indeed, but I don't live there anymore."

"Well, it was awfully considerate of him to move closer to your home so that you could see your family."

"It's not as considerate as you think. He divorced me and then sent me home on the first plane out of Nigeria." The laughter fell away and was replaced by a shuddering solemnity. Her round mouth gave into a childish pout as her eyes disappeared into the past. Asabe suddenly felt a tinge of pity for the big woman who had yet to shed her girlhood to completion. It reminded her of Fatima's desperate face when she'd first arrived no more than eight months ago.

The meat merchant's voice grew loud up ahead of them. He was arguing with the only man who had been in the line. He had been accused of favoring the ladies over him and giving them better prices on the meat.

"My meat, my price!" he said defiantly over and over again, until the man simply threw a wad of CFA francs onto the bloody table and stomped off with his bag of meat. Asabe could hear him muttering to himself as he walked away.

Asabe glanced back at the woman, still far away in thought, and saw that there was a small U-shaped scar on her left check just below her earlobe.

It was then that Asabe knew the woman who stood before her. She was not pleased at the revelation, thanks to Maryam. Asabe knew this woman because she had been partly responsible for the scar that marked her face. It had happened thirteen years prior.

Asabe had been visiting her best friend and neighbor Ladidi. They were in the process of executing a childish prank, better left secret or else they would both be caned. Ladidi and Asabe carried on with abandon in their trespasses, believing that they were alone. They were not alone.

Ladidi's younger sister had been hiding in the closet, awaiting the opportunity to step forward and divulge to the first adult the details of their questionable play. Unfortunately, she never had the opportunity.

Ladidi was enraged that once again her younger sister, half her age and every bit the imp, had not only invaded her privacy but had also promised to use it to her detriment.

Ladidi instructed Asabe to hold the young girl down, and she complied, ignoring the feeling that perhaps Ladidi's plan for retribution was a bit extreme. What came next was by now a blur in Asabe's mind.

Ladidi straddled her younger sister with a glittering silver letter opener in hand. Her sister at that point had lost all her desire to tattle and had begun to blubber apologies and promises. Asabe thought it was enough to scare the girl senseless, but Ladidi didn't agree. Ladidi had always been mild in temperament to the point of being an easy target for bullies, but she was completely transformed by the antics of her mischievous sibling.

"Don't let her go until I finish this surgery. We don't want the patient to get away, do we?" Ladidi sounded almost mad to Asabe. Although her friend's transformation made her feel nervous, she did not let pity move her; she did not let go of the girl.

Ladidi lowered the letter opener, with deliberation. The girl screamed mindlessly and began at once to thrash from side to side, but in vain. She was too small to cause damage to her assailants.

"Asabe, what do you think I should remove first? Her mouth, for talking too much?"

Ladidi traced the girl's mouth with the point of the letter opener. The tip pierced the flesh just enough to leave an impression.

Ladidi then turned her attention to the girl's eyes. With the letter opener primed below the girl's right eye, she said, "Or maybe I should take out her eyes for seeing too much."

Asabe watched her friend in silent wonder that she even had the audacity to contrive such thoughts. It was almost as if Ladidi were not Ladidi anymore, with her face so completely expressionless. *No, no,* Asabe reasoned to herself, *Ladidi has just gone away for a minute.*

"I know!" said Ladidi with sudden revelation. "This all started because she was listening to a secret conversation. So I'll just have to cut her ears off."

Asabe watched as Ladidi brought the point down on the girl's face just below the lobe of her ear, how she pressed until the tip of the letter opener disappeared into the girl's fleshy jowl, how the first bright red droplets of blood oozed out and then coursed in thick rivulets down the blade of the letter opener, how the girl froze with terror, the way her eyes looked glassy and devoid of sanity just like Ladidi's.

"Hey! Ladidi, I think that's enough." Now Asabe was afraid of the trouble she was sure to be in now.

"No, not enough. She must not listen anymore. Right?" she asked the girl. There was no answer from the girl, so Ladidi pressed harder.

Asabe searched her mind for any inkling that she might be dreaming, that she might be able to remove herself from the room by osmosis. There was nothing. All Asabe could think to do was stop the horror before it progressed any further. Instead of holding the girl down by her shoulders, Asabe took hold and snatched the girl from beneath the weight of Ladidi. The blade had still been digging in the girl's flesh, and the sudden motion caused instead a deeper more jagged scar than there would have been otherwise.

The woman who stood before Asabe in the crowded market, waiting in line to be served by the meat merchant, was that girl. Sauda. Sauda, the source of Maryam's gossip three months prior. Asabe threw her own internal guard up around herself. Not because of the incident of thirteen years past. That had been resolved, forgiven, and almost forgotten. After all, they had been youngsters at the time.

Asabe's feeling of wariness had everything to do with Maryam's assertion that Sauda had targeted Adam as her next husband. There was always the possibility that Maryam had lied. It wouldn't have been first time.

"Sauda? Is that you?" Asabe asked the woman.

"Yes, you've finally figured me out, eh?"

The line moved forward. There were only three people ahead of them now. "What gave me away?"

"The scar."

Sauda's hand went to the scar on her face. Her eyes clouded with remembrance. It was difficult for Asabe to read the look on Sauda's face. It was a peculiar cross between pain and pleasure.

"Yes, you saved me from my senior sister's edict. I never forgot that you protected me that day. I was almost convinced that Ladidi meant to do me harm." Sauda shook the memory away. "But now that I am older, I know that it was simply child's play." Asabe nodded, afraid that if she spoke at all of that day, Sauda might suddenly recall the truth about her participation in that child's play.

Asabe changed the subject. "How is Ladidi? I haven't heard from her in nearly five years since she married that brother and moved with him to the States."

"She says that she is doing well, but I don't believe it is so." The line moved forward again.

"What would make you say that?"

"I've heard things through mutual friends, things she wouldn't tell our baba for fear that he would destroy her husband. You know how fiercely protective Baba was of his girls."

"Oh," was all Asabe could say. "What of you? Is your *iddat* over?" Asabe asked, already knowing the answer.

"Sure. Has been for almost three months now."

The woman ahead of them gave the meat merchant her order.

"Be assured that I am ready to be married again. Without a doubt," she confirmed with a stamp of her foot. "I am too young and too beautiful to remain unmarried for so long, especially as I have no children."

The arrogant imp that Asabe remembered showed herself. She always did think highly of herself even when she was a tiny girl.

"Have you any prospects?" Asabe fished. Surely, she thought to herself, even if she had Adam in mind as Maryam alleged, she would never be so bold as to say so to her face.

Asabe was mistaken.

"Oh yes, and as we speak, my baba is doing his best to convince the brother of the benefits of marrying someone of my stature. His name is Adam." Sauda gazed into space dreamily. "Isn't your husband named Adam?" She asked with such seriousness as to convince Asabe that Sauda knew without a doubt that the Adam of whom she spoke was *her* Adam.

Asabe was unwilling to allow herself to be pressured into a response without first knowing the truth of the situation from Adam. He would speak the truth, she hoped.

Asabe inhaled a deep breath and lied.

"No, my husband's name is not Adam." She then gave her order, two and a half kilos of fresh lamb, to the meat merchant as if nothing noteworthy had happened. As if she hadn't just been challenged by the imp of her past. As if she hadn't just told a bold-faced lie.

And it was a lie. Both Asabe and Sauda knew it to be so.

"I AM ENGAGED to be married to no one," Adam denied. "What would make you think such a thing?"

"She told me herself that you were her prospect for marriage. So did Maryam."

"Maryam the Mouth told you that I was to be married to this, this . . . What is her name?"

"Sauda."

"You should know better than to listen to what she says. She is a gossip and a lie. Everyone knows that."

"As well as I, and when she told me about Sauda, I dismissed her so harshly she'll think twice about ever speaking to me again." Asabe flopped down on Adam's bed. "It isn't what Maryam said that caused me alarm. It's what Sauda said. She confirmed what I thought to be a lie."

"What exactly did she say to upset you so?" Asabe warmed at the sympathetic worry she saw on Adam's face.

"She told me that her father was at that moment trying to convince you to marry her. You. My Adam." Adam smiled at this.

"And you believed her?"

"Why not? It wasn't exactly the first time I've heard it said."

Adam stood akimbo in the center of the room. "Life for me is simple, Asabe. I want a good wife and a son. Allah has been kind thus far. I have *two* beautiful and obedient women in my household and, Insha Allah, two sons on the way. What cause would I have to marry that girl?"

"Well, she is from a wealthy, influential family. Perhaps her father offered you a position in his business."

"I have my own business. I have no need for his money. He has nothing to offer me that I could want at this point in my life." Adam sat next to Asabe on the bed. "I've told him as much."

"You mean it's true?" Asabe sprung from the bed. "He has been trying to get you to marry her?"

"Abu Kareem has been trying to get anyone to marry that girl. Believe me when I say that I was not the first so-called prospective husband for that girl, and I won't be the last."

Adam motioned for Asabe to resume her seat, but she refused.

"He came down to the shop today and the day before that and the day before that as well. He is desperate to be rid of her. 'Spoiled and arrogant' is what he called her. 'Having her back at home is too expensive even for a man of my financial standing,' he says. I simply don't know how he expects to ever marry her off if he is willing to list all of her faults, and believe me, they are many."

"I know. I knew her as a child. She was a terror."

"Well then, you understand that I am not marrying her, or anyone else."

"I suppose," Asabe said warily. She still did not resume her seat next to Adam.

EIGHT

Dinner consisted of *plasas* with tender oxtails and *foufou*. Fatima ate little; she did not feel well.

Asabe watched from across the table as Fatima picked indifferently at her food and then gag on a mouthful of foufou.

"Is something wrong with the food?"

"No," said Fatima between gasps of air, "the food is fine. Just fine."

As if to confirm this notion, Fatima bent over and heaved the contents of her stomach onto the floor. Asabe watched, afraid to swallow what was in her own mouth. When Fatima was finished, she sat up, remorse clouding her brown face. Then there were tears.

"Sorry," she whispered before she ran from the table with her hand clasped over her mouth. Seconds later, Asabe heard the bathroom door upstairs slam shut.

Asabe thought it odd that Fatima would experience nausea in her eighth month of pregnancy, but she'd heard stories of worse. The sickness of pregnancy is the one thing never envied about pregnant women.

Asabe cleaned the mess left behind by Fatima and then decided to finish her dinner before looking after Fatima. This would give Fatima the opportunity to clean up and relax.

Asabe was not destined to finish her dinner that day. And Fatima . . .

The scream came so suddenly and so loudly that Asabe nearly fell from her chair. It sounded like the wail of a wild animal. Asabe darted for the stairs but stopped short before taking the first step. She was afraid to encounter whatever had caused such terror in the voice of her co-wife.

"Fatima?" Asabe whispered. "Fatima?"

There was no response.

Asabe headed back to the dining room and then turned back toward the stairs. Back and forth she went in this manner several times, fighting her fear of the unknown.

"I am not a coward!" she yelled into the silence that fell over the house. "I am no coward. She is my family. How would I look deserting my family?" Asabe stomped up the staircase, thrusting against her apprehension with such force she too felt a wave of nausea.

Asabe stood immobile on the landing.

"Fatima? Where are you, little sister?" There was still no response, but by that time, no response was necessary.

Asabe saw purplish droplets on the carpet. They led to the bathroom door in an arc to the left. Then there was another line of purplish droplets, larger and more in number and newer as they had not yet soaked into the plush, standing out like stubborn beads of sweat. These led to Fatima's room.

The fear fell away like water down a fall. Asabe ran to Fatima's room and threw the door open without knocking.

"Little sister?" Asabe saw Fatima standing in the center of the room, her little feet submerged in a puddle of rich purple blood. She screamed, "Little sister!"

"I HAVE THE MONEY right here in this briefcase. It is yours when you marry my Sauda." Abu Kareem set the opened briefcase on the cluttered desk to give Adam a full view of its contents. "Come now, is my daughter so dreadful that you won't take my money?"

"She probably is," said Adam.

Abu Kareem looked insulted, but only a bit.

"Look, brother, under normal circumstances, I wouldn't dare think anything unfavorable about your daughter; but these circumstances are not normal. It is not customary for a father to bribe a man into marriage with his daughter, unless she has some defect."

"You are a good man. I have heard wonderful things about your character, namely that you are always in the mosque for prayers. You are not a young man. Perhaps with your maturity, you can be a patient partner. My daughter needs a man who is patient."

"Yes, but that man is not me."

"Why not just say that you will give the proposition some thought? At least then, you will give this old father some hope."

"If I said that, I would be a liar. Then I would not be living up to the type of man you think me to be. A year ago, I was desperate for remarriage because I wanted to have a son. Now, I will have my son, maybe even two sons, if Allah wills." Adam spread open his arms in front of him. "And though I am certainly not a wealthy man, I am doing rather well. Do I look like I need your money?"

"Sometimes marriage is charity," said Abu Kareem, trying another tactic.

"Sometimes marriage is a curse," Adam said in rebuttal.

Abu Kareem smiled in concession. He closed the briefcase with a click and offered his outstretched hand to Adam. They shook like old comrades, agreeing to disagree.

"I won't give up just yet, but for now, I do wish you luck with your soon-to-be son, and your business. I know what it is like just starting out."

With that said, Abu Kareem left Adam's office, his ebony cane clicking on the floor.

Adam sat smiling to himself at the old man's tenacity. He was a kind old man, unable to lie about his troublesome daughter, but fiercely loyal to her just the same. Adam admired old Abu Kareem, though the man was only five or so years older than he. The difference wasn't so much in age but in wisdom and experience. In the department of wisdom and experience, Adam was still a babe. It's as if he was in mental, spiritual, and moral hibernation in his twenty years in the States. It would probably take him that long to catch up.

Adam swiveled around in his chair and faced the window. The sun was beginning its decline, and the sky was streaked orange and fuchsia. From his office, he could see the street, its growing business district, and the many new foreign cars that signaled the booming financial opportunities of his city. Certainly, it didn't have the same glitter as in the West, but this was good. It proved that culture and religion could cosurvive with advancement.

The voice of the muezzin echoed from the minaret of the mosque just a block away. This particular call to prayer struck Adam more deeply than it had in a long time. He wasted no time to respond. On his way out of the office, he instructed Jamil, his press operator, to lock up, being sure to remind him to disconnect the giant new lightbulb sign he'd recently installed.

"The wiring in this building is old. I don't want the place to burn down now, just when things are looking up for me." He announced that he would not come back to the office that night but would visit the mosque and spend the rest of the evening at home with his wives. Adam was truly happy for the first time in months, and he simply wanted to be home.

Adam gave the keys to Jamil and left, ignoring the phone that rang persistently in the back room. "You answer that!" he yelled back.

AFTER ASABE HUNG UP WITH JAMIL, she decided to call Umms, the midwife. The call, however, was a disappointment. The young girl that answered Umms's telephone told Asabe that Umms would be away for the remainder of the day.

"She is having her babies now. What am I going to do?"

"Can't you deliver them?"

"I am no more capable of delivering than you. I have no experience with such things."

"Well, you can try calling Sister Maryam. She sometimes helps Umms."

"Thank you," said Asabe, hanging up. Just as she began to dial Maryam, Fatima called to her from down the hall. In panic, Asabe dropped the telephone to the floor and ran down the hall to Fatima's bedroom.

When Asabe had left Fatima just five minutes prior, she'd been sitting upon a pile of old white towels so high that her feet could not touch the floor from the chair on which she sat on. Those towels were no longer white. This time Asabe screamed, but Fatima remained calm.

"I want you to help me to my bed." Asabe continued to scream and tear at the front of her shirt.

"Asabe, you must control yourself. For my sake, and for the sake of my babies." Fatima looked up into Asabe's face with tranquillity and took her hand. Somehow this one act quieted Asabe's anxiety, and she was able to regain her composure. Asabe awaited further instruction.

"How much longer before Umms arrives?"

"She will not be coming. She is out—"

"Then you will have to help me because it is time. I cannot wait." Fatima stood up. "Help me to my bed."

JAMIL CAUGHT UP WITH ADAM just as he was entering the mosque. Adam was surprised to see him so soon. "You've locked up the shop already?"

"No, sir. There was a phone call." Jamil tried to catch his breath.

"I instructed you to handle the phone."

"Yes, sir, I understand, but—"

"But nothing. Whatever it is can wait until tomorrow. If you deem the situation that important, then I will make sure to address it as soon as I arrive tomorrow morning. Otherwise, I trust your judgment." Adam patted Jamil on the shoulder and then turned to enter the mosque.

"But, sir, it was your senior wife."

"Don't concern yourself any further," Adam said without turning back. "I will be leaving for home as soon as the prayers are finished."

"I told her that, sir, but she says that your junior wife, Fatima, is ill."

"Ill?"

"Yes, sir. And she says that the babies are coming."

Adam smiled proudly. "This is good news, isn't it?"

"No, sir. I get the impression that it is not good news. She says that there is blood. Too much blood." Jamil wiped the sweat from his brow with the back of his hand. "Far too much blood."

At first, Adam only stood there, under the welcoming arches of the mosque. Musk-scented men rushed past him, all in a hurry to make prayers. Adam looked at no one in particular but simply let his gaze slip languorously over the horizon. He barely heard Jamil ask him if he was all right. He ceased to feel the men pushing past him into the sanctuary of Allah. All he saw was the golden red in the sky. All he heard was his own heart beating in his ears.

"Should I drive you home, sir? You don't seem to be well." Jamil was holding Adam by the shoulders, shaking him slightly.

"No, no. I will be fine." He pushed Jamil off himself and dashed out to the street toward his car.

ASABE USED HER OWN HANDKERCHIEF to swab the moisture from Fatima's brow. Fatima whimpered as if such a slight touch had caused her a world of pain. When Asabe pulled away for fear of causing more harm, Fatima took a ragged hold of her arm. Her nails pierced the flesh of Asabe's upper arm.

"Promise me," demanded Fatima between hungry breaths, "that you will be like a mother to my children. Especially my girl. A girl needs a mother." Fatima's eyes darted wildly around the room as if in search of something. Perhaps she was looking for her sanity. Perhaps insanity, for it would have been the only possible sanctuary from the pain she was experiencing.

"Your babies will have a mother," Asabe tried to assure her, but she too was unconvinced.

Fatima refused to turn loose Asabe's arm when she pulled away. "You must promise me, before Allah, to nurse my babies." Her breaths were short and rapid.

"But I have no milk," said Asabe, pointing to her empty breasts. Tears rose in her eyes with realization. "These are the breasts of a barren woman."

Fatima twisted and writhed. She gritted her teeth and yelped like a dog kicked in its ribs.

"Love my daughter because Adam will not. He is too preoccupied with having a son."

Asabe began to protest, to say that it would all be unnecessary, that she would live; but Fatima shrieked, filling the house with proof of her pain.

"Promise me before Allah, with sincerity."

"I swear," was all Asabe could think to say.

ADAM RUSHED UP THE STAIRCASE, nearly tripping over his own feet, chanting, "A son, a son, a son." He raced down the hallway, his jalabiyah a billow of white floating behind him like a flag. He knocked first and then threw the door open before there was an answer. Adam found Asabe sitting at the end of the bed, looking at the place from which the babies should come.

"Are my sons here?"

Asabe swung around, feeling the calm of relief descend. At least now, she wasn't alone.

"Adam, there is a problem." Asabe hastened toward her husband.

"There is so much blood, and I do not know what to do." Fatima moaned in the background. "I haven't been able to contact Umms. Please go to Maryam."

Adam looked over Asabe's shoulder to get a better look at the mother-to-be.

"Yes, but have I a son yet?" he implored. "A son?"

"A son?" echoed Asabe. "Don't you care about your wife? If you don't go and get help, you may not have a wife or a son. Now get," she said, pushing him out of the doorway.

"If she is doing so badly, then perhaps we should take her to a hospital."

"That's almost twenty miles away." Asabe looked back at Fatima who was whipping her head back and forth in the throes of a contraction. "The babies will be here before then. We need help now."

Adam headed down the hall toward the steps.

ADAM WAS CORRECT in believing he'd have a son, but so too was Fatima about having a daughter. The son, Ali, was the first to be born. His glistening black body offered itself to the world before Adam could return with Maryam. He was a runt who did not cry at his birth.

The girl, Hadizah, was born fifteen minutes later into the open hands of Maryam. She was different from her brother, twice his size, twice as loud, with a mouth primed for suckling. She slipped into the world screaming from the moment her tiny hairy head met with the light outside of her mother's womb. Maryam cleaned and wrapped the child in a white receiving blanket. Then she was allowed to latch on to her mother's breast.

By then, Adam had already confiscated his son and had retreated with him to another room in the house. He didn't ask after his wife, whose mahogany skin had grown ashen and dull, whose eyes did not even register the faintest bit of delight at seeing the two miracles her child's body had produced. She seemed not to care at all.

The bleeding had stopped, and Fatima no longer complained of pain, but still, Asabe was concerned. Asabe suggested to Maryam that Fatima be taken to the hospital anyway.

"There is no need to send her to the hospital. The bleeding has stopped."

"Yes, but she doesn't seem well." Asabe whispered so as not to alarm Fatima. "I am worried about her condition. No one as small as she should lose so much blood."

"How would you expect her to look after having two children at one and the same time?"

"Not like that."

"Take my word. I have had six children of my own, and I have helped Umms deliver more than I can count on my two hands and feet. Fatima is tired, is all. In the morning, she will be fine. Besides, hospitals are not our way. That is the place for white people who use artificial means to cure themselves." Maryam shook her head. "No, it is not our way."

"Insha Allah, I hope that you are right." Asabe was unconvinced. Dinner turned over in the pit of her belly.

Once Maryam had left, Asabe pulled up a chair next to Fatima's bed. Fatima had fallen into a sound sleep with the hungry infant still attached to her breast. It was Asabe's intention to do as Maryam had instructed, to bathe Fatima in hot water and roots before she settled down for sleep. This, she said, would stave off the soreness and fatigue of childbirth. However, Fatima was resting so peacefully that Asabe couldn't bring herself to disturb her.

Instead, Asabe decided to take the child to her father, who upon learning her sex remained unaccounted for. It would also be time for the boy to have his first feed. Oddly, Asabe hadn't heard the boy screaming from somewhere in the house for need of milk, but then again, the child had not even screamed when he met with the outside world. Asabe waited for the infant to suckle to her fill and then removed her from Fatima's arms. They were wrapped tightly around the child, so much so that Asabe feared she would disturb her, but Fatima slept on. And on and on and on.

It was as if an invisible wall had been erected between Asabe and the doorway. She could not bring herself to set foot outside of it. She desired to leave in search of Adam and his son, but the reality her subconscious had accepted was forcing itself out into the open. Asabe fought it with all her strength.

Asabe trembled in the doorway, as if suddenly encased in ice, and she could not control it. She could not stop it. Still, she was unwilling to submit. Asabe looked heavenward and spoke the name of Allah, but her mind and heart could not change what was true.

Asabe looked to the child, who, in all her youth, looked back wide eyed and unblinking as if to say, *Yes, it is true.* Asabe turned back as it was the only rational act she could perform to prove that the screaming in her head was all a lie.

Asabe approached Fatima's bed. Fatima lay motionless, her face quiet and content.

With the child cradled in the nook of her left arm, Asabe reached out with her right hand and gently shook her cowife.

"Little sister," whispered Asabe. Fatima's head lolled to the left, facing Asabe. A trickle of saliva traveled slowly from the corner of her mouth to her chin.

"Little sister," she tried again a bit louder. This time, she did not touch Fatima.

There was no answer. Asabe called again. There was no answer. Asabe called to Fatima several more times. Each time, there was no response; and each time, Asabe convinced herself to try again, that perhaps she had not spoken loudly enough or that Fatima was just terribly exhausted. The last time though, Asabe called her name so loudly that the infant in her arms was startled.

Then she knew. Asabe knew that her sister in marriage had left them and that she would not ever return in this world.

Fatima had been correct twice, in that she would have a daughter and that she would not live to love her.

Asabe looked away from Fatima into the tiny face of the child in her arms. She had made a promise to Fatima that she intended to keep. Asabe also made a promise to herself that she would not ever treat the child as if she were an orphan. The baby girl she held in her arms would always feel wanted.

ASABE SOUGHT ADAM to tell him of their loss. She found him in her own bedroom, sobbing wildly over his son. His gaze greeted her with familiarity. He had been waiting for her. Adam always came to her in crisis.

"You already know?" she asked.

"How could I not know?" Adam's tears renewed.

Asabe laid the girl on the bed, and then she wrapped an arm around her husband's shoulders. "Don't despair of this. I loved her too, just as much as I could love a blood sister. Allah knows best. Yes," she said with a heavy sigh, "Allah knows best."

Adam turned toward his wife, his face suddenly placid. The tears were interrupted, and his eyes were wide with disbelief.

"What do you mean?" he mouthed. No sound came from his mouth, only a sliver of breath.

"The details are unimportant." Asabe squeezed her husband tightly.

"What do you mean?" he asked. "What do you mean?"

"Not so loud, the babies are sleeping."

Asabe reached for the boy, whom she'd hardly seen since his birth, but Adam pulled away protectively.

"Adam?"

"What has happened to my wife?"

Asabe was silent.

"Answer me. Tell me about Fatima."

"But, Adam, you already know. Why relate the details?"

"Tell me," he said through gritted teeth.

"Fatima is dead, but you already knew that, didn't you?"

Adam's gaze dropped to the infant he held in his arms and then back to Asabe. Again his eyes were flooded with tears, and he began to lament like a person whose world had come to an end. Adam released great choking sobs. Asabe recoiled, feeling that her own heart would explode.

"Oh, Adam, do not despair. She will be missed here, but remember that in the sight of Allah, she has died as a martyr. The reward she carries with her death is beyond compare."

"But what about my son?" he said through his tears.

Asabe held out her arms to receive the boy. Finally, Adam relented and handed the infant over to her.

"Your son will have you, as will your daughter. And they will both have the next best thing to Fatima. Me."

Unconvinced, Adam shook his head in disagreement.

"No, you are wrong."

Asabe removed the fold of blanket that covered the boy's face. She thought about how much the boy would grow to resemble his father.

"Why would you say that, Adam? Don't you believe in the infinite mercy of Allah?"

"I say so because my son is dead. The boy you hold in your arms is dead. My dream is dead."

WITHIN THREE HOURS, the entire neighborhood along with close friends and family had assembled at Adam's home to lend their support and prayers. Hannah was the first to arrive. She brought three barbecued chickens and a pot lamb and okra stew. She also brought the cloth necessary for Fatima's and Ali's burial shroud.

Jabar arrived it seemed with an entourage as so much of the neighborhood arrived around the same time as he. When Adam saw his friend coming through the front door, he rushed up from the couch to greet him. Adam shamelessly cried on Jabar's shoulder, who in his wisdom reserved the I-told-you-so and instead shed tears right along with him.

"She was too small to have a child, let alone two. Look what I have done. I've killed them both," said Adam.

"Don't be foolish," said Jabar, leading Adam away from the watchful eyes in the sitting room and into the corridor. A low din echoed into the hallway from the sitting room created by the dispirited murmurs of the mourners, and the zikr of the God conscious.

"You are but human, and in your humanity, you are weak and, quite frankly, of no real affect on the outcome of the universe. You could not wait for her because you were weak, this is true. But," he said, pointing in the face of his friend, "that pregnancy, her death, and the death of your son are by the command of Allah. You were only incidental in the scheme of things."

"I didn't want this to happen," Adam moaned.

"I should hope not, but it wasn't your choice, brother. We do not always get what we want. But we do get what we need. So perhaps in this grief, you should look to what you have."

Asabe happened into the corridor. Her eyes were wide with shock and fear. Adam knew his wife—her face, her moods, her reactions. Her expression had nothing to do with the tragedy at hand. There was something else. Adam's hand went to his chest, as if he could have stopped his heart from rising in his throat.

"As-salaam alaikum," said Asabe to Jabar, failing to acknowledge his presence with a glance. Instead, she tried desperately to steady her eyes on Adam, to keep him in focus, to be a rock for him. Already, she could see that he knew there was another blow coming.

Adam took a deep breath and said, "What has happened?" Asabe did not respond. She crumbled into his arms and released a dam full of tears into his shoulder.

"What is it, Asabe?" Adam tried to be tender and to sympathize with her pain, but it was so difficult. So hard.

Asabe could only point toward the sitting room, and she whispered the name, "Jamil. Jamil."

Adam released her and headed for the sitting room, with Jabar close behind. The sitting room had grown more crowded since he had left it five minutes prior. In the far corner by the front door, he could see Jamil. The room was dim. Even so, Adam could see the dark smoky smudges that streaked Jamil's once-white camise.

Jamil shifted from side to side while wringing his hands. When he spotted Adam advancing across the room, he tried to smile, but all that showed itself was a painful grimace. This time Adam's heart felt as if it had stopped. Something in him knew what Jamil was there to tell him.

"Jamil?" began Adam, dispensing with the pleasantries. "You forgot to unplug the light."

"No, sir, I did not. It happened when I ran up to the mosque to give you the news of your wife." His eyes darted back and forth around the room. "Has something happened? There are so many people."

"Fatima and one of the babies have died," offered Jabar from behind Adam.

"Inna lillahi wa inna ilahi rajeun," said Jamil.

"What has happened to my business?" demanded Adam. Before Jamil could answer, he asked, "How much is left?"

"Nothing. Nothing at all."

Adam turned to Jabar, an accusatory glare in his eyes, and said, "You told me not to dwell on my loss but to look to what I have. Well, you tell me. What have I?"

FOR THE NEXT THREE MONTHS, Adam lived apart from Asabe and his daughter. Certainly he did not move from their home. With the loss of his business, Adam actually spent more time at home than he had in years. It was his mind and heart that had taken leave.

Adam paid little attention to his daughter. Each time Asabe entered the room with the child, Adam promptly exited, sighting pertinent business elsewhere. Asabe knew better.

Asabe did not pressure her husband about the child, knowing that the matter of his business weighed heavily on his mind. Adam was a proud man, and it was difficult for him to go his friends for help. In the past, he had always been the one to help those in need; and now that the shoe was on the other foot, he was finding it difficult to walk.

Jabar offered his entire savings to Adam so that he could rebuild his business, but Adam refused the offer saying, "A man with six children should offer his fortune to no one." It was no fortune, barely enough to cover as much as a quarter of the expenses needed to rebuild. Jabar's offer was merely a gesture of loyalty and friendship. He knew that Adam needed far more than he could ever offer.

Hannah, knowing Adam's pride, anonymously opened a bank account in his name and sent the paperwork to his home by courier. Initially he was pleased, believing that the gesture was a peace offering from his sister. However, Adam had contacts at the bank, and it took only to call in a favor or two to learn the benefactor's name. He promptly closed the account and hand-delivered the money to Hannah at her front door.

"I was only trying to help you," she called out to him as he headed back down the walk toward his car.

"You are my mother-in-law. I should be taking care of you in your old age, not the other way around." He opened the car door.

"Then accept the money on behalf of my daughter and the child. They need to be taken care of. You promised me you'd never allow my daughter suffer."

"Insha Allahu, my promise remains, but I will not take your money." He sat down in the driver's seat and started the engine.

"Your pride will make you regret," was the last thing she said to him.

He waved as he drove off.

Attiyah was Adam's last and only hope for acquiring the funds necessary to rebuild. Adam's pride would not allow him to beseech her forgiveness, for this was the only way she would deign to speak with him. Attiyah had promised she would never again lend Adam her financial support, and she meant to keep her promise. When tragedies such as Adam's would have dissembled even the greatest feuds, between the most tenacious enemies, Attiyah coveted her anger like a lover would his greatest desire.

Asabe decided to take matters into her own hands. She called Attiyah herself.

To her surprise, Attiyah seemed in a pleasant mood. The conversation, despite how fruitless, began and ended without one malicious remark on Attiyah's part.

"You are aware of the misfortune that has befallen our household, aren't you?"

"Certainly, and I cannot begin to express how much it grieved me to know what has happened. Fatima was a good girl, and I know how much Adam wanted a son." She sounded so sincere that Asabe found herself momentarily at a loss for words.

"Then why haven't you come? When you didn't arrive after her death, I expected you to be present for the baby's *akika*."

"Why would I come, Asabe? I am not welcomed in my brother's house, the house that I bought for him."

"I know that he sent word to you and that you have been refusing his calls. If you were not welcomed, then he would not have invited you. He would not have called."

Asabe felt the heat of anger. No amount of hurt feelings was reason enough in her estimation for Attiyah to abandon her brother in his time of need.

"I know that you and Adam have had an argument, and I know that you left here hurting, but isn't this the time to let it go? He needs help."

"You weren't there, Asabe, so you have no idea how disgusting was his treatment of me, his sister, the only one who ever supported him. I didn't deserve what he said to me. I still can't believe that it came to that." Asabe thought she heard Attiyah sniffle back tears. "An apology is forthcoming before I lift a finger to help him."

"Then forget him, and do it for the child." Asabe's anger was rising to the surface. Not only was Attiyah refusing her own flesh and blood a hand up, but she was smug and self-righteous as well.

"I will not. He must come to me and apologize to my face with the same arrogance that he slandered me to my face. And," she added, "he must not do it because he is looking for my help. He must not come with any request for my money."

Asabe's anger spewed forth like a volcanic eruption. "You are disgraceful. A sad excuse for a human being. He needs your help, and in all of your arrogance, you are willing to allow your only living sibling to suffer just because your precious sensibilities were offended.

"Fatima told me what happened between the two of you, and I know that you deserved everything that he said to you. In fact, it was long overdue. Like a tyrant, you have been holding your money and your position over his head for years, using it to keep him obedient. You have so failed as a human being that there is nothing in you to respect, so you've used your husband's money to earn it. Instead, you've earned your brother's contempt." Asabe paused to avail Attiyah the opportunity to respond, but there was only the sound of her breathing.

"Attiyah," said Asabe as calmly as she could, "when will you realize that your brother respects you because you are of him? Family.

You need nothing more to have his regard. But this thing you are doing, this point you are trying to make, will not make him come to you. He has just as much pride as you. If you want to prove that you are the better of you two, then this is your opportunity. Don't lose your chance on stupidity."

There was a long pause after which Attiyah responded with "Is that all?"

"Yes."

She hung up the phone.

NINE

Adam walked among the charred ruins of his business. Shattered glass crackled beneath his feet. Twisted bits of metal jutted upward out of the rubble, casting distorted shadows in the twilight. The odor was foul and consuming. Adam never knew that fire could smell so repulsive, could be so destructive.

It was an obscure ritual of his, to visit the remains of his livelihood. He could think of nothing else to do than hope it had all been a dream and that if he returned to the site at just the right moment, it would all undo itself like loosely woven twine. A dream it was not. In his dreams, Adam imagined his son in adulthood, standing behind the counter, issuing commands to his subordinates. His son taking care of him. With the death of Ali, that dream was all gone. The burning of the business was confirmation, nothing more.

Adam did not relish his nights sifting through the nothingness of his past, as if he were a glutton for punishment, but Asabe was not available to him anymore. The child was always in the way.

Dinner would come to the table late or half cooked or nearly scorched to oblivion. A film of dust had accumulated on every flat surface. Dirty clothes piled up. His home had lost its shine, and her only excuse was "We have a new baby. She needs me."

The baby. The baby. She was loud and greedy and demanding, and she was stealing Adam's only peace, Asabe. That baby had succeeded even in pulling watery milk from Asabe's barren breasts, of making Asabe a mother when her womb had never held a child.

Adam feared the child. She had come into the world brash and demanding, outweighing her brother as if she never shared Fatima's tiny womb with another. From the start, her tiny fingers clutched anything within her grasp, and her acorn eyes would not ease away from one's face unless sleep or distance prevailed.

What Adam feared most was her spirit, her very life. She came into the world lustfully consuming her life while his son never even had a strong handhold.

"There is a lesson to be learned," Asabe preached to him daily. "Be thankful to Allah, and accept your loss. This is just a test."

Adam's reply was always the same, "Take that whining girl away from me, or I will test you."

The further he ran away from the child, the more circumstances would unite them. How could he love a being he had not wanted, a being that was stealing the only love he had left?

Earlier that night before Adam found himself traipsing among the rubble, his face streaked with soot and tears, he visited Asabe's room. She was in bed, softly purring in her slumber. His daughter lay next to her, awake and joyfully nursing at her new mother's breast.

Adam knelt down beside the bed and watched the child, a stream of moonlight illuminating her amber face. She watched him with great interest, sometimes pausing at the nipple to study his face. Adam believed he even saw her smile up at him, but the gesture was so brief he couldn't be sure.

"You're too young to smile," he whispered to her. She paused again as if to be sure that she had heard him correctly. To prove her point, she smiled again, this time longer, broader, while looking him in the eyes.

He watched her fall asleep, her tiny chest rising and falling, her pink tongue peeking from between two heart-shaped lips. He touched her hair, felt the cottony curls beneath his fingers. It was then that he decided that indeed he could love this creature, this girl, but that she would still not be enough. Adam still wanted a son; that had not changed.

Adam wished that Asabe could bear him children, then she would be perfect in all respects. Then there would be no need to look beyond his own household to fulfill his needs. But eleven years of marriage had produced nothing between them but companionship and fruitless passion. This was not enough to birth a child into the world.

Adam sat down on a pile of bricks, as red as if they were laid by the mason that day. He wiped his face on the sleeve of his shirt, grateful that the dark fabric would hide the dust. It was imperative that he be presentable, for he was expecting a guest.

A gray Peugeot passed slowly down the street. The driver craned his neck to see the spectacle, an old man sitting atop his broken empire. Adam held his head down, ashamed to be seen so vulnerable. It wasn't the ruined building that caused his face to warm with shame but the way his recent losses had aged and humbled him. Humility was a cloak he rarely wore, and it was an uncomfortable suit to wear.

Adam had exhausted every avenue possible to secure the funds to rebuild but had been unsuccessful. He'd even considered taking employment at the bank. He had friends and acquaintances there among the officials. However, he could not stomach being a subordinate after having the freedom of his own calling. Pride, he knew, was a major obstacle he had to overcome; but the time for that had not yet arrived.

There was a means to begin anew, to acquire all that his heart desired. He could rebuild, possibly in a better location, with top-of-the-line equipment as well as clientele. There was a way. He could also have the son he was so desperate to beget, the son that would fulfill all that he could not in his own lifetime. He could have it all, but not without harming Asabe.

It was a choice Adam had made almost two years ago, that he would not allow love or devotion to prevent him from having a son. He had long since decided that a son was more important than even her. His desires took fair precedence over Asabe. Adam's choice, after all that had happened, seemed perversely wicked, but not so much that he would abandon his quest.

Adam spotted the green Jaguar coming up the street toward him, the headlights beaming into his eyes. His heart quickened. "No need to be excited," he told himself. "This is no different than any other business deal."

Adam arose from the mound of bricks he'd been resting on and brushed the soot from the seat of his pants. He headed for the curb where the car slowed to a stop.

As usual, Abu Kareem was dressed impeccably. The scent of his musk wafted in Adam's direction before Abu Kareem could extricate himself from the car. His cane was trouble enough, but what really slowed his approach was his rotund paunch. It was a source of pride, a sign of health and wealth.

Adam stretched out his hand. Instead, Abu Kareem embraced Adam with full outstretched arms. They exchanged greetings.

"I was pleased to hear from you, brother. I must admit that I thought it rather strange that you would want to meet with me here and at this time of the night."

"I only made the decision this night. I wanted to confirm it with you now, before I changed my mind."

Abu Kareem patted Adam's shoulder saying, "Perhaps time is exactly what you need if you are unsure. After all, you have suffered a terrible tragedy recently. Perhaps you are not up to this." Abu Kareem smiled knowingly. He was hardly concerned with Adam's mental state.

"No. Now or never." Adam looked down at his feet, shame overtaking the pride that had only seconds earlier puffed out his chest. He knew how desperate he looked, how weak and of no account. He fought to hold back the tears.

"All right then," said Abu Kareem, rubbing his hands together. "Then this means that you will marry my Sauda. Correct?"

"Yes, and you will help me to rebuild." Adam felt as if he were making an illegal deal.

"Right. It seems we will all be getting what we want. Eh?"

"Sure," said Adam, attempting a smile. Everyone gets what they want. Everyone, except Asabe.

ASABE WATCHED ADAM WATCH THE FRONT DOOR. The chair squeaked with the incessant jittering of his leg. His forehead glistened with perspiration though the house was comfortably cool. Every couple of minutes or so, Adam would remove his spectacles and clean them with the edge of his camise.

He was dressed in his favorite garment, the emerald suit with the white and gold embroidery. He kept sucking his teeth. This annoyed and puzzled Asabe as no meat was served with dinner. Occasionally, he would rise to stare out of the window down the road. Adam was not himself.

"Are you expecting a guest?"

"A guest?" he repeated, wide eyed. "What sort of a guest?"

"I thought that perhaps you would know that better than I."

Adam remained silent, staring up at the ceiling. He was stalling, and Asabe knew it.

"Well, are you?"

"What?"

"Honestly, Adam, I don't want to play games with you. If you don't want to tell me what has you so twisted in knots, all you have to do is say so."

Asabe headed for the staircase. Halfway up, she heard Adam say, "I have done something, and I don't know how to tell you." His words were barely above a whisper, but Asabe heard them just as well as if they had been spoken through a bullhorn. Her heart raced in her chest; she could hear her blood pouring through her veins, but she was too afraid to move from the steps. She could not summon the courage to turn back to face Adam and his confession.

He was standing at the landing behind her. Asabe could sense him there, could feel his uncertainty about which words to speak next, the order in which he should reveal his tale. She could sense him pondering over whether or not to reach out to her or to turn back in silence.

Asabe did not turn to face Adam, nor did he ask her to.

"I am afraid that today you will be hurt and that it will be my fault."

He waited for her response. Asabe said nothing. "I have found a way to rebuild, of that you should be pleased."

Still silence.

"I have also found a way to have a son. Yes, all at once, I will gain a son and my livelihood."

"So you took Abu Kareem's offer after all. When is she supposed to arrive?"

"Fifteen minutes ago." Adam headed up toward his wife. It disturbed him not to see her face, to see the hurt so that he could soothe it or the anger so that he could placate it. But Asabe was not to be touched, and neither was her face to be seen.

Adam never would know how his marriage to Sauda affected her. She would never speak to him of his marriage to Sauda until the day when all was done.

Asabe left her husband standing alone on those stairs. She simply walked away. She did not retire to her room and shed tears as she had the first time. She hardly gave it much thought. She was not surprised.

Asabe knew that Adam visited her room at night while she slept. She knew that he would watch her and wish her to be just one bit more of a woman, that she might bear him sons. Asabe had heard him in his prayers to Allah, how he'd beg Allah to make him not care so much about having a son. More than anything, Asabe had long reconciled herself with the knowledge that she could not soothe the aching in his soul as only faith could. Adam was a man much without faith. As much as she loved him, he was.

Truth be told, Asabe could almost hear her heart shatter when her husband confirmed the truth she already expected, but she would never let him know.

WHEN SAUDA ARRIVED THREE HOURS LATER, she was followed by an entourage of moving men, her father, and her maid, Salimah. She carried in her body, jiggling as if it had a mind of its own, while all else struggled with her overstuffed luggage.

There came in a procession of boxes and trunks and suitcases, of which she proudly announced, "These are my things." She directed the statement more to Asabe than to anyone else.

Adam watched in awe, wondering the moment he opened the door if he had made a mistake. Perhaps Jabar had been correct when he'd said that rich women make bad wives.

"They want too much, and they'll expect you treat them like their father did. That's fine if you too are wealthy, but, brother, you are not."

Sauda stank of contumacy, her head thrown so far back that the very insides of her nostrils could be seen with clarity. She was adorned in more gold than Adam had ever seen outside of a jewelry shop, and her clothes were so stiff with opulence that Adam could hear them rustle with each step she made. Her hefty bosom was thrust outward; it, in fact, preceded her entrance into the house, into every room she entered as she strolled about inspecting her new home.

Asabe laughed aloud, unable to restrain herself. The choice was laughter or tears. It was not Adam's marriage to Sauda that caused her throat to tighten in disgust. It was the pandemonium she knew the girl was bringing with her. Asabe knew Sauda; she knew the terror she had been as a child, and she could see in Sauda's eyes that little had changed except her body.

Later that evening, Asabe visited Sauda's room. Sauda was pleased to show off the varied expensive fabrics and gold trinkets she had brought with her, though Asabe showed little interest in them. She was also quick to show off her maid, Salimah, whom she bossed around the room to do one insignificant task after another.

The only thing of value that Asabe could think to show was the child she carried in her arms.

Sauda was no more impressed than Asabe.

In between strained slips of conversation, Asabe stared at the big girl. She'd thought that Sauda did not notice but was mistaken.

"Why are you staring at me? Are you afraid that Adam will think I am more beautiful than you? Or perhaps my youth is what concerns you."

Asabe smiled at the irony of Sauda's suggestion, for she was actually thinking just the opposite. Asabe wondered how Adam could marry such a girl. She was not pleasing to the eyes, but rather bland. Her skin was smooth, yes, but it was the color of dried dung, and her hair was short and dusty done up in the way of Westerners. Her demeanor was so coarse and arrogant that Asabe could see no hope in them ever becoming friends, or of Adam ever truly loving her. Asabe was positive that in Sauda, she had little to fear except her ripe womb.

Asabe pitied Sauda because she would never get what she wanted from Adam, and she pitied Adam for the sheer desperation it must have required for him to make a mistake of such enormous proportions.

Sauda would bring hell into their home. Asabe just knew it.

"You are the type of woman many men would like to marry, Sauda, but not for the reasons you think. Your beauty is overrated."

Sauda leaned on one hip, thrusting her backside into the air. "Do you think I don't know that Adam married me because of my baba's money? I'm not the insipid fool you think I am."

"Then why would you marry him if you knew this to be true? Have you no dignity?"

"I have dignity, and I have my ways. You see, I will do what none of you have been able to accomplish, and *my* husband will love me for it. I will give him a son."

Asabe roared with laughter, finding it difficult to regain composure. Hadizah smiled up at her as if she understood the joke, and this tickled Asabe even more. Sauda watched Asabe in confusion.

"What is so funny?" she asked over and over again. Her inquiry was met with more laughter. Asabe decided to leave the room to allow the new bride to prepare for her first night with her husband. Asabe would not say why she was laughing. She would not tell Sauda that Adam would never love her. She would not say that Sauda was a very ugly girl with nothing in social graces or beauty to attract Adam. She would not say that desperation was the only eventuality that drove Adam to her. Asabe decided to let the girl learn on her own.

"Insha Allahu, you will give birth to many sons," said Asabe as she left the room.

TEN

Asabe watched from the window as Adam walked through the garden, holding Hadizah in his arms. Despite the sun's glare, Hadizah kept her tiny face turned upward to catch every word her father spoke to her. Adam had no choice but to love her. Asabe heard the joyous giggle of the infant, and she could see the overwhelming adoration on Adam's face.

Adam was amazed that such a small creature could so captivate him that he had all but forgotten the young woman that bore her into the world. It had been the look on her accepting face that convinced Adam that her birth and the subsequent death of his son and wife were simply to be. It was her trusting nature, when she crawled into his lap to fall asleep, even when he was sure he could never accept her, that he realized that she would have his love whether he willed it or not.

Asabe was proud of the six-month-old, for she had managed to do for Adam and their home what no one would have been able. Hadizah brought with her light and, despite her sex, hope for a better future. She caused Adam to confront thoughts he had never dared, to ask questions his mind had never been able to conjure.

"Why does she awaken whenever I enter the room? Does she sense my presence? Do you suppose she will be a bright girl? Certainly she knows far too much for her age. If I read to her, do you think she will understand? Do you think that I will live to see her have children that will resemble her as she does her mother?"

Adam would go on and on about his daughter. In the beginning, she was *that whining girl.* Then she was *the child.* Soon enough, she was *my daughter.* Don't yell at *my daughter.* Don't stop *my daughter.* Go feed *my daughter.* I will buy this for *my daughter.* I will do this or that for *my daughter.* When *my daughter* is older . . . And Hadizah was Asabe's daughter as well.

Outside, Adam sat beneath the gnarled arches of a baobab tree and laid his daughter on her tummy across his lap. Asabe watched Adam caress the infant's back. Hadizah's excitedly kicking legs relaxed as she drifted into sleep by the touch of her father's hand.

If a wall had grown up between Asabe and Adam over the past few months, that wall was now gone as they had a shared interest, a shared joy. Their affection, not for each other but for the child, had united them. It had effectively suspended any mistrust or uncertainty or anger that existed between them. Hadizah's birth was a blessing. The child had made a barren woman a mother, and an old man youthful in spirit.

Loving husband and wife with child, they were a perfect unit—almost. There was Sauda to think of.

Since Sauda's arrival, Adam's home had become an asylum of mental warfare. She was like the weather, never predictable and liable to change without a moment's notice. She was the master of passive aggression, insinuating the worst about Asabe to Adam, but never willing to truly speak her heart.

She was always trying to gain Adam's good favor, showering him with gifts of costly trinkets and specially tailored clothes and fistfuls of money. But his gratitude was not enough. His kind treatment was not enough.

In the three months since their marriage, Abu Kareem had visited their home on nine separate occasions, demanding from Adam what he simply could not offer, that his daughter be assured that she is wanted and cared for.

"You need not profess undying love," he'd tell Adam. "At least tell her that you desire her presence in your home. She feels as if you don't even like her."

Adam would go to her and tell her what she wanted to hear. This too was not enough.

Sauda wanted to know why Adam never looked at her the way he did Asabe. She wanted to know why he never sat on the floor in her room to the wee hours simply chatting with her as he did with Asabe.

She wanted to know why it was always Asabe that he wanted to cook his meals. Why he never wore her gifts. Why he never laughed at her jokes. Why he never came to her unless it was her *night*, and even then he would have devoted most of the day to Asabe and that orphan girl. As many concessions as he made to assure her that her position in his house was firmly in place, it was not enough.

Asabe pitied Sauda, who tried so hard to defame her character in order to shed a favorable light on her own. She pitied Sauda because she tried so hard for what seemed unattainable. She pitied Sauda for being jealous of an infant she was sure had stolen the love Adam should have saved for her. She pitied Sauda who, despite her lofty attitude, was no more than a vulnerable child in search of acceptance.

Another woman would have hated Sauda, for she had the ability to bring a lion to tears with her ugly ways. But Asabe could not hate Sauda because she feared the wrath of Allah.

Adam approached the house. Hadizah was asleep in his arms, her small head resting on his enormous shoulder. Adam walked slowly, afraid to disturb the child. He stroked her black curls. Often Asabe would catch Adam sinking his nose into the ocean of curls and inhaling deeply. She would often do the same.

Asabe had grown comfortable with her loneness and was startled when she heard, "They do look very nice together, don't they." Sauda pointed in Adam's direction.

"Yes, they do." Asabe smiled proudly.

Sauda rubbed her stomach. "If I were you, I wouldn't get too comfortable with his infatuation with that girl. It won't last much longer." Then Sauda began to thoroughly massage her undulating paunch.

"Is that so?" Asabe passed her cowife and went to the refrigerator on the opposite end of the kitchen. She opened the door and removed a few items from inside. "Which would you rather have for dinner tonight, chicken or goat?"

"I'm not sure if I'll be eating tonight," said Sauda, trying to bait Asabe.

"That's too bad. I was just thinking that we could ask Adam to go for barbecue."

This time Sauda stood swaybacked in the center of the kitchen while digging her fingers into the small of her back. She grunted in pretend discomfort and then lowered herself into a chair at the table.

"I know that you are trying to ignore the obvious, Asabe. But I understand. I know that it will hurt you to see me carrying Adam's son because you know that he will quickly lose interest in the happy little threesome that you have created with him and that orphan girl. But listen, I will be sure to remind him of his duties to the two of you."

"A son would be a wonderful thing," Asabe countered. "No one would be more happy than I to see Adam's dream come true, but it would take a lot more than a son to erase the eleven years of history between the two of us."

Adam entered the kitchen, slipping his thongs off at the door. He raised a finger to his smiling lips to signal everyone into silence so that the child would awaken. He passed through the kitchen and exited through the corridor on his way upstairs to lay the child down.

Sauda picked up where Asabe left off. "I am pregnant."

Again, she was patting her stomach.

"I figured that much. Only a fool would have trouble deciphering your hints. You are not exactly subtle."

"Tonight is my night with my husband. I will tell him then."

"I'm happy for you," said Asabe as sincerely as she could. "How far along are you?"

"About two or three weeks, as best as I can tell."

"And already you're patting your tummy as if it is a thriving life?"

"It is a thriving life."

"It is a clot of blood."

"It's mine."

"Yes, it's your clot of blood." Asabe began to clean the chicken in the sink. She smiled inwardly, knowing that her refusal to fully acknowledge Sauda's baby would drive her to distraction.

"It's not a clot of blood."

"Sure it is. If you gave birth to it right now, do you think that it would have arms and legs and a face? No, it would not. Because it is a clot of blood. No more."

Sauda's lips were drawn tight across her teeth; her eyes narrowed in her effort to control herself. Finally, she said, "I believe that you are just jealous." She beamed triumphantly.

"Jealous?"

"Yes."

"Of a clot of blood?"

"Yes."

"Why should I be jealous? I pass several clots of blood every month."

Sauda let out an infuriated howl and stormed from the kitchen, nearly knocking Adam to his feet as he came through the door.

"What's wrong with her?" he asked.

"Just hormones," said Asabe, laughing.

BY THE FIRST DAY OF RAMADAN, Adam's business was completely restored. The only signs of the fire that remained were those that lingered in the memory.

On the curb, Adam stood along with his oldest employee, Jamil, as well as five new employees. With Abu Kareem's assistance, Adam had been able to not only rebuild but also expand. The new three-story building stood on a new lot closer to the center of town. It wasn't the type of crude brick-and-wood structure as before; but instead, it was modern, made of glass and steel. Abu Kareem called it a work of art within itself.

There was an elevator, a grand lobby with a receptionist, lush potted plants, a small fountain, a modern computer system, central heat and air-conditioning, stylish furniture, a waiting area for visitors, and the coup de grace was Adam's office on the top floor. Adam's office was furnished masculinely in leather and dark woods. "Like in the magazines," he'd whisper to himself each time he entered.

Mu'min Printers would no longer be limited to printing business cards, invitations, and pamphlets. Now, that was merely a department in the greater scheme. Adam would now expand into books. Mu'min Printers had become the Mu'min Printing Company Inc. This name was chiseled in the enormous marble slab at the entrance.

Adam raised the camera that hung around his neck and took his first photograph of that very marble slab glowing pink in the sunlight. The Mu'min Printing Company. If his son would not man the desk in the top-floor office one day, then at least the building would bear his name.

Next Adam rallied his new employees in a semicircle before the front entrance. They were the second photograph. Then Jamil offered to take a picture of Adam next to the marble slab. Adam walked slowly to the marble slab, checking his gait, not wanting to seem proud or arrogant. Nothing he did could mask his happiness. The sun shone brightly, and the glass building glistened like a sheet of diamonds. The varied bright flowers that formed the landscape of his building were like an ocean of swirling rainbows. How could a seed of pride not assert itself?

Just as Adam was wishing he could share that moment with Asabe, he noticed a yellow taxi pull up to the curb. There was Asabe with a sleeping Hadizah tied to her back. The picture that Jamil took of Adam caught him not poised distinctively before his new business, but rather a green and brown streak racing toward Asabe.

"I'm so glad that you came." Adam was a bit winded. "I was just thinking of you."

He reached over Asabe's shoulder and stroked Hadizah's cheek.

"She is tired. Why didn't you leave her with Sauda?"

"Sauda has asked me to send her regards. She wanted to be here on your opening day, but she had a doctor's appointment. Something about an ultrasound."

"Is there something wrong?"

"No, I don't believe so. She says that she is anxious to know the sex of the child."

"Why then didn't you leave Hadizah with Salimah?"

"Sauda took Salimah with her to the doctor's office."

"Oh," was all Adam said before dragging Asabe by the hand inside the new building. With Asabe, Adam felt free to brag about every new gadget or piece of machinery. He bragged about the acquisition of each piece of furniture, the procedure for forwarding calls on the automated telephone answering system, the air-conditioning, the gardener that would come every other day to tend the grounds, the cafeteria . . . He was pleased to share with her because she would be more awed than he, and this would reinforce his pleasure, somehow justifying his marriage to Sauda.

Since Sauda's arrival, he had truly done his best to inculcate within himself deep feeling for her. It was his marriage to her that had brought his newfound prosperity and, hopefully, his posterity.

She was unlike any woman he had ever known.

In many ways, she was like Western women. She lacked modesty and common respect. She would alter the dress to just within the limits of decency, always ready to cross the line. She would often go without her hijab, exposing her hair. She would tie her wrapper two inches too high, exposing her ankles and part of her calf. She would speak to men in such a brazen manner as to shame them. She would not cast her eyes down when looking at men but often look on brazenly until she had caught their attention.

She was unlike any woman Adam had ever known.

She was loud and complained incessantly. She often swore in anger the way many men dared not. She was needy and vulnerable where she should not have been and fiercely independent and stubborn where she should not have been. She was angry in times of happiness and happy at other's anger.

Sauda was unlike any woman Adam had ever known.

There was something about her, something unreal, and difficult to trust. There was a falseness in her eyes, a vacancy of thought and dignity, of true caring, that had built a wall between himself and her. She desired his rapt attention, his love, and admiration; but all he had been able to muster was an expression of his desire to be for her what he knew he could not.

"HURRY UP! How long do you expect us to wait?" Sauda screamed at Salimah and then gave her a swift kick in the rear. With a plastic smile plastered on her face, she then turned her attention back to her guest.

"It is nice to finally meet you. How long will you be staying?"

"I'm not sure. I suppose that depends entirely upon how my brother receives me. He's quite angry with me." Attiyah allowed Salimah to refill her teacup.

"Well then, that explains why I've heard so little about you. I only knew about you because Asabe mentioned you once."

"Unfortunately, she will probably be quite angry with me as well."

"Everyone angry with you? What brings you then?"

"That is a bit private. I don't mean to be rude; but it is really between Adam, Asabe, and myself." Attiyah stirred a lump of sugar into her tea. "I see that you are pregnant. Already. You must be pleased."

"Absolutely," Sauda beamed. Sauda sipped her tea and then twisted her face in disgust. "Salimah! Get in here!"

Salimah scurried from the kitchen, face and shirt smudged with flour. She knelt before Sauda. This time Sauda slapped the girl so hard she toppled over onto her bottom.

"How many times do I have to tell you that I don't like my tea this hot? Are you trying to burn me?" She handed the cup to Salimah and said, "Put this in the refrigerator until it cools down. But not too cool." Salimah hurried back toward the kitchen with tears in her eyes.

"How could you dare to hit that girl? Do you treat all of your help that way?"

"Yes, if they are disobedient."

"I hate to see what you will do when your child is disobedient. You might kill her."

"Her? Oh no, I am having a son. I would never harm Adam's son. Not for anything."

Attiyah rose from the sofa, straightened her clothes, and stood by the window. "Will he be home soon? It's important that I speak to him while I still have the nerve."

Sauda joined Attiyah by the window, paying little attention to the view. She was looking up into Attiyah's face.

"He is most likely at his new office. Today was the first day of reopening. I don't know where Asabe is, but I suspect she is with him." Sauda coughed in an effort to clear her throat of the envy she felt for Asabe. It was too late and too weak an attempt, Attiyah heard it clearly.

"How do you and your sister get along?" asked Attiyah. She did not return Sauda's gaze.

"I suppose that we get along well enough. I personally don't believe that she will be here much longer, but I suppose Allah knows better about these things."

This time Attiyah did look at Sauda. "What makes you say that?"

"Well," began Sauda beaming, "she hasn't anything to offer a man with Adam's desires."

Attiyah's interest was fully piqued. "What are Adam's desires?"

"A deserving wife who can bear him many sons and wealth. I can give him all of the things she cannot."

Sauda thrust her bosom outward and said, "Did you know that it was my father who helped Adam to rebuild? Did you know that the new car he now drives, a Rolls-Royce, was a gift from me? And look at my belly"—she patted her abdomen—"have you ever seen Asabe with this?"

Salimah entered the room and placed Sauda's cup of tea on the coffee table. Sauda returned to her seat.

"Just today I was at the doctor's office, and she performed an ultrasound. She says that she is positive that it will be a boy. A boy. But I didn't need her to tell me that. I knew that it was since the day I learned that I was carrying his child. Adam needs me."

Attiyah marveled at Sauda whose arrogance was unmatched even by her own. Attiyah chuckled. "Sauda. Sauda." She rolled the girl's name off her tongue. "You really do think highly of yourself, don't you? Sometimes this is a good thing. Sometimes though, it sets you up for disappointment." Then suddenly, Attiyah remembered that it was

Ramadan, a holy month, and that she was fasting. Attiyah was unwilling to speak the truth as the truth was sure to cause an argument to ensue.

Why destroy the validity of her fast by engaging in a petty tit for tat with a pompous girl who hardly knew the truth or the gravity of her presence in Adam's home? Why should she hurt the woman who had built her entire life around her money and what it could buy her? Attiyah was once that type of woman, and she was happy that she had been able to see her error before her life was finished, and she had to answer to Allah. She had Asabe to thank for that.

Attiyah had traveled two hundred miles to make amends, to beg forgiveness, and to start anew while she still had the opportunity. That opportunity would soon come. A forest green Rolls-Royce had just pulled into the driveway behind her car.

ADAM GREETED ATTIYAH as if nothing had happened between them. This was a relief. Adam accepted her apology with a wave of his hand and a smile.

"It's nothing. I have no reason to hold a grudge with you. You are my sister and have done so much to help me in the past. One argument between siblings can be washed away like dust. It's nothing."

Then, suddenly it seemed, a cold silence fell between them.

"What is it?" asked Attiyah. "Let us put it all on the table."

"I can accept your mistreatment. My skin is thick. I'll admit that sometimes I deserve a tongue-lashing, but not Asabe. You truly hurt her last time. You know that you were wrong."

"Adam—"

"Before you start criticizing her, let me warn you that would be the one thing that could draw a line of division between you and me." The vision of Asabe walking out of his house floated to the surface of his memory. His heart was racing in his chest.

"I was wrong about Asabe," said Attiyah. Adam's face went placid with shock. She continued, "I now know that Asabe is the best kind of woman for you. I wouldn't have it any other way."

"What changed your mind?"

"She did. Could you ever forgive me for giving her so much grief?"

"No. That is entirely up to her."

ATTIYAH FOUND ASABE in the prayer room. She was propped up against a mound of pillows with Hadizah cradled in her arms and nursing. Attiyah heard the infant's lips smack in delight of her mother's milk. Kasuar sat, purring at Asabe's feet.

Attiyah bent down and lifted the heavy cat into her arms before she sat on the floor next to her sister-in-law. "I think that it is wonderful of you to nurse this child. One would think that you actually gave birth to her."

Asabe did not look in Attiyah's direction. "Sometimes I feel as if did. She is mine. It's my milk that nourishes her. It is me that loves her."

Silence.

"How long are you going to sit there before you explain what brings you here?" Asabe wanted to know.

"I was trying to think of a way to explain myself, but for me, it's not easy."

"Why not?"

"I am not accustomed to admitting my mistakes or of saying that I am sorry."

Asabe was moved by Attiyah's humility. Somehow it softened her ugliness.

"I don't care if you never like me. But Adam is my husband, all of the good and the bad of him. I don't like seeing him hurt or disappointed. It's funny the way the people you love the most are the ones who can cause the most pain." Asabe shook her head.

"You have no idea the pain my husband was in. He lost all that was important to him in one single day, and you refused to come to his aid.

"Now I know that the two of you are from the same stubborn stock, but if there was ever a time to let a grudge go, that was it. I swore after I spoke with you that day that I would never speak to you again." Asabe sighed heavily, releasing her burden. "But this is Ramadan, the month of forgiveness through fasting. If Allah can forgive worse crimes, then so can I. Besides, it was Adam's transgression that caused me to leave that day. You were simply acting true to form."

"I knew that I was wrong about you that day when you called. Even I couldn't have defended Adam any better." Attiyah looked away. "I am sorry, Asabe. I was wrong."

"You need not speak of it again. Your presence here is enough." Asabe reached out for Attiyah's hand.

Silence.

"May I ask a question?" said Asabe.

"Anything."

"When are you going to stop stroking that silly cat and hold your niece for the first time?"

THAT NIGHT, ADAM SLIPPED FROM ASABE'S ROOM and went to Sauda's room. For several minutes, he stood in the hallway, drawing lines in the carpet with his toes. He wanted to enter, to be in close to the child that Sauda carried within her. He wanted to be near to his son.

Adam fought with pangs of guilt that he would desert Asabe on her night in order to visit with Sauda, but he could not help himself. Asabe was not having his son. Sauda was.

It no longer mattered that Sauda was a crass character. It no longer mattered that she had done everything in her power to draw him away from Asabe and his daughter. It no longer mattered that she was temperamental and childish. It no longer mattered that she was not genuine and that sometimes she lied. It no longer mattered that he found it difficult to be in her company because with one word, with one promise, it was all nothing. She was having his son, and regardless of how wonderful or loving a wife Asabe was, she had never done this for him. Hadizah, as delightful a joy as she had been, would never be a son. They would not ever be enough.

In the darkness of the hallway, Adam whispered a promise, "I will learn to love her the same as Asabe, for my sake and for the sake of my son. We will be the family I wished for, and he will be my missing limb. I will name him Mu'min, after the son that I've lost." Adam could not help smiling, for guilt or no guilt, he was on the verge of realizing a dream long in coming. It was Sauda that he had to thank for delivering him from the torment of his loss. Asabe and their daughter, Hadizah, had served as a comfortable diversion from his pain; and he was grateful. But Sauda would be giving him a son, and this made his grieving seem all the easier to relinquish.

Adam entered Sauda's room and was surprised to find Sauda awake and sitting up in her bed. Her features were indistinct in the darkness, but he could see her eyes and teeth shining clearly. She smiled up at him knowingly, and although he found her unattractive, he returned the smile.

"Did you know that I was coming?" Adam closed the door behind him.

"I figured you might."

Adam turned on the lamp on her bureau and sat at the end of her bed. In the light, he decided, she wasn't as unattractive as he thought.

"I couldn't stop thinking about what you said. Did the doctor really say that you would be having a son?"

"No. She said that *we* would be having a son. She also said that this would be a delicate pregnancy, and undue stress and fatigue should be avoided at all costs." Sauda smiled inwardly at the concern and awe on Adam's face. "I'll need your help. I'll need your attention."

"Anything. I'll do anything."

Adam could see in his mind the day Fatima and his son were lowered into the earth. He didn't think he could do it again. He knew he couldn't do it again.

"You just say the word, and the deed will be done," he promised.

Sauda smiled again. This time Adam thought she seemed almost beautiful. That night, Adam did not return to Asabe's room.

ELEVEN

Asabe moved down the rows of her garden, picking the most succulent vegetables she could find. Since the night before, she'd been craving a fresh salad, with olive oil and vinegar drizzled on top. Asabe intended to break her fast with cool salad later that evening. Hadizah, sound asleep, was tied to her back. Kasuar purred at her feet, licking her toes with his sandpaper tongue each time she stood still for more than a second. The wind, light and mild, crept beneath her blouse.

The day had begun favorably. That morning, the entire family united in the prayer room and made dawn prayers together. They shared a pot of sweet millet cereal for *suhur* and talked among themselves about nothing in particular and anything that came to mind. Hadizah had been full of happy giggles all morning long and spoke in her twelve-month-old tongue, "Mama," for the first time. Yes, the day had begun favorably, but it would not progress in the same way.

Asabe's face was turned upward to catch the welcoming yellow rays of the sun and the soft caress of the wind as it pushed along to the west. Her eyes were closed tight against the delightful onslaught. She breathed deeply. Just then, her pleasurable train of thought was interrupted by a sudden crash and then shrieking so violent the baby sleeping on her back shuddered awake. The cacophony of sounds came from the opened window of the kitchen.

"You are so stupid! Stupid! Stupid! Stupid! Can't you get anything right? I don't know why my baba hired you anyway. Incompetent is what you are." No doubt the braying came from Sauda.

After nine months with Sauda, still, Asabe could not decipher the relationship she had with Salimah. So insulting and violent was Sauda's behavior with the girl that it hurt her own soul to witness. It angered her as well because Salimah refused to defend herself. She would not even speak up to protect her own interests. To make matters worse, she would burst into tears at even a harsh glance on Sauda's part.

Again, the yelling stretched its hand out into the garden.

"You pick up every piece of glass. You hear me? I hope you cut yourself, you nasty wench." It was not the first time that Sauda had behaved in such an appalling manner. Asabe was ashamed that she had never spoken up in defense of Salimah, for she could feel the anguish just as if it were herself being abused.

By the time Asabe reached the kitchen, Sauda had already exited to another part of the house. Asabe could still hear Sauda curse Salimah in the distance. Salimah was kneeling on the floor, doing as she was commanded. She was picking up the remains of a shattered teacup and plate with her bare fingers. She looked as if she were trying to cut herself.

Asabe knelt down, took the girl by her hands, and encouraged her to get up from the floor. She escorted Salimah to the table and sat her down in much the same manner as she would have done a child.

"You sit here and relax. I'll clean this mess."

The girl said nothing.

Asabe removed an old straw broom from the dustbin and swept up the scattered pieces of china. Hadizah enjoyed the side-to-side motion and gurgled in delight as if she were on a theme park ride.

"She certainly has a temper, doesn't she?" said Asabe in reference to Sauda. Asabe tried to make light of the situation. Salimah said nothing; her eyes were cast toward the floor.

Asabe continued, "Allah must be very pleased with you. Not many people would be so patient. This is probably why she doesn't fire you, though she is constantly threatening to do so."

Asabe looked back over her shoulder at the silent girl. She behaved as if no one had said a word to her.

"You must be the shy type," Asabe surmised, "the type who is afraid to speak out, especially with aggressive people. I was the same as you when I was a young girl, but no more. I got tired of being taken for granted."

Asabe bent over to sweep the remains onto a dustpan.

"Although there is always room for patience and modesty. I can tell you are both patient and modest."

Asabe emptied the dustpan into the garbage and returned the broom to the dustbin.

"Would you care for a cup of tea?" asked Asabe from the stove. Still the girl did not answer. This time Asabe found Salimah's silence more than shy, but extreme and slightly annoying.

"Salimah?" she called, with no reply. The girl simply kept her head lowered and her eyes on the floor. Asabe squatted down in front of Salimah's chair. This time the girl looked up into Asabe's eyes, and for the first time Asabe actually *saw* the girl who had been sharing her home for the past nine months.

Something in her frightened, wild face was so innocent and pure that Asabe could think of no other person than Fatima. They did not share the same features, but there was a continuity of simplicity and gentility that made them as akin as sisters. Now, Asabe could see why Sauda hated the girl. She was jealous.

Sauda was not jealous of Salimah's beauty. Salimah was a plain-looking girl, almost boyish, with tight Asian-looking eyes and a mouth as round and luxuriant as any peach. She was not a natural beauty. Her beauty needed taming.

Sauda could not have been jealous of Salimah's social standing; the girl was just a maid. The one thing that Salimah had that Sauda did not was innocence and sweetness, a quality more comely than external beauty or money or social standing. Sauda hated Salimah because she was everything that she was not, everything she could never be. And she intended to make her suffer for the insult.

Asabe cupped the girl's face in her hand. "Have you heard anything that I've said to you?"

Salimah shook her head in the affirmative.

"Then why haven't you answered me? Certainly you aren't afraid of me, are you?"

Salimah vigorously shook her head in the negative.

"So what is the problem? You *can* speak, can't you?"

Nothing. Salimah again lowered her head, but Asabe forced it back up.

"You can't speak?"

Salimah shook her head again, in the negative. Asabe's mouth fell open. Hadizah giggled at nothing, in the way that only babies will do.

Just as Asabe was going to ask Salimah the condition of her affliction, down came Sauda's course bellow from upstairs.

"Salimah," she yelled, "come here now!" Salimah slid from the seat, an apologetic look on her face, and disappeared quietly from the kitchen.

Later that evening after dinner and prayers, Asabe found herself wandering in the silence of Fatima's room. Salimah had in some strange way conjured up the feelings she had finally begun to allow to settle in the recesses of her mind. Asabe had almost forgotten that she missed her cowife.

"Little sister?" she whispered into the stillness, knowing there would be no reply. She simply wanted to hear the loving phrase once more, for it evoked happy memories of the girl she had no choice but to love. She pushed back a reserve of tears.

Many of Fatima's belongings still cluttered the bureau. Asabe held in her hands a silver bottle of kohl. It had never been opened. She fingered the heavy gold earrings that Adam had given to Fatima when she was only a week old in the house. With a smile, she remembered how the earrings seemed to weigh down the fragile young bride. She put them into her pocket. Later, she would put them in a safe place. She would save them for Fatima's daughter.

Asabe sat down on the bed that Fatima had once slept in, had conceived in, had given birth to Asabe's joy in, had given her daughter her first suck in, had died in. Now it was without an occupant, without life. It almost ceased to be a bed.

Next, Asabe fingered the tiny clothes. The clothes of varying colors still held the scent of Fatima's favorite perfumed oil. The closet is where Asabe felt her most, is where she felt the most anguish, is where she decided that it was time to let go so that she could heal.

"It was simply Allah's will," she whispered to herself.

Asabe removed Fatima's set of designer luggage from beneath the bed and filled them with the clothes in the closet. Asabe worked quickly and recklessly. She just wanted to be finished. She wanted to release Fatima from her mind, though deep in her heart, she knew that it would not be entirely possible. Each day when she looked into Hadizah's face, she saw Fatima's eyes looking back at her.

In the shoulder bag, Asabe put all of Fatima's jewelry and cosmetics. That finished it. As best as Asabe could, she carried and dragged the two pieces of heavy luggage and the shoulder bag out to the servants' quarters about seventy-five yards back. A small light shone through the window, illuminating her way through the darkness.

Asabe tapped on the door, but there was no answer the first or second time she knocked. Asabe set the luggage down on the front stoop and walked around to the side of the small domicile where the light was emanating from.

Asabe saw no one. There was only Salimah's sparse quarters. There was a desk cluttered with papers by the window in the foreground and a modest dining table and kitchen in the background. To the left, partially obscured from view, was a small living room decorated with as many as fifteen luxuriously stuffed pillows and several potted plants whose foliage spilled over onto the floor. There was an ajar door on the right, the entrance to a short corridor down, which was Salimah's bedroom and bathroom.

In the ten years since Asabe and Adam occupied their home, Asabe had only once been into the servants' quarters. They had never had any servants to occupy the space.

Asabe went back to the front door and tried the handle. Certainly, Salimah would not mind if she let herself in, in order to leave the clothes. The door was not locked. Asabe entered. Asabe liked the tiny apartment; it smelled of sandalwood musk and coconut. Salimah was fond of burning incense.

Asabe left the luggage to the left of the doorway and turned to leave but decided that she should write a note so that Salimah would know from where the clothes had come.

There were many papers scattered about on the desk by the window, all of them were covered with Salimah's hurried scribble.

Asabe tried the drawer and removed a red booklet in hopes of finding a blank sheet of paper. What she found though was something altogether different. The entry was dated on that day and read,

Today Sauda became very angry with me. I dropped a teacup by mistake and she became so angry that I feared she would strike me again. The bruise she gave me last week has still not faded.

Something else happened, Asabe came and cleaned the mess for me. It was very kind of her, but I knew that she was a kind soul from the first time I saw her. It is a shame that no one else appreciates her kindness. Misses Sauda has so turned their husband's head with her artful deceptions that he no longer knows if he is coming or going.

Asabe will surely be harmed in this all. In the end so will Adam. But this is not the worst. Only Allah knows what Misses Sauda has in store for the innocent one.

"Artful deceptions . . . innocent one . . . ?" Asabe recited to herself. "What does that mean?" she said a bit louder. When Asabe heard her own voice resound in the small room, she felt great shame for having read the private entry. This was obviously Salimah's private journal. Asabe had unwittingly intruded where she would not have been welcomed. She replaced the book and turned to leave, forgetting about the note she had intended to write.

Asabe was angry with herself. This type of invasion had happened before, almost two years earlier. Asabe's hand went to the left side of her face, to the place where Adam had left his mark of violence.

"Never again," she promised herself. "Never."

Asabe hurried through the darkness back to the house. The air was cool, and the wind had picked up. Asabe glanced up into the clouds; it seemed a storm was headed their way.

A storm yes, but which kind?

"What sort of deception?" Asabe whispered into the darkness. "What has my co-wife done that will harm Adam and me?" Asabe could not shake from her mind the words she had read in the journal entry: *Only Allah knows what Misses Sauda has in store for the innocent one.*

ATTIYAH WAS PLEASED TO OBLIGE ADAM'S request to assist him in the choosing of the perfect gift for his wife.

"I need a woman's opinion," he'd said, "to find the most beautiful garment for the most beautiful wife a man could ever have."

It was the day before the Eid, a day to mark the end of Ramadan and the beginning of three days of celebration, and he was running out of time.

After five hours of searching, they finally agreed on a dress. Adam informed Amina, the owner of the small boutique sporting her name, that money was no object. With those words as encouragement, she disappeared into a room behind the counter and emerged with a black garment bag.

Adam and Attiyah stood in rapt attention as if she were about to unveil a priceless piece of art. It came close. The dress was the color of a ripe cherry, red threatening to be black. The silky sheer fabric was sewn layer upon layer in long flowing waves. The neck and hemline of the dress was decorated with a bold stripe of gold lame, and dozens of tiny gold buttons trailed their way from the neck to the hem.

Adam stood with his mouth agape. Attiyah stroked the fabric as if she were caressing the cheek of a sleeping babe.

"It won't fall to pieces if you touch it," assured Amina.

"But it's so soft. Almost like the petals of a flower."

"I only bring it out for special customers." Amina grinned pretentiously.

"You mean for the customers who have lots of money to spend," said Adam. Before Amina could become offended, Adam said, "There is certainly nothing wrong with that. If you hadn't saved this dress, surely someone else would have bought it by now."

A trio of talkative women entered the boutique. Amina excused herself and left to greet them.

Attiyah removed the dress from the hanger and held it up to herself before the mirror. "Yes," she said, "this will fit her perfectly. I can virtually see her in it now."

Adam approached Attiyah and inspected the garment more carefully. "It looks far too small for her, especially now since her pregnancy is beginning to show."

Attiyah spun around. "Asabe is pregnant? Since when? Why hasn't anyone told me? In the name of Allah, why are you allowing her to fast? It may harm the baby."

"I'm not referring to Asabe. She hasn't become pregnant in the entire twelve years since our marriage. I don't believe that she will ever give me a child."

"Everything is by the will of Allah. It isn't up to you to decide if she is capable or not."

Attiyah glanced down at the expensive garment in her hands.

"All of this talk about buying a beautiful gift for a beautiful wife has been about Sauda?"

"Of course. I can't think of anyone who deserves it more than she. She is accustomed to the best, and I intend to give it to her."

"What about Asabe? Aren't you pleased with her anymore?"

"Why shouldn't I be? She is a wonderful mother and caretaker to my daughter. She is honest and obedient. And patient. I've never known anyone more patient in all of my life. Asabe is my wife, and if Allah has any mercy on me, he will allow me to live out my last days with her."

"You profess your love about her loud and clear, my brother. I believe you. It seems though that at this moment, your only concern is Sauda. This is an extravagant gift. Have you already bought Asabe's gift?"

"No, I haven't."

"Tomorrow is the Eid. When do you intend on doing it?"

"To be honest," he said, lowering his head, "I really had no intention of buying her anything."

Attiyah replaced the garment on the hanger. Attiyah tried to think of just the right words to say, words that would make Adam see how wrong he was.

"Asabe is your wife. How do you think she will feel when she sees that you have given this overpriced dress to Sauda while she gets nothing?"

"A moment ago, the dress was so like flower petals that you were afraid to touch it. Now you describe it as if it were repulsive."

Attiyah could not cage her words. "On some people, it would be repulsive, particularly spoiled, ugly women who haven't even the tact to appreciate the gift."

"I take it you don't care for Sauda."

"I don't see how you could. She's horrible. Anyone could see that. Even Satan would stay away from her."

The three talkative customers, now silent, were casting inquisitive glances in the direction of the arguing couple.

Attiyah lowered her voice. "It is only because she is your wife and carrying your son that I have held my tongue with her, but I have seen her say and do things that no respectable woman ever would."

"I don't care what you think of her. Just last year, you couldn't stand the sight of Asabe. Now you're rallying in her defense."

"She is your wife."

"I know that," Adam yelled, "but she isn't the one who is having my son! Asabe is many good things, but she has never given me a son. That deserves my loyalty more than anything else."

"Allah is the giver of life. Not man. Not you."

Adam turned to walk away, but Attiyah continued talking.

"It has been promised by none other than Allah that the man who is unjust between his wives shall be raised on Judgment Day with his body as lopsided as his affections. That man will be marked with his injustice so that all who look at him will know his misdeeds."

Adam ignored his sister and approached the counter where Amina stood watching their tit for tat.

"If you have that dress in a larger size, you've got a sale."

Amina smiled up at Adam.

"I do. It's very good doing business with a man who knows what he wants."

SAUDA STUFFED THE LAST TWO CRACKERS into her mouth and washed them down with half a glass of warm milk. She attempted to throw the empty cracker box into the trash can ten feet from her bed, but it landed on the floor with a hollow thud, along with her other failed attempts.

Her bed was cluttered with the wrappers of cookies and candies and the crumbs and silt of cheap delicacies, all testimony to her night of bingeing. Each mouthful was one more brick in the wall she'd built to damn her tears and drown her uncertainty.

The time glowed a neon 5:10 a.m., and her hope had finally dissolved.

Adam would not be coming to her room. He had promised her the prior evening that he would forgo his night with Asabe to attend to her. In her excitement, Sauda had spent the following hour attempting to mask the unsightly countenance that plagued her pregnancy.

She had wanted the pregnancy so badly and had spent endless nights supplicating to Allah. Allah granted her desire with such might, its presence was consuming; and at times, she'd wondered if she truly wanted it at all.

There were dark blotches around her cheeks, and her eyes were reminiscent of a raccoon. Her nose and lips seemed swollen as water blisters, and her feet reminded her of the flat, clubbed feet of an elephant. Her protruding stomach replaced her bosom as the part of her body that preceded her into any room.

Despite this, she adorned herself in the only gown that still fit, pressed powder onto her shining face, rubbed on scented oil, and waited for her husband. Her husband never came.

Sauda had sat up in her bed all night wondering where Adam was and what he was doing. Countless nights in the past, Sauda had pressed her ear against Asabe's door in the quiet hours of the night, nights when he was supposed to be with her, only to hear them giggling with each other like two silly teenagers. Though his propensity to desert her had waned since the announcement of a son, she could not help but fear his disinterest in her.

He had been more attentive to her, filling her jewelry box with more of the expensive gold trinkets she loved so well. He started bringing her sweetmeats from town, which she would devour in his presence, to show her appreciation and, of course, to keep them coming. His gift to her for the Eid hung in her closet. With all her father's money, she had scarcely ever owned a garment as beautiful.

She should have had no reason to fear his love for her, or the lack of it, but despite it all, she could not change the look in his eyes. It was not the look of love, or even longing, but rather determination. He was determined to do his duty, determined to make things right, determined to have a healthy son.

Sauda squeezed her eyes shut so tightly that stars appeared behind the lids. The dam threatened to give way. It was a sudden rush of emotion that came with the thought of Adam holding their son. Their son. Then perhaps the sense of duty in Adam's eyes would turn to love.

Or hate.

"What would he do," Sauda asked herself aloud, "if it is not a son but a daughter? What would he do if he found out that my ultrasound confirmed no son? That I lied?" Sauda shook her head from side to side as if to shake away the thought. "Oh, Allah," she said, looking up, "let it be a son. Let it be a son."

THAT IT WAS THE EID meant little as regards to Sauda's disposition. It seemed, in fact, that Sauda was even more onerous than usual. Sauda screamed words at Salimah that even she thought Sauda would never dare to use.

There was no cause for Sauda's ill behavior. Salimah had been timely with the breakfast, and it had been prepared with as much efficiency as was possible. She hadn't dropped or soiled anything. Although it was much deserved, she hadn't even given Sauda a cross look. It was the previous night that Sauda spent alone that made her so disagreeable.

Sauda sat at the kitchen table, her legs spread wide open in the manner of a man so that her protruding belly could rest comfortably on the chair. Her feet were swollen and bare, and her hair was disheveled. To Salimah, Sauda looked wild and uncertain, as if she was ready to deliver her burden. Sauda wore Adam's Eid gift. She could have been dazzling had she not seemed so undone.

"You hurry up and finish with those dishes. You hear me?"

Salimah nodded.

"I want you to braid my hair. It wouldn't be such a mess had you done it last night like I asked you to. I had to iron my own dress this morning because you were late getting over here. Where were you? Huh? What were you doing?" Sauda sucked her teeth. "You're lucky that I wasn't in the mood because I was tempted to go right down to your quarters and whip you. I would have whipped you real good too."

Over a heaping spoonful of oatmeal, Sauda's eye was drawn to a golden tassel that hung from Salimah's scarf, a scarf she didn't recognize.

Everything Salimah owned Sauda had provided for her, and she would have never given Salimah anything as expensive as the ensemble she was wearing.

Salimah was wearing a jalabiyah the color of the sun. Its bell sleeves and neckline were embroidered with black thread that possessed occasional flecks of gold. The matching scarf was the same, with golden tassels dangling from the four corners. Sauda stared at Salimah, wondering how she could have missed the sight of her maid. The girl did not look at all like herself. She looked almost . . . normal.

"Hey," said Sauda, standing up. "Where did you get that dress?"

Sauda approached Salimah, who was at the sink, and grabbed her shoulders, turning her so that the girl would face her. Salimah's slight eyes were lined with kohl, and her lips were shiny and tinged with pink. With so little makeup, Salimah's boyish face had overnight changed into one of a blossoming young woman.

Sauda released the girl and stepped back as if she had received an electric shock. Just the day before, Salimah was a homely-looking wench.

Sauda repeated, "Where did you get that dress?"

"I gave it to her, along with a few other things," answered Asabe from the kitchen doorway. "Doesn't she look beautiful this Eid morning?" Asabe said this more to Salimah than to Sauda, and they smiled at each other from across the kitchen. Sauda stood looking from one to the other, uncertain if she had missed a private joke between the two of them.

"Well," said Sauda, resuming her seat, "you shouldn't have given her something so expensive, especially not to a maid."

"Why not?"

"It gives them pretensions. Before you know it, she'll be thinking that she's as good as you and me. She must be kept in her place."

"She is no less than either one of us. In fact, before Allah, she may even be better. Besides, there is no chance of her getting out of place. You are particularly diligent about reminding her of her place every chance you get."

Before Sauda could find insult in Asabe's words, she added, "This is the Eid, and everyone will be dressed in their finest. You have a sweet nature, and I know that you would want the same good fortune for your maid."

Asabe was in a good mood and was willing to use subtle manipulation to get what she was after—a peaceful, joy-filled day.

"I suppose," said Sauda, succumbing to Asabe's compliments as unlikely as they were. Not even Sauda believed Asabe's talk of her sweet nature, but it sounded nice to her anyway.

"She can keep the clothes as long as she doesn't let it go to her head."

Kasuar crept under the table and purred around Asabe's legs. She knew what he wanted. Asabe removed a can of sardines from the cabinet. When Kasuar caught sight of the shiny silver and red can, his purring grew louder, and he began to lick at Asabe's toes in his excitement.

The doorbell rang. Asabe asked Salimah to answer the door.

"It's probably Jamil. He and Adam are riding to the mosque together this morning to attend Eid prayers. Please go and let him in."

Salimah left immediately.

"That's an impressive garment," Asabe said to Sauda.

"I know." Sauda puffed out her already-heaving bosom. "It cost a lot of money too."

"I can tell. Was it a gift from your father?"

"No. *My husband* gave it to me."

"Adam?" Asabe put the tin of sardines just outside of the door on the back porch. Kasuar followed it out.

"Who else? I am his wife after all. I am worthy of such gifts, even if you don't think that I am."

"Of course you are worthy," Asabe cooed. "You are his wife, and I know that he has a great deal of affection for you."

"Affection? No, ours is love."

"I'm sure that it is. This dress is proof of that." Again, Asabe turned on the false sweetness and charm. "It fits you perfectly. Obviously he put a great deal of thought into this purchase. Money too." Asabe tried to laugh, but it came out a cough. "Of course you deserve it. You are the soon-to-be mother of his first son."

Sauda relaxed in her chair and resumed eating her breakfast.

"That's right. Don't you forget it either." After a few seconds of silence, Sauda asked, "What did he get you?"

"I don't know," Asabe almost whispered.

"How could you not know?"

Asabe said nothing to this.

"You mean he didn't get you anything?" Sauda raised up her heavy legs, dropping her fat feet against the floor. She clapped her hands like an excited child.

"Ha! So the *favorite* wife didn't get an Eid gift while the one he only has *affection* for gets a gift that costs enough to buy everything in the favorite wife's closet. Ha!"

Asabe poured herself a cup of tea.

"Well, don't feel too bad. I warned you before that he would soon turn away from you." Sauda proudly rubbed her stomach. "Don't worry. I'll remind him from time to time that you are still his wife. I'll make sure that he gives you and that orphan girl some bit of attention." Sauda laughed aloud.

"You sure are an arrogant one, aren't you?" said Attiyah from the doorway. She was dressed all in white with sparkling silver embroidery. Huge silver domes hung from her distressed earlobes, but as usual, her fingers sparkled with nothing but gold. Under her left arm, she held a large brightly wrapped box. She held a small blue velvet jewelry box in her right hand.

After kissing Asabe on the cheek, Attiyah said, "This big box is from Adam. He asked me to give it to you. And this small one is from me."

Attiyah rolled her eyes at Sauda, who in her shame cast her eyes down into her bowl of quickly cooling oatmeal.

"Go on, open them."

Asabe began with the small velvet box. Inside was a heavy gold chain, the links designed to resemble the weaving of a basket. Asabe allowed Attiyah to put it on her neck.

"It's so pretty, don't you think, Sauda?"

"It's okay." Sauda barely looked at it.

Next was Adam's gift. Asabe tore the wrapping from the largest box and snatched the top off. The thrill ended there. Asabe stared at the scarf, sheer and red. Red, red, red. It wasn't as costly as Sauda's gift, nor was it inspired. Asabe knew the moment she laid eyes on the silky red material that the gift was not even from Adam.

There wasn't a stitch of red in Asabe's closet because she despised the color. Adam knew this. He'd known since the days before they married when he brought her a similar red scarf as a gift, and she asked him to take it back. Adam had never made the mistake again.

Despite the unequal quality, the gift would have been enough had it come from Adam. It was then that Asabe knew that Adam had not intended to give her anything for the Eid and that Attiyah was only attempting to compensate for his insensitivity.

It didn't work.

This explained Adam's behavior earlier that morning when she handed him his gift. For weeks, he'd been saying that he needed a new prayer rug, how his old rug was tattered and unraveling around the fringed edge. When he opened the bag and saw the royal blue rug with a picture of the sacred house printed on front, he behaved as if he hadn't really wanted it all along.

"I appreciate this, but it wasn't necessary," was all he had said.

She had tried to speak with him, wanting to know why he had not come to her the night before; but he was in a hurry to shower, in a hurry to dress, in a hurry to do a million other chores. He hardly looked in her direction, and now she knew that it was because he could not.

"Well, let us see it," said Sauda with a mouthful of biscuit.

Asabe held the scarf up.

"Now that's pretty." Sauda's eyes burned with admiration. "Red is my favorite color."

"It will go beautifully with your skin," said Attiyah to Asabe.

"It would go even better with mine," said Sauda.

"Get your own scarf. This one isn't for you." Attiyah sucked her teeth.

"You know," Asabe began, "I think that I agree with Sauda. Perhaps it would look better on her."

"What?" said Attiyah and Sauda in unison.

"And since I have failed to buy you a gift for the Eid, I'll give you this scarf. That is, if you'll have it."

Sauda's face lit up.

"You're not really going to give *her* your gift, are you? Adam bought it for you."

"Did he?"

Attiyah did a double take and stared at Asabe. Sauda again looked back and forth from one woman to the next, trying to absorb what was taking place. She knew that something had just occurred and that she was miserably outside of the loop.

Asabe knew something, of this Attiyah was positive. Too much of a protest on her part would only confirm Asabe's suspicions, and then it would have all been for nothing. Perhaps her knowing about Adam's neglect wouldn't be so bad after all. He needed to be found out, and she surmised that she should not have tried to cover for him in the first place.

Attiyah shrugged her shoulders, "It's your scarf. You do with it as you please."

Asabe passed the scarf across the table. "Eid Mubarak." Asabe offered a crooked smile.

"Eid Kareem."

HANNAH STOOD IN THE KITCHEN DOORWAY and stared down the corridor into the sitting room. There, the men congregated, sitting, standing, leaning, and reclining with plates of food piled high. They ate like gluttons now that the fasting of Ramadan was done and the Eid had commenced.

Hannah recognized only a few of the men. Adam was there of course, and there was Jabar who's loud and gossiping wife was in the garden, entertaining the ladies with the latest news of who had divorced whom and who had recently given birth and when. Abu Kareem sat on the couch with his cane propped up against his knee and a plate on his lap. Attiyah's husband, Mahmoud, had arrived only ten minutes earlier, carrying gifts of clothes and food and spouting stories of his many moneymaking trips abroad. Jamil was there, the youngest and least pretentious of the bunch. He leaned in a corner, and unlike his cohorts, he nibbled rather than devoured his food. His attention was not on his plate but rather on Salimah.

Salimah moved around the room in silence, hardly noticing the attention that she received. She was too busy retrieving empty plates, filling empty glasses, and taking orders for more of this or that food. She was the servant, but today she did not look like the servant. She was the same in character, silent and obedient, but this day her back was straight, and her head was held high. And Jamil noticed.

Salimah, with skin was as black as rich earth, looked like a little bumblebee in her sun-colored dress. And Jamil noticed.

"What are you staring at?" asked Asabe from behind her mother. Asabe had just come in from the garden.

Hannah pointed down the hall and said, "Look."

All Asabe saw was a roomful of greedy men telling one preposterous lie after the other in order to impress the others. "What am I looking at?"

"Jamil. See how he's looking at Salimah."

"So what? Is that supposed to mean something?"

Hannah crossed her arms over her bosom and turned to Asabe. "Can't you see that that boy is interested in her? Sometimes I wonder if you're blind. I wouldn't be surprised if soon that boy came around asking for her hand in marriage."

"Mother, she is a maid. Not many men would reduce themselves to marrying a maid, especially a mute maid." When Asabe saw the astonishment on her mother's face, she quickly spoke to defend herself. "I think that Salimah is wonderful, mute or not, but you know how men can be. He's a college boy, trying to move up in the world. I don't think he'd look back to pick up a little village maid for marriage."

"You're wrong. He's still young, and I don't think he's acquired those arrogant ways yet. Besides, it would be a hypocrisy on his part if he did."

"What do you mean?"

"I mean that his own mother worked in our house when I was still married to your father. His own mother was a maid years ago."

"Sauda won't like this, if it's true."

"When it comes to matters of the heart, what Sauda thinks means absolutely nothing. She won't lose anyway. The way she treats Salimah, you'd think the girl was a bad maid."

Hannah left the doorway and went to the window. She stared out into the garden full of women. "There are lots of good maids to be had, but not many people find the perfect mate. I think Jamil has seen his perfect mate."

Asabe replaced her mother in the doorway and noticed something herself. Abu Kareem kept looking up and into the corridor.

"I know something else Sauda won't like," Asabe said.

"Who cares about Sauda," said Hannah, waving her hand in dismissal.

"You will, soon enough. You've been spending so much time noticing Jamil noticing Salimah that you didn't notice who was noticing you."

"Who?" Hannah stood up on her toes to get a better look.

"Abu Kareem."

She laughed out loud. "You must be joking. What would he possibly want with me when he could have his pick of young virgins? I'm too old for him."

"He's at least fifteen years older than you."

"Asabe," chided Hannah, "by now you're old enough to know the way of things. Old men can have mere children for brides up until their last breath while women like me . . ." Her voice trailed off.

"Women like you are strong and wonderful and knowledgeable and patient and wise and just as marriageable as any young nymph. Some old men still prefer mature ladies."

As if she were beginning to believe her daughter, Hannah stood up straight and threw her shoulders back as if to say, *Yes, you are right.* However, when Hannah caught a glimpse of Salimah, simply blossoming with youth, the very promise of fresh starts and fertile beginnings, she resigned herself to the truth she'd already told herself.

Hannah's chest deflated, and her shoulders dropped. "Like I said before, I'm too old for him."

FAR MORE PEOPLE than Adam expected had to come to his home for the Eid. Most were young women, some married, but most not; and Adam suspected that many of them were simply on the prowl, hoping to be seen bedecked in their best dress and taken interest in by one of the male guests in attendance.

Most were friends of Sauda's, women he had never seen until that day. All were still fairly young, between the ages of nineteen and twenty-two, too old to find young men to marry; and this particular group of women was far too challenging for any mature man to bother with. Like Sauda, they were haughty, privileged, and problematic.

Adam lay back on his bed and closed his eyes.

"Tired?" Asabe was standing in the doorway of Adam's bedroom.

"Very much," he answered without opening his eyes. Adam felt tiny damp fingers grasp at one of his toes. Asabe had brought Hadizah with her. He sat up on the edge of his bed and took the gurgling child into his arms.

"Today was busy. Lots of people." He tried to rub the sleep from his eyes.

"Yes, but it was nice. Don't you think?"

Adam nodded. Asabe watched her husband, unsure of how to begin, of what to begin. She wasn't altogether positive of why she was there. Asabe had never been at a loss for words with Adam, but this time, he was different. There wasn't much she could say that would be of consequence, for she knew her husband, his moods, his motivations. Asabe knew why he had so blatantly done injustice between her and Sauda. Because of this, Asabe could not be angry with Adam. Asabe knew that he would not succeed.

Sauda was a different breed of person than they, desperate and needy and willing to jealously defend her interests, whatever she deemed them to be. Sauda was angry and in pain and in need of far more than Adam could offer. Sauda was not easy to love or even to respect. Adam had made the terrible mistake of thinking that by slighting Asabe, he would be doing justice to Sauda. Instead, Adam was doing a disservice to his own soul. He was lying to himself. Outwardly, he seemed attentive and interested in Sauda, but his eyes could not veil the disgust he felt whenever he looked at her.

Asabe did not want to quibble about his latest attitude toward her—that he was frequenting her room less and less, that he had so abruptly ceased their familiar discussions, and that after twelve years of marriage he failed to give her a gift for the Eid. Asabe wanted to assure Adam that she would not desert him even though he had deserted her.

Asabe leaned down to show Adam her new necklace. "Did you see what Attiyah gave me?"

"Yes, she showed me the day she bought it," Adam yawned. "I thought that it would be a bit imprudent considering your tastes, but she insisted. She said that you would love it."

"I'm glad she did insist. I think it's about time that I have at least one imprudent item in my wardrobe." Asabe ran her fingers over the slick gold. "I think that I deserve it. Did she show you the scarf that she gave me?"

"No."

"It was quite beautiful, silk. I think it was of the highest quality." Asabe watched for a reaction when she said, "She told me that it was from you, but I knew it was a lie."

This time Adam looked up. The sleep had fallen away. Hadizah tugged at his ear. He tried to think of something appropriate to say, but Asabe spoke first.

"I knew that it wasn't really from you because it was red. Redder than blood. I knew you'd never buy me anything red. I've always hated that color."

"Did you tell her that you knew?" Adam's voice was unsteady.

"No. But she knows. I gave it to Sauda." Asabe sat in the chair at Adam's desk. "So in actual fact, you have given Sauda two gifts this Eid. At least she thinks so, and what she thinks is all that matters, right?"

Adam was silent. He wasn't afraid of Asabe, but he could not read her mood, and this unnerved him. She should have been angry, but anger manifests itself in shouts and ugly words. Asabe was as pleasant as ever. She should have been hurt, but her eyes were not damp with tears; instead, she almost smiled at him.

"I'll admit that at first, I was a bit insulted that Attiyah would cover for you with me, your wife of twelve years; but I realized that she is the one who has suffered the most insult."

"How was she insulted?"

"You are her junior brother. She practically raised you. I think it is a shame that at the age of fifty-four, your behavior is such that she still feels the need to act on your behalf."

"No one asked her to do so. I told her that I had my reasons for not buying you a gift. She didn't have to give you anything in my stead."

Adam's voice had an edge so pronounced that Hadizah paused her usually cheerful gurgle to look up into her father's face.

"You're correct. She didn't have to, but I think that she was just trying to be polite. After all, you weren't." Asabe wanted to take the words back; they didn't come out the way she intended.

"I was impolite? How?" Adam stood from the bed. Hadizah's eyes opened wide and watchful of his face. "Because I didn't get you a gift?"

Asabe refused to speak for fear that the words would not come out right.

"I don't think that you deserve anything."

"Why not? I cook, I clean, I nurse and love your baby. I tolerate you and your unruly, arrogant wife. I deserve all that you have to give and more. I am your wife, a position few women would want." Asabe didn't care anymore. She would not tolerate his disdain.

"If you think that life with me and my wife are such a hardship, then you can leave. She can do all of the things that you do, and she is giving me a son." He handed the baby to Asabe. Hadizah began to whimper but stopped when she heard her mother's good-natured laughter.

"What's so funny?"

"You are," said Asabe between gasps of air. "Adam, I wouldn't leave you, not now anyway. You're going to need me." Asabe laughed some more.

"I don't need you for anything."

"You believe that now, but soon you will know better. I didn't come here to argue with you. In fact, I came here only to say that I love you and that I understand. I do. But you have been very ugly with me just now, and Allah doesn't like ugly."

Adam tried to speak, but Asabe silenced him by holding up her hand. "You will fall from your lofty seat, and you will be hurt. I don't hope this to be, but it isn't in my control. When you do, I will be there to help you pick up the pieces of your broken life because I do love you and because I am your wife. Sauda may be having your son, but she will not be a loyal wife. I know her type, and so do you. If you have made yourself believe that she is better than me and that you love her more, then you are more delusional than I figured."

"I don't think so."

"Oh, you'll see," said Asabe, leaving the room. "You'll see."

TWELVE

Jamil's car jolted forward when the asphalt ended and the dirt road began. Dust climbed into the air in large smoky clouds, making it nearly impossible for him to see more than twenty feet ahead. He slowed his car to twenty-five miles per hour. The decrease in speed nearly drove him mad.

"Slow down," chided his best friend and escort, "the village won't disappear before you get there."

Jamil was in a rush to reach the village of Salam. It was the village of Salimah's father.

For three months, Jamil cultivated an innocent relationship with Salimah. He would visit her each Friday after congregational prayers in the mosque. They would speak in the garden; or rather, he would speak, and she would listen, at first with her head bowed and her arms crossed over her chest. However, Salimah's seeming disinterest did not sway his determination. Jamil knew that he wanted to marry Salimah, and soon enough, she knew that she wanted to marry him.

Each time Jamil came to visit, he would bring a gift, a box of chocolates or a bag of roasted peanuts until he was positive that he would have no other for his bride. Then the sweets became silken scarves, leather sandals, handfuls of wadded money, and promises of a happy future. Though she had never spoken a word to him in thanks or in love, he was well aware of her feelings for him, for he would barely pull his car into the drive before she was racing outside to greet him with bashful smiles.

The previous week, Jamil's parents drove out to the home of Rahman, representing him. They asked on his behalf for Salimah's hand in marriage. Rahman, they said, was undecided and had insisted on seeing the face of the man who wanted his daughter's hand. And so Jamil was on his way to greet the father of the woman he desired for his wife.

Only two hours previous, Jamil had left Salimah. She waved good-bye to him from the front porch of Adam's house. She wore the same sun-colored dress he'd first seen her wear on the Eid, except this time, her wrist was stacked with the four gold bangles that he had given her. He'd never seen anyone become so animated over anything material. Jamil found her reaction charming. It made him want to give her more and more.

As Jamil's car came over the crest of a small hill, Siddique pointed to a rusted and sun-bleached sign that read Salam in dingy red letters.

"This is the place." Jamil glanced over at his friend and smiled so broadly his cheeks ached.

"You look like a hyena, grinning that way. I almost expected you to cackle like one." Siddique nudged his friend in the ribs. They both laughed.

Considering the locale, Rahman's home was quite well off, more so than his neighbors. His home was reminiscent of an adobe, molded with black clay instead of red and squared edges instead of round. Despite its seemingly primitive materials, the house was grand and almost elegant with its large wooden front door painted chalk white, white shutters, and lush flower garden, all surrounded by an eight-foot-high wrought-iron gate.

Rahman answered the door himself. Rahman was a raisin of a man, small and shriveled and black. He had large rheumy eyes with which he seemed to peer right into the soul of Jamil. His back was slightly humped over in his old age; but he seemed strong, even feisty, judging by his combative stance.

Rahman hardly noticed Jamil's travel companion.

"So you're the one who wants my daughter's hand." Before Jamil could offer a reply, Rahman continued by saying, "Don't stand out there like a fool, young man. You and your friend come in."

Jamil and Siddique followed the old man out of the foyer and down a cool dark corridor that extended from the front of the house to the back.

"Kubrah," he yelled, "bring my guests some refreshments out back! And hurry!" In the backyard, there was a mango tree and two lemon trees perfuming the entire backyard. There was a worn patio set with a green umbrella, which had many holes, and four chairs that squeaked when any amount of weight was placed in them. It was here that they sat.

"Tell me, why do you want my daughter's hand?" Rahman wasted no time on pleasantries.

It was a simple-enough question, but somehow it left Jamil dumbfounded. Jamil looked to his friend for help, but Siddique shrugged his shoulders as if to say, *If you don't know why you want her, then how could I?*

Then the words came to him. "She is beautiful and kind."

"She may be, but beauty fades, and kindness has the habit of shifting as quickly as the winds when problems arise. I know, I've been married four times. Women can be a trial."

"Yes, but she is different."

"All women are the same."

"Not Salimah. She is special and innocent and pious. She is patient and understanding."

"When a man sees the woman he wants, she will always in his eyes seem *special.* Until you get her home. And then her true colors will show themselves." Rahman was smiling now, but Jamil did not see the humor in this inquisition. "You haven't married her yet. How would you know how patient she is?"

"Because she works for Sauda, and that woman is a terror," responded Siddique

"Now there, you have definitely spoken the truth. It is that woman's stubbornness that has my family living in the best house in this village. Her father, Abu Kareem, pays my daughter well for her patience. My daughter's patience has helped put her senior brother into university in London, and it has helped to pay for two of my daughters' weddings. Patient, she is." And then as if it was a new realization, Rahman added, "She is also mute. Hasn't spoken a word in seven years."

"I know that she is mute, but surely that doesn't lessen her value, at least not in your eyes."

"Oh no, not in my eyes. She is my daughter, I would willingly take care of her until my last day, but I don't have to marry her. These days, young virgins are many, all vying for the same scarce men. Surely there is someone more to your standards that you could marry."

A young woman stepped out into the backyard, carrying a silver tray with glasses of iced tea, a plate of cookies, and a bowl of peanuts still in their shells. She smiled uneasily and offered them the salutation, "As-salaam alaikum."

As she walked away, Rahman leaned forward and whispered across the table, "See her?"

Jamil nodded belatedly, still trying to process Rahman's last remarks.

"That is Salimah's senior sister, Kubrah. She is eighteen, she can sew, cook, and clean. She is very obedient, and she won't give you cause to argue. She is beautiful too, don't you think? She is quite religious, can recite the whole of the Qur'an by heart. Out loud. By mouth. See what I mean? She can talk. Why not marry her instead?"

"Your daughter is indeed very lovely, but I don't want anyone else. I want Salimah despite the fact that she cannot talk. I would want her if she had a clubbed foot, if she were in a wheelchair, blind and cripple. There is no one in this entire world like her, and she is the one I want. Nothing and no one else.

"I came here for your blessing. Just tell me what I have to do. I'll beg you. I'll come here every day and harangue you or serve you, whichever you choose, just as long as when it is all done, you will consent to allowing her to be my wife."

Rahman took a long sip from his tea and then leaned his head back to peer through the largest hole in the umbrella up to the darkening sky. For a long time, he said nothing. Jamil feared that he might have lost his chance. He looked to Siddique, but his friend could offer nothing.

"Sir?" said Jamil, breaking the silence.

"You shouldn't call me sir," said Rahman, still looking heavenward. "You might as well start calling me Baba if you're going to be marrying my daughter." He smiled at Jamil. Rahman extended his hand. They shook heartily. "I only wanted to be sure that you were sincere. Salimah is my favorite. Don't tell anyone I said so, and the man who marries her must be exceptional. He must be worthy."

"She is my favorite too, Baba, and you can tell the whole world."

SAUDA TASTED THE LENTIL SOUP and then spat the repulsive concoction into the sink. She added half a cup of sugar where there should have been a tablespoon of salt and an overdose of ground red pepper. This wasn't her kitchen anyway, and she was not accustomed to cooking. Had Adam not insisted, Sauda would never have ventured into the kitchen for any reason other than to partake of a meal that someone else had prepared.

Three months prior, around the time of the Eid, something momentous had happened. Adam ceased almost all relations with Asabe. He would not visit her room. He would not allow her to clean his room or wash his clothes. He would not sit in her company. He would not even eat her food. When the time came to visit with his daughter, Adam would take Hadizah from Asabe and visit with her in Sauda's room or in the living room or outside or anywhere other than with Asabe as he had before.

Sauda had no idea what caused Adam's displeasure with Asabe, but it pleased her nonetheless. To a point. When the chores that were once Asabe's fell into Sauda's lap, she began to wonder if Asabe wasn't useful after all.

Adam was a big man, not simply by the placement of genes. He was a man with a hearty appetite and a great love for good food. So too was Sauda. She often wondered if perhaps Adam had made a mistake in abandoning Asabe. He had to have missed her food. Sauda did.

Cleaning was a chore that Sauda disliked but could do with some efficiency. Sometimes though, she would fake discomfort due to her pregnancy and manipulate Salimah into doing her chores for her, as she had that day. Sauda intended to order Salimah to do the cooking as well.

Adam had instructed Salimah not to cook to allow Sauda to prove her worth and thereby disproving Asabe's, but Sauda wasn't feeling well. Nor was she in the mood to begin the meal for the third time.

Sauda stood over the sink and looked with disgust at the remains of the last pot of lentil soup she'd poured down the drain. Sauda turned on the hot water and flipped the garbage disposal switch. The soup disappeared down the drain in a muddy-looking swirl.

Sauda turned her attention out of the window in search of Salimah. Earlier after Jamil had left, Sauda saw her heading out back toward her quarters. Sauda turned off the bubbling pot and slipped on her sandals at the door. She pushed her way out of the screen door using her mound of protruding belly and tottered out to Salimah's quarters.

Sauda did not knock, entering as if it was her own room. She found Asabe and Salimah sitting cross-legged on the floor, smiling at each other as if they were the best of friends. Hadizah was toddling around the room, a glittering string of saliva stretching from her mouth to the floor.

Sauda had no way to rationalize her feelings, but the scene she beheld annoyed her.

"Do you usually sit with the help?" asked Sauda.

"When they're interesting company, I do." Asabe smiled up at Sauda and excused herself to the bathroom. Hadizah watched her mother disappear down the hall, and then she turned her attention to a piece of loose thread on the carpet.

Asabe seemed too happy to Sauda. Abandoned, barren women shouldn't be happy.

Sauda sat down at the desk by the window. She was winded from her walk. The baby attempted to stretch within the restricted confines of her belly. A foot to her rib cage caught her off guard, and she hiccupped.

"I'm not feeling well today." Sauda began by trying to gain Salimah's sympathy. Sauda may have lied about not feeling well in the past, but today she could not have been more serious. "I need you to do something for me."

Salimah nodded, waiting to hear what Sauda wanted.

"You know that I am not a good cook. I'm horrible at it, that is no lie. I can't help it. I've never had to cook for myself." Salimah seemed unmoved, uninterested even.

"I've ruined dinner twice this evening, and Adam is due home at any minute. I want you to go and prepare something for him. Anything you want, just as long as it's finished within an—"

Salimah shook her head vigorously in the negative. Sauda countered by shaking her head in the positive.

"Oh yes, you will. I don't care what Adam told you. He doesn't pay your salary. My father does, and he hired you to be my helper, my maid. That means you do as I say."

Sauda hardly realized the time when she rose from the chair and hovered over Salimah, who still sat cross-legged on the floor.

"I don't have to negotiate with you. Get up and go to the house."

Sauda grabbed Salimah by the arm, pulling her to her feet. Sauda noticed the new golden trinkets that clattered on Salimah's wrist. This annoyed Sauda.

"Did Jamil give you these?"

Salimah smiled proudly. This too perturbed Sauda.

"Expensive items don't make you more important. You are still a maid. You are still no one special. Don't let the attention go to your head. You have a job to do." Sauda heard the crunch of gravel and the hum of Adam's engine outside. "Hurry up, he will already have to wait for his dinner. I don't want to waste even more time arguing with you."

Salimah continued to shake her head in the negative. This act of defiance, as passive as it may have been, ignited a fury in Sauda that she could little control. It wasn't until Sauda felt the stinging on the palm of her hand that she realized she had struck Salimah.

Salimah had stopped nodding her head. She was as immobile as a statue, stupefied by what had just happened to her. Unquestionably, it was not the first time that Sauda had struck Salimah; but this time, Salimah did not even see it coming.

Hadizah crawled across the room and pulled at the hem of Sauda's dress. Without thought, Sauda reached down and roughly pushed the child backward.

"Get off of me, orphan." Sauda assumed that Hadizah would land on her padded bottom. Instead, the toddler twisted and then toppled over landing with a resonant thud of her head on the edge of the coffee table.

Asabe saw it all from the entrance of the hallway. She screeched and ran for the child. Sauda struggled to control the rage and malady that was having its way with her. Sauda covered her face with her hands, hoping that when she finally emerged, all would have been miraculously righted.

Salimah forgot her own injury and knelt down with Asabe and the child. There was no blood, but there was already a bit of feverish swelling in the center of the baby's forehead. Salimah carried Hadizah into the kitchen so that she might cool Hadizah's face with a damp towel.

Asabe snatched Sauda's hands from her face, her entire body quaking.

"Tell me something good. Tell me that you had good reason to harm my baby. Tell me something before I harm you."

Sauda could not help herself; remorse was quickly replaced by arrogance. "I didn't mean to hurt Adam's baby. Adam's baby, not yours. I wouldn't hurt anything of Adam's."

"Well, you did, and I want to know why."

"It was a mistake. I'll explain it to Adam when I speak with him. I would explain it to the child's mother, but she isn't here." Sauda showed a triumphant grin.

That was her next mistake.

Asabe reared back and slapped Sauda as hard as she could. She had never hit anyone in her life. She had wanted to strike Sauda many times before but had restrained her anger. This time her self-control disappeared. Asabe had calculated the blow—where she would hit Sauda, how hard, and if she would allow Sauda to strike back.

It felt all too satisfying, hitting Sauda.

"You can't hit me. I'm pregnant."

Hadizah let out a howl from the kitchen. To even the score, Asabe hit Sauda again.

"Why did you hit my baby?"

"I'm pregnant. You can't hit me."

Asabe hit Sauda again, this time causing a slow red drip of blood to run from Sauda's nose.

"When I hit you in the stomach, then you can complain."

"Just because you're barren doesn't mean—"

Asabe hit her again, causing Sauda's lower lip to split and bleed.

Asabe enjoyed the hitting. She liked it a lot. This time, she decided that she would use her closed fist if Sauda could not produce just cause for harming Hadizah.

"I'm waiting to hear why you pushed my baby, for why she's crying her eyes out over there." Asabe raised her clenched fist as a warning.

Sauda stuttered something unintelligible, clutched her belly, and then doubled over.

"Something is wrong," she moaned. Then came the dull splatter of liquid on the carpet.

Sauda's water had broken. She was in labor.

There was a knock on the door and Adam's voice calling, "Sauda? You in there?"

Sauda managed to call him in. She was still clutching her belly and standing in a soggy puddle of her own fluids. Her face was twisted in pain, and her nose and bottom lip were both bejeweled with glistening trickles of blood.

Adam looked to Asabe whose clenched fist still hovered in the air.

"What have you done to my wife?"

"She hit me," answered Sauda. "Can you believe she hit a pregnant woman?"

"She hurt Hadizah, she deserved it. It was her fault." Thereafter, Asabe decided on silence as every syllable she spoke only came out sounding petty and childish. How does one defend oneself against the accusations of a woman in the throes of labor? Asabe knew that there was virtually no way.

Adam helped Sauda to the chair and then turned to Asabe. "If anyone would have told me that you had beaten Sauda or anyone else for that matter, I would have called that person a liar. I'd say that you didn't have it in you. No, not Asabe. She's better than that. I thought I knew you."

"You do know me. All you have to do is ask yourself, ask your wife what would have provoked me to act as I did."

"Are you trying to justify what you have done to her?"

Asabe felt her conscience fold. She had never hurt anyone, had never before been able to conceive the thought.

"No. I was wrong, but so was she."

"I don't see any marks on your face. I don't see you in pain."

"Yes, but your daughter is. Can't you hear her?" Asabe pointed in the direction of the kitchen.

"Adam," whined Sauda, "I'm in labor." She added for effect, "I'm about to have our son."

"If anything has happened to my son, I don't think that I will forgive you." Adam threw his hands into the air. "I can't stand here and argue with you. I have to get my wife to the hospital."

Adam helped Sauda out of the chair and to the door.

"When I return, I want you to be gone. Go to your mother's house for a while. Just go. I don't want to see you, and I'm sure neither does Sauda."

DR. HALIMAH SULAIMAN USHERED ADAM DOWN THE HALLWAY, toward Sauda's room. He sat uninformed in the waiting room for more than four hours and had begun to worry. This was not the first time that Adam sat in wait for the birth of a son. The last time, he had been somewhat unwilling, even incapable of understanding what a joyous occasion it should have been. He was a different man then.

That had been twenty-two years ago, less four days. This time he was much more a man of understanding as well as desperate. Adam fully intended to be the father to this Mu'min, that he was not to the last Mu'min.

For three months prior to this birth, Adam had spent countless minutes with his ear pressed against Sauda's bare belly, trying to hear the beginnings of his son. He would cup his hands over his mouth and whisper secrets and promises to his unborn son. He had said things to his son that he had never told another soul.

Adam was ready to be a father.

"Is Sauda all right?" he asked the doctor. Dr. Sulaiman had been silent since she retrieved him from the waiting room.

"Yes, *she* is fine."

Adam felt a wave of uneasiness. It chilled him to the bone. He stopped walking and stood in the middle of the hallway, obstructing the movement of an orderly pushing a linen cart.

"What of my son? Is he all right?"

"Technically, the child should be fine. There are some things to discuss however. If we could just get to your wife's room," she said, pointing down the hall, "we can all discuss it together."

Adam heard Sauda long before he reached her room. When Adam heard her screams, he ran to the room, leaving the doctor behind. Adam opened the door and saw Sauda thrashing her head from side to side. A nurse stood next to her bed, holding a swaddled infant in her arms. Sauda spat at the nurse.

"That is not my baby! I'm not going to nurse it. I'm not!"

"Please, madam," said the nurse, trying to coax her, "I know that this is a shock to you, but you must think of the child."

Sauda spat at the nurse again.

Dr. Sulaiman instructed the nurse to hand the baby over to her and leave the room. The nurse was visibly shaken by Sauda's attack; she quickly did as she was told. Sauda crossed her arms over her chest and pouted like an unhappy child. Adam was stifled by his ignorance.

Dr. Sulaiman was an average-sized woman with tremendous presence. She quickly took control of the situation. Sauda did not offer the same resistance with the doctor.

"This is your baby," began Dr. Sulaiman. "I know because I delivered her. I know that you wished for a son, and I understand that you are disappointed, but you have absolutely no right to abuse my nurse. And you have no right to refuse giving your daughter suck."

"Daughter?" Adam stared at Sauda. "But you said we were having a son."

Sauda ignored Adam and said to the doctor, "But something is wrong with it. It doesn't look right. It can't be my baby." Sauda turned away when Dr. Sulaiman attempted to hand her the baby. "I won't."

"Sauda, you said we were having a son. You said the ultrasound showed a boy."

The infant whimpered. Adam approached the doctor and pulled the blanket away from the baby's face. Adam propelled backward as if he had been pushed.

"No, that's not my son, is it?"

"What is wrong with you, people? Are you human beings that you would run from your own child?"

"Dr. Sulaiman, my wife said that you did an ultrasound three months ago. You told her it would be a boy. You promised us a son."

"She did have an ultrasound, but I never told her it was a boy. In fact, I couldn't tell her much of anything, considering the way the baby was positioned in the womb."

Adam turned back to Sauda. "You promised me a son."

"No one except Allah could make such a promise, Mr. Abdulkadir."

The infant's whimper grew into a plaintive wail.

"That baby isn't normal. It just isn't mine. My baby was supposed to be a boy. That baby is a girl. My son was supposed to be normal and healthy and beautiful. I don't know what that *thing* is."

"This *thing* is your daughter. In all respects, she is a healthy infant girl. You have Allah to thank for that blessing. However, she is different, and she will be for the rest of her life. She has Down's syndrome. It is not a contagion, it's a condition. You better learn to accept it because you can't put her back. She's here, and she is yours." Dr. Sulaiman again attempted to hand the infant over to Sauda.

"No," refused Sauda.

"You said that I was having a son," said Adam.

"I don't want to touch that *thing*."

"If I have anything to do about it, you will," insisted the doctor, snatching loose the tie on the back of Sauda's hospital gown.

"You said we were going to have a son."

"Don't you touch me. You can't make me." Sauda attempted to retie her gown, but the doctor snatched it down, exposing Sauda's right shoulder.

"Sauda? You promised," Adam pleaded.

Dr. Sulaiman laid the infant in Sauda's lap. "If you allow this baby to fall, you will regret it. Now, give her suck."

"No."

"Yes."

"What about our son, Sauda?"

Finally, exasperated and cornered, Sauda purged herself of the lie she'd told Adam for three months.

"No! There is no son. Do you see a son? I lied. I told you a lie. Can't you see that now? See?" She held out the baby, who with the sudden movement stopped crying. "This is not a boy! Not a son!"

Sauda crumbled into exhausted tears.

"But why?"

"Because you wanted a son, and because I wanted you."

Dr. Sulaiman pushed Sauda's nipple into the infant's hungry mouth.

"I told you that I don't want to."

"Oh, shut your stupid lying face!" Adam screamed from across the room. "Feed your baby." Adam turned and walked from the room.

THIRTEEN

Asabe knocked on the door for the third time, wondering if perhaps she should have called first. What would she have said had she called ahead? *As-salaam alaikum, Mother. I beat up my co-wife, and my husband kicked me out of his home.* It sounded so unlike Asabe that she cringed at the thought.

Asabe knocked again, this time harder. Still, there was no answer. Asabe looked down the driveway. Her mother's white Toyota was parked in the curve of the horseshoe driveway. Parked behind it was a green Jaguar. Hannah had to be home because she had a guest.

Asabe knocked again, and after receiving no answer, she left her suitcases on the front stoop and walked around toward the back of the house with the sleeping Hadizah cradled in her arms. Perhaps Hannah was entertaining her guest in the garden too far from the front door to hear her knocking.

Asabe stopped short behind a tree and watched her mother laughing aloud. Hannah reached across the table and familiarly rubbed the hand of . . .

"Is that Abu Kareem?" Asabe whispered to herself. "What's he doing here, alone, with my mother?" Asabe's heart was pounding in her chest.

Abu Kareem sipped from a glass, the ice tinkling like chimes.

"You are a dear woman. I haven't been this happy in a long time." Abu Kareem passed something across the table to Hannah, but Asabe could not see what. There were no lights, and dusk hovered in the sky a brilliant blend of pink and orange.

"Oh, Abu," cooed Hannah. "You give me so much." Asabe hardly recognized her mother's voice; it was soft and young, as if the age had been washed out of it.

"What?" said Asabe into the trunk of the tree she was hiding beneath. It was not Asabe's intent to hide in the shadows eavesdropping, but what would she say if she had made her presence known? No decent woman would ever sit *alone* with a man she was not married to, exchanging gifts and stroking hands. It was not their way as Muslims, as people with a culture that had clearly defined rules about decency. This was a crime that could shame whole families if it would be known.

"I give you this for your services," said Abu Kareem. To this, the two laughed in unison.

"What exactly do you mean by that?" asked Asabe, stepping from the shadows.

Hannah shot up from her chair so quickly it was as if a fire had been lit beneath her. Abu Kareem rose too, only not as quickly, using his cane for support. They both looked blindly in the direction of the tree, Asabe was still obscured in the shadows.

"That you, Asabe?" called Hannah.

"It is." Asabe approached them.

"What are you doing here?"

"I was going to ask you the same about Abu Kareem," said Asabe as if he were not standing right there.

Hannah and Abu Kareem looked at each other, and then both began to laugh until they were teary eyed. Asabe shifted the baby's weight to her other arm and tapped her foot impatiently.

"I don't see what is so funny. I come to my mother's home and find a so-called respectable man giving my mother gifts for her *services*. What in the world is happening here? What kind of woman are you, Mother?"

"You hold on one minute. If it weren't my fault for this misunderstanding, I would lash you for talking that way to your mother."

Abu Kareem pointed his cane in Asabe's direction. "I asked her not to tell you."

"You asked my mother not to tell me that the two of you were carrying on in an ungodly fashion? As if I'd ever want to know that."

"What is so ungodly about a married couple having drinks together in their garden? Since when has it been a crime?"

For the next hour, Hannah and Abu Kareem explained how they'd come to be married. They told how Abu Kareem had pursued Hannah as if she were the last woman alive as well as Hannah's initial refusal. She was afraid to marry him for fear that he would eventually lose interest in her.

He'd sent gifts and money and letters. He'd call and arrive unannounced with an escort whose job was not only to serve as a chaperone but also to wax eloquent about the possibilities of marriage with him. Not that Hannah had ever doubted him; he was polite, dignified, and admittedly handsome even with the severe limp and ebony cane. The fact that he was an incredibly wealthy man certainly did not detract from her interest in him. Hannah's problems were her own insecurities and the wonder that he would actually want her for a wife.

There had been many women in Abu Kareem's life after the mother of his children died seventeen years prior. Five times he'd married since then, becoming a running joke in the community. Every two or three years, he would take a new wife, always young, each more beautiful than the one that preceded her, but none able to withstand the horror of a family that he had raised. Or to be more exact, Sauda.

Sauda managed to terrorize each wife until she could not take being with him no longer. He loved them all the same, but he could not make them love him or tolerate Sauda's deliberate sabotage. Finally, Abu Kareem came to the conclusion that he could not have a wife and Sauda too.

Abu Kareem had done fine alone and was content in his solitude, especially after Sauda had married Adam. When he wasn't acquiring new properties or making important deals abroad, he would sit alone in his favorite recliner and stare out of the window. He'd listen to himself think. As of late, his own thoughts had become too cumbersome to bear alone. Solitude became a vacuum of silence. Contentment became loneliness.

No man is an island, how well he'd come to know that old adage. Abu Kareem had wanted to hear his thoughts, but he also wanted a response to his old man's ramblings. Abu Kareem wanted a new voice, one that was wise enough to relate to his plight, one that would tell him that he was not just a crazy old man but a man with value beyond his buying power. He wanted a woman, not a girl, who had more to offer than her youth and beauty and physical charms. Abu Kareem wanted a woman who could see the man he once was before the broken hip and the cane, before the balding head and the deep creases that framed his face, before his voice cracked from old age, before he lost some of his teeth, before his joints popped when he stood up or lay down or for nothing at all. He wanted a partner who could understand old Abu Kareem because she was growing old right along with him.

It took nearly two months of convincing, but Hannah finally agreed to marry Abu Kareem, and for two weeks, they had been happy together. Abu Kareem was afraid that the news of their marriage might upset Sauda so completely as to put the unborn child in danger. Together, he and Hannah decided to keep the marriage a secret until the child's birth.

This explained what Asabe had seen, but still it didn't explain why she'd arrived at her mother's home unannounced, and with her luggage.

"All right, now that you understand what has happened, why don't you tell us why you've come?" Hannah placed a cup of tea before Asabe and urged her to drink.

Asabe wasn't terribly surprised by their news; she'd seen the way Abu Kareem looked at her mother during the Eid three months prior. However, it complicated the tale she now had to tell.

"Adam kicked me out."

"What?" Hannah's hand went up to her mouth. "Why? What happened?"

Before Asabe could answer, Abu Kareem said, "I know that Sauda must have had something to do with it. She's a troublemaker, I know."

"She did, but not the way you think. This time I was the one in the wrong." Tears slipped from Asabe's eyes. Her hands trembled in her lap. "I have done something unspeakable, and, Abu Kareem, you won't like it."

"So you've finally hit her, huh?"

Asabe's mouth fell open.

"I don't blame you. She's probably had it coming to her a long time. Someone had to do it," he said, shrugging his shoulders. "I could never bring myself to discipline her, and as a result, she has grown up to be an unbearable woman. She was my youngest child and a girl. I felt sorry for her, being motherless. I allowed her to cling to me and to manipulate me. I spoiled her, and I'm ashamed to say that I taught her no manners. I made her what she is. I take full responsibility."

"She may be lacking in manners, Abu Kareem, but I had no right to strike a pregnant woman. I just hope that I didn't cause any damage to the baby."

"You didn't hit her in the stomach, did you?" the married couple asked.

"No, but she did go into labor. You may be a grandfather tonight, Abu Kareem."

ADAM WROTE,

Dear Mu'min,

Today I was supposed to have a son, a son I would have named after you. He was to be the joy that I failed to allow you to be so many years ago. This time the child did not die only minutes out of his mother's womb as did Ali, but the child was born a girl. She is a retarded girl, who will only serve to be a burden for the rest of her life. I shall accept her as I have my other daughter, for she is at the very least of me, but she will never be a son. She will never be you.

I know that I do not deserve you, for I was such a horrible man to your mother and a resistant father to you. I do regret it. Allah has not only deprived me of you, and of any other son, but he has also deprived me of the only precious thing that I could have left. Your memory.

There was a time when I could recall your every feature, down to your very fingertips without the assistance of a photograph, but no more. I am now an old man and all I can recall of you, my son, are your last words to me those fourteen years ago. You were begging me to stay, not to leave you. You wanted to know why I was making your Mother cry and why I hated you.

Your words have haunted me ever since. I was a fool. And now your father, the fool, has only his own mistakes to serve as a legacy because Allah is most certainly not giving me the only thing that I hold to be valuable.

Perhaps you don't care about my mournings, and I'm not sure that I would blame you, but if it means anything to you, my dearest Mu'min, I miss you terribly and I wish with all of me that I could have you back.

Happy birthday, my only son.

Your Baba, Adam

Adam sealed the letter in an envelope addressed to his son in the States. This time he did not cry. There were no more tears. Adam laid his head on his desk in the fold of his arms, but comfort did not come. He climbed into his bed and wrapped himself in the covers as if he were in a cocoon. He wanted to be his own support, wanted to soothe away his own pain, but he had never had to do it before because there had always been Asabe.

"How can I go to her now, after what I have done?" Adam shivered beneath the covers.

Adam raced down the hall in his bare feet toward Asabe's room and threw the door open. Asabe's scent rushed him at the door, and at first, he just stood there inhaling her. Adam imagined Asabe telling him to come in.

"It will be all right," said the imaginary Asabe. "I know that you are hurting, but I will not leave you. Trust me," she said. "Trust Allah."

Adam smiled at the Asabe in his imagination, accepting her invitation to nap in her bed while she gingerly massaged the worry from his head. He climbed between the satiny covers of Asabe's bed and drifted off to sleep just as she was saying, "I'm so sorry, Adam. I'm so sorry."

ASABE WATCHED THE INFANT through the nursery window. Sauda's baby lay in her crib silent and awake, sucking vigorously at her tongue, which seemed too large for her mouth. Even in youth, the infant was markedly different from the other infants that occupied the cribs around her. Her small black face was flat and broad, and her eyes were little more than slits. She was an odd-looking baby, and by most assertions, she'd even be considered ugly, but Asabe threw away that thought.

"It is a child," she whispered into the glass, causing a cloud of steam. "In that alone she is beautiful, a miracle from Allah."

Asabe stopped the nurse in attendance as she passed by the window and mouthed through the glass, "Is it a boy or a girl?"

"Girl," said the nurse.

All came to light. Now Asabe understood the meaning of the cryptic entry in Salimah's journal, the one she pilfered in innocence months earlier. The words had haunted her, whispering themselves in her head over and over again.

Misses Sauda has so turned their husband's head with her artful deceptions that he no longer knows if he is coming or going. Asabe will surely be harmed in this all. In the end so will Adam.

Asabe thought of Adam, that his heart was probably broken into a million pieces, that he had probably crumbled inside.

Then there was Sauda. Asabe should have been very angry with Sauda for deceiving Adam about the sex of the child. Sauda knew that the prospect of having a son would make Adam turn to her, would make him forget everyone else. It was not just Asabe that suffered the loss of her husband for nearly four months, but there was also Hadizah. Adam had not been the same with her either.

Despite her naiveté, Hadizah could sense Adam's sudden dissatisfaction with her. The promise of a son had transformed his daughter into a substitute until something better came along.

Asabe should have been angry, but she wasn't. What Asabe felt was a strange mix of concern and pity. Only a desperate woman, an insecure and afraid woman, would prey on the hopes and dreams of a similarly desperate man for three months of attention, with a lie that could undo itself so easily. Asabe decided to go to her cowife.

Abu Kareem warned Asabe not to enter Sauda's room.

"She is too emotional," he said. "I've told her about my marriage to Hannah, and for a second, I thought that I had lost her. Her head just fell to her chest, and she cried. She isn't the Sauda that I know. That girl is not my daughter, and I'm afraid that more stress will push her over the edge."

Asabe nodded, but she still walked past Abu Kareem toward Sauda's room. Abu Kareem hobbled in front of the door, blocking Asabe's entrance.

"Please leave her alone. I don't want her hurt any more than she already has been." His eyes were moist with sincerity.

"Abu Kareem, I only want to help. I won't cause her any more harm. It's time you stop protecting her. Right?" Abu Kareem sighed heavily with resignation and waved Asabe toward Sauda's door.

The room was dark and warm. The bedside lamp stood unused, and the television remained silent on its perch on the wall. The curtains were drawn shut against the yellow light of the moon. The room smelled stale and acrid. At first, Asabe stood with her back to the door, thinking that perhaps she had made a mistake in coming.

"I don't want my temperature taken," croaked Sauda from somewhere in the room. "I told you people to leave me alone."

Asabe thought Sauda's voice lacked conviction. Indeed this did not sound like the Sauda everyone wanted to love but could not.

"I haven't come for your temperature," said Asabe, feeling along the wall for a switch. In the light, Asabe found that Sauda looked even less like herself than she sounded. Her eyes were nearly swollen shut and what one could see of them were red. Her hair was matted in some places and standing up on end in others. Her scarf appeared to have been thrown across the room, where it lay crumpled beneath a chair. There were salty tracks on her face where the tears had streamed down her cheeks, unchecked by a handkerchief or hand. Sauda looked beat.

"What are you doing here? Come to gloat, to make fun? Go on ahead then and have your laugh. Just hurry up so that you can get out." Her bottom lip trembled.

"Those are your ways, not mine."

"Get out then." Her voice had recovered some of its gumption, but Asabe still heard the pain.

"I saw your daughter. She is a beautiful baby.

Sauda glared at Asabe.

"You're a liar. You didn't see my baby because if you did, you would know that she isn't beautiful. She is . . . is . . . is . . ."

"She is yours."

"I wish she weren't."

"Months ago, when you first announced your pregnancy, you threw it in my face. Remember that? When I told you that the pregnancy was no more than a clot of blood, you told me that it was yours and that I was simply jealous because you were having Adam's son. You were an arrogant imp. Remember that?"

"So now what? Is this where you throw my retarded daughter in my face? Is this where you laugh at me, where you tell me that I get exactly what I deserve?" A tear slipped from the corner of her eye.

"No."

"So say whatever it is you have on your mind. Go on and get it over with."

"What I wanted to say is that this is the time when you should draw on your pride because it is your strength. Be proud that you have had a child because many women would give anything to be a mother. Even if the child is a girl or retarded or even deformed. Believe me, I would know.

"You have been given the honor, by Allah, to have the ability to produce, to bring another being that is a part of yourself and your beloved into the world. Some of us will never do that. You should be proud. Look at you. You are a big strong woman, with health as an ally. Insha Allah, you will have more. A son may still be in your future."

"But I've lied to Adam," she bellowed. "What if he divorces me? What if he hates me?"

"You may have lied, but so did he. He allowed you to believe that you were more than a vehicle through which to have a son. He allowed you to believe that he was genuine because you wanted it so much. He has no one but himself to hate right now."

"Why don't you hate me? You should."

"Believe me when I say that if it were not for my love of Allah, I'd not only hate you, but I would have long ago acted on that hatred. You have not made it easy to love you."

"You don't even like me. You proved that earlier when you hit me."

"I was wrong to strike you. I would never try to justify my own wrongdoing, but, Sauda, don't you think that it is about time that you take some of the responsibility for what happened?"

"I can't help it. You are a delight to talk to, according to Adam. The best cook in the entire world, he raves. So special and patient and accepting and smart and beautiful and on and on and on. All of this from a woman who has done little more in her life than be a wife. How can I compete with you? How can I win his favor? I am traveled and educated abroad. I have more money than I would ever know what to do with. My womb is fertile. I have said and done all that I could think to make Adam notice me, but still . . . How could I be civil with you?"

"You could, if you realized that I am not your competition. The relationship that you have with Adam has little to do with me. That is between you and him. You and I could be friends. I couldn't have been closer to Fatima if I had tried. We were like sisters from the same womb. You and I could be the same way, like sisters."

Asabe was unsure if she meant all that she said, but submitting to gentility and compassion was easier for her than to anger and vengeance. Seeing Sauda as she was, defeated and unsure of herself, allowed Asabe to witness the humanity in Sauda and that there might be something within her worthy of adulation.

Asabe sat in the chair next to Sauda's bed and held her hand while she purged her woes in great sobs. When Sauda finished, Asabe found a hand towel in the bathroom and dampened it with water. She used the towel to wipe the tears from Sauda's face. With that done, she brushed Sauda's hair until her eyes began to flutter, and she hummed with pleasure. By then, Sauda was finally ready to sink into sleep. She slid beneath the covers and fell asleep. Sauda never thanked Asabe, but the look in her eyes was thank you enough for Asabe to recognize.

Asabe spread open the curtains and pushed the window open. She then turned off the light and closed the door behind her as she left. Abu Kareem met her at the door, eager to know the details of their discussion. Asabe told him that he would have to wait for the details.

"I have to go home."

"All right. I'll go get your mother from the lounge, and then we can leave."

"I don't mean my mother's home. I'm going to my husband."

ASABE WATCHED ADAM FROM THE DOORWAY. In his slumber, without the tension of the day clouding his face, Adam looked most like himself. It was a face she hadn't seen in a long time. In the past, Asabe had always thought Adam looked at least ten years younger than his actual age; but this time, it seemed that his age had indeed caught up with him. Adam looked all his fifty-five years.

Adam had fallen asleep with his glasses perched crookedly upon his nose. These days, his hair was more gray than black. The gray hairs, like the years, were catching up with him. Asabe saw in her bed a man for whom pity was an easy emotion to adopt, but she refused to let pity move her.

Asabe had not returned home to make amends. She had not come to coddle her husband or to take his side. Asabe had come to make right far too many wrongs to number, for the sake of people who weren't capable of righting the wrongs for themselves. It wasn't a task she wanted, for she was tired of setting aside her own woes for the sake of others. Asabe realized, though, that if she did not, then no one else would.

Asabe sat on the edge of her bed. She ran her fingers over Adam's tight gray peppercorns and his large black face.

"I'm so sorry, Adam. I'm so sorry."

Adam's eyes fluttered open, and he gazed up at her knowingly. "I knew you'd come. At least I hoped you would." His voice was hoarse.

"You said it right the first time. You knew I'd come here once I'd heard the news because you know me. And I knew that I would find you in my room because I know you."

Adam smiled tentatively, relieved to see his mate. He reached up for Asabe to hold her or to be held, but Asabe stood up and walked across the room and sat in the chair. Adam was left alone on the bed, his arms still stretched out in front of himself, grasping at air or perhaps the imaginary Asabe he had dreamed.

"We need to talk, Adam." Asabe crossed her arms over her bosom.

"Don't worry. I forgive you for hitting Sauda. She probably deserved it. I forgive you for anything you may have done wrong."

Asabe smiled. "I haven't come for your forgiveness, Adam."

"No?"

"No. Earlier when I hit Sauda, you said that you didn't know who I was anymore. Those words hurt me. Now, you say she probably deserved it. Why?"

"Because now I know what type of woman she is. She is a liar, a manipulating liar. She is a bad woman. Did you know that she lied about having a son? I can't believe that she did that."

"I can. I may have done the same in her place."

"How could you say that? I've never known you to lie and connive. Never."

"Then why wouldn't you listen to me earlier when I'd hit her? Why did you question my motives? Why kick me out of our home?"

Adam's eyes darted as he searched his mind for the correct response. All he could do was nod his head.

"Sauda is your wife, and if she is bad, you have made her so."

"What?" Adam hopped from the bed and began straightening his crumpled clothes. "I made her bad? So that must mean that you think I am bad as well. Is that what you think of me?"

"No, I don't think that you are bad, but I probably should. Do you realize that this is the first time you have been in my bed in almost two months? You spent every night in Sauda's room, the one who would give you a son. If I were a different kind of woman, a woman with little fear of the consequences such a deception would have before Allah, I too would have lied to have your affection and undivided attention. If Sauda was ever good, you made her to be bad; and if she was already bad, then you made her to be wicked. You promised her that if she could produce a son, there was nothing in the world you would not give her."

"I never promised her that," said Adam, shaking his head vigorously. "I never said that."

"No, not in those words, but the intent was implied. You told her which buttons to push, and she pushed them. She said the word *son*, and your disgust of her became utter devotion. She said the word *son,* and your daughter became a temporary distraction. Sauda said the word *son*, and I ceased to exist."

"But as you can see, there is no son."

"And for this, you are willing to slander her? For a thing that she has no control over? If she had a choice, don't you think that she would have chosen a son?"

"She lied." Adam crossed his arms. "She didn't have to do that."

"Yes, she did. How else would you have shown her any tenderness? She behaves foolishly a lot of the time, but she is not stupid, which is more than I can say for you."

Adam opened his mouth to protest, but Asabe ignored him and continued.

"She played you for a fool, and you were too caught up in yourself and what you wanted to realize it. You thought that you were getting what you wanted, and because of it, you refused to be a husband to me on even the most basic level. You became blind to the truth."

"You're right, she made a fool of me, but it isn't too late to remedy that."

"How? Divorce?"

Adam shrugged his shoulders.

"You'll do no such thing." Asabe stood up and crossed the room. She placed a firm hand on his shoulder. "You've got a wife who needs your forgiveness and your help, and you're going to give it to her. The two of you have a daughter with a special condition who needs to be raised, knowing that she is wanted. You will do that too."

"I don't know if I can."

"I know that you can because I know you. Remember?" Asabe smiled up into her husband's aging face, a face she could never get enough of. It was as smooth as silk, never having been able to grow more than a short rough patch of kinky hair under his chin. She reached up to stroke his face and then stopped when reality reasserted itself. Adam though caught her hand in midair as she withdrew. He pressed her hand against his cheek, closing his eyes.

"I've missed you," whispered Adam into the palm of her hand.

Asabe pulled her hand away.

"But I've always been here. I've been here waiting for you to remember me."

"I promise that I won't ever treat you that way again. I promise you."

"Just promise me that you will always do what is right, and I will be a very happy woman."

"I promise."

FOURTEEN

Sauda was perched on the sill of the opened window in her hospital room. She angled herself so that her face would catch the cold droplets of rain as they fell from the charcoal sky. She wanted to wash her tears away.

Sauda broke down while trying to imagine her future life as a two-time divorcee, Abu Kareem attempting to bribe any man worth the distinction to marry her, and they turning him down flat. A woman divorced twice in three years was less likely to find a husband than an unproductive woman.

Sauda had no reason to expect Adam to forgive her. Why should he? It wasn't as if he ever loved her, and she certainly had done nothing to prove that she was worthy of his love. Sauda resigned herself to returning to her father's home upon release from the hospital.

Ismael, Sauda's first husband, would not have forgiven her most recent trespasses. He forgave nothing.

When dinner was set before him late, or if it came to him not quite warm enough, he did not forgive. When a wrinkle remained in his camise, or even if she wore the wrong perfume, he would not forgive. If she ate heartily, she was to him a glutton. If she refused to eat, she was a fool.

He would not forgive.

How many times had she begged him, tears wetting her face, hands outstretched, to forgive her weaknesses, her minor trespasses? She did not know, could not recall, the number of nights that she spent alone. Or the nights she spent wrapping her wounds in gauze, wondering if it had really been so serious.

Sauda envisioned a future without a husband, but with a child it sickened her to lay eyes upon. That was no future at all.

Then came a flood of harsher tears, burning her eyes, mingling with the rain. Sauda glanced down at her blouse. It was saturated with sticky milk.

ADAM STOOD IN THE HALLWAY, grasping the door handle with such resolution that he could feel the skin of his knuckles stretch. He did so to stop the trembling in his hands.

It was time to bring Sauda home, and he had delayed in coming to retrieve her for so long that he was sure she had begun to entertain fears of abandonment. Only twenty-four hours earlier, he had contemplated doing just that. Until he'd asked himself why.

Would he abandon her because she had given birth to a less-than-perfect child? Would he abandon her because she had resorted to the only objective that would gain his consideration? Because she cared for him and was desperate for reciprocation? Because she had told him the one thing that could guarantee his pleasure for nearly four months?

She had lied, but that fabrication had given him more hope and pleasure than he would have ever gotten otherwise. Perhaps he should be thanking her. Perhaps not, for a lie is and will always be nothing more than a lie.

He would not abandon Sauda, though not for the sake of love, for Adam could not honestly claim that he carried within his heart even a thin thread of love for her. It would not even be for the sake of the imperfect girl-child she had given birth to.

Adam would allow her to remain with him for two reasons, reasons for which he bore no shame, reasons he would soon divulge to her so that there would never be any mistake as to love or allegiance. Adam would bid her stay, firstly, because even after their most recent trial, all was not lost. Her womb was still healthy, and a son was not an impossibility. Moreover, a son was almost imminent, considering his great desire. Sauda would also stay because Adam had promised to do what was fitting, and forgiveness was fitting. How could he forgive himself and not forgive her as well?

Adam pushed the door open and walked in.

"I forgive you," he said.

SAUDA TURNED TO FACE ADAM, unsure if she should trust her eyes. In her heart, she was already divorced.

"What?" She heard him the first time, but the words were ones she only imagined she would hear in a dream. "What did you say?"

Adam sat down on the edge of her bed, the white sheets twisted into wrinkled knots.

Adam spoke without ceremony, "You know why I married you, don't you?"

Sauda shook her head. It was true, she knew.

"My father never lied to me. And I have not ever been a fool." Sauda cringed at her own words, for this latest episode was proof to the contrary.

"I know what motivated you to marry me. Money and the desire to have a son."

"That is where I went wrong, Sauda."

Shrugging her shoulders, Sauda said, "There is no wrong in it. These are all valid reasons for marriage, even before Allah."

"Valid for some men, but not men like me. I don't know how to pretend, and I am terrible at dispensing justice between two women. I lied to myself that I could love you both the same. It simply wasn't possible. Even Allah said that no man can control the feelings in his heart."

Sauda found a white hand towel in the top drawer of the nightstand. She used it to dry the rain-mingled tears from her face.

"Is this what you have come here to say? That you cannot love me like Asabe? That you have finished with me?"

"I have come to apologize to you, for ever allowing you to believe that there could be anything else. I didn't really want another wife when I married you. What I wanted was a son. But how else to have a son than through a woman? After Fatima, I felt that the last thing I needed was another wife. Your father, I think, would have sold you for any price. He hunted me down at every opportunity to number your good qualities, which even he said were few."

"Sold me?"

"I don't mean it the way it sounds. It's just that he was desperate to be rid of you, to marry you off." Adam looked to the ceiling, trying to collect his thoughts. "I mean—"

"You mean that my father met your price." Adam flinched. Sometimes the truth could be so coarse. "I already know this," Sauda assured Adam. "But I wanted to marry you anyway. Married people do not always love each other at first. These things take time. I knew this." Sauda felt almost as if she were begging. "It isn't easy for a nineteen-year-old divorcee to marry the man of her choosing. I was fortunate."

"You're not complaining? For many women, it isn't enough to know that they have the man of their choice. They want also to have their feelings returned. They want to receive honest emotions meant for them alone."

"I always believed that you would come to feel the same for me as I do for you."

Adam shook his head. "I thought so too, at first, but I think that I have failed us all."

Adam motioned for Sauda to sit at the table in the far corner of the window wall. Adam joined her. He leaned forward, his elbows resting on his knees and his head hanging between his hunched shoulders. Adam removed his glasses and pinched the bridge of his nose. Sauda waited for him in silence, scratching her wrist where the IV had been removed.

"I want you to come home with me. But there will be conditions on us both."

"They are?" Sauda's heart leaped madly in her chest.

"No more lies of the heart or otherwise." Adam sat back in the chair and stared ahead. "Also, Asabe must be respected, as my first wife, as a fellow woman, as a human being. Don't you women believe in some sort of universal sisterhood?"

"Not when we are competing for the same husband."

"There is no competition here. My feelings are my own, and I will place them where I please. You must show her the same respect that you accord for yourself."

Sauda surprised Adam when she said, "I agree. It was jealousy that made me hate her. It was knowing that I would have to fight to carve out my own small piece of affection from you. How does a woman like myself, with no skills and purchased beauty and, admittedly, stunted graces, contend with an Asabe? It's impossible, like a lamb trying to tame a lion. I was doomed to fail from the start. So I fought dirty."

"There was no fight but the one that you instigated. It must not happen again."

"It won't." Sauda's breasts began to ache and burn. The throbbing caught her breath.

Not noticing, Adam said, "Good. We'll both try harder."

"Do you still want a son?" Secretly Sauda hoped that Adam would not. *No, I don't care about a son, only you* is what she wished he would say. As she had earlier attested, she was no fool. Only fools bought into delusions and fantasy.

"Of course," said Adam. "I fully intend to have a son. With you."

There was a knock on the door. In came the nurse that Sauda anointed with her spittle just the previous day. She held Sauda's tightly swaddled baby in her arms.

"I trust that you are feeling better today?" The nurse stood close to the doorway, just in case.

Sauda intimated nothing. She had nothing against the nurse. It was the baby that she didn't want.

The nurse approached the table slowly, still cautious of Sauda's mood. Adam nodded to the nurse, as if to say, *Don't worry, she won't bite.*

"She was a bit fussy, madam. I thought that perhaps you might want to feed her before you finally left for home."

"Can't you give her a bottle?"

"No," said Adam. "You must nurse her. I want all of my children to be nursed until they reach two years."

Sauda reluctantly accepted the infant into her arms. She removed the fold of blanket that covered the infant's face. Sauda tried not to turn away, but she could not help herself. Sauda didn't want to see the round flat face, the vapid black eyes, the fat pink protruding tongue, the almost-nonexistent neck. It was a face that one couldn't even begin to pretend was normal. It was a face that repulsed Sauda to see nursing at her breast.

Sauda sensed Adam was watching her. She feared that Adam would see the worst part of her, would see her reject her own flesh and blood, and then decide that he didn't want her as his wife after all.

Sauda forced herself to look into the infant's face, attempted to feign the look of amazement and adoration all new mothers have. She unbuttoned her saturated blouse with slow sick fingers. She allowed her baby to latch on.

Sauda swallowed hard and loud and then again to push back the threat of vomit she could feel rising in her throat. It was her baby, yes;

but may Allah help her, she wished it wasn't. She would have preferred Asabe's orphan girl to this . . . this . . . this . . . baby any day.

SEVEN DAYS LATER, Adam took his daughter into his arms for the first time. The hour was 4:00 a.m., and the entire house hummed with silence. Sleep had not been his friend that night. Each time it seemed sleep would come, it eluded him. It was the coming day that took over his thoughts and stole away his peace.

It would be the day of his daughter's *akika.*

On the west side of his home, the side that faced Jabar's house across the field of grass, there was a she-goat tied to a wooden post. Later, the she-goat would be slaughtered by Adam's own hand in his daughter's stead. Her head would be shaved of the fine black hairs she wore in her mother's womb, to ensure good health and to make way for her true hair to grow. All their friends and relatives were expected to come and share in the celebration.

Adam's hands trembled as he lifted the sleeping baby into his arms. Her small flat head lolled limply to the side, oblivious of his presence. Sauda was just as oblivious, snoring lightly in her bed across the room.

Adam crept from Sauda's room, the sound of his bare feet muffled by the thick carpeting. He pulled the door closed behind him and headed down the stairs to the prayer room.

The room was cool. The windows had been left open overnight. There was an easterly breeze that caused the sheer curtains to billow and flutter. Adam did not turn on the lights. He sat on a pile of embroidered pillows in the corner of the room beneath a window so that he might catch the moonlight through the nearly transparent curtains.

Adam held his tiny daughter against his chest, her head beneath his chin. He pressed his lips against the soft spot in the center of her head to feel her silky hairs on his lips. Then he pressed his nose to her head to inhale the sweet fleshy scent that only babies have. His mouth watered.

Adam whispered the azan into her ear so that she would always be familiar with the words. He also whispered the *kalimah* so that she would always know the name of Allah, so that she would always know that he is one.

Through this all, she remained submerged in sleep, her chest rising and falling in perfect smooth rhythm.

Adam caressed his daughter's small naked back, and then he held her up so that their faces were leveled.

"Now that you know the name of Allah and who he is, it is time that you know your name. From today on, you are Lailah Adam Abdulkadir, my third child, my second daughter."

At this, she opened her eyes as if having been summoned, and she looked at him. Her gaze was direct and steady, as if she was cognitive of what had been said to her, as if she had been waiting to hear those very words to awaken.

Adam looked into her eyes, the yellow glow of the moon streaming through the window into them, and he swore that he saw her soul. He did not regard her abnormal features, nor did he regard her sex. Adam concentrated on her eyes, small and brown and slightly slanted; but more than anything, they were intelligent, soulful, and fearless.

"You are my daughter, aren't you?"

Lailah opened her small mouth with a stubborn snort and let out a hearty wail. Her thick pink tongue was curled up at the sides, and her moist little lips trembled. Adam smiled, his chest puffed out with pride he never thought he'd have for the child.

Adam laughed aloud, joining his daughter in a melodious bellow.

FIFTEEN

It was a warm day, humid enough that it seemed one could wring the moisture from the air itself. Rahman drove seventy-five miles from his village of Salam to Adam's home in a car that predated his eldest child. The thirty-three-year-old car had no air-conditioning, and the two passenger-side windows could not be opened for fear that they would remain forever lost inside of the door.

It was a journey that he was pleased to make, for it was on behalf of his favorite child, Salimah. Since she was thirteen years old, she had been in Sauda's employ, tolerating unheard of abuses so that she could help her family. She was an asset to him, but soon she would be leaving his care in order to move on to more important things. The time had come for her to make a home for herself.

There was never a shred of doubt as far as Rahman was concerned as to Salimah's status as a marriageable virgin, but not everyone agreed. Salimah's silence was perceived as a defect, and most thought she would live out her life as a spinster. In the past two years, five men had come to Rahman seeking the hand of his daughter, horrid men older than himself. Rahman was harsh in his refusal. For Salimah, he would hold out for the best. And now his desires and prayers were about to be realized.

In three months, Salimah, Rahman's youngest child, would be married to a man of even greater stature than he had hoped. Jamil was not wealthy, but he was ambitious. He was not well socially connected, but he was religious. He was not the most handsome man, but he did have a patient heart. He was what his daughter deserved.

Today Rahman was going to liberate his daughter from Sauda and bring her home with him until the time came to hand her over to her new husband. Rahman also planned to offer Sauda his last remaining unmarried daughter, Kubrah, to take Salimah's place.

Kubrah would be an equal match for Sauda and her tantrums. She was not easily taken advantage of. Kubrah had her voice and was known to readily administer serious corporal punishment onto anyone who had offended her.

Salimah reached the car before Rahman turned off the grumbling engine. After embracing her elder sister, Salimah greeted her father by offering him a broad smile and nodding her head so that he would know she was well.

"Good, good," he said as if she had spoken an entire paragraph. "I am pleased to know that you are doing well. Your brothers have been asking of you. We will all be happy when you come home."

"Except for me," said Kubrah. "You will be going home, and I will stay here to take your place. All we have is now, before you leave." Kubrah mock pouted, but Salimah knew her sister was sincere.

Salimah urged her father to follow as she dragged her sister by the hand toward the house. Salimah brought them glasses of cold water and a bowl of kola nuts.

By then, Adam and Sauda joined Rahman in the living room. They anticipated his arrival, but both were unsure as to the intended nature of the visit.

Rahman emptied the glass of water in great noisy gulps and a smack of his lips, then Rahman requested more water and handed the glass back to Salimah.

"It is a hot day," he exclaimed as if just privy to the realization.

Adam and Sauda both nodded in agreement.

"I understand that you have been recently relieved of your burden," he said to Sauda.

She shrugged, not cognizant of his meaning.

"You had your baby," he said, clearing up the confusion.

"Oh yes. We have named her Lailah."

"Alhamdulillahi. Salimah's mother was named Lailah. She was a beautiful woman, and very religious. Insha Allahu, your daughter will be the same, beautiful as well as religious. It is an odd combination, you know. Women who are aware of their beauty are often too vain to be worried about their relationships with Allah."

Adam grunted in agreement. Sauda said nothing. In her heart, she believed her daughter would never have the capacity for such qualities.

Salimah returned, placing the glass of water on the table in front of her father. Taking her sister by the hand, Salimah led her to the garden where they sat in the shade of a tree.

Rahman produced a small rectangular box from the pocket of his dusty jalabiyah. It was the type of box jewelry is often displayed in. Rahman offered the box to Sauda who sat across from him to his right. Sauda accepted the box, a pleased grin on her face. She loved gifts.

Sauda opened the box, and the pleasure fell away from her face like rushing rain. Inside was a handsewn one-by-one-inch pouch made from bright yellow fabric. The pouch was sewn closed on all four sides, leaving no way to determine the object inside.

Sauda stared incredulously at Rahman. She then looked to Adam for an explanation, but he hardly acknowledged her confusion.

"I heard about your baby, her condition." Old Rahman shifted uncomfortably in his chair. He didn't care for Sauda or her antics, but he was not a man insensitive to the anguish of a mother concerning her child.

"I wanted to bring your new child a gift. I am an old man, and all of my children are grown up. I don't know anything about picking out baby clothes or these new baby gadgets that seem to me useless and rather superfluous. We didn't have all that stuff in my day, baby swings and baby walkers and special baby bathtubs. So I decided to give your daughter the one thing no one has ever given any of my children. A lasting gift." Rahman pointed in Sauda's direction. "What you have in your hand is an amulet. You are to pin it into Lailah's clothing as a protection from Satan and any of his imps. Special children like yours are especially susceptible to the workings of Satan. They need extra care and protection."

Adam praised Rahman for his foresight and kindness. Sauda dropped the amulet back into the box as if it were a hot coal.

"Brother Rahman, when you called, you said that you had some important news. Sauda and I have been very anxious to hear. I hope that nothing is wrong."

Rahman helped himself to a handful of kola nuts from the table, half emptying the bowl, and deposited them into his pocket.

"On the contrary, I haven't been this happy in many years." Rahman looked out of the window where he could see Salimah sitting with her sister beneath a tree. Her head was resting on her elder sister's shoulder. Her eyes were closed, and a content smile was on her face. She had always been a great source of pride for Rahman. Rahman frowned to push down the smile on his lips.

"The date has been set," announced Rahman.

Adam and Sauda looked at each other, unsure. "The date for what, Brother Rahman?" asked Sauda. Sauda was the only person in the room who did not know. Jamil had been bragging about his impending marriage in the office, but Adam refrained from telling Sauda, fearing her reaction. He had been astute in his fears.

"The date for the *nikah* of Salimah and Jamil, of course. You know that they have been intended for several months now."

"Of course." Sauda looked more closely at the old man. His faded gray jalabiyah had almost certainly once been blue. His shoes were so worn that the big toe of each foot protruded grotesquely from the end. There was the matter of his embarrassment of a car, a Fleet Morris that grumbled and roared and pitched so terribly the passengers were sure to develop a headache.

"You need our help with the expenses? Is this why you have come so far?"

Rahman nodded, trying to swallow a tart mouthful of kola nut. "No, no," he said, nearly choking. "There is no question of money. On that account, we are fine."

"You needn't worry, brother. She can retain her employment with me. Her marriage will not affect her job."

"I'm afraid that it will. I have come today to take her home. This will be her last day."

"We will miss her," offered Adam. "Won't we, Sauda?"

Ignoring Adam, Sauda said, "Why does she have to go? Don't you all need the money? I could talk to my father. He could pay her more. She is very important to me here, especially since I've had my baby."

"Oh? I've always had the impression that you don't much like my daughter."

Sauda was temporarily stifled. Adam grinned.

"What makes you think that? I've always liked her. Often we don't see eye to eye, but there is nothing unusual in that. I care very much for her. I do. And I don't know how I could do without her." Sauda turned to Adam. "Tell him, Adam. Tell him how much I need her. Come on, convince him to let her stay."

"No convincing is necessary, madam. It isn't my choice. Jamil wants her to be a housewife. She has also expressed the desire to go to school."

"School? What about me?" whined Sauda.

"This isn't about you," said Adam through his teeth. "I can't believe that you are being so selfish."

"Don't be so hard on your wife," defended Rahman. "She is accustomed to being served, of having her way. She can't help herself. You can't blame her. Besides, I have a solution."

Sauda sat forward in her chair, ignoring the faint whimper of her daughter upstairs and the burning sensation it triggered in her breasts. "What kind of a solution?"

"My daughter Kubrah"—Rahman pointed out of the window in the direction of his daughters—"is willing to stay and take Saliamh's place."

"Yes. I think that will work." Sauda rubbed her palms together.

"No, it won't." Adam was unwilling to remain quiet while Sauda brought another woman into their home for her to abuse. Adam consented to allowing Sauda to retain Salimah only because she had been in her employ long before their marriage. But no more. Sauda was a spoiled, tyrannical ingrate. If she hadn't been, she may not have ever lied about having a son. If she hadn't been, he might have been able to love her.

Rahman was correct in saying that Sauda's attitude was not her fault. Much of the blame lay with her father. As her husband, Adam was willing to divest her of her supercilious behaviors.

"Salimah is a good girl. She is obedient and endlessly tolerant. Rahman, you have raised a fine girl, and I am sure that your other daughter is just as wonderful, but we won't be hiring anyone else to take her place."

"Why?" Tears pooled in Sauda's eyes. "I need her."

Adam ignored Sauda. "I hope you can understand, Brother Rahman."

Rahman nodded. He was amused by Sauda's display. He would have never allowed such insolence from any of his wives or daughters. He demanded greater respect. When respect didn't work, he could instill fear.

"But I don't understand. I want her to stay."

"No," said Adam.

"I need her. I can't take care of Lailah by myself."

"You don't need anyone to help you take care of Lailah. She's an infant. How hard can it be? Feed her and put her to sleep."

"It is hard," she complained. "I have to wake up at night, and I have to wash her and feed her all of the time. I need help."

Rahman followed the conversation, as if watching a tennis match, trying to withhold his laughter.

"Asabe is nursing a child that isn't even her own by birth, and not once have I heard her make complaints. Not once has she asked for extra help. Plus, she takes care of this house. She cooks all of the meals. She tends the garden. She—"

"I don't care what she does."

"Well, you should. Maybe you could learn a thing or two about how to be a good mother and wife."

Adam may as well have slapped her face. It would have been a less painful blow. Adam's words hurt Sauda, but pride kept the tears from falling.

"My father pays Salimah's salary, not you, so it doesn't matter what you say." To Rahman, Sauda said, "You can leave Kubrah here with me. I'll speak with my father, and he will settle the matter of money."

"Miss, I couldn't do that unless your husband consents." Rahman looked to Adam.

"If you hire on Kubrah, you had better do more than call your father. You had better tell him to come and get you because you won't be staying here," said Adam as he crossed his arms.

FOR FIVE MINUTES, Asabe tried to ignore the whimpers coming from Sauda's room. Since Sauda brought the infant home two months prior, she had been fiercely protective. Sauda rejected assistance in even the most basic care of her child.

Asabe stood in the opened doorway of her bedroom and listened to the angry voices downstairs. She was able to decipher only bits and pieces of the conversation. Regardless, it was obvious that none of it concerned attending to the weeping infant.

Asabe glanced back at Hadizah, who was napping in her crib, before heading down the hallway toward Sauda's bedroom. The door was open a sliver. The bedroom was dark despite the harsh sun outside.

Asabe pushed the door open and was met by a wall of thick, putrid air. It was the smell of old diapers, stale food, and sour milk. Asabe reeled back as if she had been pushed, her nose stinging. Her mouth watered, and her stomach cramped.

Asabe turned to looked down the hall, hoping to see Sauda rush up the stairs and declare that she had just heard her baby crying and that she would take care of her. But Sauda was not there, only remnants of her disturbed voice floated up the stairs.

Asabe shook her head. She did not want to go into Sauda's bedroom, but listening to the child whimper and whine struck a maternal chord within her, and she felt as if she had no choice.

Asabe felt along the wall for the light switch. In the light, the room was far cleaner than its odor suggested. The bed was neatly made, with a candelabra perched in the center of the mantle. Neat rows of glass bottles filled with an assortment of perfumed oils lined the dresser top. The contemporary dark wood nightstands were polished until gleaming and were topped with hand-crocheted doilies. The room, decorated in pastel pink and yellow, was remarkably frilly for such a boisterous woman.

Asabe threw open the heavy drapes and opened the windows on both sides of the room. The air outside was humid, but a slight breeze still moved through the room. The room quickly began to smell better.

Lailah quieted when Asabe stood over her crib. Her small black eyes struggled to find Asabe's face. Asabe patted Lailah's stomach, reluctant to pick her up for fear of angering Sauda. Sauda had been adamant about allowing Asabe to hold her child, though she never could understand why.

Since the day Asabe visited Sauda in the hospital, when she dried her tears and consoled her, they had been more than civil to each other. They had, in fact, become friends and trustees of each other's sensitivities. This made Sauda's attitude seem all the more strange.

The quiet lasted only a brief moment. Lailah began again to whimper, her flat face twisted. With her short plump fingers, Lailah scratched at her diapered bottom, her fingers moving as fast as they could. Asabe noticed also that the poor infant's pink T-shirt was damp and stained.

"I know, poor baby. Her doesn't feel too good, does her?" Asabe removed Lailah's rubber pants. The cloth diaper was saturated.

And the odor. The odor was sickening. Asabe choked back her repulsion.

Lailah's bottom was coated with feces, although there was no evidence of a bowel movement in her diaper.

"Did she change your diaper without cleaning you first?" Asabe asked herself more than the child. This was not the worst of it.

There were five raw blemishes as red as cherries on Lailah's tiny black bottom. Three of them were bleeding; the other two were seeping yellow pus.

Asabe removed the rest of Lailah's clothing and carried her naked into the bathroom. Asabe filled the sink with tepid water and commenced to washing the child from head to toe. Dry skin flaked from the child's head. Soured milk was trapped in the creases of Lailah's neck. Dirt was under her fingernails, in bad need of clipping.

The child lay still in the water. On occasion, she would close her slight eyes and sigh, her bottom lip shaking. Asabe had never seen such relief on a face as young. Lailah was relieved and comforted, but Asabe was not. She could barely hold the child for the trembling in her hands.

A month earlier, when Sauda had rejected her baby, calling her an ugly aberration, still Asabe thought that she would eventually come to accept her lot. Asabe believed that like any other mother, Sauda would not be able to resist loving her own child regardless of her defects. However, as Asabe washed the child, sighting her condition, it was obvious that Sauda had not accepted her lot. It was obvious that Sauda had not grown to adore the child.

Lailah was filthy and unkempt. She had gained little weight since her birth; her ribs bulged clearly from beneath her thin coffee skin. No loving mother would neglect her child in such a way.

"If she didn't want to take care of you, she could have asked Salimah. She could have asked me." Asabe bit her bottom lip. "This won't happen again," Asabe promised as she lifted the baby from the foul water. "I won't let it."

Asabe found a yellow tube of antibiotic ointment in the medicine cabinet. This she would use to treat the baby's raw bottom.

In the bedroom, Asabe laid the infant back into her crib while she searched Sauda's room for a clean diaper and a set of clean clothing. There were two bureaus in Sauda's room, but not one drawer was occupied by baby clothing.

Asabe tried both nightstands. In one nightstand, she found books and papers, candles and incense. Asabe opened the double doors on the bottom of the second nightstand. Two bottles rolled out onto the floor. There were twenty-three used and unwashed bottles inside the nightstand. Asabe knew because she counted them, lining them up on the floor in front of her like an isle display in a grocery store. The insides of the bottles were coated with congealed and spoiled milk and spores of green mold. There were also two cans of unopened baby formula.

For two months, Asabe had thought Sauda exceedingly modest. She would never nurse her baby in the presence of others. She wouldn't even nurse before her own husband, claiming embarrassment. Each time the baby would cry in hunger, she would leave the room to feed her. No one knew that she was using bottles.

It was not *their way* to deny their children to nurse but the way of unbelievers. It was the way of the West. Any woman who would deny her child the breast was no woman at all. A woman like that was lower than a cur in the street—filthy, uncultured, unworthy of the status of motherhood.

Lailah, growing hungry and impatient of lying alone in her crib, showed her disapproval with an occasional moan. This forced Asabe to focus on the task at hand, finding suitable dress for Lailah.

Next came the closet; it was the absolute source of the fog that contaminated the air in Sauda's room. On the floor of the closet were two plastic garbage bags partially concealed by Sauda's expensive clothing. The first bag was filled with weeks and weeks' worth of baby clothes. All dirty.

The second bag was heavy with soiled cloth diapers. Some were black with days-old excrement.

Two days earlier, Sauda begged Adam to buy the baby new clothes. She told him that Lailah had grown too large for the ones that she already had. Now, Asabe knew that Sauda had simply been too lazy to wash the garments. Too lazy or too trifling or too full of bitter disappointment.

The oppressive stench weighed as heavy on Asabe's chest as an iron weight. Or was it her anger?

Asabe dragged the two bags from the closet, and without forethought, she emptied them both in a stinking heap atop Sauda's bed. She then scooped the cooing infant up into her arms and left the room.

"What are you doing with my baby?" asked Sauda as she came down the hall.

Asabe pushed past Sauda, nearly knocking her from her feet.

"She is also Adam's baby, and if he knew how you were taking care of her . . ." Anger stole Asabe's words.

Sauda followed Asabe into her bedroom. With the child held tightly against her bosom, Asabe removed a cloth diaper and a yellow kimono T-shirt from a drawer. They were garments long outgrown by Hadizah. Asabe massaged ointment onto Lailah's infected rump. She then dressed the child while cooing and talking to the child in baby speak as if Sauda was not standing in the doorway.

"What were you doing in my bedroom? You have no right. We may be friends now, but unless you want to make an enemy of me, you had better stay out of my room, and you had better leave my baby alone." Sauda attempted to lift Lailah away from Asabe's grasp.

Asabe bared her teeth, giving Sauda cause to pause. The taste of iron shavings flooded Asabe's mouth. She had been biting her tongue, trying to push back the urge to do her cowife harm. She would have overlooked almost anything to keep the peace with Sauda; but a child, harmed or neglected or even the least bit resented, Asabe would not overlook.

Asabe swallowed the puddle of blood in her mouth.

"I am already your enemy."

Sauda forgot her previous diatribe. "But I thought we were friends."

"I was willing to hurt you after what you did to my Hadizah. I'd be willing to do the same for this child."

"There is nothing wrong with my baby." She tried again to remove Lailah from Asabe's embrace.

Asabe pulled away. "Before I give her to you, we must come to an understanding."

"I don't have to understand anything. She is my baby and my business. You take care of that orphan girl. I'll take care of mine."

"I do take care of my daughter. But do you really take care of yours?"

Sauda said nothing to this, her face collapsing as if a firecracker had gone off inside of her head.

"You promised Adam that you would nurse his daughter."

"I do."

"In that case, for whom are those twenty-three bottles in your nightstand? Surely you haven't taken a liking to baby formula at the age of twenty-one."

"I only use the bottle when I'm too tired to nurse." Sauda crossed her arms over her bosom.

"Then why hide twenty-three bottles in the nightstand? Twenty-three bottles for the occasional bottle-feeding? Tell me the truth, Sauda."

"I don't like nursing her. I don't like . . ." Sauda covered her face with her hands.

"You don't like your baby?"

Sauda shook her head. "You think I'm a bad person, don't you?"

"I want to believe that you have some redeemable qualities, but I simply do not understand you. I am as barren and unproductive as a rock. There isn't much that I wouldn't give to be able to have a child of my own. If only for one time I could know what it is like to carry another life within my body, I would be satisfied. It wouldn't matter to me if the child was not normal because the ability to give birth is not a right of passage into womanhood. It is a privilege.

"Your baby has been lying in her own filth for so long and so consistently that she has infected sores. Her clothes were piled in a dirty heap in your closet." Asabe sucked her teeth. "The odor in your room bears testimony to your neglect."

"I need help. I don't know what to do for her the way she is."

"She is a baby regardless of her differences. Feed her, dress her, clean her, love her is all. If you can't or won't, then allow someone else to do it. This innocent child should not suffer because of your ignorance. I heard you downstairs, fighting to keep Salimah in your employ. What for? You haven't allowed anyone in this household to help with Lailah."

"I need Salimah for other things."

"For what?" she yelled. "To convince yourself that there is at least one person you can dominate? If you want to dominate someone, try yourself because you are nothing more than a vulgar woman in fancy attire. You have no real substance and no heart. No self-control."

This time Sauda succeeded in wrestling the child from Asabe's arms. Lailah immediately began to wail her discontent. Hadizah sat up in her crib, startled and dazed from sleep.

"You don't know how I feel. You don't understand what I'm going through. Hadizah may not be your real baby, but at least she is normal. You don't have to be ashamed to let people see her because they might think that because you had a retarded baby, there must be something wrong with you."

Sauda held the screaming child, her maternal instincts so suppressed she didn't attempt to rock or quiet Lailah.

"I can't care about your pain when that baby has to suffer." Asabe stood at her window. Adam was outside escorting Rahman and his daughters down the driveway to their car. What she said next was in Adam's defense as well as that of his daughter's.

"If I come to know that you have continued to bottle-feed that child, I will inform Adam. If ever I witness that child as filthy and degraded as I have today, I will inform Adam. If you continue to discard her dirty clothes like disposable tissues, I will inform Adam. Do you understand me?" Asabe turned to face Sauda. Their eyes locked in a silent battle of wills.

Sauda left Asabe's room, her ego deflated, her will overcome, for the time being.

SIXTEEN

For the first time in more years than he could remember, Adam awoke long after the sun made its ascent into the sky. He sat up in his bed among the wrinkled sheets. A harsh stream of morning light splashed across his face. The warmth did not burn away the guilt.

Adam had heard the azan that morning at exactly five thirteen, but this time, it failed to move his heart as it once had. Strangely it made him crave even more the comfort of his bed, though there was really no comfort there at all.

When he didn't descend the stairs thirty minutes after the azan, as was usual, to take a cup of tea before racing to the mosque to share his prayers with other men of faith, Asabe came. Adam heard her too. He only pretended that he did not hear her knocking at his bedroom door. When she entered his room, calling his name, shaking him, he turned over in his bed, feigning deep sleep.

This was not the first morning that Adam had not attended morning prayers in the mosque. As of late, he had simply opted to make them at home, with his women. This was the first morning though that he had failed to perform his prayers at all.

Adam stared straight ahead into the sunlight, eyes watering, as if this confrontation would scare the sun back into its sheath of darkness. It did not, and so neither did his guilt.

After showering and getting dressed, Adam made ablution with intent to perform his prayers despite the tardy hour. But when he stood on the masala, he could not. Would not. There was a lurking sense of guilt, a darkness enveloping his heart. By making dawn prayers nearly three hours late, after the sun had long since announced the day, it seemed that somehow he was reaffirming his guilt.

Adam stepped away from the masala. He did not look back. He did not give in to the compunction of his failing faith, for that is exactly what it was.

There was a time before, in his blemished past, when faith was like an enemy to him. In being so, he was actually an enemy to himself, though when the realization was evident, it was sadly too late. When it was too late, by then, he had lost all that was dear to him in the world.

A son.

A woman almost as devoted to him as she was to her god.

This time was different, for it seemed that he had lost all that was dear to him in the world long before his faith had failed.

Another son.

A jewel of a bride.

The promise of a son.

Until this morning, Adam had not had the courage to be honest with his feelings. Until this morning, Adam had not even been able to confront the truth in himself. Adam wanted to know why. Why would a man of faith, such as himself, a man who prayed diligently, timely, and with spirit and belief, be denied the only thing he truly wanted in the world?

"Lesser men than I have sons. Don't I deserve to have a son as well?" Adam asked aloud.

Adam dropped his head into his hands. He shuddered against the shame, the anger, the inexhaustible feeling that he had been somehow slighted. Failed.

Asabe entered the room, carrying a serving tray. There was a highly polished brass teapot, a teacup, and a saucer that tittered with each step she initiated, and a plate of buttery rolls filled with cream cheese.

Asabe looked lovely, a broad relieved smile on her face. Her lips were shiny with pinkish gloss. Her eyes were lined with black kohl. Her hands were decorated with ruddy henna. Her presence was sweetened by the scent of perfumed oils. And she, a sweet apparition, was smiling at him, loving him and wanting to know, "Are you feeling better? I was afraid you might be ill. I expected you to sleep in the entire day."

Adam attempted a response, but the guilt got in the way and pushed the words back into his stomach. At that very moment, Adam saw the very reason why he should be prostrating himself to Allah.

After belief in the oneness of Allah, there is no greater treasure for a man than a pious wife.

His father had recited those words to him many times before his death, but until now, they had never resonated with such truth. Adam's pious wife was standing before him. Asabe was his greatest treasure. He knew that he should have been showing his gratitude for such good fortune, but at that moment, he was simply unable.

"Nothing for me this morning," he said, checking his watch.

"Why not? You must be hungry." Asabe stepped closer to her husband. She wanted to see him, his face, his eyes. "Is something wrong?"

Adam removed his glasses and dropped them into the front pocket of his camise. If he couldn't see her face, then he would not have to look into her eyes when he pretended to be pleased with himself and his life. He would not have to see the questioning in her eyes when he told her the lie.

"All that's wrong is that I am running late for work. I have got to get going." Adam brushed against Asabe as he left the room. He couldn't hear her following him down the carpeted hall in her bare feet, but he felt her there. He felt her eyes burning into the back of his head. He felt her wanting to ask him again what was wrong but deciding instead to hold her peace.

Adam slipped on his shoes at the front door, and without looking back or saying a word, he walked out. The screen door clashed against its frame.

Asabe set the tray down on the foyer table and followed Adam outside.

"I can wrap your breakfast!" she yelled down the driveway. "You could eat it at the office!" Asabe wanted to give her husband the opportunity to . . . She just didn't know.

Adam waved as he backed out of the driveway.

ASABE HAD JUST SLIPPED ON HER SLEEPING GOWN when she heard light tapping on her door. Before she spoke a word, Sauda entered, smelling of rich cinnamon musk and wearing a silky white ensemble alluring enough to make a blind man see. She was smiling.

Sauda twirled around in the center of the room with the attitude and confidence of Western runway models.

"How do you like my new gown?"

"Ooo, so pretty. So pretty," said Hadizah, pointing at Sauda. She stood up on Asabe's bed but lost her balance and fell onto her padded bottom.

"It's very pretty," admitted Asabe. "And so are you. Pregnancy did not agree with you, but since you've had Lailah, you have bounced back to your usual self. Your shape is back."

"I know, and so is my husband." Still smiling.

"What does that mean?"

Sauda sat on the edge of Asabe's bed. At first, she said nothing but only stared into the palms of her hands. Hadizah crawled to Sauda, and using her stepmother's shoulders as support, she stood up. The eighteen-month-old gently stroked Sauda's freshly braided hair.

"It has been two months since Adam has stayed with me in my room. Two months is a long time. I was lonely."

"You've only just had your baby, Sauda. There is nothing so unusual in that."

"Yes, but you know that having a child is not the only reason Adam has not been to my room. Besides, I missed him."

Hadizah pushed one of Sauda's skinny braids into her mouth and began to chew. Sauda pulled the robust toddler into her lap and held her tiny face against her shoulder. Asabe had never seen Sauda show such affection to anyone, including her own child.

"I take it you're pleased to have Adam tonight."

Sauda answered with a profuse grin.

"Then I am happy for you."

"Happy enough to take Lailah for the night?" Seeing the questioning on Asabe's face, she added, "It has been so long, and I don't want to be disturbed. Please."

Asabe didn't realize the time she relented and agreed. But she had. Sauda was Adam's wife, the good and the bad of her, and Lailah was her daughter as well. It would be selfish, even petty, of her to deny Sauda a few moments of solitude with her husband because these were the times when Adam was at his best.

Adam had been a poor student in the school of tact and understanding, but he was a star pupil in the subject of tenderness. Unable to feign affection, Asabe knew that if Adam had finally consented to resuming his nights with Sauda, it was because he wanted to. Sauda had every reason to be pleased.

Seconds later, Sauda slipped back into Asabe's room holding her two-month-old daughter in her arms. She handed the sleeping child over to Asabe along with a bottle, which Asabe promptly handed back.

"You're still bottle-feeding this child?" Asabe didn't want to be angry, but she could feel its attempt to rise to the surface.

"No, no. I just thought that you might not want to nurse her."

"I'm not like you, Sauda. I would not deny her because of her condition, even though she isn't mine."

Sauda seemed not to notice Asabe's scathing commentary, or otherwise, she did not care because the smile reappeared on her face. She turned to leave.

"Pretty, pretty," squealed Hadizah, jumping from the bed and running to Sauda. She grabbed a tiny handful of Sauda's hem. "Pretty, smell good. Pretty hair."

The memory of the last time Hadizah grabbed Sauda's hem flashed in Asabe's mind. She stepped forward to restrain her daughter.

"Leave Mommy Sauda alone, Hadizah."

"Don't worry," defended Sauda. "I don't mind."

Sauda bent down and cupped Hadizah's face in her hands. She kissed Hadizah's tiny heart-shaped mouth and tenderly embraced the child.

Sauda looked up at Asabe and said, "I wish my little girl could be this beautiful. I wish . . ." Sauda's voice trailed off hauntingly. There was such defeat and complacency in her voice. It chilled Asabe's heart.

"Good night," said Asabe.

"Insha Allah, it will be a very good night."

AT 3:00 A.M., LAILAH AWOKE, screaming violently into the silence. Hadizah did not stir in her crib by the window. Asabe was not as fortunate. She awoke with a start and was quite annoyed.

Asabe had been dreaming. In this dream, Asabe's figure was distorted by her protruding belly, so huge and round that she had difficulty walking through doorways.

In this dream, she sat in her rocking chair next to her bedroom window while watching her children play in the front garden. Her three hardy little boys, dirt smudged and sweaty, giggled wildly as their father tickled them senseless. Hadizah was there, her only daughter, digging soil from the flower beds to make mud pies.

All of them were beautiful little black replicas of Adam, who appeared strangely as a young man in the dream. His gray hairs were gone. He had no more use for his glasses, and he was thirty pounds lighter, revealing the muscular frame he once sported.

Asabe stroked her belly, round and comely. She knew that she carried in her belly another boy because in her dream, she knew everything.

Asabe experienced the pains of labor and lay on her bed to give birth. She did not give birth to another infant boy but to a grown man, fully clothed, and speaking to her in a voice as smooth and as deep as Adam's.

Just as Asabe was about to learn his name, she heard the screaming. She jumped from the bed and ran to the window to see which one of her children had been hurt, but when she leaned out of the window, all she saw was blackness. Once her eyes adjusted to the dark, she then realized that she was no longer in her dream. Asabe was in her own bed, and Lailah was lying next to her.

Asabe sat up lifting the child into her arms and rocked her until her screams had subsided to weary hiccups. Once the child was calm, she then held her to her breast. Lailah turned away her head. She was so thoroughly uninterested in suckling that Asabe knew right away that Lailah was still not being breast-fed. Sauda had lied.

It was too late to be angry, and she was too tired to judge Sauda.

"You will nurse this night, little one," cooed Asabe into the child's ear. Asabe began to explain as if Lailah could understand, "This is not a bottle. This is a breast. It doesn't feel the same in your mouth as a bottle, I am sure; but believe me, once you taste it, you will definitely like it better."

Lailah ceased to whine and squirm. Indeed she responded as if she understood.

"Now," said Asabe, holding her nipple against the infant's cheek, "I'm going to put this in your mouth, and you do what comes natural. It isn't as bad as you think, and it tastes a lot better than a rubber nipple. Ask your big sister, she'll tell you."

There was little light in Asabe's room. Heavy clouds hid the moon that night. Still, Asabe could see Lailah's eyes in the obscure shadows of her room. Lailah knew. She knew that she was being spoken to. Lailah knew that she was being loved. Lailah knew that this moment was about satisfying her needs. To this, Lailah responded by trusting the words she heard, though she did not quite understand, and by relaxing in Asabe's arms.

This time Lailah did not turn her head away when Asabe pushed her nipple into her mouth. She accepted it cautiously, giving a tentative suck. Before long though, the child was nursing so vigorously that Asabe once caught her breath at the discomfort.

WHEN ASABE AWOKE THE NEXT MORNING, before the roosters cackled, before the call of the azan, it was with a start. She sat up in bed, searching the blackness with wide eyes.

Asabe felt along the bed, searching the cool sheets for the infant. Lailah was there sleeping, her round diapered rump raised up in the air. Then Asabe listened for the steady whispering breath of her sleeping daughter. She cocked her head and leaned forward. The room was silent.

Asabe rose from her bed, stepping lightly on the floor, making sure not to create too much motion and wake the sleeping baby. She headed for Hadizah's crib across the room. Just as she was reaching Hadizah's crib, Asabe stubbed her toe on the dresser. Some of the glass bottles of perfume and lotion on the dresser fell over and rolled off onto the floor.

This did not awaken Lailah, but she did turn over onto her side with a muffled grunt.

Asabe put her hands into Hadizah's crib to feel for her warm body. She was not there, only wrinkled linens. Asabe heard her voice. Hadizah's voice as it filtered up from below. Hadizah was downstairs.

"How did she get out of her crib?" Asabe whispered. Asabe rushed from the room, forgetting her robe. "Hadizah? Where are you?" Asabe turned on the living room light. On the couch, she saw Hadizah's stuffed elephant. But no Hadizah.

Asabe heard her daughter's voice again, hysterical, screaming. The smell of smoke. Asabe stood at the end of the corridor leading to the kitchen. Puffs of white smoke seeped from the seams of the doorway.

Asabe started forward and then stopped halfway. She wiped her damp palms on the back of her gown, trying desperately to swallow back her fear, but it was quickly getting the best of her. Asabe opened her mouth to scream for Adam. Instead, a belch of spontaneous giggling escaped from her throat like air from a pierced balloon. She couldn't stop. The closer Asabe came to the kitchen door, the worse the giggling became.

Stop it! Stop laughing! she screamed inside of her head. *What if Hadizah is . . .* Asabe clipped the morbid premonition, unwilling to succumb to the terror it suggested. Asabe stumbled ahead, her hysterics turning into tears. She pushed the door open and . . .

Sauda stood at the sink with her back to Asabe, Hadizah propped up on her hip. Sauda held a smoldering pot under a cold stream of water from the tap.

"Momma Sauda wanted to cook her favorite girl a nice breakfast, but she messed up and burned it." Sauda was talking to Hadizah. Hadizah had a handful of Sauda's ear in her hand.

"As soon as I get this pot cleaned up, I'll try it again. Your momma is going to be so pleased when she sees you all cleaned up and fed when she gets up."

Sauda lowered Hadizah to the floor and scrubbed the pot. When Hadizah saw Asabe standing in the doorway, she squealed, "Momma!"

In unison, Asabe and Sauda answered, "Yes."

Sauda smiled broadly at the sight of Asabe, but her voice did not convey the same warmth. "Oh. You're awake."

"Yes," said Asabe. "I am. What happened here?"

Still smiling, Sauda said, "I came to your room this morning to get my Lailah. I figured that maybe she would be ready to nurse. I didn't knock, didn't want to disturb you. Lailah was sleeping just fine. Right next to you. But Hadizah was sitting up in her crib awake, so I decided to take her out and give her breakfast so that she wouldn't wake you and Lailah." Still smiling. "So that's what happened."

"You came to nurse Lailah?"

Sauda nodded her head. Licked her dry lips. More smiling.

"Nurse? Lailah?"

"Yes, but she was sleeping, and Hadizah was awake."

Sauda lifted Hadizah from the floor. She walked across the kitchen and handed Hadizah to Asabe.

"Here she is. Just fine. I took her out because, you know, I didn't want her to wake you up."

Asabe refused to reciprocate, and so Sauda's smile finally fell away.

"What is this really all about?" asked Asabe.

"Nothing. What do you mean?"

"You've never come to get Hadizah before."

"I came for Lailah. I wanted to nurse her."

"You're lying. Lailah is not a nursing baby."

"I do nurse her." Sauda pretended to be outraged.

Lailah's vibrant wail wafted downstairs, slicing through the silence.

"Here is your chance to prove it. Go on up and feed your baby."

Sauda threw her hands up. "Okay, okay. Just don't tell Adam. He wouldn't forgive me."

"Why shouldn't I?"

"I tried to nurse her, but she wouldn't take my breast."

"How hard did you try?"

Sauda lowered her head. Smiling again. "Not very hard."

Asabe waved away the indiscretion, too weary to fight. "All right, Sauda. The matter is between you, Allah, and Adam. But why did you come into my room and take my child?" To Asabe, the inquisition felt strangely petty.

"To be closer to Lailah." Sauda closed her eyes. "I pretend that she is my baby. Perfect. Beautiful."

"But you have a baby of your own, Sauda."

"But she isn't—"

"Don't say it, Sauda. Just go and tend to your baby."

Asabe watched Sauda as she left the kitchen, the way she didn't once take her eyes off Hadizah. Sauda eyed Hadizah even as she was passing through the swinging doorway. She walked backward even, nearly tripping over her robe.

Hadizah began to whine and squirm in Asabe's arms. It was then that Asabe realized how tightly she was squeezing her daughter.

SEVENTEEN

Mu'min leaned over his mother's hospital bed, the raised railing digging into his ribs, and kissed her forehead. The usual deep creases of her forehead were smooth and as cool as satin against his lips. Khadijah was not merely asleep but floating in the black waters of a coma.

Next to Khadijah's bed, the monitor produced a continuous stream of green spiked lines meant to represent her heart rate. If not for the redundant pattern, Mu'min would have long since thought her dead. There was little proof to the contrary.

Khadijah had suffered so much pain. Nothing the doctors could have administered would have calmed her tears; stopped her from writhing in her hospital bed, tearing at the sheets; or silenced the many times she shouted the name of Allah into the universe. Nothing helped except the drugs the doctors used to induce a permanent sleep until the cancer had its fill of her, until the angel of death was deputed to reclaim her soul.

Mu'min sat in the chair next to his mother's bed. He reached through the railing and took one of her icy hands in his. He could almost feel her impending death seep into his skin and crawl up his arm, the coldness of it. Part of him wanted to throw back her lifeless hand and scrub the scent of death away.

Khadijah's hand was a bookmark in the book of life and death. She may still have been among the living, but any page now, and she would be among the dead. Still, Mu'min held on. He would not let her go. He would confront anything because she was his mother, the first woman he had ever loved.

"Mu'min, it is late. Come, honey, let's go home." Zulaikah stroked her husband's back. "You can sleep for a few hours, and then in the morning, I'll make you a nice hot breakfast. Then you can come back."

Zulaikah was the second woman Mu'min had ever loved, and she had been a gift chosen for him by his mother.

With each feathery stroke of her hand, the tension and fear in him ebbed just a little. She had that way about her. Every word she spoke, whether in haste or in passion or in normalcy, sounded like relief. Every time she touched him, it felt like home. He wanted to leave, to close his eyes and forget the hospital and his mother's blanched face and the memory of her collapsing onto her kitchen floor, but he would not go home and enjoy his young wife until he had done his duty by seeing his mother off on her journey into the next life.

"No. I'm not ready to leave."

"You're tired, Mu'min. If you don't rest, you'll end up a patient in the hospital."

"Good. That way, my mother and I can share a room."

No one laughed.

"Take the keys," he said, reaching into his jacket pocket. "You go on home, and I'll call you to come and pick me up when I'm ready."

Zulaikah refused the keys. "If you stay, I stay."

"You don't have to. She's my mother."

"She's my mother too. Remember?" Zulaikah smiled down at him. That smile was like icing on an already-perfect cake. He loved that smile since the first day he saw her, since the day his mother dragged Zulaikah home with her from the mosque.

"This is the girl you are going to marry, son." It was eerie the way she spoke those words, like a soothsayer in the midst of her craft. It made him almost afraid, until like now, Zulaikah smiled at him. Then somehow he knew his mother was only speaking the truth as she knew it. Anyone with eyes could see that there could be no other girl for him.

Looking up into her face as round and as ripe as a peach and the color of just-right toast, he wanted to leap from the chair and seize her in his arms; but he did not, straining against the impulse. He did not want to dishonor his mother's suffering by seeking such carnal pleasures.

"I'm glad you're here."

"Where else would . . ." Zulaikah's voice trailed off. She stared at the door, a look of puzzlement stealing away the smile from her face.

Mu'min followed her gaze but saw nothing except a door, painted puke green but a door nonetheless.

"What is it? Did you see something?"

"I thought I saw someone looking in through the little window."

Mu'min shrugged his shoulders, and her hands fell away. "Probably just a nurse."

"I don't think so."

Then Mu'min saw the face. No, two faces, pushed together, cheek to cheek, as both tried to look in through the tiny square window of the door. When the two faces caught sight of him watching them, they disappeared.

"I'll be back."

Mu'min left Zulaikah standing by his mother's bed.

CHARLES AND MARGARET BRADY stood arm and arm in front of Khadijah's hospital room door when Mu'min came out.

He was a much larger man than they ever imagined he would be. To them, he was like a mountain, his head stretching toward the heavens. His shoulders were as wide and solid as steel beams. This he did not inherit from his mother, they knew, but evidently from his father along with his rich coloring.

Standing before Mu'min, they knew that they must have very much resembled the Munchkins from *The Wizard of Oz*, their heads bent way back to look into his heavy face.

The man standing before Charles was not the grandson he'd watched secretly through the hospital nursery window twenty-three years prior. That grandson was tiny, sleeping serenely, the color of coffee watered down with too much milk, wrapped in a pink receiving blanket because the hospital had run out of blue ones.

That grandson of so many years ago, he could envision bouncing on his knee. Charles could see himself showing that grandson off to his friends, telling them, *No, he ain't got no black in him. We got some Indian in our blood. That's where his color comes from.* This boy—man—was nothing like that baby, nothing like the possibilities he once envisioned. The man standing before Charles Brady was a black man. In this black man, this grandson of his, Charles Brady saw nothing of himself.

Margaret felt Charles growing tense. She released his arm and stepped forward. Her hands and arms ached to embrace the giant standing before her. Instead, Margaret fidgeted with the strap of her pocketbook. It would have satisfied a longtime yearning of hers to hold Mu'min's face in her hands and kiss both cheeks and then his forehead and say, *Do you know who I am? I'm your grandmother, that's who, and I love you.*

But Margaret would not embrace Mu'min or even divulge her identity because she had promised Charles.

It was Charles's stubborn pride and unjustified shame that made them stay away from their only child for twenty-four years, until it was almost too late. And now, the best they could get of her was a stolen glance of her on her deathbed.

Margaret held out her hand. "Hello. My name is Margaret, and this here is my husband, Charles. You can just call us Maggie and Chuck."

"Can I help you?" Mu'min asked, ignoring her outstretched hand.

Charles and Margaret looked at each other, as if the answer was hidden somewhere within the folds of their aging faces.

"We've come to visit Karen Brady," they said in unison.

Mu'min searched his memory for that very familiar but alien name.

"Karen Brady," he whispered.

"I believe that she is now known by the name of Khadijah," assisted Margaret.

"Khadijah, my foot. You won't never hear me calling her by that name." Charles crossed his short solid arms over his chest.

"You hush, old man," said Margaret, giving him a tap on the arm. "After all of these years, can't you just give it up?" She turned back to Mu'min, smiling as if she had not just been scolding her husband like a child.

"You've come to see my mother?"

"Yes, son," she said, still smiling, her lips forming bright fuchsia crescents on her chalky face. "We heard that she was ill. How is she? She getting any better?"

"I'm afraid not. It's only a matter of time."

"Oh," she gasped, clamping an age-spotted hand over the fuchsia crescents. It was all she could do to suppress the scream she felt welling up in her chest. Charles instinctively took her hand and pulled her closer to him. Margaret laid her head on his shoulder.

"How do you know my mother?"

"We know her from way back when she was just a little girl."

"That's right," said Margaret, pulling a handkerchief from her white patent leather pocketbook. "She was a joy to her folks."

"Yeah, until she broke their hearts." Charles crossed his arms over his chest again.

"She did no such thing. She was a free spirit is all. She had her own path to follow, and she wasn't afraid to do that, even if it meant leaving her family." Margaret dabbed the tears from the corners of her eyes. "She caused her family no harm. None at all. So don't you go feeding this boy none of your crazy mixed-up stories. You hear me, Charles Eugene?"

Charles grunted.

Smiling again, but with less conviction this time, Margaret asked, "You must be her boy, Mu'min."

"Yes. So you knew my grandparents?"

Charles and Margaret glanced at each other, both of their faces gone crimson.

"What'd the doctor say is wrong with Karen? She got the cancer or something?" asked Charles.

"Breast cancer. She's been fighting the disease for five years now. They couldn't help her." Mu'min lowered his head. "The disease just got the best of her, I guess."

"Poor boy," cooed Margaret. She started forward to comfort her grandson, but Charles blocked her way.

"Maggie, I think that we had better be going now," Charles said this, not once taking his eyes off Mu'min.

"But I was hoping I could go in and see her," she whined.

"I only agreed that we could come and check on her condition," he said through his teeth, "but I didn't agree to going into the room."

"Damn it, Charles, too many years have passed for you to keep on this way about that girl." Margaret stood belly to belly, toe to toe with her husband and looked him in the eyes. "I never in all of my life thought that I'd say this to you, but get with the times, old man. This is the new millennium." Margaret stomped off, her fat sandaled feet making slapping sounds against the tile floor.

Charles turned to Mu'min, an uneasy smile on his face. He tried to initiate a laugh, but he stopped when he heard how unconvinced he sounded of the humor in his wife's display.

"Women can be touchy. It doesn't matter how old they get. They always find a way to nag the hell out of a man."

Mu'min stared at the man in front of him. Stout, balding, with blue eyes as dark as the bottom of the ocean. Those were the eyes of his mother, murky from a past full of secrets and shame.

"Well, you can't blame her. She came all the way to the hospital for nothing."

"Not for nothing," defended Charles. "She came to see how your momma was doing, and now that we know, we'll be going." Charles held out his hand, but Mu'min seemed not to notice the gesture.

"I know who you are," said Mu'min. "What I don't understand is why you've come now. You disowned my mother twenty-four years ago. Although she never told me why, I have a fairly good idea. Many years have passed, many circumstances. After my father left, my mother suffered trying to take care of me. Did you know that we once lived in a tent in a friend's backyard? Where were you then?"

"If you had hard times, then you should blame that *African* your momma married." Spittle flew from his mouth. He wiped it away with the back of his hairy hand.

"That *African* is my father."

"That *African* had no respect for us. He came to this country with his accent and his ways and brainwashed your momma. She used to be a good churchgoing girl. She was smart, the first in our family to go to college. She could have married any man she wanted. Instead, she dropped out of school, left the church and my home in order to marry that man, and adopt his heathenistic religion. As if that wasn't bad enough, she started calling herself by some damned weirdo name we couldn't hardly pronounce."

"After so many years, you can't get past it. You're still stuck in the past. Your only child in all of the world is about the die, and all you can think about is *that African.* You should have stayed home, Grandfather."

Charles flinched as if he'd been pinched. *Grandfather.* The word strummed in his head like a harp.

"I came for Maggie's sake. I came to make her happy."

"She didn't look happy to me. What mother would be happy leaving her daughter to die? What father, for that matter?"

"It doesn't make me happy."

The deep ocean behind his eyes began to swell, leaving heavy puddles on the verge of tumbling out onto his rough windburned cheeks.

"I have been agonizing over your mother ever since the day she walked out of my house with that Afri—, with your daddy. I tried to tell her that she was making a mistake. I told her that she was ruining her life, but she didn't listen to me. I haven't known a day of happiness since."

The tears that Mu'min saw in the old man's eyes washed away his own hurt and anger and had replaced it with pity. It was the eyes, so much like his mother's, that moved his heart and made him want desperately to understand his grandfather's pain, however unjustified.

"Couldn't you have been happy knowing that she was happy? Couldn't that have been enough?"

"It might have been enough had your momma really been happy."

"For the most part she was. You might have known that had you been around."

"You never saw me, boy, but I had my ways of knowing how you all were doing. I was there for your first day of school." Charles eyes were glassy, seemed almost to smile. "I can't count the number of times I sat in my old pickup outside of your school and watched you coming and going. You were a happy little boy, and so was your mother until your daddy left. Nobody had to tell me when that man left y'all. I could tell by the look on your little face when I watched you out on the schoolyard. I could tell by the look on your momma's face. That's when I knew that I had been right about your daddy all along. He did exactly what I said he would."

"This pleases you?"

"Naw, son, it doesn't. It makes me sad. I'll admit to one thing though. Habits are hard to break. I never could get over your mother's decision to be with your daddy. It was against everything that I believe in. It was against everything that I was taught about right and wrong. Like should be with like, I've always said."

"Did it ever occur to you that you might be wrong?"

"Sure it has. Fact is, I probably am wrong." Charles ran a callused hand over his shiny, balding skull. "But I'm sixty-eight years old, emphasis on the word *old*. It's too late for me to change. I just can't do it."

"That is a shame," was all that Mu'min could think to say to his grandfather.

Mu'min realized that he did not hate his grandfather. How could he? He was very much a product of his upbringing, and for that, he could not be blamed; however, he could be blamed for opting not to recognize his failures and rise above them.

"I hope that one day you will realize that you are the one who has lost. The good thing is, when you're ready to change, you can." Mu'min held out his hand. "When you do, I'd like to have you around. And not just in the shadows."

Charles looked at the outstretched hand of his grandson. It was large enough to envelop both of his. *My grandson,* he marveled. Somewhere within this massive black man ran *his* blood. Somehow this man was a part of him. The very idea caused a ripple of inexplicable pride to course within him.

Instead of taking Mu'min's hand, Charles did the very last thing he would have expected of himself. Charles embraced his grandson. He wrapped his stout arms around Mu'min's waist. Charles shut his eyes tight against the part of him that kept whispering what a fool he was making of himself. In that moment, he heard nothing, and he thought of absolutely nothing.

Mu'min looked down at his grandfather, a virtual stranger. Nothing of him was familiar as it should be between two so closely related. He didn't know the man who smelled of Old Spice and seawater. He had never had a chance to love him, but he would not reject him. He would not allow his grandfather know the pain of rejection. Mu'min held his grandfather.

Finally, Charles pulled away, refusing to meet Mu'min's gaze.

"I'd better be going now. Maggie is probably waiting in the car to cuss me out right proper. I know she's mad at me."

Mu'min watched Charles disappear down the hall, past a cart of linen, past a row of chairs and a table, past a soda machine, past three nurses racing down the hall toward him.

The door to his mother's hospital room flew open. Zulaikah stumbled out of the room, her face twisted with grief and panic. She didn't need to say a word.

Mu'min rushed past her into the room to his mother's bedside. She looked no different, still pale, still motionless. The monitor next to her bed no longer featured a pattern of consecutive green spikes.

Flatline. And that maddening sound, *Teeeee.*

In came the three nurses and, seconds after, the doctor. There was no attempt at resuscitation. It was simply too late. Khadijah's time had come and gone.

The doctor, a thirtyish Hispanic man, used a stethoscope to locate her heartbeat.

Nothing.

"Mark the time of death as 11:43 p.m.," the doctor said, looking at his watch.

EIGHTEEN

Jamil married Salimah after Jumah prayers in the courtyard of the mosque that sat squarely in the center of the village of Salam. The entire village was present for the sacred event.

Salimah sat inside the mosque surrounded by her three sisters, close family and friends, and those who were merely curious to see the little girl they'd once referred to only as No Mouth. No one ever thought that she would marry such a young man, let alone one that was handsome and educated.

Salimah wore an ankle-length dress with a raised waist made of Chinese silk. The bloodred dress glowed like neon against her black skin. Salimah's hands were decorated with intricate designs created from henna applied the night before at her henna party. On each finger, she wore a gold ring as well as a small loop in her left nostril. Her eyes were lined heavily with kohl. Salimah's face was hidden by a veil made of the sheerest black fabric garnished with small golden disks that tinkled each time she moved her head, a gift from her brother's Moroccan-born wife.

The elder women watched Salimah, their eyes moist with pride. They congratulated her profusely, hugging and kissing her. Most of her peers and childhood friends were happy for her, though some hung back and watched enviously.

When the completion of the nikah was confirmed by Imam Latif, the women let out a shrill cry and escorted Salimah outside to the courtyard where her groom awaited her. A crowd of clapping men parted to allow the bride to pass through to her groom. There, in the pocket of musk-scented men, Salimah saw her husband waiting for her, his face serious but pleased. He held in his hands the reins of two horses. Each horse wore rows of colorful woven belts with dangling tassels around their necks.

Suddenly, Salimah's future flashed before her eyes. She could see herself in Jamil's home, cooking his food, loving him more than she already did, carrying his child in her swollen belly; and it scared her. She stopped and turned back. All she wanted was to return to the inside of the mosque. Perhaps there, *it* would all undo itself.

The village women who had followed her outside burst into a cloud of hysterical laughter. They pushed her back into the direction of her husband chanting, "Get out! Go home! Get out! Go home!" As much as she wanted to, they would not allow her retreat into her sudden attack of modesty.

The first time that Jamil ever touch his wife was that day when he put his hands around her thin waist and lifted her onto the white horse. The warmth of her frail body left an imprint on his palms as potent as an electric current. Secretly he wanted to repeat the action, lifting her over and over, again and again, reliving the first feel of her on his hands.

Jamil wasn't the only person who enjoyed this first contact. The entire village roared with excitement. Children whose lips and tongues had turned pink from the wedding candy pointed and giggled. The elder women, round as gourds and happier, it seemed, than the bride, let out another ecstatic round of the shrill cry. The men clapped again.

Keeping the reins of his Salimah's horse in his hands, Jamil mounted his own horse, a handsome auburn colt. Jamil looked over to his bride and found her looking back at him, into his eyes. She had never looked into his eyes before.

Tugging lightly on the reins of Salimah's horse, Jamil drew her nearer to him. He whispered to his bride, "Do you dare to burn a hole into my heart with your eyes?"

Then he saw her smile at him through the sheer veil, a row of perfectly straight brilliantly white teeth. He could tell that indeed that is what she intended to do.

Together, they rode their horses out of the courtyard and onto the main road that ran directly through the center of the village. Their wedding guests followed, the women and young ladies on the right side of the road, the men on the left. The children following behind the bride and groom received a generous dusting of the dirt kicked up by the horses.

Jamil saw his best friend, Siddique, amid the crowd of men. He too was clapping and chanting, "Get out. Go home," but his eyes were not on the newly married couple. He was eyeing Salimah's elder sister, Kubrah, who walked on the opposite side of the road. Jamil also saw his family, his mother, sister, and two uncles.

Adam walked among at least 150 men, but he seemed alone. He did not join in the chanting. He did not clap. He showed no emotion at all. Adam may as well have not been there.

Salimah saw Asabe waving frantically from the crowd. Asabe carried Lailah on her back and held Hadizah by the hand. Salimah did not see her former mistress, Sauda. This neither concerned nor surprised Salimah.

Up ahead, at the junction where the main road met the edge of the village, a brand-new Toyota was parked. Beneath the gleaming sun, the burgundy finish shone as red as Salimah's dress. It was a wedding gift to the married couple from Adam.

Salimah watched her husband dismount his horse. The very sight of him, his skin glittering beneath beads of perspiration, dressed in a finely embroidered white gown, his mouth smiling at her, his eyes looking only at her, sent her heart into hysterics. She closed her eyes to push back the vision of him. Before she could check her emotions, he had his hands again around her waist, pulling her down from the saddle. Salimah leaned against her horse to steady herself.

The men along with Jamil crowded around the new car. Some stroked the hood, admiring the color and sleekness. Others patted the new groom on the back, winking at him knowingly. A virgin is a prize to any man.

The women circled Salimah and the horse. Two elder women took turns whispering advice on how to satisfy a husband into her ear.

Salimah nodded, thankful the veil concealed the emotions she was still having trouble recovering from.

Kubrah stepped forward through the crowd. With a wave of her hand, the crowd of tittering women was hushed.

"My sister does not speak," she began, "but anyone who knows my family knows that we are masters with words. We are poets and writers, people knowledgeable in the art of manipulating words."

Many of the women shook their heads in affirmation. Salimah's father, Rahman, was a regular at social events. He was always asked to orate on such occasions. Their uncle was Imam Latif, the man who performed the new couple's nikah. He was a hafiz and a writer of poetry.

Kubrah continued, "I will follow in the tradition of my forefathers and foremothers."

With trembling hands, Kubrah unfolded a piece of paper pressed into her damp palm.

"Salimah is my junior sister and the gem of my family. I wanted to tell her that, but those words don't seem to truly express how much we love her. So I have written her a poem."

Kubrah advanced forward and stood directly in front of her sister.

You little sister, are like the dawn

on the very threshold of a new day,

fresh and aglow with beauty,

burgeoning on a newness unknown to man.

There you stand,

so pure we want to save you
to hold you and cage you,
to preserve your unique and undeniable status.

But, alas we cannot,
and as a butterfly you will flit and flutter away,
leaving us behind,
and so too the dawn that you are.

You little sister will cease to be like the dawn,
becoming something even grander
though less sweet.
By, the will of Allah you shall be like the day
shining in all of your glory,
warm and sunny, bitter and sweet,
glorious, brilliant, resilient, seasoned.
Your light shall not falter, but will simply be,
for that is the nature of day.

We will still know you,
our love for you shall not cease,
but you will no longer be the little sister we once knew,

that dawning day.

But, more little sister, much more.

The two sisters fell into each other's arms, holding each other in a way they had not done since they watched their mother burn to death in a car wreckage eight years prior. That day, they clung to each other in pain and fear, but this time it was for the sake of happiness. This time, there was no horror, no feeling of helplessness. This time, they were happy to release each other because this day was beautiful, incorruptibly joyous.

Hand in hand, Kubrah escorted her sister to the shiny new vehicle. Jamil was already waiting for her in the driver's seat. Amid another round of clapping and cheering, Salimah joined her husband in their new car. They drove away, the village of Salam disappearing in a cloud of dust.

THE WALIMAH BEGAN immediately following the wedding. By the time the bride and groom arrived to their new home, many of the guests were already in attendance.

When Jamil bought the house a month ago, it was no more than a shell with electricity and running water, until Salimah's sisters. It was Salimah's family that purchased all the furnishings from beds to dishes to shower curtains. Much of the merchandise Salimah had never seen, leaving her sisters to do the decorating of her future marriage home.

Outside in the garden, the men congregated in as many as six different groups. Some crowded around the buffet table bedecked with every delicacy imaginable. There was barbecued lamb, tender and moist. Skewered and roasted fish was arranged on a platter. There were platters of seasoned rice and trays of fresh vegetables, two stockpots brimming with stew, boiled and fried potatoes, boiled and fried plantains, fresh sliced pineapple and mango, homemade ginger ale, coconut and chocolate cakes, buttery tea biscuits, bean cakes . . . It was a glutton's paradise.

Other men chatted among themselves, complaining about their wives or bragging about a new addition to the family.

Still, other men were circled around a man who stood shirtless and seemingly in a trance. In his right hand, he held a sword. His eyes rolled backward in his head, and then with a primordial bark, he lifted the sword and began to carve the flesh from his arm and then his hard stomach.

His skin stretched and rippled beneath the stress, but miraculously he did not bleed. There was not a single injury on his body.

It was so remarkable a sight that many of the men could find no utterance. Silence was the only sign of awe or approval they could muster.

Most of the men crowded around two men, naked except for their loincloths and the feathered charms of protection they wore around their arms. They circled around each other like mighty predators and then flew at each other savagely. The taller man sank his teeth into his opponent's shoulder, slobber running down his hairy chin. His opponent yelped excitedly, as if he enjoyed the pain. The wrestlers fumbled with each other, locking arms, foreheads pushed together, their painful grimaces like smiles. They kicked up clouds of dust with their bare feet as they performed defensive moves. They looked like lovers in a dance of courtship. The crowd clapped and cheered, at first softly and then with vigor.

"Bring him to his knees! Bring him to his knees! Bring him to his knees!" they shouted.

Finally, the stout round wrestler hooked his left leg around his opponent's right leg, causing his knee to buckle. He fell to his knees. The crowd cheered again.

The scene inside of the house was much different. Rainbows of decadently dressed women in every shape and size lounged on the new furniture beneath cool fans, their lips and fingers oily from the food.

There was hardly an available seat in the house. Many of the women present had not been present at the actual nikah. The village of Salam was many miles outside of town. Similarly, most of the village women, excluding those Salimah was personally related to, did not make an appearance at the walimah.

When Asabe arrived with Lailah and Hadizah in tow, Sauda had already arrived. She'd taken a ride with her father, Abu Kareem, and Asabe's mother, Hannah. As soon as she saw Hadizah, she crossed the room and scooped her up, whisking her across the room to where she had been talking with her lady friends.

Asabe searched the room for Attiyah. She'd promised that she and her husband would attend the nikah and walimah. Thus far, she had arrived at neither.

Maryam was there, entertaining a handful of women with her gossip. She had them enraptured with the story of a woman from town who'd refused to donate blood to her ill cowife, saying that she'd rather see her die.

Asabe was reunited with a few of her old classmates from fifteen years past. They had so much yet so little to catch up on. Most of their stories were the same. Marriage, husband troubles, cowives, children. Nothing was new or out of the ordinary.

The old midwife Umms was there, dispensing advice to the younger ladies about pregnancy and childbirth. Mostly she was directing her talk to Salimah, who she said would probably be pregnant in no time.

"I saw the two of you looking at each other when you drove up," she said. "When a man looks at his wife that way, babies are close behind. Insha Allah."

The entire room erupted at the old woman's observances.

Shortly thereafter, the entire living room of women rose from their seats and commenced to dancing to a popular traditional song.

A man sang,

My wife,

she is good

when she brings me food

she bows way down

so I can see the crown

of her head

I don't want her to fret

I won't ever get

another wife

in all my life.

Sauda led the room in the dance, her loose and heavy body rolled and swayed to the music. On her hip Hadizah bounced, her head leaning back, an impetuous grin on her young face. The other women joined in, giggling like children.

Salimah sat alone in a dim corner, smiling and eating from a plate piled high for the second time.

Asabe wanted to join the group. It had been a long time since she had danced since her own walimah. She leaned forward in her seat, her body arched, her foot tapping to the beat. This was as close to dancing as she would get that evening.

Asabe had a nursing infant to tend to. Lailah was presently nursing at Asabe's breast. It didn't matter that the child's own mother was no more than fifteen feet away because ever since the first time Lailah nursed from Asabe, she would have nothing else. She would not accept a bottle. She would not even agree to latch on to her own mother's breast.

Umms hobbled across the room through the mass of moving women toward Asabe. On occasion, she would stop and join the dance for a few seconds before moving on. Finally, she dropped her old body onto the couch next to Asabe.

"So this is the new baby in Brother Adam's home." Umm's leaned over to peer into the infant's face. "How old is she now?" Umms hardly seemed to notice Lailah's abnormalities.

"Five months," said Asabe.

Umms shook her head but said nothing for the next few minutes. Umms watched Sauda with Hadizah across the room. Umms may have been silent, but she wanted to say something. Asabe could feel the premonition lying heavily on her chest.

Finally, Umms said above the music, "Why do you nurse Sauda's baby?"

Asabe shrugged her shoulders. "I nurse her because she needs to eat."

"Yes, but why do *you* nurse the child?"

Asabe smiled because she could think of nothing else to offer the old woman in response. Umms smiled back, shaking her head. Her loose jowls oscillated with the motion.

"In my lifetime, I have had two husbands and as many as six different cowives. I have nursed many babies that I did not give birth to."

"Well then, you understand."

"Oh yes. I understand many different scenarios which might lead you to nurse your cowife's baby. This is not my question. I suppose I should have asked you why your cowife does not nurse the infant herself."

"She does," lied Asabe.

Umms shook her finger in front of Asabe's face as if she were a small child.

"It is against the law of Allah to tell lies."

"But, Umms, I tell you the truth."

Umms glanced across the room at Sauda. She scrutinized her with intense little eyes and then sucked her teeth, making a slurping sound because two front teeth were missing.

"What are you going to do when she has another child? Will you take care of that one too? Like a maid?"

"I don't mind helping Sauda with her child. Besides, I don't think Sauda has to worry about having another child for some time now."

"Oh no?"

Umms stared across the room again. The music had since stopped. Sauda was sitting this time, sipping grape juice from a glass and telling jokes to the women crowded around her.

"In the West, women use artificial means of birth control to create desirable spaces between their children. They are a godless bunch. But here, we need none of that because Allah has equipped us with a natural means. Nursing our young is the best form of birth control, the best way to create spaces between our children. The more you nurse, Asabe, the longer it will take for you to become pregnant with your own child."

Asabe was again stifled; she shook her head to assure Umms that she was paying attention.

"This is how I know that Sauda is not nursing her baby."

"What?" asked Asabe incredulously.

"You mean you don't know?"

"Know what, Umms?"

"I've been a midwife for more than fifty years now. I know what an expecting woman looks like when I see her."

"What are you saying Umms?"

"There will soon be another new baby in Brother Adam's home."

NINETEEN

Adam stood over Attiyah's bed. He hardly recognized her. She didn't seem so old the last time he saw her. Now, her face was a tapestry of rivers running in every direction. Her forehead was a broad valley, her hair a snowy mountain.

"Is she sleeping?" Adam asked Mahmoud. What he'd really meant to ask was if she was alive. She was so still, so . . .

Attiyah's eyes flew open. "I was." She tried to smile. Instead, a moan escaped her lips. Her eyes slipped wildly around the room. "Mahmoud? You in here."

"I am." Mahmoud stepped forward out of the shadows. "What is it?"

"Pain," she gasped. "The pain. Bring my pills. Hurry. Please."

Mahmoud rushed from the bedroom, calling the name of their youngest daughter, Saffiyah.

"Can I do anything?" asked Adam.

"Yes. Stop wringing your hands. Stop staring at me. Stop worrying." This time she managed the smile.

"Oh," was all Adam could muster.

"It's dark in here. Open the curtains, and throw open the window. Let us get some fresh air and sunshine."

Once Adam obliged his sister's request, he took a seat on the window's ledge. "Why was I the last to know that you were ill?"

"Because I am not ill."

"You had surgery. That sounds serious to me. That sounds like ill to me."

"I broke my hip is all. Not an uncommon thing to happen to women my age. At sixty-two years, I can't expect everything to be running perfectly anymore."

"Yes, but you had the surgery almost a week ago. If I hadn't called to check on you, I might never have known. Mahmoud said that you made him promise not to tell me. Why? As your only brother, haven't I the right to know?"

Saffiyah entered the room, carrying a tray with a glass of water and a small plate with two tiny blue pills in the center. She was very pregnant. When she saw Adam, she smiled bashfully and greeted him.

Nearly eight years had passed since Adam had seen Saffiyah. Then, she was a seventeen-year-old newlywed. Now, she was the mother of four children, not including the one she carried so laboriously in her belly.

Attiyah's eyes radiated when she saw her daughter coming. Suddenly, she became like a child. "I want to lie on my side," whined Attiyah.

"You know better. The doctor said that you have to lie flat on your back. As straight as possible."

Saffiyah lifted her mother's head in her hand and held the glass of water to her lips.

"Take a big mouthful this time so you don't choke on the pills."

Attiyah choked anyway, sputtering and spitting dramatically. "I told you that I hated those pills. They taste foul, and they make me choke."

"Aren't you the one who asked for them? Aren't you the one in pain?" scolded Saffiyah.

Attiyah nodded.

"All right then. Stop complaining." She turned to Adam. "How are things with you, Uncle?"

"Alhamdulillahi. Things are fine."

"What of your newest wife? I hear she's a handful."

Adam laughed out loud. "You're just like your mother, you know that? As for Sauda, she is pregnant again. Perhaps next time when your mother comes to visit, your husband will allow you to follow her. Then you could finally meet her and my girls. Perhaps by then, I'll have a son for you to meet."

"I might just do that." She set the half-empty glass on Attiyah's nightstand and headed with the tray to the door. "How is Asabe doing?"

"The two of you have been chatting over tea for the past hour now. Haven't you asked her?"

"I have. She says that she is fine." Saffiyah nodded her head. "But I don't believe it. She's as nervous as a hyena in lion territory. Something has your wife very preoccupied." Saffiyah shrugged her shoulders and left the room saying, "I'll bring your lunch up in about thirty minutes, Mother."

Attiyah sighed heavily. "It's so good to have her here. Children are a trial when they are young, but when they are older, they become the most blessed gifts that Allah could ever bestow on a human being. As soon as Saffiyah heard that I'd taken a fall and hurt myself, she was here. Cooking, cleaning, nursing me. Everything I've done for her, she now does for me. Allah knows I never thought I would so enjoy being catered to, but I do. I love being taken care of by my daughter. She wasn't the only one to come to me. All six of my children were crowded around me in this very room last night. My four daughters. My two sons. Insha Allah, you will come to know that same joy, Adam."

For a long time, Adam stared out of the window. He didn't see the flower garden or the stone wall that surrounded Mahmoud's home. He saw his son, fourteen years ago. Mu'min was holding his mother's hand and stroking her arm in an effort to comfort her.

Khadijah was telling Adam how important it was for him to stay with her and their son. Her words reverberated in his memory like the waves of the ocean. "Take me with you, Adam. Please. We could be so happy, you and me and our son. He will be our crutch in old age. He will take care of us. We can take care of each other."

But Adam walked away. Three thousand miles away, his father was dying, with no one to take care of him. He had to go. But not with her. His dying father wanted to see him married to a good Muslim girl from their own tribe before he died. A girl who shared their traditions and beliefs. A girl from a good family, with an exceptional upbringing and strong ties to religion.

Adam cared about Khadijah as well as their son, but how could he disappoint his father while he lay on his deathbed? How could he break his father's heart by bringing home a woman with no family background, with no discernible culture, and no religion other than the one he gave her? She was a Westerner. She was white. She was rejected by her own family. She was not the type of woman he should be married to. She was beneath him.

These are the matters about which Adam contemplated when he left Khadijah fourteen years past. He had forgotten to consider his son. He'd forgotten how much Khadijah had sacrificed to be his wife. By the time he had the prudence to regard the family he'd left behind, it was too late.

"What are you thinking about?" asked Attiyah.

"I was thinking how fortunate you are to have children."

"You are just as fortunate. You have two women vying for your affections and two pretty little girls."

"Yes. But no son."

"Allah knows better. Speaking of which, Asabe tells me that your prayers are scarce these days. Perhaps that is part of your problem."

"What do you mean by that?"

"She means to say that you have not been very diligent these days as regards the worship of your Allah," came Asabe's voice from the doorway. "In other words, you have become like an unbeliever because you no longer make your prayers."

Asabe crossed the room, took Attiyah's hand in hers, and bent over to kiss her sister-in-law on the forehead. "How are you feeling today?"

"Alhamdulillahi."

"I do pray," announced Adam.

"It's a lie, Adam. You may be able to tell Attiyah that lie, but don't forget that I live with you. In the early hours of the morning, when the azan is waking the earth, you lie in your bed, dead to the world. At night, when I come to pray, I do so alone. I was once accustomed to following you, but that is no more. Your best friend, Jabar, has been asking if you are ill. He wants to know why you no longer frequent the mosque. I don't know what to tell him."

Adam looked to Attiyah and smiled. "What she says is not true. I assure you."

Attiyah looked away. "There is no need to convince me. This is between you and Allah."

"Why would you try to embarrass me in front of my sister?" Adam chuckled. His palms were damp and his fingertips icy.

"Have I?" Asabe shrugged her shoulders. "Someone needs to embarrass you. The sad thing is, you have neglected Allah, yet once again he is giving you a chance. A possibility." Asabe turned to Attiyah. "Did you know that Sauda is pregnant again? By now she should be at least five months along."

"You may get your son after all, not that you deserve it."

"I hope that he gets his son," said Asabe as if he were not standing in the same room. "I hope that he gets all that he wishes for. I just pray that he doesn't lose his soul in the process."

MARYAM BANGED ON THE BACK DOOR for the second time. Then she peeked into the kitchen window. She could hear the hysterical cries of both Hadizah and Lailah. It seemed that she could hear Sauda, also crying.

"Open the door, Sauda!" yelled Maryam, but she knew that Sauda could not have heard her through the chaos of voices inside. Maryam decided to enter of her own accord; after all, she had been invited.

Maryam found Sauda in the living room. The child's face contorted and glistened with tears. Hadizah stood in the center of the room. Her head was thrown back as she screamed on unabated.

Sauda cried just as seriously as the children.

"What happened here?" Maryam lifted Hadizah from the floor. Hadizah bucked and squirmed until Maryam had no choice but to allow her to fall to the floor. "Where is Asabe?"

"She went with Adam to visit with his sister," sniffled Sauda.

Maryam looked around the room. Two half-eaten plates of food and a bottle sat on the table. A plate lay overturned on the floor. The air was thick with the odor of soiled diapers.

"She left you here to take care of the babies?"

Sauda shook her head, bouncing Lailah on her hip. "Actually I insisted. I wanted to take care of them myself."

Maryam removed the infant from Sauda's arms. "You should have known better. No one can tend to these two like Asabe can."

Sauda's tears stopped. Her eyes narrowed. "I can tend to my own baby just as well as Asabe. Even better."

"Oh." Maryam's voice was flat with sarcasm. Maryam headed for the stairs. "Part of the problem with this one is her diaper. It's as loaded as a sack of potatoes."

Sauda followed, leaving Hadizah alone in her tantrum.

"I suspect that this little one is also hungry. Why haven't you fed her?"

"I tried to, but she wasn't hungry."

"She's gnawing at her fingers. Either she's teething or she's hungry, and she's a bit too young to be teething."

Downstairs in the living room, Hadizah let out a great whoop. She screamed for her mother.

"She won't nurse."

"Probably because you haven't a drop of milk in those great big breasts of yours." Maryam reached the top of the stairs and started down the hall toward Sauda's room. "This your room here on the left?"

Sauda nodded.

"Get me a damp towel and a fresh diaper," instructed Maryam.

Sauda left for the bathroom and did as she was instructed. Maryam diapered her baby. Lailah quieted down as soon as she felt the cool towel against her bare bottom.

Downstairs grew suddenly quiet.

"I should go downstairs and check on Hadizah."

"No, you shouldn't. Leave her alone."

"She could be hurting herself."

"Trust me, she has tired herself out and is probably sprawled out on the floor, sleeping."

Maryam sat down on the edge of Sauda's bed. Without a word, she unbuttoned her blouse and pushed her breast into Lailah's mouth. At first, Lailah turned her head away, spitting out the first drops of milk. With a firm hand, Maryam turned the child's head back toward her breast.

"Eat," she commanded, looking at Sauda instead of the child.

"I do nurse her," protested Sauda.

"You don't need to prove it to me. I am not the one that you are depriving."

Lailah sucked noisily. The slurping sound made Maryam giggle.

"Everyone knows that you don't nurse your baby. Everyone."

"Asabe lied. She's jealous because she can't have her own baby."

"Asabe and I aren't friends, but I won't allow you to speak badly of her. Any woman who would nurse a dead woman's baby is deserving of respect. She also suckles your baby. Why? I hear it is because you're too lazy and selfish."

Maryam's observation silenced Sauda. There was too much of the truth in Maryam's words for Sauda to argue the point. Sauda had begged Maryam to come help with the children. Maryam was her final resort before she would be forced to call for Asabe over two hundred miles away.

What would she have said to Asabe? How would she save face while simultaneously admitting that she was unfit? How could she save her pride while admitting that Lailah, as retarded and defective as she was, longed for Asabe, *her* scent, *her* taste, the cadence of *her* voice. Lailah longed for everything that Sauda could not offer her, a mother who was not truly her own.

Lailah eventually fell asleep at Maryam's breast. She laid the child in her crib, covering her with a blanket, and left Sauda's room.

"What else did Asabe tell you about me?" Sauda rushed behind Maryam.

"Asabe tells me nothing."

"I don't believe you."

"I help Umms with her midwifery at times. She is the one who told me about your neglect."

"Umms has never tended to me."

"She saw you at Salimah's walimah three months ago. Remember? Even then she knew that you were pregnant, could tell by looking at you. She knows that you don't give your own baby suckle. She can tell by looking at Asabe."

Maryam found Hadizah. She was curled into a fetal position, her thumb pushed deep into her mouth, and her face streaked with salty tracks where her tears had dried. Maryam took a pillow from the couch and pushed it beneath Hadizah's head, leaving her on the floor.

In the kitchen, Maryam sat at the table. "I'll have a cup of tea."

Sauda sat across the table, unwilling to oblige her neighbor. "You mean to say that old woman told everyone who would listen that I am a bad mother?"

"She told no one except me that you do not suckle your daughter. As for being a bad mother, your actions speak for themselves."

"Then why do you say that everyone knows?"

"Because I told everyone."

Suddenly, Sauda felt the urge to use the bathroom. She squeezed her thighs together to keep from wetting herself. Sauda gasped for air in an effort to maintain her composure. She was barely successful.

"Get out, Maryam, and go home. You've done enough."

"Angry, are you? Your anger will not serve you today. If you throw me out, I will not come back again. And then, you will have to call Asabe and admit to her your incompetence. It is a shame, isn't it? A woman who has never in her life birthed a child is a better mother than you are."

Maryam giggled again. Such an insufferable laugh. To Sauda, it was worse than the raking of fingernails on a blackboard. The urge to use the toilet grew stronger.

"We'll be fine."

"How far does Attiyah live? A few hours, isn't it? A long way to return just because you can't control two babies."

"Get out."

"All right, if you insist." Before closing the door, Maryam said, "Thank you for the tea. As-salaam alaikum."

SAUDA LAY DOWN ON THE FLOOR next to Hadizah. She lay on her back, gazing into the child's sleeping face. Hadizah's round cheeks were a delicious temptation. Sauda wanted to feel the tender flesh of them between her teeth. She wanted to inhale Hadizah's quiet breaths, the sweetness of them.

Sauda wanted a daughter as perfect as Hadizah. Any child as perfect as Hadizah.

But Hadizah was Asabe's baby. Hadizah belonged to her. If Sauda had ever forgotten that fact, Hadizah reminded her the entire afternoon. She cried until her eyes had swollen shut. She incessantly called for Asabe. Part of Sauda wished that Hadizah would call for her.

Ummi?

And Sauda would have answered, *Yes, my daughter. Yes, my child. My perfect, perfect child.*

But of course Hadizah wanted no one other than Asabe. Her own daughter, the one whom she often wished had not been born, didn't want her either.

"What's so good about Asabe?" asked Sauda. Hadizah turned over on the floor next to her but did not awake.

Sauda stroked her slightly swollen abdomen. Already, the child within was beginning to make his presence known. Each night, just as she was on the verge of slumber, the baby would flutter in her belly, as he was now.

He? She hoped. She prayed. She dreamed of having Adam's son. Perhaps if she wanted it enough, Allah would give her a son in life. Maybe make her dreams come true. Maybe give her some worth as there was nothing else she could offer Adam that he might want.

She couldn't be Asabe.

Upstairs, Sauda heard Lailah whimper as she awoke from her short sleep. Sauda sat up.

"Maryam is right about me," she whispered. "I am incompetent, selfish, a horribly vain and ungrateful mother. Allah help me, but I am."

Sauda wrapped her arms around herself to stop the trembling, to keep the tears from rushing out.

Once Sauda regained her composure, she did the only thing she could. Sauda picked up the telephone and dialed Attiyah's home.

Saffiyah answered.

"As-salaam alaikum. This is Sauda. Please put Asabe on the line."

Adam and Asabe returned, covering over four hundred miles in less than four hours.

TWENTY

Mu'min pushed open the front door of his mother's home. He stood on the front stoop for a long time, peering into the house much as a stranger would. Mu'min knew the house and recognized the furnishings and the scent of lemon oil and baking bread. But without his mother there, it ceased to be a home.

"How long are we going to stand out here on the porch?" said Zulaikah.

Mu'min smiled down into his wife's face. "This is harder than I imagined, returning to my mother's home. The last time I was here, my mother was baking cookies. They burned. She rushed to the stove, but she never made it there. That day, when she fell to the floor, was the last day she ever walked, the last day that I heard her voice."

"You've had many days with your mother. Surely, that isn't the day she would wish you to remember."

"You're right."

Mu'min stepped inside of the house, carrying a bucket of cleaning supplies and a mop. Zulaikah followed, also carrying a bucket as well as a broom and a bag of rags for cleaning.

"My mother left this home for me. And I want to make it a special place for you and my children."

"That's right. And it will be special because your mother once lived here," said Zulaikah, patting Mu'min's shoulder. Zulaikah believed the mantra, but she wasn't so sure about Mu'min. She knew that he was reluctant about moving into his mother's home, but with the both of them in school and a baby on the way, money was scarce.

The house was paid for. The taxes were current. It belonged to them. There really wasn't much choice.

Outside beneath the midday sun, the temperature was ninety-three degrees and climbing. Inside was at least ten degrees hotter. Their clothing clung to their flesh, especially Zulaikah. She wore a deep violet overcoat over her clothing as well as a broad hijab that she pinned under her chin.

As soon as the door was closed behind them, Zulaikah peeled off the excess of clothing. Mu'min removed his camise and then turned on the air-conditioner.

"I'll take the kitchen, you take your mother's bedroom," suggested Zulaikah.

"I'd rather not do my mother's room. Too much for me. Too soon." Without another word, Mu'min disappeared into the kitchen.

Despite the film of dust on every surface, Khadijah's bedroom looked as if she had just left it. The bed was made, the sheets and bedspread taut except for a small round indentation on the left corner where she probably sat to pull on her socks.

There were worn lines in the royal carpet beneath the rocking chair, where she must have reclined and rocked while she read the Qur'an that sat in a basket to the left of the chair. The back of the chair wore Khadijah's old cream-colored sweater. Zulaikah remembered that sweater. It had coffee stains all down the front.

Khadijah's dresser was nearly naked as compared to most women. There were no bottles of cold cream or collections of perfumes. No vials or compacts of makeup. There was only a bottle of no-name brand lotion, a tub of petroleum jelly, and a fingernail clipper.

There were two plants on the windowsill, dead and collapsing over the rims of the pots. Some of the leaves, shrunken and brittle, littered the floor beneath the window. The tops of the white sheers were yellowed from the collection of dust.

On the far side of the room, the closet door stood ajar like an opened mouth, calling to her. Zulaikah answered.

In the light, Zulaikah could see that Khadijah had few clothes. Only three dresses, four knee-length blouses with matching harem pants, two overcoats, both black, two nightgowns, and one housedress hung in the closet.

Zulaikah removed a plastic trash bag from a box in the bucket. She neatly folded each garment and placed them in the bottom of the bag.

Three pairs of shoes were lined up on the floor of the closet—two brown, one navy, all worn. Still, to someone less fortunate, such shoes would be a prize. Zulaikah laid the shoes into the bag on top of the clothing, topside down.

Three shoeboxes and a stack of eight telephone books. Only one set was current. The rest stretched back for three years consecutively. Zulaikah placed all eight directories into a separate bag meant for trash.

Zulaikah removed the three shoeboxes one at a time and placed them side by side at the end of the bed. The first box, blue and tattered, was full of old bills, telephone and electric. The postmarks on some of the envelopes dated as far as five years back, to 1995. Inside each envelope, there was either a canceled check or money order receipt that matched the amount on the bill.

There were no cable bills. Khadijah did not watch television. No credit card bills, because she avoided interest at all costs. No rental invoices. No car or mortgage notes. If Khadijah couldn't pay for a thing outright, she didn't want it.

This box, including the contents, was trashed along with the telephone books.

The second shoebox was an ocean of receipts. None were for major purchases. Many of the receipts listed items as mundane as bread, flour, and eggs. On each receipt, along the right margin, Khadijah had added each item in red ink. This also went into the trash.

In the third box, Zulaikah found an object wrapped in a piece of brown velveteen.

"What do we have here?" Zulaikah said, prodding the object with her finger. The object beneath the peachy fabric was solid. Then she tapped the surface with her finger. The sound produced was muffled but definitely the sound of wood.

"Did you have any secrets, Mother Khadijah?" Zulaikah was startled to hear that she had spoken the words aloud.

Zulaikah lifted the edge of the fabric away from the object, revealing a patch of loud crimson. The hairs on the back of Zulaikah's neck stood on end, a shiver darted down her back. She had the curious feeling that she had discovered something grave with serious consequences and that she should give serious consideration as to whether to proceed. She might regret it. Mu'min might regret it. Khadijah hadn't hidden the box beneath a swatch of fabric, within another box, for not.

Curiosity won over trepidation. Zulaikah pulled the fabric back some more, uncovering a cherrywood box decorated with bold hand-painted flowers in yellow, fuchsia, red, blue, and green. The hinges and latch of the box looked like brass. Dangling from the latch was a tiny brass lock, much like the type found on luggage. The box had an antique quality to it.

Zulaikah lifted the box, surprised to find how heavy and substantial the wood was. She shook the box next to her ear. It sounded like papers, slipping from one side of the box to the other.

"Can't be more receipts and bills," Zulaikah deduced. "Maybe important documents. Maybe money. Ooo, ooo, maybe there are some stocks in here. Maybe Mother Khadijah was wealthy, and no one knew about it."

Zulaikah's mouth watered as she searched the shoebox for a key that would undo the lock. There was none. She glanced around the room. "Where would you have put such a key, Mother?"

Zulaikah heard the cabinet doors slamming shut in the kitchen downstairs and the familiar swish-thud that occurred when Mu'min slam-dunked an item into the lined trash can. The sudden realization that she wasn't alone in the house startled her. She could hear her heart thudding in her ears. She thought of Mu'min, that perhaps she should tell him of the find, but locating the key thoroughly intrigued her, and she decided it could wait.

She checked both drawers in the nightstand—only magazines, bottles of prescription medicine, and stationery. She tried each drawer in the bureau. Top drawer, undergarments. Second drawer, socks and pantyhose. Third drawer, two crocheted shawls and five old sweaters. Bottom drawer, nothing.

She looked under the bed. On the windowsill. She even felt along the bottom of the closet shelf and underneath the drawers to see if perhaps the key had been discreetly taped.

"What am I? A spy?" Zulaikah laughed at herself.

"Laikah! Would you come here a minute!" called Mu'min from the kitchen.

Zulaikah reluctantly headed for the door. "Coming," she answered, looking back at the box.

In the kitchen, Zulaikah found Mu'min standing at the window. A harsh line of sunlight slanted across his face. His eyes were closed, his arms crossed over his chest.

"Come here, look out of the window, into the backyard. Tell me what you see."

Zulaikah stood beside her husband, her head barely reaching his shoulder. "I see an overgrown flower bed. I see bushes in need of trimming. Grass in need of mowing. An old swing set. A severed clothesline." Zulaikah gave her husband a cutting stare. "I hope you don't intend to ask me to clean the yard all by myself. It's too hot out there, and don't forget that I am pregnant. I'll help you a little, but I'm not going to do it all by myself."

"I wouldn't think of asking you to."

"Well then, what?"

"Look at the swing set. Notice anything?"

"No. Nothing."

"It's been painted yellow."

"That's right. It was blue before, wasn't it? Who painted it?"

"About a week before my mother was hospitalized, she told me that she thought you would become pregnant anytime soon. She wanted to do something to welcome a new baby. She said that she was going to childproof the house, buy baby things, car seats, and stuff. She wanted to know what color to buy, and I said yellow.

"That day when she collapsed, she'd wanted to show me something. That's why I came over. She said it was a surprise for the future. Something yellow, she said. Something big and familiar. She never had a chance to show me that day. There it is." Mu'min pointed to the swing set. "She painted my old swing set yellow."

"She was right about a baby coming soon."

Mu'min placed his hand on his wife's flat tummy. "She was right about a lot of things."

"This is a special surprise."

"Yeah, and it took me three months to find it."

"I found something too."

MU'MIN TURNED THE BOX OVER IN HIS HANDS. "No, I've never seen it before. I couldn't begin to tell you where she may have put the key. But," he said, shaking the box next to his ear, "knowing my mother, she kept the key in a very practical spot."

"Why would she hide the box and then hide the key?"

"I doubt it's as mysterious as it seems, Zulaikah. My mother was an open book. She believed that everything had its place, and it just so happens that her place for this box was in a shoebox in the top of the closet." Mu'min set the box down on the kitchen table. "No big deal."

"I want to know what's inside." Zulaikah stroked the surface of the box as if she were caressing a baby's cheek.

"Nosey."

"Not nosey, just curious." Zulaikah retrieved a butter knife from the silverware drawer and handed it to Mu'min. "Open it. Please."

"I won't break the lock, Zulaikah. I don't care how much you smile at me."

"Not break. Look," she said, pointing to the latch, "it has little screws. Just take the whole thing off."

Mu'min relented saying, "You had better be glad that you're pregnant. Right about now, I'd do most anything for you."

Zulaikah smiled. Such a precious smile. Mu'min always loved that smile.

The entire operation took less than five minutes. Once the latch was removed, Mu'min pushed the box across the table toward his wife and said, "Enjoy, Nosey." They both laughed.

Zulaikah lifted the top off the box, her eyes hungry orbs. She stared into the box for a long time. Zulaikah said nothing, stifled by what she saw. Her previous fears and premonitions proved true.

"So what is it?" He watched his wife. What he saw in her face caused his smile to slip away. "Is it a dead rat or something?" He tried to laugh.

Zulaikah replaced the top and looked into her husband's eyes.

"What is it?" This time Mu'min could not have been more serious. He stood up from the table.

"You should be sitting."

"Why? Is something wrong?"

"You be the judge of that." Zulaikah pushed the box across the table. "Open it."

Still standing, Mu'min lifted the top. First he saw his name written in jerky penmanship. The stamp, the postmark, all foreign. The envelope, red and blue stripes around the perimeter. Par avion. He lifted the first of a least a dozen letters from the box and turned it over in his hands. On the back, he read the sender's name.

Adam Abdulkadir.

The letter slipped from his fingers and landed with a soft slap against the tile floor. He slumped backward into the chair.

"My father." His voice was little more than a whisper.

"Your mother must not have been the open book you thought her to be. She had secrets just like the rest of us."

Mu'min's face grew dark. His eyes narrowed. "I can't believe it. I can't believe that all along . . ."

"You must be pretty angry with your mother right now. But that letter is postmarked this year. It's not too late for you to get in touch with your father."

"I will never get in touch with him."

"Why not? You've always spoken highly of him, of what you remember of him. Now you know that it was your mother who kept you from him all of these years. Now you know that he did not abandon you."

"My mother was a good woman. She was like a mother lion. She would go to any length to protect me. If she would do this, hide these letters from me, then she must have had a very good reason. And that reason must have been that my father was not as good a man as I remember him to be. Remember, I was only eight years old when he left. Mine is the memory of a child. Children don't know everything."

"If what you say is true, then all you have to do is read the letters. Decide for yourself."

"I won't read them. I don't need to. My mother always knew what was better for me. Always. I just have to assume that this time, she was right."

"But he's your father, Mu'min. Aren't you being hasty in this decision?"

"No." Mu'min left Zulaikah at the table and began to tie the full trash bag.

"Don't you at least want to know why he never came back for you?"

"He left me and my mother. That is all I need to know."

"Allah is the best of forgivers. Can't you find it in your heart to forgive your father?" Zulaikah picked up the letter from the floor. "For all you know, there may be nothing to forgive."

"I don't care."

"You're lying."

"I don't care," said Mu'min, kicking the trash can. It overturned, causing bottles of old food to roll out onto the floor.

"You will be a father soon, Insha Allah. We don't know what the future holds, but what if for some reason you and I were separated? What if you left me for some reason, and then later you realized that you had made a mistake and that you wanted to come back home? Wouldn't you want that chance?"

"I wouldn't need a chance because I would never leave you or my baby." Mu'min righted the trash can and began picking up the contents.

"Maybe your father said the same thing. Maybe it wasn't his idea. Maybe your mother *told* him to go."

"No way. My mother lost her family and every friend that she had because she married my father and became a Muslim. My mother begged him to stay. That much I remember. She begged him. I begged him."

"You're the one who said that yours is the memory of a child. Maybe you have the events mixed up in your head."

"Then explain the visit from my grandfather in the hospital. Was he lying when he admitted to me that he disowned my mother?"

"Maybe."

"You're grasping at straws. Why do you care if I read those letters? He wasn't your father, and therefore not your problem."

"I care because how you react now is a reflection on how you may behave with your own child."

Mu'min's fists clenched shut then open. Shut then open. The muscles in his jaw rippled. The vision of his wife blurred. Mu'min closed his eyes to push the fire in his head away. He started forward, first slow, uneasy steps. And then quickly. Zulaikah matched each step that he took moving backward until she found herself standing with her back against the wall.

"Know what? This conversation is over."

Mu'min took the box of letters and dropped them into the trash. He then tied the liner, lifted it from the trash, opened the back door, and threw it out into the backyard.

"No more talk about my father. Okay?"

Zulaikah nodded, hoping that he couldn't see her hiding the letter behind her back.

MU'MIN TURNED LEFT INTO THE DRIVEWAY of Emerald Lawns Cemetery. He followed the gravel road east for an eighth of a mile before he turned left. This small trail was paved and led to a part of the cemetery fractioned off for use by Muslims. Here, there were few headstones. Only rounded mounds of soil marked the existence of a grave. Because of the absence of coffins, within a year, nature would flatten the mounds of earth, leaving their existence privy to the memory of loved ones.

The cemetery was littered with trees. Bushes lined the perimeter of the graveyard, providing a natural fence to block out the sight and sounds of the traffic from the major road it was located on.

It was beginning to cool, but only a bit. The sun stubbornly hung in the sky though it was nearing eight o'clock.

Only a flowering cactus with a fuchsia bloom marked Khadijah's grave. Mu'min had planted the cactus by his own hand a week after her burial. Her grave was under a tree, next to the grave of an infant who had died during birth.

Mu'min stood over his mother's grave, his tears falling onto the soft earth beneath him. He cupped his hands before his face and spoke a silent prayer, requesting Allah to pardon his mother's sins, affording her comfort from hell.

This done, Mu'min sat down at the end of his mother's grave. He wanted desperately to speak with her, to tell her about the events of that day. He wanted to know why she had hidden the letters from him for so many years. He wanted to know who his father was and if he should love him or be angry with him. He wanted to know, but she wasn't there to tell him anything.

Mu'min did not hear the man walk up behind him. He was too submerged in his own pain and confusion to sense the presence of another person. The man watched Mu'min clandestinely from beneath a tree for close to five minutes before he finally spoke.

"I'd hoped that I would see you again. Unfortunately, the circumstances aren't choice."

Mu'min swung around. His heart was thumping in his chest.

"I thought that I was alone. You scared me."

"I'm sorry. It wasn't my intention, but I didn't want to intrude."

Charles Brady stepped forward out of the shadow of the tree. He held a blue baseball cap against his chest.

"It's been three months, and still you . . . I guess a boy never gets over his mother's death. I never did anyway."

Mu'min stood up and shook his grandfather's hand.

After an attenuated silence, Charles finally said, "How have you been since I last saw you?"

The image of Khadijah lying dead in the hospital bed, pale as dough paste, flashed in his mind. That was the day half of his existence perished. Ironically, today he threw away his only connection to the other half of his existence.

"Honestly, I was fine until today."

Charles cocked a bushy eyebrow. "What happened today?"

Mu'min stared incredulously at his grandfather. The last time he had seen this man was also the first. That was the same day that he lost his mother, the same day he learned that for twenty-three years, he had been denied by his own grandfather for having an African father.

Charles cleared his throat. "Oh. I'm sorry. It's not really my place to be asking you such personal questions, is it?" Charles backed up. "Maybe I should be going. I'm sorry that I intruded." Charles turned to leave.

"Please stay. Maybe you could help me."

"I'd be happy to." Charles's face turned crimson; his azure eyes widened.

"I want you to tell me about my father."

"I don't think that you do. Last time we spoke to each other, you defended your father. I can't blame you for that. I would have done the same thing if someone had spoken ill of my daddy, even if he was a murderer. Every human being wants to love their own parents. Even if those parents are not worthy of that love, a child will always find something to elevate that parent and make him or her special. Now, if you are asking for my opinion of your daddy, you won't be hearing what you want."

"What I want is the truth."

Charles took a deep breath. He shook his head. "I don't know much about him. I didn't want to know about him. He was black, a foreigner, and a heathen. That was enough for me."

Charles flinched when he heard the words coming out of him. For the first time in more than twenty years, he had said the words out loud. He had said them to his grandson, forgetting for an instant that Mu'min was the very image of the man he was speaking so ill of. Only a slight variation in the hue of their skin marked their difference. Try as he might, Charles could not help feeling the most sincere affection for the replica of the man he once despised for taking his daughter away from him.

"I'm sorry that I said that. I didn't mean—"

Mu'min waved his hand, unaffected by Charles's slip of the tongue.

"In the hospital, you told me that you would sometimes come around and watch us. Did you ever see anything that would give an impression about what my father was like?"

"I saw some things." Charles shifted from one foot to the other. He brushed beads of sweat away from his forehead with the back of his hand. "What exactly are you looking to know, son?"

"Specifically, I want to know if my father loved me."

Charles glanced heavenward. "I saw your daddy set you up on his shoulders as he walked you to the park to play. I saw him playing with you in the front yard. I saw him pick you up from school. I saw him swing you up in the air and catch you before you hit the ground. I heard your laughter, and I saw the way you looked at him. It was almost like there wasn't another soul on this earth worth your time.

"I saw so many things, but it was the way that you looked at him that almost convinced me that maybe I was wrong about him. For a while, I felt like a fool for disowning my daughter and giving up a chance at having such a perfect grandson. I almost believed that I was the fool, until the day I didn't see him anymore. That was the first time I saw your mother's head hang so low she didn't know what was in front of her. That was the day I saw you sitting alone in the front yard. Alone. No more laughter. No more smiles. No more happiness. And I knew that it was because of him."

Again, Mu'min's heart thundered in his chest. His palms were damp. His mouth was dry, but he did not once take his eyes off his grandfather. He devoured each word that Charles spoke.

"You wanted to know if he loved you? Only the god in the heavens knows the answer to that question. But if you want to know my opinion, I think he might have. I think. I just don't understand how a man who loves his child could leave just like that."

There was little said thereafter. Charles invited Mu'min back to his home for a cup of coffee, but with dusk clouding the horizon and the time for evening prayers approaching, Mu'min declined. They exchanged telephone numbers. Charles's face brightened, and for a second, Mu'min saw his mother's face.

MU'MIN TURNED OFF THE ENGINE, allowing his truck to coast into the driveway. It was close to midnight, and all except the porch light were off. Mu'min imagined that Zulaikah had tried to wait up for him, but since her second month of pregnancy, her energy had waned. She slept more than ten hours a day now.

Mu'min decided to enter the house through the back door so as not to disturb Zulaikah. They had agreed to sleep on the foldout couch in the living room until they had redecorated his mother's bedroom. He walked along the side of the house and unlatched the fence into the backyard.

Standing in the backyard, Mu'min felt like a child again. He sat on one of the swings, allowing the breeze to rock him gently. Nothing in Khadijah's house had changed since the day that his father left. The swing set remained, as did the old patio set, as did the wildly growing flower beds, as did the six-foot fence that she repainted red every June. Now it was his home.

Mu'min headed inside. At the stairs, he was confronted with the trash bag he'd earlier discarded in anger. It sat at the foot of the stairs, gleaming like a beacon in the moonlight. Inside of that bag, along with old and rotten food, was his past. If he were willing, it could also be his future.

Mu'min removed the bag and propped it up against the house. He quietly unlocked the door and went inside. Inside the kitchen, slivers of silver moonlight sliced the darkness. He saw his mother sitting at the kitchen table, with the box of letters in her hands. She held the box out in front of her.

Mu'min trembled, his heart shuddered in his chest. He closed his eyes, hoping that he could wash the vision away. When he opened his eyes, his mother was gone. It was Zulaikah sitting at the kitchen table, the box of letters stretched out in front of her.

Mu'min let out a heavy labored sigh.

"I took them out of the trash. I was afraid that you wouldn't."

Zulaikah placed the box on the table and headed for the doorway.

"If you're not ready to read them, then just put them away until . . . Just in case." Zulaikah left the kitchen.

Mu'min watched the box as if it were a living entity. His fear of the unknown overcame his curiosity. He wasn't ready to read the letters just yet. He wasn't prepared to confront the truth, whatever it may have been.

Using the back stairwell just off the kitchen, Mu'min carried the box of letters to his mother's bedroom and put it back on the top shelf of the closet.

Just in case.

TWENTY-ONE

Asabe rubbed her naked belly. It was as smooth and round as a globe, the brown skin as silky as the petals of a rose. She was sitting in the rocking chair by her window, watching Adam in the front garden, rolling about on the grass with his brood of young sons. She listened to their hysterical giggles and the sweet melody that their only daughter, Hadizah, hummed to herself.

That is when the pain came. The contractions surged up and down her back and abdomen like the waves of a sand dune during a storm. Her heart lost rhythm. She gripped the arms of the chair and hungrily gulped the air. With her head thrown back, Asabe hiccupped a scream so alien she did not recognize her own voice. She slid from the chair onto the floor and crawled to the bed.

On the bed she pushed, desperately trying to discard her burden and free herself of the intolerable pain. Once the contraction died, Asabe leaned back on her bed and waited for the next wave to arrive.

It did not come. With her eyes still closed, she ran her hand along her belly and found that the silky globe was gone. Her belly was as flat as when she was a fourteen-year-old virgin.

A young man, dressed, surrounded by white, stood at the end of her bed. He was tall and handsome with eyes the color of acorns and skin the color of creamy peanut butter. At first, she thought that this young man was her son, one of the many she had given birth to in her dreams. But he was not as pleased to see her as she was to see him.

His eyebrows were a single thick stitch across his forehead. His nostrils were flared. His fists clenched tight against his sides. Asabe had seen this man before, standing in the same spot at the foot of her bed. He was not her child. Asabe did not know who he was.

"What do you want?" Her voice came out in a whisper.

The young man growled. It was a vicious primitive sound that instilled fear and hatred.

"What do you want?"

Again he ignored her, pacing the length of the room. His breaths were loud and ragged. His solid footsteps shook the floor and vibrated in the walls. The bed jerked wildly, Asabe holding on like a man riding a bucking bronco.

"What do you want?"

A flood of laughter floated up from the garden. The young man stopped in the center of the room with his head cocked like a confused puppy. He approached the window and stared down into the garden.

"Who are you?" asked Asabe, rising from the bed.

He murmured his name, but Asabe could not hear him. His body convulsed, and his face was streaked with tears. He sank to the floor.

"Who are you?"

He looked up at her, the tears replaced by calm knowing, and pointed out of the window.

"Ask him. He knows who I am. He knows."

The young man was pointing at Adam.

"No. He doesn't know you."

"Yes, Adam knows who I am. He has known me forever."

Asabe's belly began to ache again. Each word the young man spoke punctuated a new wave of pain. Asabe grabbed her rapidly growing belly, her mouth filling with sour saliva. It was as if air was being pumped into her.

"At first, I thought that you were my boy, but you are not my boy." Asabe fell to her knees.

The young man kept nodding his head. "Yes yes yes yes," he said. His insistence angered Asabe.

"No! We don't know who you are," said Asabe, doubling over. The pain of labor had never been so intense.

"Adam has known me forever. And you, Asabe," he said, pointing in her face, "you know me too. Remember me?"

The young man knelt down onto the floor, bringing his face so close to Asabe's that she could see the pupils of his eyes, deep as the black heavens.

"Look at me," he demanded. "Look at me, and you will know who I am."

Fear crept into Asabe's heart. She squeezed her eyes tightly closed, shaking her head from side to side, afraid to see.

The young man held Asabe's face in the palms of his hands, trying to steady her, but Asabe struggled even more, thrashing wildly against the stranger, screaming, "I don't want to see you. I don't want to know."

"Asabe, open your eyes. Look at me."

"No!"

Asabe sprang up. She was no longer looking into the face of a stranger, but into the face of Adam.

A dream. It was only a dream.

Adam placed his hand over her left breast and then her forehead. "Your heart is speeding like a race car, and you are sweating. What has you so afraid?"

"I didn't want to see him." Asabe swallowed hard. Her stomach was heavy, as if she had swallowed a rock.

"Who didn't you want to see?" Adam used the corner of the sheet to dab the moisture from Asabe's forehead and nose.

"He said that you would know who he was." Asabe searched Adam's face. "Do you?"

Adam smiled, cupping Asabe's face in his hands just as the young man had. "How would I know the person in your dreams?"

Asabe pushed his hands away, the anger resurfacing as well as the pain gnawing in her belly. Her mouth watered, and she belched a noisy gaseous retch.

"You don't look very well, Asabe."

Asabe headed for the door, swallowing hard against the nausea. She ran down the hall, reaching the bathroom just in time, and emptied her stomach in painful heaves.

Adam's muffled voice came to her through the locked bathroom door. "Should I stay with you tonight?"

Just then, she heard the cackle of Jabar's rooster in the distance. "It's nearly five. You should be getting ready to go to the mosque."

"We have time. I could help you chase away the bad dreams."

"You should be getting ready for the mosque."

Nothing else from the other side of the door.

Asabe stood in the shower, scalding beads of water spattered on her back. Each time Asabe closed her eyes, she saw the strange young man's face, grinning at her, reveling in her dismay. Such a blatant face, a pervasive knowing face, a terrifyingly familiar face. It was a face that Asabe did not want to know.

Once Asabe was dressed, she headed for the kitchen as was her usual morning routine. She passed Adam's room on her way downstairs. The door was partly opened. The room was nearly pitch, but Asabe could see her husband, an immoblie lump in the center of his bed, his snoring ragged and consistent. His snoring was his only consistent quality these days. He should have been in the mosque that very minute, thanking Allah for his good fortune. Instead he lay in his bed, lazy, void of purpose, like an unbeliever.

Seeing Adam fueled Asabe's anger; although she did not know from what source her anger originated, she knew that Adam gave her anger direction.

She wrestled the urge to wake Adam. He would only turn over and pretend that he was too exhausted to be roused from his sleep.

Asabe was tired of waking Adam, tired of reminding him of who he was, what he was, and what his priorities were.

"Be as you are, if you like," Asabe spoke into the darkness of his room.

The snoring stopped, but Asabe continued on.

Asabe found Sauda in the kitchen, feeding Lailah watery porridge with a spoon. Lailah dribbled a mouthful of porridge on her bib and screeched when she saw Asabe enter the kitchen.

"Sit down, Asabe. Let me get you a cup of tea." Sauda ambled to the stove. The child in her abdomen seemed heavy. Asabe felt guilty having Sauda serve her, but she did not argue with her cowife.

"Feeling better?"

Asabe shook her head. The malaise was still with her. That face was still with her. The anger was still with her.

"I heard you screaming this morning. Bad dream?"

"Very much so."

"What was it about?" Sauda stirred two teaspoons of honey into the amber tea.

Asabe was silent. How would it sound, her admitting that she dreamed of having Adam's son nightly? It would sound desperate. How would it sound her dreaming about a man, not her husband, who watches her while she is most vulnerable, while giving birth?

"Asabe?"

"I don't remember."

ATTIYAH'S HOME was as silent as a graveyard. When Adam finally arrived, it was nearly 2:00 a.m., but every light in her home burned.

Asabe and Sauda, along with the children, escorted Adam to Dakar. He came at Attiyah's bidding. She had been asking of him for nearly a week.

Saffiyah answered the door. Her eyes were puffy, and her lips trembled like the leaves of a tree during a windstorm. She held her newborn, only two weeks old, with one arm.

"As-salaamu alaikum, Uncle. We have been waiting for you." Asabe and Sauda took turns embracing Saffiyah before they passed on into the living room. Each toted a dozing child of her own.

"How is she?" Adam wanted to know.

Saffiyah shook her head, the trembling in her lips increased. "Only Allah knows. The illness came so suddenly. One day she was back to normal—cooking, cleaning, digging in her garden. She was even visiting the sick. Imagine that. Then the next day . . ." Saffiayah's voice faded. She shook her head, eyes full of disbelief.

"I should have come a week ago, when you first called. I should have come." Adam pounded his fist into the palm of his hand.

Saffiyah had called several times a day for the past week. At first, Adam was truly too busy with one problem or another at work to be bothered with taking a call from his niece. In the past, she only ever called him to ask for money. However, after the fifth or sixth call, Adam was simply too annoyed with her persistence to be bothered. Until the chilling message she left for him with his secretary.

Will you wait until your only living sibling dies before you call us back?

Adam spoke with his niece at nine the previous evening. She said that Attiyah demanded to see him and would not rest until he arrived. So Adam packed up his family and made the trip to Dakar that very night. Having Asabe sitting in the front seat next to him, sometimes reaching out to stroke his hand on the dark highway, made it so much easier for him.

Saffiyah stared at her uncle. Adam's eyes had glazed over. He seemed to be struggling with mania, as if he were deciding whether or not to violently break down. Saffiyah stepped back, shifting the new infant in her arms.

"Where is Mahmoud?" asked Adam, glancing around the foyer.

"I am here." Mahmoud descended the staircase to the left. He stuck his head into the living room, greeting Asabe and Sauda. Mahmoud then offered his hand to Adam.

"Go bring tea for them while I speak with your uncle."

Saffiyah started and then halted, looking unsure. She didn't trust Adam, the wildness on his face, that look of being so close to the edge of rage.

"Go on," said Mahmoud, urging her down the corridor. "Go tend to your aunts. They've come too far for you to be a rude hostess."

Saffiyah hurried away as if she was a girl of no more than ten years.

Mahmoud led Adam in the opposite direction into a large cold room. Heavy red drapes hung from the windows, a large potted plant with white blooms sat in the corner, and a picture of the Kaaba hung from the wall. The room was otherwise bare.

"I didn't want the others to hear," said Mahmoud. He glanced around the room as if to be sure that no one else was present.

Mahmoud's eyes were so red, so tired. The room was so cold. *Dead.* Adam shook his head.

No. Not dead.

"She sleeps sometimes. Usually no more than five or ten minutes at a time. Then she wakes up and asks of you. She hardly ever asks to see me or even her own children. Only you." Mahmoud sighed heavily. His breath stank, stale and old and tired. Adam closed his eyes.

Mahmoud continued, "And when she sleeps, even then she speaks of you. She laments over your soul, over your missed prayers, your lost faith." Mahmoud offered a dry laugh. "In the best of health, she was never this self-sacrificing. What does it mean?"

Adam crossed his arms over his chest. His eyes grazed the ceiling. Adam wanted to find a single spot to focus his eyes upon. Something to help steady himself. Everything was moving. Mahmoud's face and hair was a sinuous swirl of brown and white. The wall became the floor, became the ceiling, and it would not stop. Adam inhaled deeply, wanting to flush the sticky premonition of death away. It was no use.

Mahmoud grabbed Adam's elbow. "Steady, brother. It's too soon to give in just yet."

"What happened? I thought that she was doing well since the surgery. I thought that she had recovered."

Mahmoud shrugged his shoulders. There was such defeat in that insignificant movement. "Infection, that's what the doctor says."

"You don't think so?"

"It is what it is. Nothing more, nothing less. Dying doesn't always have a label."

"Dying?"

Again, Mahmoud shrugged his shoulders. "When the doctor tried to tell me how long she expected Attiyah to survive, I told her to shut her mouth. Doctors these days think that they know everything. She may have been educated in London, but she still cannot predict the hour of anyone's death. If she could, then perhaps she would have foreseen this."

Mahmoud giggled like a drunken clown, though his voice lacked the spirit to be convincing. He stopped so suddenly it was as if he had never laughed at all. His face fell sullen and cold.

"She will die, Adam. The minute, the hour even, I don't know. No one does, but she is dying. And if she is not dying, then this is the cruelest illness I can think of because it has brought her so close to death that I have heard her whispering in her sleep for Allah to take her soul."

Mahmoud closed his eyes and recited the forlorn plea of his wife. "'Ease my suffering . . . Take my soul . . . Have mercy, Allah, and prepare me for paradise.' You should go see her now." Mahmoud patted Adam's shoulder and left him alone in that barren room.

ATTIYAH WAS NOT ATTIYAH ANYMORE. She lay in the same position on the same bed as the last time Adam had seen her, but she was not the same. Adam was barely able to distinguish where his sister ended and the bed began. She looked so small and weak. One would never believe that this was a woman reaching no less than six feet three inches. No one would ever believe that this woman, who lay like a wasted sheet on her bed, nearly reached to the clouds when she stood upright. No one would believe that she was once able to instill fear even in men.

Attiyah was not Attiyah anymore.

Adam stood over his sister for several minutes, trying to find one part of her that he could recognize. She was sleeping, her eyes squeezed so tightly that her brows were furrowed. Her hair was tightly bound in a deep violet scarf. Attiyah's cheeks were sunken into her face like little ditches. Her lips, as thin as shavings of ice, were ashy and peeling. Adam breathed through his mouth. He did not want to smell her.

"It took you so long to come," said Attiyah. Her voice was coarse and low. She spoke without opening her eyes.

"I should have come sooner. I'm sorry that I took so long." Adam kneeled down so that he could hear her more clearly. "How do you feel, sister?"

"I feel like it's a good day to die." Attiyah's cheeks inflated like balloons then collapsed.

"Such a morbid thing to say."

"I suppose it is, if you are afraid to die."

"Aren't you?"

Attiyah smiled. "I saw Israfel seven nights ago. He was standing by my window."

"Israfel?" Adam sat back on his heels.

"Yes, the angel of death came here. I saw him with my own two eyes. Up till that moment, I was doing so well. And then I was an old woman stuck in her bed about to die."

"You don't know that you will die. You may recover and outlive us all."

"No, I won't. Besides, I wouldn't want to." Attiyah coughed. "I wanted to see you, little brother, because you are the most unhappy, bitter man that I know. At the same time, you are probably the most fortunate man that I know. I wanted you to see me so that you might know what it is truly like to have no reason for hope. I will not live, and so the only thing that I can hope for now is that Allah will forgive me for all of my sins. All I can hope is that he will find some miniscule deed of mine worthy of saving me from the fire of hell. That is all I have left, the hereafter."

"Then you should not worry yourself over me."

"I practically raised you, and so in a way you are more like my child than my brother. Especially since you often behave like a child." Attiyah's cheeks deflated, her ragged breathing eased into silence. The silence was a disgrace, for Adam wished to hear the racket of life. Noise. Sound. Something.

"Attiyah?" Jewels of sweat forced themselves from the pores on his face. "Attiyah?"

Attiyah's cheeks inflated, and her breathing again grew coarse. This time her voice sounded muffled and weak. "When I die, will you pray for my soul?"

"Of course I will. Always. Of course."

"Why?"

"Because you ask it of me, because I am your brother, because it is my responsibility, because—"

"Why would you pray for my soul if you will not even pray for your own?"

"But I do." Adam was no more convinced by his profession than Attiyah.

Attiyah's eyes fluttered open for a second or two, and then they closed again. Her cheeks inflated only a bit this time. Her voice was even more faded than before. "Do you mean to say that you will begin? I know that you have become a stranger to faith."

"You don't understand."

"Oh, but I do. I know that you long for something that you have only just learned is not within your power to acquire. I know. I know that because of this, you have turned away from the only thing that can give you what you want."

"I want so little. I want only a son."

"Only?" Attiyah coughed again. Her voice was warbled, as if she was speaking from underwater. "If it is so easy, then why haven't you produced a son on your own?" Attiyah's cheeks sank deep into her face, and again her breathing grew silent. Too silent.

Adam raised off his heels to peer into Attiyah's face. Her lips were slightly apart, and he could hear the low whistle of her breathing. Every other part of her was inert. But she was still alive. Still. For now.

"Well, answer me," she hissed. "Why haven't you got all that you want yet?"

"You know that it is not within my power." Adam pushed himself off the floor and stood over Attiyah's bed. He was ready to leave. He did not want to be a witness when death claimed her soul. "You are not well. I should leave and let you get your rest. This is not the time for you to worry about me." Adam started toward the door.

"How will . . ." Attiyah's voice tapered off, but her lips were still moving.

"What did you say?" Adam stood in the center of the room, halfway between the door, freedom, and Attiyah with her desire to preach to him while death hung above her head like a thundercloud.

Attiyah's lips flapped away, her cheeks puffing up with air, the sound of muffled gurgling; but Adam could not understand one word that she spoke.

Adam took one step forward. Only one step. "What did you say?"

Flapping, puffing, gurgling. Not one intelligible word.

Finally, Adam gave in and went to Attiyah's bedside. Her eyes fluttered open. All Adam could see were the whites of her eyes, rolling in their sockets.

Attiyah mouthed Adam's name. He submitted and knelt back down by Attiyah's bed. Her cheeks slowly inflated. "How will you . . . ," she began again.

Adam leaned closer, his face only inches from his sister's. "What did you say?"

"How will you pray for my soul when you will not even pray for your own?" she whispered.

"I will, I promise." Adam started again to push himself off the floor.

"Good," she whispered, opening her eyes wide. This time she was seeing, and she focused her eyes ahead of her. Adam lowered himself back to the floor and leaned closer to hear his sister.

"La ilaha illa lah," she hissed into his face.

Attiyah's breath fell on his face like a mask, heavy and dank with death. Adam reeled back on his haunches as he slapped nervously at his face, trying to wipe the scent away, the feel of the dry wind of death coating his skin.

Get it off. Get it off. Get it off of me.

A slow high-pitched shriek blared incessantly in Adam's head, like the sound of a teakettle at full boil. He covered his ears, but Adam could still feel the hot, dry breath on his face, digging into his pores, contaminating his skin with the decay of nonexistence. His hands went back to his face, slapping and scratching, slapping and scratching. And then back to his ears to block out the horrible noise.

Within a few seconds, Mahmoud, Asabe, and Saffiyah were circled around Adam in Attiyah's bedroom. They all stared at him, mouths open, eyes fearful and ashamed at the same time.

It wasn't until Adam found himself looking up into Mahmoud's ancient black face that he realized that he was the one screaming. Mahmoud held Adam by the shoulders. "It is all right, brother. There is nothing on your face." Mahmoud ran his hand over Adam's face and showed it to him. "See?"

Adam crumbled into a heap at Mahmoud's feet. His entire body shuddered; he breathed deeply as if he had never before drawn breath. "Nothing is on my face?"

"No. Nothing," assured Mahmoud.

Adam glanced over at Attiyah's bed. Everyone in the room followed his line of vision. Everyone else knew what Adam knew, that Attiyah could no longer be numbered among the living.

SAUDA STOOD AT THE FOOT of the staircase. She had actually been in the forefront when everyone else raced upstairs to Adam's aid. Earlier that morning, while they drove the two hundred miles to Dakar, Sauda saw Adam's and Asabe's fingers locked on the front seat. She saw the way Adam clung to Asabe like a child. Now it was her turn. Sauda wanted to be Adam's comforter too.

Just as her foot landed on the first stair, a spasm gripped her abdomen more torturous than the stabbing of many tiny knives. She could not go further, could scarcely inhale a single breath. In the fever to reach Adam, who wailed and moaned upstairs, no one noticed that Sauda had been left behind.

The pains as quick and hot as bolts of lightning seared down her back and belly, landing in her pelvis. And then as quick as lightning, the pain subsided. A bit. Still clutching the banister, Sauda smiled in relief. If the pain had continued, it could mean only one thing. Labor. And it was too soon to have the child. Too soon.

Sauda could no longer hear the whine of her husband, but different sounds. She heard wailing so painful that she could feel her insides churn. It was Saffiyah's voice. Sauda knew what that sound meant. She had heard that sound before when her own mother had died. No one thought that she could remember that day; she was so young, but she did, as if it had happened only an hour ago. The wail of grief never changes, no matter who the griever may be. The tonation of the voice is always the same, a deep quavering cry that comes from a reserve so deep one never knew it existed.

The pain came again, this time stronger and more persistent. It was an urgent, tenacious throbbing that spiraled in her abdomen like a runaway tornado. Sauda wiped the tears from her eyes and sucked in a mouthful of air. She closed her eyes and prayed because it was too soon to have the child. Too soon.

The pain dissolved slowly and sweetly like a cube of sugar in boiling tea. Sauda welcomed the end of that ribbon of pain because it was too soon to have the child. Too soon.

They would wonder where she had gone, why she had not come to console her husband, so Sauda started up the staircase on unsteady legs.

I'm fine. Every pregnant woman experiences pain sometimes. This is just routine. It is nothing.

One, two, three, four stairs.

No, no, not again. I'll stand here, and maybe it will go away. Oh, Allah, it feels like when I had Lailah, it feels like real labor. Pain. No, it's too soon. I'll just stand here. It will go away. It will. It will! See? It is going away, just like I thought. See? Just a couple of nice deep breaths, and it will be just fine. It will be nothing, just a false alarm, just a joke. Just nothing.

Five, six, seven, eight, nine, ten steps.

The pain crept back like a slow and heavy fog. Consuming, pervasive, tenacious, and very real. It was not going away, but Sauda continued up the staircase, unwilling to submit to its will. The pain wasn't so bad when she pretended it wasn't there. A soothing warmth washed over her from the quiet of her belly down to her toes.

Attiyah's bedroom was the second door on the right.

Only five or six paces more, and I will be by my husband's side.

"Adam?" called Sauda as she came to stand in the opened doorway of Attiyah's bedroom. She wiped away the perspiration that accumulated on her brow with the back of her hand.

Sauda saw Adam on his knees, his face buried in his hands. Mahmoud was trying to coax Adam from the floor. Saffiyah was pulling a navy sheet over the body of her dead mother, covering her from head to toe. Asabe was silent with shock.

"Adam, I'm here now." Sauda's voice quavered, the pain reasserting itself like a familiar old friend.

It's too soon for the child to come. Too soon.

Sauda forced herself to stand straight, grunting with the effort. More warmth through her pelvis, down her thighs, anointing her calves, tingling in her feet. It was a curiously soothing sensation.

Everyone turned to face Sauda, alarmed by the note of panic and struggle in her voice. Their attention was focused at her feet.

"Sauda?" Asabe started forward, with her arms outstretched, but she halted as if she had run headlong into a wall. "Sauda?" she croaked.

Adam stumbled forward on his knees, his eyes as glassy as marbles. Sauda reached out for her husband, intent on being his rock, his helpmate. "I'm here, Adam. Don't worry, I'm here now."

Sauda heard a peculiar squishing, sucking sound when she started for her husband. She would have ignored it had everyone in the bedroom not gasped, their faces contorted with terror.

"What is it? What happened?" she asked impatiently, glancing down.

Sauda was standing in a puddle of her own fluids. Water and blood were rushing out of her as if an invisible tap had been opened.

It's a dream. I'm still pregnant with Adam's son. Our son. I'll wake up in the morning as I always do, and everything will be as it should.

This is not pain, and I am not losing my baby. Perhaps I've only eaten the wrong thing for dinner. Yes, Asabe's fish stew always gives me the gripe. It is only the gripe, though I have never felt any pain this intense. Except, of course, when I gave birth to Lailah. But this is not the same thing. I am not in labor. Oh, Allah, don't let this be the same thing because it's too soon to have the child. Too soon.

THE NEXT MORNING, a Friday, Adam watched his senior sister and son being committed to the earth. He did not cry. To most, Adam seemed courageous, stoic; but really, his heart was as vapid as the inside of a balloon. Only, Adam felt as if all the air had been let out of him, all the life.

Within an hour of the burial, Adam insisted on returning to Diourbel. Attiyah's house was the last place that he wanted to be. Attiyah's memory inundated that house, filling each corner. However, her memory is not what chased Adam away.

Everything Attiyah had been was in that house, an unfinished afghan rolled up in the corner, her favorite tea set, her scarf draped over that back of a chair, her scent permeating every dusty corner, her six adult children. Attiyah had two sons, both in their thirties, one a physician, one a businessman like himself, both of them exact replicas of Mahmoud.

For the second time in less than two years, Adam found himself mourning the death of a son. Inevitably this brought to the surface regrets about the son he left behind. Mu'min. Adam was alone in his grief, but Mahmoud was not. Mahmoud was surrounded by his two sons, who doted on their father like he was a child.

How could Adam remain in that house when there was nothing there for him except catalysts to bad memories and regrets?

This time, Sauda sat next to Adam in the front seat of the car. Twice her hand crept across the seat next to his, her fingertips touching his only slightly.

Through her fingertips, Adam felt her wanting him to reach forward and lace his fingers with hers. But he could not. Twice he pulled his hand away, looking for Asabe's face in the rear mirror.

TWENTY-TWO

Over the next month, Sauda's bedroom became a sort of sanctuary, which she left only in the instance when she had to use the bathroom or when the time for prayers commenced. Lailah became her new interest. With Lailah, Sauda was like a child with her favorite babydoll. Sauda spent the greater portion of the day dressing and redressing Lailah. She would groom her daughter's hair daily, plaiting dozens of tiny braids, thin as threads. With her new supply of milk, Sauda even began to nurse Lailah, as if she had never harbored adverse feelings against her own child.

Sauda lost more than a son that day. In her estimation, she also lost any hope of making Adam truly appreciate her, of wanting her with the same devotion that he had for Asabe. In Sauda's distorted view of her predicament, she was worse than barren. At least Asabe was cherished by her husband, despite the fact that she had never granted his greatest desire. Sauda could claim only to have given Adam an imperfect daughter, the complete opposite of what he wanted from her. After her past antics, the way she misled and manipulated Adam, he had remained with her only to conceive a son. That too was gone.

When Sauda was not attending to the every whim of her daughter, she would cuddle up with her on the bed and sleep. Sauda would sleep sometimes as many as eighteen hours in the day. The land of dreams seemed a more acceptable place to be.

Sauda ate her meals in her bedroom, which Asabe would bring up to her. Although Asabe had never experienced the distress of losing a child, she was determined to be sympathetic to Sauda's grief; however, after an entire month of Sauda's reclusive behavior, her patience wore thin.

To Asabe, Sauda's behavior seemed excessive, even ridiculous. She considered going to Adam with the dilemma; however, Adam was no more receptive than Sauda. Adam was hardly ever home, and when he was home, he was as much a stranger as Sauda.

Asabe went to the home of her mother and Abu Kareem.

Hannah and Abu Kareem sat side by side at the kitchen table. Asabe sat opposite from them. Hannah nursed a cup of tea as she listened in silence to Asabe's complaint.

"I'm worried about her, Abu Kareem. Her behavior isn't normal."

"Are you so sure about that?"

"What do you mean?"

"You have never lost a child, seen him, held him in your arms, *named him*, and then put him in the earth. She has to recover in her own way. Her own time."

Hannah was irritated with Abu Kareem's insensitivity. She spoke up. "Asabe's ability to have a child is irrelevant in this matter. Let us keep Sauda in sight, she is the real problem here."

Asabe continued, "Abu Kareem, I have been very patient with her. I have babied her, washed her clothes, cooked her food, taken over all of her chores and responsibilities. It has been a month, Abu Kareem. I think that it is time for her to get out of the bed and move on with her life. It isn't over. She is healthy. At least she can still have another baby."

"Yes, but you know as well as I do that the loss of this baby is not her only ailment. Sauda is afraid that she has displeased her husband," reasoned Abu Kareem.

Hannah snorted into her cup of tea.

Abu Kareem leaned back, the chair squeaking beneath the strain of his ample physique, and gave his wife a harsh glance. "Did you want to say something?"

"I was only thinking that if Sauda is having problems pleasing Adam, it is partly her fault. Her past behavior bears testament to the relationship that she has fostered with Adam. She is fortunate to still have a husband."

"That is a harsh thing to say," scolded Abu Kareem.

"But it is the truth. The sooner that we admit it, the sooner and the better we can help Sauda."

"Abu Kareem is correct," said Asabe. "You are being hard on Sauda. Adam is just as culpable as she is. The situation at home has become more than I can bear. Both of them behave as if they want to crawl back into the womb and disappear."

"Adam is the one I sympathize with," said Hannah. "He lost a son and a sister. It is with him that I would be most patient."

Abu Kareem shot his wife another hard stare. "Adam's loss is no more important than my daughter's."

"You're right. Adam had problems before this all happened," said Asabe. "It's almost as if he has turned on the world. I don't remember the last time I've seen him pray, and when I broach the subject with him, he pretends to be tired or asleep or too busy to be bothered. Since the loss of Attiyah and his son, he is even worse. I have tried to help Sauda. I've talked to her, done everything she requested of me; but I am her cowife, not her spouse. If there ever was a time for Adam to step forward as the head of his household and prove his worth, this is it."

Abu Kareem leaned forward with his elbows on the table, his face in his hands. He sighed heavily, frustrated with the idea of having to accept that once again his daughter needed to be dealt with.

"I have two daughters. Ladidi, my eldest, and Sauda. Ladidi lives in the States with her husband. She has a happy marriage, one son and one daughter. From day one, she was a joy, I never had a single grievance about her, but Sauda . . . Sauda creates enough drama for them both."

Abu Kareem pushed away from the table. With much effort, he stood up using his cane for support. The years were creeping up on him more swiftly now. Hannah rose from the table taking old Abu Kareem by the elbow, unable to conceal the concern on her face.

"Where are you going? You want something? I'll get it for you. Just sit back down."

Abu Kareem waved Hannah away. "I'm a grown man. Stop treating me like a child. I just want to straighten out my legs. I can't sit down all day."

Abu Kareem paced from one end of the kitchen to the other, slow as a turtle and just as round. His face carried an expression so intense, Asabe was unsure if he was in pain or simply deep in thought. Probably both. Hannah did not leave his side. She continued to hold him by his elbow, making laggard laps around the kitchen with him.

"I was hoping that you could come to the house, maybe have a talk with Sauda. Adam too. Maybe they'll listen to you."

"I have an even better idea," said Abu Kareem. His eyes beamed with satisfaction. "Give me time to arrange everything."

"What do you have in mind?" asked Hannah.

"You'll see," he said, grinning profusely. "It will be the best thing, not just for Sauda and Adam but for you and me as well."

SAUDA AWOKE to the sound of banging on the front door. Asabe had left nearly four hours earlier. If it were her, she would have let herself in as well as Adam. The person at the door was probably a well-wisher, one of the many neighbors that had come over the past month to console Sauda on her loss.

Sauda had long since grown annoyed with the harassment, women preaching to her, using insipid anecdotes as proof of her actual good fortune. Sauda was not interested in hearing how fortuitous her life was when she felt so alone.

It was a boy. A son that Adam named Abubakr. Just two or three months longer and Sauda would have been able to present to Adam the culmination of all his hopes and dreams and of her prayers for months. Now, Abubakr was gone, along with the dreams, the prayers, the hopes that finally when Adam looked at her, she would see something more than pity or annoyance or shame in his eyes. Now, Sauda could not recall the last time Adam had looked at her at all.

The banging was louder and closer than before. The visitor had evidently walked around the house to the back door. Probably to see if perhaps she was in the kitchen.

Lailah was lying next to Sauda with her face buried against her mother's chest. She slept soundly, her breaths a low hiss like the sound beads of cold water make on a hot burner. Her fat crimson tongue lolled out of her head, her slanted eyes opened just a peek. These days, Sauda found so much joy in her daughter's face, with her broad ridged forehead, squint eyes, and perpetual half-moon smile. It was a face Sauda once thought heinous. Her son may have been dead, but at least she had Lailah. At least she had someone of her own.

Hadizah was snuggled against Sauda's back, her leg thrown unceremoniously over her hip. Asabe asked Sauda to keep Hadizah while she ran an errand. Now that Sauda gave it thought, Asabe never mentioned where she was off to.

The knocking came louder still. The visitor, obviously determined, was willing to knock until she relented and answered the door. Sauda finally got up, being careful not to disturb the girls. Both girls routed toward the center of the bed in their sleep as if in search of her presence. Instead, they found each other, cuddling together like newborn kittens.

The knocking grew more demanding, but Sauda was not going to rush. She didn't want a visitor anyway.

Sauda stopped first in the bathroom. She sprinkled her face with cold water, brushed her teeth, and applied kohl to her eyes. Sauda noted how faded her skin appeared, almost ashen. It was as if an eraser had been used to rub the color from her face. Her cheeks were not as plump as before. Despite the abundance of sleep, Sauda wore bags under eyes like a woman three times her age.

Sauda stared at her face for a long time, lost in the oddness of her appearance, of how unfamiliar she looked to herself.

"What happened to me?" she whispered to herself. Sauda was startled to realize how close she had come to the mirror. A circle of steam had developed on the cool glass.

Sauda heard movement coming from downstairs. Unsure, she also thought she heard a voice, slight and musical like the tittering of a bird. Sauda rushed from the bathroom and raced to the head of the stairs.

Salimah, Sauda's former maid, stood at the bottom of the staircase. Salimah smiled impishly, a wristful of gold bangles rattled as she waved up at Sauda. She wore a royal blue wrapper with a matching blouse and sea green mules. Her head was wrapped with a matching scarf, and a sheer white throw was draped over her shoulders. Sauda stared down at Salimah for a long time before she realized who was standing there.

"Salimah?" Sauda headed down the stairs.

Salimah nodded.

"Who brought you here?" asked Sauda, looking around the room. She knew that Salimah could not drive. Someone would have escorted her.

Salimah only smiled. She leaned forward, firmly embracing her former mistress. Sauda cherished the contact; it had been a long time since she had been embraced with such sincerity. Salimah pulled away, gazing into Sauda's eyes as if she was looking for something she lost. She did this a long time before she hugged Sauda again.

"I wish you would have had Jamil call to inform me that you were coming. I would have been quicker to open the door."

Salimah smiled, silent as ever. Sauda took comfort in Salimah's silence, in the absence of anecdotes and preaching. With Salimah, Sauda would talk when she was inclined, and Salimah would do all the listening.

Remembering the voice she thought she heard, Sauda asked, "Is someone with you?"

Salimah nodded.

"I thought I heard someone call my name."

Salimah smiled again. "You did," she said in that tittering birdlike voice.

Sauda stepped back abruptly, as if someone had stabbed her with a hot poker. She blinked, unable, unwilling to believe that she had heard mute Salimah, No Mouth, speak.

"What did you say?"

"I said, you did hear someone call your name. It was me. I didn't call because I wanted it to be a surprise. *Surprise.*" Salimah held out her arms.

SALIMAH VISITED WITH SAUDA for three hours. They sat side by side on the sofa in the living room with their fingers locked as if there had never been the slightest bit of animosity or mistrust between them.

Salimah was definitely not the same meek child that Sauda knew only four months earlier, who scurried around dusty and silent and weak. It was Salimah's weakness that had made her such an easy target for Sauda because she would not fight back, wouldn't show the slightest hint of displeasure of fury. That Salimah was not easy to respect, not for Sauda.

The new Salimah was a different person altogether. She was bright and strong. Happy. Although her voice was as small as the smallest hummingbird, she had many big things to say.

When Sauda asked what made Salimah begin speaking, she simply answered by saying, "I realized one day that I had not done everything in my power to make my husband happy. I imagined how it would please him to hear me speak his name aloud. So I did."

The old Salimah was not as decisive or determined. Sauda liked this version of Salimah better.

Salimah waited for Asabe to return. It was her she had really come to see. However, as agreed, Jamil arrived at nine to retrieve her. The horn wailed outside.

"Tell Asabe that I came. Tell her that I'll try to visit again."

"I will," promised Sauda as they embraced by the door. Sauda waved out to Jamil. "Asabe will regret that she missed you. In a way, I'm glad that no one else was here. I got to have you all to myself."

After Salimah left, Sauda headed back upstairs. The girls were awake. Hadizah was speaking to Lailah in baby talk while holding her in her tiny lap.

When Hadizah spotted Sauda, she immediately asked of her mother. "Was that my ummi"

Sauda flopped down on the bed. "No, that was Salimah. Remember her?"

"Salimah?" repeated Hadizah, a quizzical look on her face. "Where my umma?"

"I don't know. Insha Allah, she will be home soon. Don't worry."

ADAM ENTERED THE MOSQUE just as the azan was called. The voice of the muezzin—loud, deep, and soulful—reverberated in his heart like the treble of a drum. He halted in the entrance of the mosque to breath deeply and steady himself. He felt subject to swoon.

Months had passed since Adam had been to the mosque, months since his forehead touched the floor in prayer. Though no one else was yet present in the mosque, he felt as if he was being watched, judged. There was no one there to curse him for his arrogance, except himself, the memory of Attiyah, and Allah.

For the past month, in his sleeping and waking hours, Adam heard his sister's voice reprimand him for his weak faith, battering his brain with promises of a life filled with grief because he had deserted his faith. The curse had already asserted itself in his life. Within seconds of her soul's departure, the son he desperately wished for was born, dead.

The misery was worse because no one could help. Asabe had pulled away from him, seemed always to be angry with him, judging him with her eyes. Sometimes he even thought that he saw disgust in her eyes. This wounded Adam in a place so deep he never thought that it would go away.

He couldn't go to Sauda. What could she say to him. *I'm sorry?* It wasn't her fault that the baby died. Still, somewhere deep in his gut, Adam wanted to blame her. If not her, then who?

Adam sat on the rich verdant carpet just as men mingled into the mosque; he was waiting for *Isha* prayers to begin. The imam was sitting at the head of the masala, with his back facing the men. He was bent over the Qur'an, reciting the Arabic in a temperate fluid voice.

One of the men that entered sat next to Adam, smelling heavily of rich musk. His thigh grazed Adam's. Adam moved to his left to give the worshiper room to sit, but the man moved back toward Adam.

"This is a large mosque, brother," said Adam, without looking up. "You don't need to sit so close to me.

"It's been a long time," said the man.

Adam was surprised to see his best friend, Jabar. His face warmed. What would he say to the man that he had been avoiding for months? Adam tried to swallow back a nervous giggle, but he was unsuccessful.

"As-salaam alaikum," said Jabar, extending his hand.

"Walaikum as salaam." Adam took his friend's hand, refusing to meet his eyes. "I know that you must have wondered why I haven't been to the mosque."

"I have."

"I can explain." Adam felt like a child. Tiny beads of perspiration collected on his scalp.

"You don't need to explain anything to me. All that matters is that you are here now."

Adam breathed a very audible sigh of relief. His eyes were burning with repressed tears.

Jabar patted Adam's back. "I hear that your household has experienced some very serious tragedies. I didn't come because I figured that you didn't want to see me. For the past few months, you haven't returned my calls or visited. You have made yourself scarce. I assumed you wanted it that way, so I kept my distance."

The mosque was now more than half full. Some of the worshippers had paired up and were speaking among themselves. The imam stood up about to begin the prayers.

"I've been a fool, old friend," whispered Adam. "If I ever act so foolishly again, pester me until I relent."

"Sure?" asked Jabar, grinning.

"Absolutely."

TWENTY-THREE

Macaroni and cheese, fried chicken, fresh snap peas, and butter-honey corn bread. Zulaikah had prepared Mu'min's favorite meal. She wanted him to be in a good mood.

Upstairs, Mu'min washed away the remnants of a hard day's work while Zulaikah set the table. She listened to the muted hiss of the shower to gauge how long it would be before he descended the stairs. She checked her watch. The time read, 5:50. He'd be out of the shower any minute.

Zulaikah put down two straw place mats and folded two paper napkins into triangles, placing a fork and knife on top of each. The platter of fried chicken was positioned closest to Mu'min's plate because she knew it would be the first thing he reached for.

Zulaikah removed a small spinach salad from the refrigerator. She needed the vitamins and would probably be the only one to have any. Mu'min wasn't much for uncooked vegetables. He preferred all his food to be well seasoned and warm.

Lastly, Zulaikah removed a box of matches from the cluttered junk drawer by the sink. Everything from useless business cards to nuts without matching bolts, screwdrivers, tacks, restaurant napkins, and dozens of condiment packages found a home in that drawer.

Zulaikah lit the candles on the table, submerging the cold white kitchen in a warm tawny glow, softening the jagged shadows that lurked in the corners by the refrigerator and the back stairwell.

The shower stopped. She heard drawers in the bedroom bureau opening and closing as Mu'min searched for a fresh T-shirt and a pair of socks.

Zulaikah's heart fluttered in her chest. *How would she convince Mu'min?* She dried her damp palms on her blouse. In doing so, she felt the stiffness beneath the thin fabric. She pulled the envelope from her pocket, holding it to the light. *How would she convince Mu'min?*

"My mouth was watering just thinking about dinner," came Mu'min's voice as he thundered down the back staircase into the kitchen.

Zulaikah slipped the envelope into the drawer along with the matches. "How was work today?"

"Work is work. What can I say?" Mu'min patted her slightly bulging tummy. "How were you and my baby today?"

"All is well, Daddy." Zulaikah tried to sound cheerful while really she was afraid. *After the last time . . .*

Mu'min made a beeline for the table and sat down. He grabbed three pieces of chicken at once, piled a mound of macaroni and cheese in the center of his plate, and sliced himself a massive piece of corn bread.

"Aren't you going to eat?" asked Mu'min.

Zulaikah stood still at the counter, watching her husband demolish the meal and hoping that she could broach the subject without incident.

"Yeah. I'm eating." Zulaikah sat down across from Mu'min. "How is dinner?"

"As always," he complimented with a full mouth, "you have done an excellent job. But you know that I don't eat fried chicken without hot sauce." He smiled at his wife, but she didn't seem to have heard what he said. "Zulaikah?"

"I'm sorry, Mu'min, I forgot to get another bottle at the store."

Mu'min stopped chewing, dropping his fork onto the plate. "Okay, tell me, what is wrong? You haven't been my Zulaikah all evening. It's not the baby, is it?"

"No. I'm fine. The baby is fine."

"You sure?" He seemed unconvinced.

Zulaikah nodded. As if to prove that she was fine, she too began to fill her plate with food, although she wasn't a bit hungry. "I could use some hot sauce too."

"What about the junk drawer?" asked Mu'min. He stuffed a forkful of macaroni and cheese into his mouth.

The envelope.

"No, there's none in there."

"Bet there is," he said, rising from the table.

Zulaikah jumped up quickly. Her chair teetered on its back legs before toppling over onto the floor with a clatter. "Let me get it for you." She sounded out of breath.

Mu'min stopped in midtransit and went to his wife. Mu'min righted the chair. "You don't look good. I thought the morning sickness was gone."

"It is." Zulaikah offered a smile so artificial looking it was more a grimace. "Nothing wrong with serving my husband, is there?" Zulaikah headed across the kitchen to the drawer.

The envelope. Get the envelope.

Mu'min took hold of her arm. "You sit down and get your bearings. Let me get my own hot sauce."

"But you've been at work all day. You must be tired."

"Work isn't such a difficulty that I can't walk across the kitchen and open a drawer." With a firm hand on her shoulder, Mu'min prodded her to sit down. He crossed the room to the drawer. Before opening the drawer, he turned back—it seemed like slow motion to Zulaikah—and said, "Are you sure there isn't anything wrong?"

Zulaikah nodded belatedly, a thoroughly unconvincing gesture. She watched as his hand went to the drawer handle. Her eyes widened into two small moons.

The envelope. The envelope. The envelope.

Mu'min's hand paused in midair. "What is it?" he wanted to know.

Zulaikah shrugged. "Nothing. It's just that I don't think that there is any hot sauce in that drawer."

Mu'min watched his wife a second longer, unsure. Nervous energy charged the air. He could feel it bouncing off the walls and onto him, his skin soaking it up like a sponge.

Mu'min slowly opened the drawer, his eyes never leaving his wife, who sat fingering her napkin. Mu'min rummaged through the drawer, which was overstuffed with unnecessary items, all of which probably belonged in the garbage. The condiment packages had sifted to the bottom of the drawer, so Mu'min removed the items from the top, beginning with the box of matches.

"What's this envelope?"

Zulaikah stood up. The chair fell over again. "Uh . . ."

Mu'min stared at the envelope for a long time. It appeared familiar—blue-and-red-striped fringed edge, foreign stamps, par avion. He read his name aloud as if he had never heard it. "Mu'min Abdulkadir. That me," he said, looking up at Zulaikah, an uneasy smile on his face.

"Yeah, that's you."

Mu'min turned the envelope over in his hands. "Adam Abdulkadir." Mu'min let out a long, hollow sigh. As if nothing occurred, he let the letter fall from his fingers onto the floor. He turned his attention back to the drawer, rummaging through it until he found what he thought to be four packages of hot sauce. Mu'min returned to the table, stepping on the letter in the process.

"Told you there would be hot sauce," he said, passing two of the packets across the table to Zulaikah. Mu'min tore the corner from the hot sauce and squeezed the contents onto a chicken breast. "Oh no, this is salsa." Using his knife, he tried to scrape the salsa from the crispy golden crust.

"Aren't you going to open the letter?" Zulaikah was still standing.

"I can't believe that I put salsa on the chicken. Now it's ruined."

"Mu'min?"

"I ruined my chicken. Who eats salsa on fried chicken?"

"What about the letter?"

Mu'min slammed his fist down on the table. The orange candle flames flickered as if they were cowering. "I ruined my chicken."

Zulaikah reached across the table and removed Mu'min's plate, depositing it on the counter next to the sink. She then retrieved the letter.

"Forget the chicken. Let's talk about the letter."

Mu'min turned to face her, his head rotating on his neck as if he were possessed. His eyes narrowed into mere slits, boring imaginary holes into her head. Zulaikah stepped backward, as if readying herself to run.

"No." Mu'min's voice was as weighty and solid as a boulder. "No." With that, Mu'min left the kitchen and headed up the back stairwell. Their bedroom door slammed shut, the house reverberating with the force.

Mu'min had to read the letter, just had to. If she had been someone else, perhaps she would not have cared if Mu'min never gave his father the time of day. But she was not someone else. Zulaikah knew what it was like to want her father but never even have the choice. Her father had died before he ever knew that she was conceived. For her, there had never been a second chance. There had never even a first chance.

Cynthia, her mother, eventually remarried. Together, she and her husband had one daughter only eighteen months younger than Zulaikah and two sons. Technically, they were a family; but she was always the one with the dead father or the first, the one who came before, an outsider. There were no mysterious letters to be found, no address or phone number overseas or even across the street. Her father was simply dead, gone, and nothing could make him come for her.

Since the discovery of the letters, Mu'min acted as if a grave wrong had been done to him. He was unwilling to see how truly fortunate he was to be given the chance after so many years to reconnect with his father, his flesh and blood, his history. Mu'min seemed not to care while Zulaikah was often filled with such overwhelming jealousy, the poison of it threatened to spill over into their marriage. If given the same opportunity, she would not have allowed a single second pass without trying to find her father.

Zulaikah did not want for her husband the emptiness and misery of never having all the parts to make himself a whole person, as she had all her life. Mu'min had to read the letter, just had to.

Zulaikah stared at the letter in her hands. Mu'min Abdulkadir, along with their address, was written in jagged, shaky script. It looked like the writing of someone nervous or upset or old and unsteady.

Maybe Adam Abdulkadir was ill or dying or just plain desperate to make contact with his son. Maybe he cried over the letter as he wrote it. Perhaps the shattered pieces of his heart littered the paper inside the envelope. In which case, it was even more imperative that the letter be opened.

Before Zulaikah could check her impulses, she had already torn off the edge of the envelope and was pulling out the thin letter.

She didn't read the entire letter. Her eyes and her mind were racing too quickly for that, but she did manage to ingest bits and pieces.

She was able to sense Adam's fear and uncertainty as well as the consuming presence of guilt.

I dream my son, that one day you and I will come back together. . . . You are my missing limb . . . two daughters that cannot take the place of you.

My son . . . It seems that the mistakes of my life began to compound the day that I left you and your mother behind. I keep trying to mend that mistake by committing yet another. Now I have two innocent daughters, an infant son born dead only hours ago, and a heart without faith to show for my efforts. Allah help me. I am a man without faith or a son.

Zulaikah's nervous fingers left damp prints around the edges of the paper. Her hands trembled slightly. It was as if the letter had been addressed to her. It was as if she had been waiting all her life for this letter.

"Anything in that letter I should know about?" Mu'min was standing at the far side of the kitchen at the foot of the staircase. He was smiling, but to Zulaikah, he looked more like he would cry.

"You have no idea. Did you change your mind?"

"Not really. I decided that I better come back down and take my medicine. You were going to force-feed me anyway. Weren't you?"

Zulaikah smiled at this. Mu'min rarely ever denied her. This would be no different. He was right; she would have forced him by any means necessary.

"You are a very lucky man. You have a father who loves you. He wants to reunite."

"If he had never left me in the first place, there would be no need for a reunion." Mu'min crossed his thick arms over his chest.

"But he did. You can't change what is past. Besides, you don't know why he left. Maybe he had good reason."

"He thought he had good reason, at first. But he came to realize very soon that he had made a mistake. In a way, I can understand why my mother never told me about the letters."

"How do you know all of this?" Zulaikah refolded the letter and slipped it into the envelope.

"I read the other letters."

"When? Just now?"

"About a week ago." Mu'min motioned for Zulaikah to sit down. He joined her at the table.

"Why didn't you tell me?"

Mu'min shrugged. "Nothing to tell. My father made a terrible mistake by leaving behind a devoted wife and son. He came to regret it later, but by then, he was too far away and too helpless to do a thing about it. I didn't grow up with my father, and sometimes it hurt me not knowing why. Believe me, it hurt him the most."

Mu'min's face softened a bit, the angry creases fading just enough to expose the Mu'min that Zulaikah knew as tender and compassionate. Zulaikah reached across the table and took her husband's hand in hers. It was such a nice hand, belonging to such a good husband.

"What are you going to do now?"

"What do you mean?"

"I mean, when are you going to go see him?"

"Why should I? He left me, remember?"

Zulaikah released Mu'min's hand as if it were a hot coal. "I can't believe how stubborn you are being."

"Texas is a long way from Senegal. Even if I wanted to, we can't afford it."

Zulaikah hopped up from the table. In the refrigerator, she removed a can of Coke. The Coke was actually a decoy safe used to dupe possible burglars. Zulaikah unscrewed the top and removed a roll of bills ranging from ten- to one-hundred-dollar denominations.

"One hundred, two hundred, three hundred, four hundred, five hundred, six hundred, seven hundred, eight hundred, nine hundred, nine hundred and twenty, nine hundred and forty, nine hundred and fifty," she counted. "I don't know how much a ticket would cost, but I'll bet that this would do it. If not, I work, you work, and we could always borrow the rest from my mom."

Mu'min nodded his head. "No way."

"Why, Mu'min? This is the chance of a lifetime."

"Maybe so, but you seem to have forgotten that we are going to need all of the money that we can get with the baby coming soon."

"We could make due. All you have to do is want it."

Mu'min was silent. He hadn't told her about reading the letters for this very reason. He wanted to decide on how to proceed on his own in his own time. Mu'min's memories of his father were all positive. He could still see his father's face in his mind, always smiling, always pleased, so much like the one he saw when he looked into the mirror. But as Mu'min looked across the table at his pregnant wife, he could in no way fathom leaving her or the unborn child. Therefore, how could his father?

He had read his father's letters. There was talk of the bonds and expectations of culture, all of which sounded like faltering excuses, wrapped up in flowery, well-meaning words. Adam Abdulkadir had left fifteen years ago because he was too ashamed to present his wife and son to his family.

How could Mu'min rush off to another country to greet a man who was once so ashamed of him that he abandoned him?

"You do want to see your father, don't you?"

"Sure. One day."

MU'MIN STOOD BY THE WINDOW, watching the deserted street. The rains had just stopped, leaving an oily gloss on the black asphalt. The yellow moon peeked timidly from behind the charcoal clouds, though it seemed that any minute the rains would return, the clouds once again engulfing the moon. At that moment, the moon was like his heart.

Zulaikah slept less than twelve feet away. She looked like a little girl with her fisted hands positioned under her head, and her long legs drawn up against her chest. She snored in her sleep, like an old man, since her pregnancy had begun to show. Since they had retired to bed at ten thirty the previous evening, Zulaikah had not moved a single inch, nor had her rhythmic breaths been interrupted.

Now, the time was 2:48 a.m., and Mu'min had not experienced a single moment of sleep. He couldn't forget his father. Each syllable that his father wrote in the letter churned in his mind like debris in a tornado.

Adam's words were intelligent, and his sentences were well formed and concise; however, he sounded no different than a beggar. Sometimes the indigent beg for food, money for the rent, a job. They beg for the things that they need.

Adam didn't need food or money for the rent or a job, but these were the things Mu'min might be able to give. Adam needed his son and absolution. Adam needed to reclaim the past he gave away fifteen years ago. But he couldn't do that on his own. It was up to Mu'min, and Mu'min knew it.

Mu'min closed the bedroom door behind him when he left. It was colder downstairs. The aroused tingle of chill bumps rose on Mu'min's naked arms. He grabbed an old afghan from the back of his mother's antique sofa and wrapped it around himself. It still did not diminish the chill that coursed through him.

Mu'min turned on the lamp on top of the marble fireplace mantle. He stood looking around the living room, which hadn't changed since he was a child. His mother had lived in the house for more than twenty-four years since before his birth and before his father's departure.

Same sofa, same coffee table, same fireplace that never held a fire, same writing desk with lion's feet sitting beneath the window. On the writing desk was a neat stack of blue writing paper and a black ballpoint pen. He stared at the paper for some time. Zulaikah had left it there before she went to bed, knowing that he would end up roaming the house that night. She knew him so well.

It may cost hundreds of dollars and a lot of confused feelings to go to Adam in Senegal. To write a letter costs only a few cents and the smallest bit of courage, read a note next to the stack of writing paper.

"I can handle that," said Mu'min out loud. He glanced suspiciously around the room, surprised to hear his own voice. Then he smiled to himself because it was true. He could say all the things that his troubled heart and mind could conjure, fold them into an envelope, and mail them to Senegal for only a few cents. He could expel years of delayed fury and never have to look his assailant in the face. He could do that, no problem.

It was as if Mu'min had awakened from a long sleep, as if the clouds had parted allowing his heart to shine through, to heal for the first time in years. Mu'min did not struggle for inspiration. The words tumbled forward as if being poured from a bucket. He wrote his first letter to his father without feeling the slightest bit of doubt, without shame or fear.

TWENTY-FOUR

More than two months passed before Asabe heard from Abu Kareem. She had begun to think that Abu Kareem had forgotten his promises to help her with Adam and Sauda.

Abu Kareem arrived on a Friday afternoon about an hour after *Jummah* prayers had ended. Hannah led him into the house by his hand, with him protesting the entire way. His body was quickly succumbing to old age, but in his mind he was still as spry as a twenty-year-old man.

The day was clear and bright, but the temperature was abnormally brisk. Hannah wore a plain black *jilbab* and white hijab. Unlike her husband, she seemed to be thriving. No one would guess that she was a forty-seven-year-old woman.

Asabe was surprised to see them but was pleased nonetheless. She escorted them into the living room before she headed out to the kitchen for refreshments. "Do you prefer tea or coffee, Abu Kareem?"

"Nothing," he said brusquely, slumping onto the sofa. His breathing was labored. The short walk from the car to the house had winded him.

"Bring him a glass of water," said Hannah. "He is thirsty."

"No. I don't want water. We don't have time for that."

Hannah removed a handkerchief from the pocket of her jilbab and handed it to Abu Kareem. He accepted it begrudgingly.

Abu Kareem waved Asabe to a chair. He leaned forward in his seat. "You thought that I forgot my promise to help with Adam and Sauda, didn't you?"

"No, Abu Kareem, I knew that you had not forgotten. You're a busy man."

"I am never too busy for my family. I made the necessary arrangements the day after we talked, but I decided not to announce my intentions until now because I knew that if I gave Adam and my daughter the opportunity to think on it, they would surely renege at the last minute."

"It was actually my idea to wait," added Hannah.

Abu Kareem placed his hand on Hannah's knee. "Where is Adam?"

"He should be on his way home. He left for Jummah at the mosque more than an hour ago. He said he would be back soon."

"Good. What of my daughter?"

"She hasn't left her bedroom in the past two months."

"I'll need your cooperation in this matter, Asabe. I won't be able to execute my plan without your complete assistance."

"What do I need to do?" asked Asabe, half afraid.

Abu Kareem and Hannah grinned at each other, snickering like a couple of teens.

"Two things. I want you to pack a small bag for Adam, including only necessary items. Hannah will go up to help Sauda pack her bag." Abu Kareem prompted Hannah by patting her hand. She headed upstairs.

"We'll be down shortly," she said, smiling at Abu Kareem.

Abu Kareem glanced at his watch, "We only have five hours, so be quick." To Asabe, he said, "Go on. Hurry up and pack your husband's bag."

"What do you have planned for them?"

Asabe knew that Abu Kareem and her mother would never harm Adam or Sauda, but she couldn't displace the feeling that Abu Kareem's mysterious plan would in some way harm them. Abu Kareem saw the worry on her face.

"Why are you so disturbed? You don't really think that I would do them harm, do you?"

"You are being rather mysterious. I suppose I'm simply curious to know what you have in store for my husband. I worry about him."

Abu Kareem chuckled, but something must have caught in his throat because it turned to a cough that caused his entire body to quake. Abu Kareem dabbed his damp eyes with the handkerchief, inhaling deeply to regain his composure.

"Of course you worry about Adam. He is your husband, and you are a good wife. When you came to me, you described Adam as well as my daughter as having lost faith. I have to admit, there was a time in my past when I was a less-than-worthy worshipper. Fortunately, my father was still alive, and he was wise enough to recognize my dilemma. He didn't preach to me or demand from me obedience. He did for me exactly what I am doing for Adam and Sauda. He packed my belongings, escorted me to the depot, and sent me on the long journey to Mecca. In those days, few people flew. In fact," he said, laughing again, "many people still went by way of caravan.

"My father didn't ask my permission. He didn't even entertain a discussion on the matter. I was going, and that was it. I think I was twenty-three. I was already a very wealthy man, but I hadn't married yet. I was young and stupid and had forgotten my mortality. I had forgotten how temporary and useless this world really is."

"Your father sent you on hajj?"

"He certainly did. It was the single greatest act of love he ever performed on my behalf. My life was forever changed the day I stood in the shadow of the Kaaba. I will give this gift to my daughter and her husband."

Asabe was unaware of her own tears until Abu Kareem handed her the handkerchief. She dabbed her eyes with the soft fabric. Asabe was happier than she had been in a long time. She was pleased to know that she wasn't alone and that she wasn't the only person who wanted to help her household. However, Asabe also felt a bubble of jealousy rising in her gut. For more than thirteen years, Asabe had solved all of Adam's problems. She had been the one to comfort Adam in his times of grief and disappointment. It was difficult for Asabe to acknowledge that she could not be everything for her husband. He would sometimes need other people. Mostly, he needed to nurture his relationship with his creator. That, he needed to do on his own.

"You said that I needed to do two things. What's the other."

"While we are gone, you will have to be responsible for the children."

"You need not say a word. They are both my daughters as well. I wouldn't let any harm come to them."

Abu Kareem reached into the pocket of his jalabiyah and removed a thick envelope. "This should be enough CFA to cover any of your expenses. Unbeknownst to Adam, I have arranged for Jamil to assume Adam's duties at the office until he returns. He will also be responsible for getting Adam's mail at the post office. He'll drop it off here at home. On the days when he come, if there is anything that you need done, feel free to ask him. He has been instructed to tend to your requests as a favor to me. Besides, I'm tripling his salary in Adam's absence."

"You've taken care of everything."

"Not quite." Abu Kareem turned to look out of the window. He had heard the quiet purr of Adam's engine as he drove up to the house.

"What else is there?"

"Convincing Adam."

ADAM'S FIRST FLIGHT was nearly thirty years ago. He was on his way to the United States then, a young man anxious to experience life in the West, away from the village and his father's groundnut plantation. His second airplane flight took place sixteen years later. That flight wasn't as promising. It was the day he left a part of himself behind.

Now, on his third airplane flight, Adam was unable to determine exactly how he felt. He was definitely afraid, but he didn't know why. He was also overjoyed, for no explicable reason.

Adam gazed out of the tiny portal at the billowing clouds piled up beneath the airplane. The clouds seemed to be holding the plane up in midair. Hannah and Abu Kareem occupied two seats directly in front of Adam. Sauda sat to his right; her eyes were fixed on her hands, which were clamped together in her lap. She hadn't spoken a word since they left Diourbel for Dakar four and a half hours earlier.

"Is something wrong?" asked Adam.

Sauda said nothing.

"Sauda?"

"Nothing is wrong."

"I don't believe you. You haven't said a word in hours. Are you afraid to fly?"

"I've been flying all of my life."

"Then why are you so sullen? I've never seen you like this."

"You haven't really seen me for the past two months. How would you know?"

Sauda spoke the shameful truth, and Adam had to admit to it. He had practically ignored her very presence for the past two months, not feeling the least bit guilty about his neglect until the moment Sauda said it out loud.

"I deserved that, didn't I?"

Sauda shrugged her shoulders. "I didn't expect better from you."

"I'm your husband."

"I was beginning to wonder."

"Is this why you're behaving as if someone has snatched your heart from your chest?"

"No. Like I've said, I didn't expect better from you. I miss my daughter. I don't want to leave her."

"She'll be fine with Asabe."

"I know she will. It's just that she and I have only just begun to know each other. She is just realizing that *I* am her mother."

ASABE AWOKE SUDDENLY AT 3:01 a.m. She had forced herself awake, something she had grown adept at doing over the past month. The same dream haunted her, the same young man with the handsome face who wanted her to see something.

Nothing in the dream seemed dangerous or particularly terrifying, but for Asabe, it was a nightmare. That young man wanted to tell Asabe a secret, but for some reason, the very prospect terrified her.

Earlier, Asabe had put the girls to sleep in Sauda's room. Hadizah had asked to sleep there, and it seemed to ease Lailah's anxiety. Both of them had become very attached to Sauda over the past two months and were upset at her departure. Asabe had fallen asleep on the living room couch, something she rarely did. The house just seemed so empty without Adam and Sauda.

Asabe turned off the living room lights and went into the kitchen with the intentions of putting on a pot of tea. She was exhausted, had been for weeks; but after the dream, she always found it difficult to find comfort in sleep.

After Asabe put the water on for tea, she removed a fresh loaf of French bread from the pantry. She sliced herself three large pieces of the crusty bread and spread a thick layer of cream cheese on each piece. There was a mango in the fruit dish on the table so ripe it perfumed the entire kitchen. Asabe cut the mango in half and sliced the soft flesh from around the pit.

By then, the water had come to a boil, and Asabe's mouth watered. Her growling stomach was proof of her hunger.

Asabe quickly devoured her late-night snack. Though her hunger was abated, she did not feel quite satisfied. Her stomach grumbled even louder now. It bubbled and pitched inside her gut violently. Now, Asabe's mouth watered for an entirely different reason.

Asabe knew that she probably could not make it to the bathroom, but vomiting in the kitchen sink where she washed and prepared her food seemed unreasonable. She took the stairs two at a time, grasping the railing, fighting a wave of vertigo.

For the third time in as many days, Asabe emptied the contents of her stomach into the toilet. Her throat was sore from the effort, and her mouth burned from the acid, but she felt relieved.

Asabe put down the toilet lid and flushed her snack away. It seemed such a waste. She brushed her teeth and splashed her face with cold water. In the mirror, Asabe's mahogany face was flushed with a healthy ruddy glow. This was curious, for she didn't feel as robust as her appearance suggested.

Asabe watched her reflection for a long time, wondering how she had managed to look better than she had in a very long time when her household was in a shambles and she couldn't seem to get enough sleep. The whites of her eyes were so bright they appeared almost blue, and her cheeks were fuller than usual. Her skin was silky and unblemished.

Asabe closed the bathroom door to avail herself of the body-length mirror hanging on the back. She removed her scarf, exposing the hair she had paid little attention to grooming over the past few weeks.

Asabe scrutinized her reflection, starting from her head, slowly moving her eyes down her entire frame, ending at her feet. Asabe had gained weight. A lot of it. She removed the scale from the cabinet beneath the sink. She hadn't been on the scale since before Fatima had come to live with them, at least three years ago. She weighed around one hundred and thirty pounds then, rather thin for a woman standing five feet ten. Now Asabe weighed one hundred and fifty-seven pounds.

She tugged at her blouse. "This explains why my clothes don't fit as well," said Asabe to her reflection. "When did this happen?" she asked herself. She was smiling now. Over the past two months, Sauda's ample girth seemed to shrink while she hid away in her room. "Did I pick up the weight that you lost, Sauda?"

Asabe turned sideways, still gazing at her reflection. She pulled her blouse tight against her belly to get a better look at her waist. "Not so thin anymore," she said. "In fact," she said, pulling her blouse up over her stomach, "I look almost . . . pregnant. Pregnant?" Asabe belted out a ruckus laugh, startling herself.

She snickered to herself all the way down the hall to her bedroom.

"Imagine me pregnant after thirteen years of marriage. Imagine that!" Asabe was laughing and crying at the same time. The very idea was both amusing and terrifying. After so many years of heartache and disappointment because her blood arrived at exactly the same time every month, it was preposterous to think that she could be pregnant.

"My blood," said Asabe as if it was the name of a dearly loved one. "When is the last time I've seen my . . ." Asabe's voice trailed off as she tried to calculate the number of weeks using her fingers. It had not been weeks but months.

In her bedroom, Asabe frantically stripped off her blouse and again stared at her reflection in her dresser mirror.

"Am I?" she asked herself, half afraid.

Asabe turned to her left and then her right, inspecting her silhouette. She lowered the waist of her wrapper.

"How could I have missed it?" she said, rubbing her slightly rounded belly. "Shouldn't I have seen it earlier?" Then Asabe began to laugh again; it was a hearty, joyous bellow. "I have to tell Adam." Asabe ran from her bedroom down the hall to Adam's room.

"Adam! Wake up!" shouted Asabe, throwing Adam's bedroom door open. It wasn't until Asabe saw the neatly made bed that she remembered that Adam had left the previous day for Mecca. She was all alone.

TWENTY-FIVE

An elder man wearing a deep azure turban and stark white jalabiyah met Abu Kareem and his family at the King Abdulaziz Airport in Jeddah. His name was Hasan, and he was a close friend of Abu Kareem. They met each other nearly forty years earlier on Abu Kareem's first trip to Saudi Arabia and had remained close friends ever since.

Hasan rushed forward and embraced Abu Kareem, placing a generous kiss on each of his cheeks. He stood back to get a better look at his old friend and shook his head when he saw how heavily Abu Kareem leaned on his cane.

"As-salaam alaikum. You are not well," Hasan proclaimed in guttural Arabic.

"Alhamdulillahi. Taiyib." Abu Kareem tried to assure his friend that he was well in unsure Arabic. After a few seconds longer of concerned scrutiny, Hasan finally relented with a broad smile. He turned his attention to Abu Kareem's family.

Abu Kareem introduced Adam, whom Hasan embraced with the same enthusiasm and love as he had with Abu Kareem. Although Abu Kareem explained that no one else in his group spoke Arabic, Hasan still rambled off question after question to Adam as if he could understand.

Hannah and Sauda stood back a ways. Hasan nodded in their direction, offering them polite salutations.

Hasan was a man of great wealth and position. He was a very distant cousin of the king through marriage, and although that tie was now severed by divorce, he was still afforded many of the privileges of royalty. With only a few words, Hasan was able to circumnavigate many of the formalities of customs and handling and deliver his entourage from the bustling airport in less than twenty minutes. This was the season of hajj, and they were not the only people who had flocked to Saudi Arabia to partake of the right of pilgrimage.

Abu Kareem requested that Hasan deliver his family to a hotel, where he had made reservations, but Hasan would not hear of it.

"You must come to my home in Medina," he insisted in Arabic. "You can meet my family and rest a bit. I will take you to the tomb of Rasoolulah." The tomb of the Prophet Muhammad was second only to the Kaaba in importance to Muslims.

More than ten years had passed since Abu Kareem last saw Hasan, so he gladly accepted the invitation.

The black Mercedes jeep sped along the highway, the tepid desert air rushing in through the half-opened windows. Brother Hasan looked almost like a dwarf behind the driver's seat, but he handled the machine with ease. He rambled on and on to Abu Kareem, who sat in the front seat alongside him. However, even Abu Kareem did not understand everything that his friend said in his excited Arabic tongue.

Adam sat in the back, behind Hasan, mesmerized by the surreal beauty of the open desert that passed by in great monotonous sheets of yellow sand and the blue-gray mountains that climbed out of the desert floor toward the seamless afternoon sky.

Hannah sat behind Abu Kareem. On occasion, she would reach forward to remove a piece of lint from his camise or to whisper something in his ear or to adjust the folds of his turban; she offered him a tissue when he sniffled, a bottle of water from her purse just because he cleared his throat, and Rubb for his lips because the weather was dry. Hannah doted on Abu Kareem as if he were a child. She wouldn't leave him alone.

He was as enamored with her as he was annoyed.

Sauda sat silently between Adam and Hannah. She focused her eyes on the palms of her hands to steady herself. Her stomach was still uneasy from the flight, and her heart was still in Diourbel, Senegal.

Two months ago, when she thought that she was pregnant with Adam's son, Sauda was little concerned about her daughter. Now, Sauda was distressed without the child close by. Allah took away her son before he had a handhold on life. It was then that Sauda was forced to finally confront her own mortality. She learned just how human and weak and how little she had control over the affairs of the world and even her own life. She had to face the possibility that like Asabe, Allah may never favor her with a son. It simply was not within her control. That being the case, she wasn't going to allow another day to pass when she did not do justice to her daughter; after all, Lailah might be the only child she ever has.

After five hours of coasting down the highway, listening to the hurried unintelligible garble of Hasan, the Mercedes jeep pulled into the gate of a sprawling estate. The home looked like a replica of an old southern plantation house. The gracious lawns were as clean and green as emeralds. There were few flowers, except for those that formed the immediate perimeter of house. They looked like millions of colored popcorns, each in a different hue—mandarin, carmine, violet, peach, white, and fuchsia. Each color was sufficiently intense to induce a headache.

Inside, Hannah and Sauda were hurriedly escorted to another part of the house while Abu Kareem and Adam were entertained in a spacious sitting room. The floor was covered nearly wall to wall with a giant cherry and black Oriental rug. The perimeter of the room was lined with rows of pillows, all in different sizes, shapes, and colors. A rainbow of comfort.

Adam assisted Abu Kareem to the floor before he dove into the pillows. Both were spent from the long flight, but Hasan would not allow his guests to rest until he had fed them.

Shortly thereafter, a weathered old man entered the room carrying a brass serving tray. They ate gluttonously; neither could remember the last time they had eaten such a satisfying meal. There were three whole roasted chickens, couscous, and lamb smothered in a curry yogurt sauce, sweet pistachio baklava, and potent syrupy tea.

The caffeine wasn't enough to feign off slumber. Both Adam and Abu Kareem collapsed into a sound sleep after they had filled their bellies.

Hannah and Sauda were entertained by the eldest two of Hasan's four wives. Coincidentally, both of the women were named Ruquaiyah, but their similarities ended there. They were at least twenty years apart in age. The older of the two was thin with a face and body full of angles and with pale olive skin. Ruquaiyah number 2 was so plump that when she smiled, her eyes seemed to disappear into her face. She had bright gray eyes and skin the color of wet desert sand.

The two women were gracious hosts. Like their husband, Hasan, they chattered in Arabic to Sauda and Hannah although neither could grasp the language. Nevertheless, Hannah and Sauda were comfortable despite the obvious differences because their hosts were exceedingly warm and compassionate.

After a meal similar to the one their husbands ate, Sauda and Hannah were escorted to separate but adjoining bedrooms where their luggage had already been discharged. Sauda was unable to rest until she had called home to hear Lailah giggling in the background as she spoke to her cowife. Asabe seemed somehow different, her voice light with expectation as if she had a secret to tell. She asked that Sauda have Adam call home as soon as possible.

Hannah showered and retired to her bed after Isha prayers.

Sleep claimed them both as surely as the day must eventually end.

LUQMAN WAS ADAM'S GRANDFATHER. He was a large man, much as Adam, but remarkably frail for his size. His strength was in his intellect. Luqman was not a man of formal education; he had little knowledge of the West or of any of the occurrences of the world outside his own sphere.

Luqman was born in the year 1888 in a tiny farming village fifty miles north of Dakar. He could neither read nor write. Being born blind made these tasks impossible for him. Still, he was a scholar. He could recite the Holy Qur'an from start to finish without a mistake in a voice so fluid and melodious those who listened to him wept. His greatest knowledge was in history, particularly the history of the prophet of Islam, Muhammad.

As a child, Adam heard none of the West's time-honored fairy tales. No *Cinderella*, no *Hansel and Gretel*, no *Jack and the Beanstalk*. Every night Adam and his siblings gathered in a circle around old Luqman to listen to the same story, and every night they were more riveted by the details than they had been the previous night. Luqman would sob each time he told the story. Adam never understood why the story elicited such a profound response from his grandfather. He had never been as moved.

At the age of fifty-five, Adam still remembered the history of the life of Muhammad, the prophet of Islam. Muhammad was an orphan, a humble, unlettered man who managed to change the course of the world beginning in his own backyard of Arabia. He was persecuted and despised by his brethren because he preached belief in one god. He outlawed ownership of women, the killing of infant girls by burying them alive, murder, thievery, and many other injustices rampant in his society. He did this all without an education, and oftentimes in a state of poverty so profound that he often passed his days without so much as a date to eat.

Adam had not given the story serious thought in years, but as he stood before the tomb of the much-revered prophet of Islam, every word his grandfather spoke came back in a wave so intense he could no longer tell if his heart still beat in his chest.

Adam never imagined the tomb would be so beautiful, emerald green decorated with golden verses from the Qur'an written in flowing Arabic script. But it wasn't the outer beauty that mesmerized Adam but the feeling the place evoked. All at once Adam felt pleasure and pain, shame and pride, love and hate.

In his fifty-five living years, Adam's most significant concern was how to have a son. Adam had offered nothing to the world worth mentioning, let alone respect and reverence, while the man who lay entombed before him died after having offered his very life to the world. The man who lay entombed before Adam had also desired a son, each one that was ever born of him had died in infancy; but Muhammad's insight was so great that he desired even more than a son, peace and submission to one god. His was such an admirable cause, such a self-sacrificial achievement, that Adam was for the very first time able to see himself in the proper light.

If a prophet could not demand a son from God, then who was Adam to expect more than was evidently his just due?

Adam was startled to hear himself sobbing aloud, but the pain of realization was just that great. Luqman had always preached about how grateful a man Muhammad was, despite the poverty, the persecution, and the unfulfilled desires. However, Adam, who lived free from any major want, had ceased to praise his benefactor for months on end. He had in effect denied no one but himself. If Luqman were alive, he would have been greatly ashamed of his heedless grandson.

"I've been a fool," Adam wept into his hands. A dozen men turned to glance at him, but none seemed surprised. Adam's reaction was not unusual. Some would even call it tame.

Grown men were known to faint at the site of Muhammad's tomb, overcome by the history and the wonder of the great man's life and also by the confirmation of their own mortality. A man as beloved by God as Muhammad was unable to cheat the hardships of life and even death. How could a layman? How could any man live with the ridiculous pretense that he was anything more than a glorified ape, when he had so little control over the affairs of his own life?

Abu Kareem, who stood close by, laid his hand on Adam's shoulder, urging him to quit the place; but Adam was steadfast. Abu Kareem did not disapprove. He was as touched by the reverence of the sepulcher as his son-in-law, but this was not his first time to visit the grave, and he was better able to keep his emotions in check.

"We should be leaving," he whispered into Adam's ear. "There are others who have come to witness the burial place of our Rasoolulah."

Indeed droves of other hajj goers had detoured to Medina in order to assemble and pray in the mosque of their prophet, Masjid-ul-Nabawi. Muhammad's tomb lay within the walls of this mosque.

As Adam turned to leave, passing through clusters of worshippers, he realized that he was not the only person moved to tears; he was not the only person whose very soul had been seared with reality.

TWENTY-SIX

Jamil called three days after Adam's departure to inquire about Asabe's well-being. Of course, she was better than she had been in months, although she did not tell him why this was so. He requested permission to stop by the house that morning on his way into the office to deliver the mail he'd procured from Adam's post office box and office. He also wanted to leave with her some foodstuffs, and Salimah, if she liked.

Asabe extended an enthusiastic invitation to both Jamil and Salimah. She had heard about her young friend's newfound voice from Sauda, and she wanted to hear it for herself.

Jamil dropped Salimah off at ten that same morning. It was a brilliant limpid day, but not more so than Salimah. She had only just seen her seventeenth birthday, but she looked like a woman of at least twenty-five now. It wasn't so much that she had aged in the few months that she left them; but she had definitely matured, had become more worldly, more confident.

Anxious for the company, and to see Salimah, Asabe ran outside when she heard Jamil's car pull into the driveway. Lailah was tightly tied against Asabe's back. Hadizah followed, matching each of Asabe's long strides with three or four of her own. Kasuar also followed them outside, purring and sniffing the air for prey. He waited for the car to stop before he darted into the field next to the house.

Salimah stepped out of the car, dressed dazzlingly in a lavender lace ensemble. Asabe descended on her friend like a lion on his prey.

"I don't need to tell you how beautiful you look, do I? Surely you already know." Holding Salimah by the shoulders, Asabe stepped back and looked into her friend's face. "Turn around, let me see you." Asabe beamed with pride as if Salimah was her child.

Salimah smiled.

"What are you waiting for? Say something."

"You've gained weight." Salimah's voice was soft, almost strained. That she spoke at all made it all the sweeter.

Asabe fell on Salimah again, full of cheerful giggles. "You're right, I have gained weight, among other things."

Asabe helped Salimah remove three bags from the trunk of the car before they bid Jamil good-bye. Hadizah insisted she help, so she was allowed to carry in the lightest of the bags. Jamil promised to arrive at five that evening to retrieve Salimah.

Inside, Asabe removed Lailah from her back, allowing her to crawl about on the floor. She chased her sister from room to room on her knees, her diapered rump bobbing in the air like a balloon.

Salimah helped Asabe put the groceries away. It was as if she had never left; she knew where everything belonged. Before Asabe could object, Salimah even put on a pot of jasmine tea.

"You are not the maid anymore, but my guest."

"Yes, but you are my elder. That deserves my respect and my service."

"I'm not that much older than you." Asabe used her fingers to count out the years. "I'm only twenty-eight."

"Then allow me to serve you because you are with child."

"How did you know?" asked Asabe, wide eyed with disbelief.

"It seems obvious to me. Adam must be pleased."

Asabe lowered herself into a seat at the table while Salimah removed two cups from the cupboard. Asabe felt suddenly overwhelmed, unsure if she would weep or laugh or howl with anger. If it was obvious to Salimah that she was pregnant, then why had Adam not noticed or Sauda or even herself?

With the death of Attiyah and the loss of Sauda's baby, everyone had been on edge, preoccupied and disoriented. Adam also seemed to be harboring a personal pain of his own that he had not yet seen fit to reveal. Through this all, Asabe had been patient and understanding. She had been a rock for everyone, tending to everyone else's needs above her own, so much so that she could not even realize that she was pregnant.

Hadn't the time come for her sacrifices to benefit herself? Hadn't the time come for someone else to sacrifice on her behalf?

Salimah placed a steaming cup of tea in front of Asabe before returning to the counter to collect her own cup and a plate full of fresh croissants she had brought with her.

"Is something wrong?"

"Adam doesn't even know that I am pregnant."

Salimah sipped the steaming brew and asked, "Why haven't you told him?"

"I only just realized it three days ago." Asabe looked to her young companion. "What kind of woman doesn't know that she is carrying a child until she is nearly five months along?"

"The kind of woman who has a life full of cares."

"What kind of husband doesn't notice that his wife is carrying his child? If anyone should know, it should be him, shouldn't it?"

Salimah was silent. She reached across the table and patted Asabe's hand, but Asabe would not be comforted. She wanted to know.

"Shouldn't Adam have known?"

"That is not a question that I can answer. Every man is different. Every man has his own load of concerns and fears. Perhaps he has been as overwhelmed as you."

"If it were you, wouldn't Jamil know?"

Salimah smiled shyly. "Jamil notices everything about me. Everything. But," she said, trying to wash away the look of disappointment on Asabe's face, "some men, some people, see better than others. Some people don't *see* until it is too late or just in time."

Jamil arrived at exactly five o'clock. The sun hung stubbornly in the sky, a vibrant yellow ball amid a painter's palette full of colors ranging from orange to violet. The temperature had dropped noticeably, although the weather was still mild.

Asabe had enjoyed Salimah's company and was not ready to see her leave. Asabe hadn't been totally alone in that house since before Fatima's arrival three years ago. In those days, she enjoyed the solitude; but now, even with the children, Asabe wished she weren't so alone.

"Promise me that you will visit again."

"You know that I will. All you have to do is call, and I will be here. Right, Jamil?" called Salimah into the car.

"Anytime," he assured.

"Before I forget," said Salimah, digging into her purse, "here is Adam's mail." Salimah handed Asabe three envelopes. "I was supposed to give them to you earlier."

"No harm was done," said Asabe, glancing at the mail. The first piece of mail was a card from Mahmoud, addressed to both Asabe and Adam, probably to thank them for their support at the time of Attiyah's death. The second piece of mail, addressed to Adam's post office box, was from someone named Mu'min A. Abdulkadir in the States. Asabe recognized the name Mu'min, as it was the name of Adam's business, and the name Abdulkadir, because it also belonged to Adam. Nevertheless, she did not know the person who possessed both names. The third piece of mail was addressed to Mu'min Printers Inc. It was from Bashir Construction, the company Adam commissioned during the rebuilding of his business.

Mu'min Abdulkadir. The name repeated in Asabe's head.

"Will you be fine by yourself?" asked Salimah.

"Insha Allah. Don't worry about me." Asabe embraced her friend.

"Tell Adam that all is well at the office," called Jamil from behind the wheel.

Asabe agreed, embracing Salimah one last time. She watched their burgundy sedan disappear down the road, leaving a cloud of dust in its wake.

The azan echoed in the distance, announcing that the time for prayers had arrived. Asabe returned to the house. She had left Hadizah and Lailah at play in the foyer where she could easily watch them from outside. Asabe returned just in time. Hadizah had begun to dig the soil from a potted plant that sat in a corner by the foyer table. Lailah had a mouthful of the dirt.

They both looked so innocent and content in their transgressions that Asabe could not imagine scolding them, but she did admonish them lightly so that they would not repeat their actions.

Asabe tucked the stack of mail between her teeth and grabbed one child with each arm. Despite the admonishment, both of them giggled with delight as they bounced up and down on her hip under her arm. Asabe headed for the bathroom.

Once Asabe had finished bathing the two sisters, she put both of them to bed in Sauda's room. Spooned up in the center of the bed, the girls drifted off into a complete slumber.

Asabe spent the rest of the evening in the prayer room. She prayed that Allah might comfort and soften her husband's heart and remove the veil from his eyes so that he might see. For the first time, Asabe asked Allah to grant her happiness before she asked for the happiness of others.

THE TELEPHONE RANG AT 1:30 a.m. Asabe answered the telephone on the third ring, unsure if it was really the telephone or if it was a part of her dream. Her breathing was heavy and ragged. The young man had come to her again, and he was trying desperately to force her to look into his face, to know who he was.

"Yes?" she huffed into the phone.

"Asabe? That you?" came Adam's voice amid static and a jumble of loud clicks. His voice sounded so far away, as if he was speaking to her from the bottom of the deepest well, full of echoes and obstructions.

"Yes. It is me. Adam, how are you?" Asabe sat up in her bed and switched on the bedside lamp. She had been awaiting this phone call for three days.

"Alhamdulillahi, I am fine. Are you doing well? Not afraid to be alone, are you?" Asabe heard Adam chuckle lightly over the great distance. The static surged and then faded slightly.

"No, no. Don't worry about me, I am well. The children are well, sleeping in Sauda's bedroom. They love it there. And Jamil says to tell you that business is well." Asabe paused, listened to a rapid succession of clicks. "Adam? You still there?"

"I am here, just listening to your voice. Just missing home. Should I return?"

"No"—Asabe swallowed hard—"but I have something to tell you." Asabe stroked her slightly rounded tummy. This was the first time she had done so, the first time she caressed her child from without. And amazingly, the first time she felt the life within her flutter.

"Have you enough to eat?" Adam's voice drifted to Asabe as if riding on a wave of the ocean.

"Did you hear, Adam? I have something to tell you."

"Speak louder . . . hear you very well." Adam's voice wafted and warbled through space. There were more clicks.

"I have something to tell you!" she yelled into the mouthpiece.

"Has Jamil . . . checked on you? . . . any mail? . . ." Clicks, surging static.

"Yes! He came today! You have three pieces of mail!"

Mu'min Abdulkadir.

"Hear you . . . bad connection." The static was a low rumble. "Try again later . . ."

"I have something to tell you."

Silence.

"Adam, I am pregnant."

More silence.

The rumble of static was gone; the loud clicks were gone.

Asabe dropped the phone back into its cradle and relaxed back into the bed. It was too early to be awake, roaming the house, swimming in her loneliness; besides, she had only just settled down for sleep a little more than an hour ago.

The drapes were spread open, and the light of the full moon seeped into her bedroom cold and yellow. The night seemed to be pressing against the window, trying to steal what little light was in her bedroom, and it gave Asabe an unsettling feeling. She had not felt altogether comfortable since Adam had left. Asabe would have felt better just to have Sauda sleeping in her room down the hall. Being alone wasn't the same as it used to be.

In a way, she was not really alone in that room. There was the fluttering life in her belly, like a moth trapped in a jar. Asabe caressed the child locked away in her belly.

She pulled the covers over her head and curled up on her side. Escape into sleep was the only remedy to her isolation. Even in her worst dreams, she would not be alone. Asabe was afraid to meet the young man that kept pushing himself into her dreams. At first, he only appeared on occasion; but as of late, she had grown to expect him.

Asabe's stomach barked its dissatisfaction. She was hungry and would never be able to find rest until she had eaten.

Asabe stopped first in Sauda's room. She wanted to check on her girls. The sweet sounds of their slumber created a harmonious little din. The comfort of moonlight found its way in here as well. Asabe was tempted to join them, but she decided against it. She closed the door behind her.

Next, Asabe visited the bathroom. The child moving deep within her belly had disturbed her stomach. Once finished, Asabe stopped at the mirror to examine her tired face. Her skin was as clear and supple as ever, but her eyes were red and wore dark puffy pouches. She wouldn't be able to keep on this way, battling insomnia and loneliness and the stranger in her dreams.

Asabe noticed the mail sitting precariously on the edge of the sink when she went to turn on the tap, and she mistakenly knocked them in. She must have put the mail down on the sink when she came into the bathroom earlier to bathe the girls.

The letter with the oddly familiar sender name was on top. Asabe turned it over in her hands. Through the wet envelope, some of the bold laconic print bled through, but Asabe did not read. Something about the letter, the name, felt ominous, dangerous even.

Mu'min Abdulkadir.

That name drifted into her head like a ribbon on the wind.

After Asabe washed her face, she went down the hall to Adam's bedroom where she intended to leave the mail on his desk. She could not bring herself to walk through the door, feeling as if her feet were encased in ice. Asabe glanced down the hall, left then right. She had the disconcerting sensation that someone was watching her, waiting to point out her trespass into Adam's bedroom.

She hadn't felt this way since the time she returned home after Adam's past episode of violence. It took her months to feel comfortable in his room, always afraid that she would unknowingly stumble upon some seemingly innocent item, angering him to do her worse harm than he had before.

She had never learned why Adam had reacted so violently about a worn letter and a couple of photographs. What could the letter have contained that he would want to hide from her? And the photographs of a child . . .

Her memories of that day were as old and faded as thousand-year-old parchment paper; however, the memory was steadily growing stronger, and she didn't know why. The urge to learn about the circumstances precipitating Adam's violence had long since gone; but all of a sudden, as if a flood light had been turned on, she not only wanted to know but *had* to know.

With much effort, Asabe forced past her apprehension and walked into Adam's bedroom. As if being pulled along by a rope, she headed straight for Adam's desk. Asabe may as well have been following a list of detailed instructions because her hands went without forethought to the top right desk drawer.

The pictures were there, beneath a stack of old mail. The same pretty baby with great happy eyes and buttery skin stared back at her from the first photograph. The second photograph, the one she never really had the opportunity to see in totality, featured not only the child and a Caucasian woman but also . . . Adam. He was young and thin like that Adam in her dreams.

Asabe turned the photograph over. There was no inscription on the photo with Adam and the white woman, but there was an inscription on the photo of the comely child. It read simply, Mu'min 1977.

Mu'min Abdulkadir.

The name came to Asabe again, this time in an urgent shout, though she was unsure as to what it all meant, if anything. She felt the same terribly consuming anxiety as when she was dreaming, running from the young man who demanded that she know him, remember him.

Mu'min Abdulkadir.

The name whispered itself to her in an eerily familiar voice.

Adam has known me forever. And you, Asabe . . . you know me too. Remember me? Look at me. Look at me, and you will know who I am.

"Mu'min?" Asabe said the name aloud, as if the phantom man from her dreams was standing right in front of her. "I am looking at you." And then in a voice as soft as down feathers, she said, "I see you."

She tore open the letter.

Father,

It has been fifteen years, and I'm not sure what to say. Telling you how angry and disappointed I am in you seems oddly inappropriate, though it is the truth, or at least part of the truth.

I have only recently read the many letters you've mailed to me over the years. And only recently have I come to understand the sadness that I would see in my mother's eyes when she thought that no one was looking. Perhaps this is the reason that she never gave me your letters, because she didn't want to see that same sadness in my eyes.

Khadijah, my mother, your one time wife, is now four months dead. I have tried to honor her memory, but even now, time has begun to steal the memory of her away from me. After my mother's death, when I learned of your letters, I determined that by refusing the knowledge of you, I would in fact be doing my mother the highest honor. She kept them from me, and I would follow her wishes.

Soon, curiosity about you tainted my fortitude, and then the realization that without my mother, I was an orphan, unless I chose not to be. I am choosing not to be. The truth is, my anger and disappointment in you does not exceed the affection I once had for you. Even if you don't deserve forgiveness, I deserve a father.

There. I've said far more than I expected I could. I suppose for now there is nothing left to say, so I'll end my letter here.

Your son, Mu'min

Oddly, Asabe found that she was smiling. Relief washed over her like a waterfall. Finally, she understood her husband's desperation, his motives, his true pain. The lie didn't matter to her, for now she knew that his deep hurt was not her fault or Sauda's or his innocent daughters'. The fault lay in his past, the guilty secret he lay down with, completely alone, every night.

Now, Adam would never again have to bear that secret alone.

TWENTY-SEVEN

Adam entered ihram on the seventh night of *Zilhajj*. He put aside his everyday clothes, made of the finest fabrics in the richest colors, and replaced them with the plain garb of the hajj.

Adam stood in front of the mirror. His shoulders and face were still wet from the bath. His loins were wrapped with a piece of white fabric, unsewn and many times more coarse than his expensive garments. He folded the second piece of fabric around his head and shoulders.

Adam seemed different, all his regality and wealth stripped away. His physique seemed less imposing. He looked almost weak. When he saw himself in the mirror, minus the worldly symbols he never considered being without, Adam conceived how insignificant and unessential he was in the world. He had yet to join the hajj, submerging himself in a sea of worshippers dressed like him, hungry just like him for the benevolence of Allah; but already, he understood the purpose of the simplicity of the dress. It was meant to humble him, to make him see that without the trappings of this world, without its glitter, he was just the same as every other man. Flesh and blood. Hopes and dreams. Tragedies and disappointments. Life and death.

Adam did not feel like himself. He felt as if his heart would fly out of his chest. His heart pounded against his rib cage like the wings of a powerful bird, protesting against confinement. He felt ready to submit because he had failed to do so for many months. Joy and fear competed in his belly, each one trying to outdo the other; and he reveled in the joy of it, for this meant that he was alive and that some bit of faith in Allah had remained despite his failure to recognize it.

For nearly a year, Adam had progressively lost his faith, but it wasn't something that he wished for. He wanted to regain his former closeness to Allah, the belief that Allah loved him. Without the anger and disappointment and arrogance obscuring his vision, Adam could see the simple truth. If Allah did not truly love him, he would not have given him trial after trial. He would not have given him chance after chance to redeem himself.

Abu Kareem had done Adam the greatest favor any man could do for another. Abu Kareem opened a door, the very same door Adam had previously closed, locked, and cemented shut. No man can renew another man's faith, but he can help to clear the path.

Adam wished he could share his good fortune with Asabe. She would be as pleased as he was. She would make his revelation, his striping away of faithlessness seem even more glorious.

Abu Kareem entered the room without knocking. He was dressed similarly in the traditional hajj garb. Unlike Adam, the dress seemed to reaffirm Abu Kareem's resoluteness. The weakness of old age retreated behind his spartan dress.

"Hasan is waiting to escort us to Mecca. Are you ready?"

Adam nodded. His eyes remained on his image in the mirror. "Have I thanked you yet, Abu Kareem?"

"I don't want your thanks. The *barakat* are mine, and I accept them from Allah willingly. I just pray that you benefit from this as much as I do." Abu Kareem limped over, resting his hand on Adam's shoulder. "Sauda and Hannah are waiting for us in Brother Hasan's car. Let us go."

Adam closed his eyes tight and inhaled deeply. He felt his spirit rising in the solemn winds of faith and love. He wanted to ingest the feeling, never letting it go, never to sink again to the abysmal depth of malignancy he had just been rescued from. Adam shuddered, as if a freezing blast of wind had swept through the room.

"Adam? They are waiting for us."

"I am ready."

Adam and Abu Kareem joined their wives in the car parked in front of the house. The night sky was clear and pitch. A million stars crowded in the sky. The air was sweetly chilled. There was little conversation on the way to Mecca. Even Hasan ceased his incessant babble. But they chanted the *talbiyah* the entire way.

"Labbaika Allahumma Labbaik!" (Here I am, O Allah, here I am in thy presence. Thou hast no partner; here I am.)

THEY MOVED AROUND THE KAABA, scores of the lowly come to pay homage to the one god. Tears flowed like persistent rivulets of salty ocean water from every humbled eye.

Not a single face was like the other—black, brown, tan, yellow, white, young, old, joyful, placid, mournful. Despite the differences, each intent was the same, to do their duty to Allah before Israel, the angel of death, came to claim their souls.

They circumambulated the Kaaba with swift, ready feet. With each circuit, they felt as if they were closing the immutable miles between themselves and Allah. Just above them, the angels copied the worshippers, circumambulating their own Kaaba in the heavens.

The heart of every supplicant trembled with an intoxicating mix of fear and euphoric hope, for this act of worship is promised by God to wash away all past sins, leaving the worshipper as pure as a newborn babe.

Adam was there, among the sea of humanity, just a minuscule drop of mankind. Nothing, no one worthy of mention. He was more ready than ever in his life to purge himself of the wantonness that stole away his faith in Allah. His face was slick with perspiration and tears. Adam cried for his past, the selfish mistakes that today he still suffers for. He cried for the present, that he was given the opportunity to be a guest of God before his death. Adam cried for tomorrow, that he would become the man he had failed to be for so many years because, thank Allah, it isn't too late.

Adam raced around the Kaaba, steady and strong. Abu Kareem hobbled around the house of God several feet behind. He was unable to keep his son-in-law's steady pace, but with the help of his cane and Hannah's steady hand on his elbow, he didn't drift too far behind.

Sauda walked alongside her husband. They did not speak a single word to each other, but they were closer in spirit and in love than they ever had been. Allah had been good enough to absolve his dutiful guests of the sins that dirtied their souls; therefore, how could the slightest bit of asperity remain between a husband and wife who were bound by the very same god to care for each other?

TWENTY-EIGHT

Mu'min looked out of the living room window as Zainab parked her twenty-five-year-old baby blue Cadillac in the driveway. That car looked as if it just drove off the showroom floor. The car was baby blue now, but it had once been magenta; and the time before that, the car was lime green. No one knew the original color. Zainab was a woman of great modesty and conviction, but she had an eccentric side that manifested itself in the oddest ways.

Mu'min hadn't seen Zainab since his mother's death. She had called every week to ask if he or Zulaikah needed anything, but he had always assured her that they were fine. Even at the times when they were in need, Mu'min would deny it. Seeing Zainab was far too painful.

Zainab had been Khadijah's best friend for more than ten years. They were two women on vastly opposite ends of the human spectrum. Their only similarity was their love of Allah and of fresh baked goods. Zainab had dwarfed Khadijah as she was at least five inches taller and one hundred pounds heavier. Khadijah was a thin woman, even before the illness, with refined European features and milky skin. Zainab was the shape and color of a walnut. Khadijah was quiet and analytical, unlikely to speak her mind. Zainab was loquacious and active and very creative. This made her an ideal business partner.

Sweets for the Sweet, a dessert catering service, was opened only three months after they first met each other. Khadijah was in charge of formulating new recipes, as well as the finances, while Zainab handled the clientele and the management of employees. They were a complementary pair.

Mu'min loved Zainab. She was like a second mother to him. However, despite the great number of their dissimilarities, Zainab was still an enormous reminder to Mu'min of his mother.

Outside, Zainab waved for Mu'min to come out. The day was mild, but the sun hung brilliantly in the sky. Zainab looked hot underneath the flowing brown jilbab and white hijab that was pinned crookedly under her double chin.

Mu'min raced outside in his bare feet. "Ummi. It's good to see you. I missed you."

Zainab placed one palm on the hood of the car and the other on her round hip. "You missed me, eh? Then why haven't you come to visit with me? You know where I live, and you know that you and that pretty little wife of yours are always welcome."

Her voice was light, and a smile played on her full lips, but Mu'min knew that she was serious. She had always been good to him, and he conceded that he owed her a great deal of respect.

"I am guilty as charged, Ummi. I should have come to you."

Zainab smiled broadly. "Grab those bags in the trunk. I'll get the boxes in the front seat."

"What did you do?" asked Mu'min, suspiciously eyeing the open trunk. "I told you before that we are fine. We don't need anything."

"Hush your mouth. A pregnant woman always needs something." Zainab headed toward the house carrying two cake boxes. "Where is the little mother?"

"In the kitchen." Mu'min grabbed three heavy plastic grocery bags from the trunk. "She's been excited about your visit all day."

Zulaikah put away the groceries. Zainab brought fresh cantaloupe, honeydew melon, watermelon slices, strawberries, fresh spinach, mangoes, bananas, beets, apples, oranges, and an assortment of other fresh fruits and vegetables. She also brought a brand-new juicer, insisting that a pregnant woman can never get enough vitamins and minerals. This didn't explain the two exorbitantly rich cakes she brought. One cake was double chocolate cherry fudge, Zainab's specialty and Zulaikah's favorite. The other box contained two loaves of butter pound cake. It was nothing special or terribly creative, but it was Mu'min's favorite cake. It was also once his mother's favorite.

"Won't this cake nullify the vitamins and minerals?" joked Mu'min.

"Nope. A pregnant woman can never get enough good cake either."

Like Khadijah, Zainab was in her element in the kitchen. Mu'min had no choice but to step aside and allow Zainab a space at the counter.

She grabbed a knife from the butcher block on the counter and sliced Zulaikah an enormous piece of cake. Zulaikah's eyes looked like two glass marbles the way she stared at the rich black cake.

Zainab also sliced a piece of cake for Mu'min and poured them both glasses of milk. Mu'min hadn't drunk a glass of milk since before his mother's death.

Zainab took a seat at the table between them. Like a twenty-pound sack of soil on top of a narrow barstool, Zainab overflowed from the seat. She watched them both intently, urging them to accept second helpings of the cake.

"Won't you have a piece of cake?" asked Zulaikah.

"Nope. I'm trying to lose some weight." Zainab patted her side. "Besides, I didn't come here to eat or to watch the two of you eat for that matter."

Mu'min sensed an edge in Zainab's voice. She was an easy woman to read. Her face was placid, and her small round eyes grew cloudy and narrow. Right now, she was serious.

"What's on your mind, Ummi?" Mu'min was curious and a little apprehensive at the same time.

"The two of you. Your future. Your baby."

"Ummi, you don't have to worry about us. We are fine. I promise you. I should be the one worrying about you, not the other way around.

You are the closest thing I have to a mother." Mu'min no longer had the taste for cake.

"Your mother, how I miss her, was very special to me. After my husband died and my girls were married, I felt more alone than I ever had in my life. Khadijah and our business became a welcome distraction from my loneliness. And you," she said, eyeing Mu'min, "became like my own son."

Zulaikah reached across the table to hold Zainab's hand, but she pulled away.

"I'm not going to break down and cry, if that's what you're thinking."

"Of course not," said Zulaikah, although she was unconvinced.

"Sweets for the Sweet isn't so sweet these days without your mother there. I'm no good at keeping the books, and to be frank, I don't like doing numbers anyway."

"I can come down anytime you like to do the books for you. All you have to do is ask. You know that, don't you?"

Mu'min suddenly felt very selfish. He should have been able to put his feelings of loss aside. He should have long recognized that he was not the only person who loved his mother and grieved over her passing.

"Ummi—"

Zainab silenced Mu'min with a wave of her hand. "There is no need for you to help me and especially no need to apologize. I have taken care of everything. Three days ago, I sold Sweets for the Sweet for a lot of dinero."

Zainab reached beneath the chair for her pocketbook and deposited it on top of the table. It was overstuffed and heavy, like Khadijah's used to be, but she knew exactly where to find the envelope. She slid the envelope across the table to Mu'min.

"This is your mother's half. Your half." She urged Mu'min to open the envelope, which he did reluctantly. "This should be more than enough to take care of yourself and your wife and the child you will bring into this world."

"I'll say," said Mu'min, handing the check to Zulaikah.

"Seventy-eight thousand dollars?" Zulaikah's mouth fell open. "That's a lot of money. Do you know what we could do with all of this money?"

Zainab seemed pleased. "I hope you don't mind me doing this. Maybe I should have consulted with you first."

"No, no, I don't mind." Mu'min wasn't so sure though.

"Believe me, I gave it a lot of thought. I decided to do this for one very important reason."

Zainab waited for Mu'min to question her, he knew she was, but he was afraid to ask. Zainab was a good woman, kind and thoughtful. She would never do anything to harm or begrudge even her greatest enemy; however, her intentions rarely matched her actions. With a seventy-eight-thousand-dollar check in hand, her actions didn't seem so bad. It was her intent that suddenly put fear into his heart.

Recognizing the thickening tension, Zulaikah excused herself for the bathroom. Zainab offered Zulaikah a grateful smile. Mu'min wished she would stay, guard him from knowing too much, from hearing what he wasn't sure he wanted to hear, to lessen the blow.

Zainab wasted little time. "Did you find the letters from your father yet?"

As if by command, beads of perspiration pooled on Mu'min's brow. He tried to speak, tried to breathe, tried to respond in any intelligible way. He could not. Zainab removed another glass from the cabinet and poured Mu'min a glass of cold water. Mu'min quaffed down the eight ounces of water in seconds.

"You're surprised that I know?"

Mu'min nodded because that is all he could manage.

"This last time, when your mother got sick, I asked her, no, I begged her to sell the business. I thought that it would be too much for her. She was so sick. She refused to sell. She said that it was the only thing that kept her mind off her problems. When you know that you are dying, can feel a tiny part of you surrender to illness each day, how do you keep it together? You really can't. You have Allah, you have a son who has his own life, and you have a business that is your revenue and your worldly passion. She spent her nights with Allah, and her days at work, when she could."

"She never told me how much she was suffering. She never told me about my father. Why?" For the first time, a twinge of anger and resentment surfaced in his heart. How could she keep all this from him? How could she?

"Why would she tell you about the illness?"

"I'm her son!" Mu'min was startled by the volume of his voice. His hands trembled.

"Which is why she never told you. Mothers want to spare their children the hardships and the realities of life. Your mother was no different. She protected you from her pain. She bore it alone, for your sake."

"What was she protecting me from when she kept me from my father?"

Zainab smiled and reached across the table to pat Mu'min's head as if he was still the thirteen-year-old boy she'd first met ten years ago.

"That is definitely one of your mother's greatest mysteries. She told me about your father and about the letters. She told me how she kept you from the knowledge of him, and she knew that she was wrong. Your mother wanted you to know him, she did, but I don't think she knew how to do that without destroying herself in the process."

Mu'min readied himself to interrupt, it didn't make sense to him, but Zainab held her finger to her lips, silencing him.

"Don't ask me how or why or what for or any of that because I just don't know. I don't know. What I can tell you is that before your mother died, she told me how much she wished she could go back and change things, give your father back to you. Coming between you two was her greatest mistake and her greatest regret."

Mu'min held his face in his hands, unsure if he should laugh, cry, or throw the glass across the kitchen smashing it in a million pieces.

"As it stands, I knew that if you found those letters you would probably not consider going to see your father. You would say that you didn't have enough money. You'd try to stay away, show how loyal you could be to your mother. Am I right?"

"Maybe."

"I take it that means yes. I've known you for ten years, little boy. I know you about as well as I knew your mother."

"So is this why you sold the business? You wanted to make sure that I had the money to go see my father?"

"That was the most important reason, but not the only one. Like I said, the joy left with your mother. I'm not good at running the show alone."

"I would have helped you."

Zainab shook her head. "You're not your mother. You would only have done it because I asked you, not because you have a fondness for the business, like your mom did. And I wouldn't have enjoyed you as much either." Zainab tried to smile, but it fell away like crumbs from a dry cookie.

"You sold the business because I'm not a good-enough replacement for my mother?"

"You really are angry, aren't you?"

Mu'min shrugged his shoulders. "Wouldn't you be?"

"Perhaps, but I would also feel very lucky. You had a mother who loved you, and judging from the letters, you have a father who still loves you. Your father is still alive. It isn't too late."

"Maybe not, but it is still my decision."

"Yes, it is. Which is why I gave my decision a lot of thought. My mom and dad are nearing the end of their years. I've decided to go back to New York and take care of them. I'm leaving at the end of this week."

THE DECISION WAS NEVER CONSCIOUS. Mu'min did not confide in Zulaikah, nor did he procure anyone's advice. He did not mull it over in his head or stay up nights considering the levity of his decision. Mu'min actually gave it little thought. He was, in fact, more than a little surprised when he found himself parked out in front of the Mirage Travel Agency, with two thousand dollars in cash stuffed into his cheap nylon wallet. It was almost as if he had sleepwalked there.

Perhaps it was something that Zainab had said to him that day two weeks ago when she handed him more money than he could make in three years. Perhaps it was the way he felt the last time he visited his mother's grave, sad, sorry, desperate, and curious all at once. Perhaps it was the times when Zulaikah, after promising never to broach the subject of his father again, did so anyway because for some reason he couldn't fathom, it meant more to her than it did to him. Maybe it was the wispy, smoky memories he had of his father, a giant in the eyes of the child, a hero, a saint. Or it could have been the cryptic thoughtful statement his grandfather had made about his father. *I think he might have. I think* is what Charles Brady said when Mu'min asked him if his father had loved him. It could have been the letter he received only three hours earlier from Asabe by way of DHL, begging him to come *home* and forgive his father, make his father's greatest dream come true. Or maybe his mind had long since been made up, but he just didn't know it.

Mu'min was going to see his father, that part of him that was missing, that he tried to ignore was gone all his life. He was going to make the reservations now, before he lost the nerve, before he was able to bethink another excuse for why he could not go. Perhaps this is why his unconscious mind had taken over, cutting off the part of him that would find a reason to thwart the reunion.

A burly pink-faced man with platinum hair greeted Mu'min at the door and escorted him down a hall to his office. The office was tiny, little more than a box with a window. It was much too small for the giant man. The walls were covered from ceiling to floor with posters of exotic destinations all over the world. The office smelled reminiscent of stale cigars. The nameplate on his desk read Dusty River.

"What can I do ya for?" Dusty laughed hardily at his misuse of English. His face was as shiny and red as an apple. Dusty offered Mu'min a seat and then stuffed himself into the chair behind his desk and pushed up, depositing his stomach on top of the desk.

"I want to go to Diourbel, Senegal."

"Oh yeah? Why ya wanna go there?"

Mu'min sat up straight and said nothing.

"None of my business, eh?"

Still silence.

Dusty's fingers moved swiftly over the keyboard. He squinted his eyes at the screen. "There isn't an airport in Diourbel, but I can get you to Dakar. Once you get there, you can hire yourself a car."

"That's fine. As long as I get there."

"Is this a vacation? Business or pleasure?"

"I'm not sure yet."

"Oh? Sounds awfully mysterious." Dusty raised his right eyebrow.

"It isn't so mysterious. I'm going to visit my father." *Father?*

"Oh. One of those kinds of trips," said Dusty, as if he knew Mu'min's life story. He typed some more and then asked, "When do you want to leave?"

"Soon. Within the next week."

TWENTY-NINE

Adam hung up the telephone and leaned back on the bed with his arms propped under his head. He closed his eyes, lulled into a trance by the muffled splatter of the shower running in the bathroom next door. He replayed his conversation with Asabe over in his mind.

It was a rather sparse conversation, lasting no more than three or four minutes. He had called Asabe only to inform her that the hajj was finished. He told her that he and Sauda were staying over in a hotel in Jeddah and that they would be leaving for Senegal tomorrow. Abu Kareem and Hannah were resting in their room two doors down the hall.

She seemed pleased to hear this. Asabe assured him that his daughters were well and that they had asked of him every day. She even professed her love for him, something she had not done in a very long while.

But this is not what stirred long dormant emotions within him. The emotions he experienced were intuitive, understanding that something was different in his wife. At first, Adam suspected that the change he sensed was his own; but soon enough, he knew that it was not. No matter how Adam tried to manipulate the conversation in his memory, he could not identify a single word or remark that was outstanding, that spoke to the sense he got when speaking with her.

Adam realized that it was not what Asabe said but that it was her. Something indescribable and still unknown had changed and had revealed itself to him in the very cadence of her voice, through the thousands of miles of telephone lines between them. Adam perceived a contentment, a self-assurance, a consciousness within Asabe that had not been there before.

Her voice echoed in his head, like a sweet haunting melody. Before he called home, his desire to return was a low-burning flame, but now it was a raging fire. He wasn't simply curious to be home with his first wife, to learn what had transformed her and had made him want to be with her more than he ever had. Adam also missed the predictability of home and work and friends and even days filled with nothing at all except his prayers and his wives and children.

After two weeks, it was time to return home. When he returned, he would be the husband that his wives deserved and the father that his daughters needed.

A son? Adam had not yet given up; the possibility still crept in the shadowy recesses in his mind. There, it would remain. A son would come if Allah made it so, and no sooner. That was good enough for Adam. It would have to be.

Sauda stepped from the bathroom, a cloud of steam billowing behind her. The scent of lilacs and roses sweetened her entrance. If she wasn't his wife, he might not have recognized her. She was no longer the ponderous, arrogant imp he married nearly two years ago. Her old attitude was shed with the same slow ease as her weight.

Since the birth of Lailah, the disappointment of it, the lies surrounding it, when Adam assured Sauda of how little she meant to him, she changed. She seemed to lose that part of her that was willing to fight for anything she wanted. She lost the temperament that gave her strength, but not more than after she lost their son. The day they committed that tiny body to the earth, she took leave of Adam. She took leave of herself, retreating like a turtle in his shell.

Sauda sat down on the edge of the bed dressed in a green caftan that was far too large for her. Beads of hot shower water dripped from the ends of her braids.

"Did you finally reach Asabe?"

"Yes, she says that the girls are fine. That is what you were going to ask, isn't it?"

"I miss my daughter."

"I know you do."

Adam sat up and scooted forward on the bed next to his wife. They sat together, thigh to thigh. It was the most physical contact they'd had in months. Sauda shrank away like a frightened mouse. Her reaction puzzled Adam. A year ago, she longed for this, would have accepted less even. Her new behavior, shrinking and shy with her husband, was his fault, his doing.

"You and I, we haven't been very good together since—"

"Since the start," finished Sauda.

"How do you feel about that."

Sauda turned to look her husband in the face. He wasn't the man she married nearly two years ago, but this was *her* doing. She was blind then, seeing Adam as a man with no faults, seeing herself as the woman who would encapsulate him with her love, make him want her alone. Today she could see. Sauda saw Adam as he was, cleanly and honestly. He was only a man, with weaknesses and faults and desires, just as she was only a woman. Their only difference had been their wants. Sauda had wanted Adam while he had wanted what he hoped she could give him.

"I feel like any woman would. I feel as if I have been cheated, only it was me who cheated myself."

"I know how that feels."

"I also feel . . . content. I feel right. That is also from myself."

Adam moved closer to his wife, again thigh to thigh. He took her hand in his.

"Do you think that we could ever be good together, to each other?"

Sauda stared ahead, afraid to meet her husband's persistent gaze, afraid to give in to the sweet stroking syllables of his words, his voice.

"I think we can," he answered on his own. "I know I can. I know that I want to." Adam spoke the truth. He wanted this wife of his.

"Since when?"

"Does that matter?"

Sauda finally met her husband's gaze; she saw something real and honest in his eyes. She liked the man she saw. She trusted that man.

"No. I suppose it doesn't matter at all."

CHARLES BRADY stood in front of the mirror, turning from side to side. Too big, too round, too bald, too old looking, too . . . a little of everything he didn't want to be.

He tore off the green tie; it made him look pallid. He chose instead the soft brown tie from the rack in his closet.

"Good choice," remarked Margaret from the doorway. "It looks better next to your skin."

"I was thinking the same thing." Charles was glad to have her there, echoing his feelings and thoughts, knowing as if she shared his soul, exactly how he felt.

Charles fumbled with the tie, his thick fingers inept for anything these days except skewering worms on hooks and hammering nails. Margaret sensed her husband's growing frustration and rushed to help him.

She was smiling that crooked smile she always had when she was nervous or worried. She was just as anxious as her husband.

"I haven't seen you wear a tie since your aunt Sissy passed away. That had to be a good ten years ago."

"I'm going to see my grandson today, and I want to look good. No law against looking good, is there?"

Margaret tightened the knot on the tie, too tight.

"Jeez, Maggie. You trying to choke me?"

"No. Just trying to squeeze some sense into that head of yours."

Charles yanked open the bureau drawer and removed his best dress socks, his only dress socks. He hadn't worn them for ten years either. He unfolded the socks to find that both had a hole in the toe.

"What happened? You don't darn socks no more?"

"No. I'm a liberated woman. Can't you tell?" Margaret raised her fist into the air like a militant.

"Stop with the jokes, Maggie. Can't you see how important this is to me?"

"It's only a ride to the airport, not an invitation to dinner. If his truck hadn't've broke down at the last minute, you wouldn't be running around in this bedroom making a fool of yourself."

"It could maybe lead to more. With Karen gone, he's all that's left of me."

Margaret searched the drawer and finally succeeded in finding a pair of socks without holes. They were white.

"What am I going to look like wearing white socks with black pants, a blue shirt, and a brown tie? These won't go."

"What you'll look like is the backwoods, redneck, hick that you are. You didn't really think that you were color coordinated, did you?"

Charles flopped down on the bed, which creaked under the stress. Margaret watched her husband's face, all red and puffy, and she couldn't read him for the first time in their lives together.

"Charles Eugene? Are you going to cry?"

"You sure would like to see that, wouldn't you?"

"And destroy my image of you? Mr. Superman, Mr. Macho Macho Man?"

Charles relented and pulled on the white socks. "I expected you to be happy for me, for us. Do you know how many times I wished that he would call us?"

"I know, I know. I've wished the same thing."

"Then why aren't you taking this seriously?"

"I guess I just don't want you to set yourself up for a heartbreak."

"He called me, remember?"

"How could I forget? But months have passed since you first saw him, and he is only just calling you. Not to invite you to his home, not to ask your advice, not even to see how you are doing. He needs a ride to the airport. That's all. Don't read more into it than is there. And for goodness' sake, don't try to make yourself over in ten minutes to impress him. He knows who you are and, unfortunately, everything that you are about. If you go to him looking like some badly dressed game show host, he's going to know that you're putting on airs. No one, and I mean no one, respects a fake, especially an obvious fake such as yourself."

"You sure don't spare feelings, do you?"

Margaret shrugged her shoulders. In the large walk-in closet, she removed a pair of sharply pressed Levi's blue jeans and a nicely starched shirt with a button-down collar. She carried these to the bed and laid them out for Charles as she had done all his clothes since their marriage. She returned to the closet to retrieve Charles's brown Stetson and the thousand-dollar cowboy boots she had commissioned for him five years ago. He wore them only on special occasions. This was a special occasion.

"Put these on, and you'll look very handsome and very much like yourself."

It took Charles less than five minutes to dress because it was easier this time. After he splashed on his favorite cologne and groomed his comb-over, he was ready to go.

Margaret stood at the edge of the driveway as her husband pulled out into the street. He waved as he drove away, but Margaret didn't see him. Her eyes were closed as she spoke a silent prayer asking God to make Mu'min be kind and accepting of her husband because he wanted it so much.

Once, Margaret had begged Charles to go visit Karen, if only to see the boy, but he had refused. Who would have ever thought that now, he would be sweating nervous about seeing him, desperate to make a good impression, hoping upon all hopes that he could have his grandson in his life, despite all his bigotry and anger? Who would have thought?

THIRTY

Mu'min was the last person to disembark the airplane. He walked cautiously down the steps to the tarmac behind a small woman carrying a chubby toddler in her arms. The toddler had screamed, cried, and whined the entire flight from Paris, only to finally drop off to sleep five minutes before the airplane made its descent. The woman looked as if she would collapse any moment, but the relief was evident on not only her face but also the face of every other passenger as well.

The flight had been long, from Houston to Paris, and then a connecting flight to Dakar, all in sixteen hours. Despite this, Mu'min was not tired. He checked his watch; it was four in the evening back home. Here in Senegal, it was eleven at night. Despite the late hour, the small airport buzzed with traffic. Mu'min watched as two airplanes landed on the runway after his own. Another plane made a slow, steady incline and then disappeared behind the black curtain of night.

The sky was clear, the blackest blue, the stars like blinking lights on neon signs. The sky was not like this at home, so pristine and vast that if you tilted your head back far enough, you'd feel about to drown. On a conscious level, Mu'min knew that Africa was not the big steamy jungle television hype would have him believe; still, he was nonetheless surprised to find that the air was a bit nippy.

Three male stewards in blue and red uniforms stood at the landing of the motile steps, directing the passengers across the tarmac and into the airport terminal. The over two hundred passengers walked to the terminal in a slow, steady line like ants. Mu'min followed.

When Mu'min stepped onto the plane almost an entire day ago, he possessed every classic symptom of nervousness. His palms were damp, his knees were weak, and his mouth was dry. He remained that way almost the entire flight. When the pilot announced in unsure English that they would be landing in fifteen minutes, every emotion drained away as if a plug had been pulled.

Mu'min was devoid of any emotion, as cool and dry as an arctic wind. He liked it that way because when he finally faced his father, he would have control of his emotions. Maybe he'd even be able to forgive.

He wasn't sure how far Diourbel was from Dakar. Dusty River had estimated it was close to four hundred miles. Regardless, after flying more than three thousands miles and landing in two different countries that smelled and sounded and felt so unlike home, four hundred miles seemed like only inches.

Mu'min waited an hour for his single piece of luggage to appear on the swiftly moving carousel. Another hour was spent negotiating with the immigration and customs agents. Everyone wanted a little something from the American, a few dollars to make his passage worthwhile.

When the customs officer finally handed Mu'min his old duffel bag, he was accosted by two enthusiastic teenagers, both vying for the privilege of carrying his luggage. He had wondered earlier why they were watching him from a corner near the bathrooms, whispering and snickering to each other from time to time. They had probably been discussing the best way to get large denomination bills from the generous American.

Both were about fourteen or fifteen years old, dirty and disheveled, smelling of days-old sweat, speaking fragmentary bits of English.

"We carry you bag," said the bigger of the two.

"No, thank you," said Mu'min. He reached into his pocket and handed each of them a five-dollar bill and a stick of gum, hoping to assuage their curiosity and desire to help him. Mu'min kept his bag. Dusty River had warned him not to let his bag out of his sight if he intended to keep it.

With his bag on his shoulder, Mu'min walked off into the crowd in search a car-rental booth or office. The numbers of people grew as he moved deeper into the airport. Mu'min was struck by the people themselves. Men and women, speaking French and English and African languages he'd never heard. All of them beautiful, all people of color.

Mu'min stopped to look around him. He spotted only two white faces in the entire crowd. Everyone else looked like him, the him his father had contributed—brown and tan and sable and copper skins. Already, Senegal proved to be a different world.

The two young men had followed Mu'min. "Why you don't let us take bag? We can help." They smiled up at Mu'min. The five dollars had served only to ignite their persistence. Where there was an American with five dollars, there had to be more.

"No," said Mu'min. He moved forward through the crowd. On the lower level at the far end of the terminal, a security guard in a blue-and-green uniform stood by the tall glass exit doors. Mu'min headed for him.

When the two teens saw the direction in which Mu'min was headed, they darted through a group of men and out of a side entrance.

Mu'min approached the security officer. He seemed more interested in his conversation with a smiling young woman than securing the airport. Mu'min didn't wait for the sagacious officer to finish his conversation. "Excuse me."

The officer glanced up at Mu'min, seemingly annoyed with the interruption. The young lady walked away. "Yes?" replied the officer in his thickly accented voice. He sounded like an arrogant maitre d' at a posh French restaurant.

"Where can I find a car-rental office?"

"Car rental?" The officer looked Mu'min over from foot to head, a smug incredulous expression on his face.

"Yes, I've just arrived from the United States. I need to get to Diourbel."

"Oh, you need a car. Yes?" His face grew as animated as a cartoon character's. He held out his hand. "I can help you find a car. Take you all the way to Diourbel. Take you anywhere you want to go. Yes?" The officer smiled broadly, his yellow teeth like lemon drops. He pushed his hand out farther, until his fingertips grazed Mu'min's chest.

"Yes, a car." Mu'min reached again into his pocket and retrieved his wallet. He handed the officer a twenty-dollar bill.

"You follow me," said the smiling officer.

Outside, the officer pointed to a long line of taxicabs, most marked with a company logo, some unmarked private vehicles. The drivers leaned on the hoods of their vehicles, beneath the glaring lights of the airport, shooing away moths, waiting for the next weary traveler to exit the terminal. As soon as they saw Mu'min, the well-dressed American, they swarmed over him like bees.

"They will take you to Diourbel. Anywhere you want to go." The grinning officer disappeared behind the veil of men.

ABU KAREEM SHOOK CHIEF BILAL IBRAHIM'S HAND and thanked him profusely. Had it not been for the chief's intervention, they would have had to stand in line for more than an hour to see the immigration and customs officers. Chief Bilal Ibrahim, director of the Leopold S. Senghor Airport, was one of Abu Kareem's many influential friends. As with most of Abu Kareem's friends, the chief owed him more than he could ever repay.

They stood by the main entrance of the airport. Hannah and Sauda stood a few feet behind the men, huddled close to each other to stave off the increasingly cool air.

"It's late, Abu Kareem. Why don't you and your family stay with me tonight. You can leave for Diourbel tomorrow after you all have rested."

"I appreciate your kind offer, but I called ahead before leaving Saudi Arabia to be sure that my driver would meet us."

Abu Kareem looked down the road in hopes of catching a glimpse of the black limousine. It was possible that his driver was already at the airport; however, with the predominance of taxicabs parked nose to end at the curb, there was nowhere for anyone else to park.

"In fact, he may already be here."

"That is possible," agreed the chief. He pointed at the eight-tiered parking garage in the distance to the left. "There is a section on the third floor where personal drivers often park when waiting for their charges. From there, they can see their master as they exit the building."

Abu Kareem turned to Adam. "We've been waiting nearly fifteen minutes. Maybe he has fallen asleep. Do you mind going to look for him?"

Adam left immediately.

Abu Kareem turned his attention back to his friend. "Why don't you regulate the number of taxis allowed to park in front? They seriously impede the flow of traffic. Common people like myself aren't able to get out of the airport in a timely manner."

"You are correct; however, these men are the poor and working class. Would you have me put them out of business?"

"No. I suppose not, but you've got to do something about the situation."

Ten yards away, an exasperated-looking young man was struggling to fend off a group of taxicab drivers who had surrounded him like a flock of vultures. They were arguing among each other about who would have the right to this fare.

"I take you Diourbel for five hundred American dollars!" shouted one of the men.

Another man, wearing a blue baseball cap with Yale printed on top in bold letters, pushed him out of the way. "No no no. No listen to him. You listen to me. I take you for four hundred and seventy-five dollars."

Abu Kareem pointed at the crowd. "You see? This is exactly the type of behavior that I am talking about. That young man is trying to get to Diourbel in peace, but before he gets there, he will be mauled by a bunch of sharks on a feeding frenzy." Abu Kareem headed forward as quickly as his heavy feet and cane would allow.

This got Hannah's attention. "Where are you going?"

"To help that young man."

"It's bad enough that you have to stand around for twenty minutes waiting for your driver. You've had a long flight. Please don't exert yourself any further."

"I'll be fine." Abu Kareem waved her away. The chief followed behind him. "I expect you to reprimand these men. Their behavior is not only disgusting but a disgrace to our national image and morale."

"What do you intend to do?" The chief wanted to know.

"The question is what *you* intend to do. I am going to save that young man before he loses all of his money and his senses."

The chief left in search of a security officer.

Abu Kareem pushed into the center of the crowd. He waved his cane from left to right, inadvertently striking the Yale baseball cap–wearing man in the shin. "Leave him alone." Abu Kareem led the young man out of the crowd and down the sidewalk to where he was previously standing.

No one was willing to argue with old Abu Kareem. The men quickly dispersed, some cursing under their breath. The chief returned with three security guards who cited the few drivers that hadn't already driven off.

"I sincerely apologize, sir," said the chief. The chief offered his apology more to diminish Abu Kareem's annoyance rather than the young man's.

"I hear that you are trying to go to Diourbel." Abu Kareem smiled warmly, hoping to ease the young man's obvious distress.

"Yes, I was hoping to rent a car or, at the very least, to hire a taxi. As you can see, I am not doing very well. Is it me? Do I have the word *fool* printed on my forehead?"

Abu Kareem was amused by the young man's accent. He recognized the accent as being American with a Midwest twang. Abu Kareem was fond of old black-and-white westerns. The young man sounded like a cowboy.

"Where are you from?"

"The United States. I just flew in tonight. The flight was so long, I wondered if I'd ever make it here."

Abu Kareem patted the young man's shoulder. He was a large man, solid and strong with an open, honest face, although Abu Kareem sensed that there was a darker agenda hidden beneath the young man's casual demeanor.

"What brings you to my country of Senegal?"

The young man shrugged his shoulders. "I've been asking myself that question ever since I stepped foot on the airplane back home in Texas."

Abu Kareem was intrigued. "Surely you didn't come across the world for nothing. I heard something about you going to Diourbel?"

"Yes. My father lives in Diourbel. I haven't seen him in fifteen years."

"So you're going for a reunion?"

"I'm not sure what you would call it. He doesn't know that I am coming."

"I have lived in Diourbel all of my life, more than sixty years. Perhaps I know him. Tell me, what is his name?"

A horn signaled behind them. A black limousine pulled up to the curb next to them. It gleamed in the blinding lights surrounding the airport's entrance. Adam stepped out from the front passenger seat. "You were right, Abu Kareem. Your driver was sleeping soundly behind the wheel."

The driver held open the back door to allow Sauda and Hannah to take their seats inside. He then made his apologies for the delay and returned to his seat behind the wheel.

Adam joined old Abu Kareem and his new friend.

"Allow me to give you a ride into Diourbel. We have plenty of space."

The young man silently considered Abu Kareem's offer. "I wouldn't want to inconvenience your family."

"Of course not. It's no inconvenience at all."

"You had better take the offer, or Abu Kareem will not leave you in peace," added Adam jokingly.

The young man relented. "Fine. I would be honored to accept the invitation."

"Good." Abu Kareem already liked the young man. "As you have probably guessed, my name is Abu Kareem, and this is my son-in-law, Adam." Abu Kareem extended his hand. "What is your name?"

The young man shook Abu Kareem's hand and then Adam's. "I'm glad to meet you both. My name is Mu'min Adam Abdulkadir."

Epilogue

Mu'min stepped from the passenger seat of Jabar's new red Honda into the rain. He removed the brown suitcase from the trunk and set it on the ground in front of him. At Asabe's request, Jabar met Mu'min at the airport and escorted him to his father's home. He surmised from Jabar's taciturn resistance to revealing any real news of his father's condition that Asabe had made him promise to hold his silence. This made the three-hour drive from the Dakar-Yoff-Leopold Senghor International Airport difficult and slightly tense. After telling Jabar about his family and work, there was nothing else between them to talk about, except his father.

Mu'min looked around, pleasure and disappointment welling up in his chest like unfurling wings. Nothing about his father's home had changed since his third and last visit almost four years ago. The bowed branches of the two mango trees that flanked the entrance were heavy with ripe fruit. The yard of white gravel appeared gray in the rain. The air had a sweet, slightly musty quality so thick he could almost taste it. This was his father's home, his home in effect; but now as with each other visit, he still felt somehow alien to this place. He still felt as if he did not belong.

Mu'min always wondered what the outcome would have been had his father not abandoned him, if he had traveled home with his father since he was a child, had known this home and the people of this country, the relatives that he now knew well, but who had not taken up residence in his heart. Nothing of this place had ever remained with him when he went home because even though his father had said and done everything in his power to prove otherwise, Mu'min still felt as if he was only a visitor. His only connection was to Adam, as tenuous as that relationship was.

Jabar called out from the car, "Tell him I will come tonight after Maghrib. Tell him, understand?" Mu'min nodded absently and waved his father's friend off without a second thought.

Mu'min could see Asabe as she stood looking out of one of the red-trimmed arched windows that had always looked to Mu'min like the mouth of a laughing woman. Moments after she disappeared from the window, the front door flew open, and she came rushing out. She stopped in front of him, her face streaked with wet from the steady rain.

Looking into her face, glowing with both happiness and sorrow, Mu'min was struck with the overwhelming urge to embrace this woman, but propriety and modesty would not allow this. Despite being only a few years older than himself, Mu'min regarded Asabe in every degree as a mother figure. With wisdom rarely granted to one as young, she had been instrumental in uniting him with his father, the final impetus to convince him to come to Senegal that first time seven years ago. When that first visit had threatened to end in misunderstanding, because forgiveness is only easy for those who preach about it, Asabe spoke to him with the kind of mellifluous influence that only a mother or a lover could have over a man.

"I had no idea," said Mu'min. His eyes went from her glistening face to her belly.

Asabe nodded and smiled up at Mu'min. "It will be soon." Her hand went to her pregnant bump, but her eyes never left Mu'min. "I hope this one looks as much like Adam as you."

At this, Mu'min's throat grew tight. Not even Zulaikah could bring him so close to tears with so few words. He closed his eyes for a moment.

"It seems that each time you visit, Allah blesses me with a child. I believe that each pregnancy, each child, is a special gift to me from Allah for bringing you and Adam together."

Mu'min opened his eyes. "How is he?" His voice was thick.

Asabe's face brightened. "What a couple of fools we are to be standing in the rain. Let us go in." Before Mu'min could respond, Asabe grabbed his single piece of luggage and headed toward the house. She didn't move like a woman eight months pregnant.

Asabe set the bag down just inside the front door and waited for him to enter before closing it. Nothing had changed inside the house either. The air smelled of cloves and plumes of amber smoke of myrrh swirled in the foyer.

"I smell your tea," said Mu'min, smiling. Memories of Asabe's expertly cooked dishes came back to him. His mouth watered with latent thoughts of her spicy lamb stew with rice, her special tea, her coconut cookies. Mu'min glanced around and was immediately struck by the absence of sound. The silence was so dense it was almost palpable. His smile faltered. "Where is everyone?"

"Everyone?" Asabe's strong, smooth face seemed in that moment to lose years. She looked like a child, confused and lost. Then she seemed just as quickly to find herself. She straightened, pulling her shoulders back. "They are with Adam."

"I should see him."

Asabe nodded, her face in shadows as the clouds outside shifted, blocking the light coming in through the windows. "Yes, but I must speak to you first. You must be warned about what to expect." She headed down the corridor to the left. "Come, let us have tea. Let us talk."

Asabe shifted in her chair as she watched Mu'min take a bite of a coconut cookie. She had placed a plate heaping with them on the table in front of him, along with a brass teapot and tiny glass teacups. "Good?" she asked.

Mu'min nodded. He was sure that the cookie was good, but his mouth was dry and tasted faintly of bile, but he couldn't tell her that. "Aren't you going to have some?"

"No." She sighed. "How is your family?"

Zulaikah and their two sons, Ibrahim and Idris, had been a joy for the last eight years. They still lived in his mother's home, and he had finished college and now owned his own landscaping business, Flowers of Faith.

Zuliakah had remained home and helped him around the office by answering phones and running errands when the boys were in school. His family was healthy, and he was happy with them, but he was not going to talk about that now.

"My father. What has happened to him?"

Asabe opened her mouth, but no sound came out. Her eyes shifted to a place over his left shoulder. Mu'min swiveled around in his chair and saw two girls enter the dining room. They were both wearing red and white flowered dresses. Both had heads full of tight plaits and tiny gold balls in their pierced ears. These two girls, his sisters, were the same ages as his sons, seven and four years old. Mu'min looked from the girls to Asabe. "Don't tell me," he said, his eyes widening, "that these two pretty girls are Safiyyah and Saba."

Asabe nodded. "I have been blessed," she said with a proud smile on her lips. Mu'min couldn't blame her. Asabe had waited thirteen years for her first child, thinking that Allah had ignored her pleas. Now she had two daughters that were the very image of her, as if Adam had not been involved in their conception.

The eldest of the girls, Safiyyah, stood next to her mother, her head resting on her shoulder. The youngest of the girls climbed up into Mu'min's lap. She held his face in her two tiny hands and looked into his eyes. "Mu'min?" she asked. Her black eyes twinkled.

"She knows me?"

"I have been telling them about their elder brother since they could understand. She knows you as well as anyone." She stroked Safiyyah's back then used her thumb to smooth down the unruly edges of the girl's hair. "When I told them you were coming . . ." Her voice trailed off. "When I told Adam, he opened his eyes. He smiled."

Since being told that he should come to his father, Mu'min had envisioned dozens of different scenarios. Asabe had refused to divulge the details. She would only say that Adam was unwell, but no more, insisting that she didn't want to worry Mu'min too badly. Mu'min understood her reasoning, but the effect had been unbearable. Of course he had made immediate arrangements, booking a flight within three days and flying out of Houston two days after that.

He had imagined that his father had been in a car accident and that he was paralyzed, permanently crippled, breathing with the help of a machine. Understandably, this idea brought back the nightmarish vision of his mother's death, the way the cancer had taken over, sapping her of her flesh, her strength, and the light in her eyes. This made Mu'min wonder if his father too had been afflicted by the same horrendous disease, and it was in that moment that he contemplated not coming to Senegal because he knew he could not tolerate seeing his father suffer and die in the same useless fashion, with no choices and no power. When his imagination had gotten the better of him, catapulting him into uncertainty, into sickening fear, Zulaikah had been his comfort and his voice of reason. Zulaikah had reminded him that he did not have the details and that every awful thing that he had envisioned could be wrong. Zulaikah had forced Mu'min to sit, and as she did with their boys when they were upset, she pushed his head into her lap and massaged his temples and the nape of his neck until he could think more reasonably. He would only know his father's condition when he arrived in Senegal, and until then, he would have to have faith that whatever Allah makes is what is best. He had always believed this, but Zulaikah made him remember this. She helped him return to himself.

But now, as Asabe eluded to his father and some of those visions came back on a tide of fear, Mu'min knew he could only stay afloat if he had answers. Knowledge of his father's condition would give him power over his fears.

"What has happened to my father?" Mu'min remained controlled, but from the resignation in his voice, Asabe understood that he would not accept anything other than direct answers.

Asabe sighed, sounding as if she had been holding her breath for a long time. "A stroke."

Mu'min's heart quickened. A stroke? This was easy, wasn't it? People recovered from strokes every day. Zulaikah's uncle Zachariah had a stroke a year ago. He wasn't totally back to normal, but he could take care of himself and had returned to work as a mechanic within three months.

"Then he'll be all right. He'll recover."

Asabe smiled the kind of smile one wears when placating a child having a tantrum or an unhinged person blabbering gibberish. "It will not be as easy as that, I think."

"Why?"

The child sitting on Mu'min's lap slid to the floor and reached up to the table to remove one of the coconut cookies. Safiyyah followed her younger sister's example and took a cookie from the plate then whispered in her mother's ear while sneaking glances at Mu'min. Asabe nodded. "Take two more for Lailah and Hadizah." Safiyyah took two more cookies then her sister's hand and led her from the room.

Asabe turned her attention back to Mu'min. "He recovered nicely from the first stroke. But there have been three, and he has been worse with each one."

"Three? What do you mean?" Mu'min's voice rose causing his voice to crack. "My father had three strokes?"

Asabe nodded.

"When?"

"The first one happened two years ago."

"I never knew."

"He did not want you to know."

"Why would he hide that?"

Asabe's eyes steadied on her knees. In a voice Mu'min could barely hear, she said, "He did not want you to feel obliged."

"I am his son." Mu'min leaned forward in his chair. His voice was shaking now. His hands trembled. His stomach tightened sickeningly. "I had a right to know that my father was ill."

Asabe smiled that poor, gibbering fool smile again. "You are the son. And he is the father." Her smile broadened, and Mu'min sat back in the chair.

"He is my father, and I had a right to come to him, to take care of him and do what a son should. He's already robbed me of fourteen years. He had no right to rob me of this chance to be a son to him, to do my duty."

Again, in a near whisper, "He has a right to his dignity. Yes?"

"There is nothing undignified about a son coming to his father's aid."

"What would you have done had you known?"

Mu'min opened his mouth but could find no words in response. Truth be told, there were words, but none of them could answer Asabe's question to even his own satisfaction. He didn't have the power to undo a stroke let alone the thing most crucial in his relationship with his father, time. He couldn't undo the lost years, the time that would have been spent in his father's care, the care that would have indebted him to his father to such an extent that no distance would have ever kept him away.

Mu'min instantly understood. Adam had been afraid to ask him to come because he didn't feel he had the right to ask. Adam had felt he didn't deserve to call on his son. Mu'min marveled that even after the last seven years, his father begging forgiveness and he promising to accept, this issue remained so central, so essential to their relationship.

"I would have come. I would not have denied him."

At first, Asabe said nothing. She stroked her belly, smiling as if in silent reverie. When she spoke next, her voice had changed, brisk and matter-of-fact. "Your father, Adam, cannot move at all on his left side and only a little on the right. He cannot walk or feed himself. He does not look like the Adam you recall, strong and heavy. He is much like a child now." She chuckled quietly.

"You find this funny?"

"You're father's condition? No, no. I hate his condition because it pains him so much. For his sake, not mine, you see. I laugh because it is all I can do in this situation. It is at times like this when you know that Allah tells us the truth always." Asabe's eyes were glassy and distant. "We come into this world helpless; and we grow so strong and independent that we sometimes forget that we are nothing, soft flesh, thin skin, weak hearts. All we are is by the will of Allah, and yet we forget until the day when—"

"When can I see my father?"

Asabe refocused on Mu'min. "Now. Let us go."

Mu'min followed Asabe to the masala, the room they once used to offer prayers. The room had been converted into a bedroom for Adam, with a hospital bed positioned in the center and two deep-cushioned armchairs on either side. Mu'min's four sisters—Lailah, Hadizah, Safiyyah, and Saba—were all piled onto the bed with Adam. Sauda sat in the armchair to the left of Adam's bed, reciting in a low voice from the Qur'an. When she saw Mu'min, she rose from the chair and greeted him with a broad smile. She was nothing like the woman he had first met seven years ago upon her return from Mecca. Today she was quite thin, her skin seemed brighter, and the thin wisps of hair that escaped her scarf were silvery. Younger than either himself or Asabe, Sauda seemed to have aged a lifetime in a few short years. Her eyes and the set of her face bespoke a resignation born of wisdom that was somewhat alarming. Sauda shifted her gaze to Adam, and then in a voice he could barely hear, she ordered the girls to leave the room. Sauda followed them out of the room but stopped briefly as she passed Mu'min. "I am happy that you came."

"She has been talking about you all week," said Asabe.

Mu'min did not hear her; his eyes locked on Adam. He moved toward the bed, as if beckoned by an unheard voice. Propped up, Adam was dressed in crisp white pajamas, and he smelled faintly of musk oil. His arms were positioned neatly, palms down on either side of himself. Adam's hair had been tidily trimmed, and a white cotton kufi was positioned on his head. Adam squinted as Mu'min approached. Asabe slipped past Mu'min, and removing a pair of horn-rimmed reading glasses from the nightstand, she carefully placed them onto Adam's face.

"There, now you can see your son," said Asabe. She smoothed the fabric of his sleeve and removed a piece of lint from his shoulder.

Adam's eyes widened when he saw his Mu'min. The smile that reached Adam's eyes had missed the rest of his face, which was slack and devoid of any sign of emotion. Adam's right arm twitched, the fingers of his right hand contracting slightly.

"Look at that," said Asabe, pointing at Adam's right arm. "He is so happy to see you."

At this, Adam's eyes brightened even more before redirecting to Asabe's face. Adam and Asabe stared into each other's eyes for a few seconds, some unheard conversation passing between them. Asabe nodded a couple of times. The deepest sense of awe filled Mu'min as he wondered if he and Zulaikah would ever be like that, able to silently convey meaning to each other. Mu'min already loved his wife more than he could have ever thought possible. He would readily sacrifice his life for her and their sons, but to have such understanding that words would become obsolete, this was beyond anything he could imagine.

"Adam wants me to leave," said Asabe, still locked in silent exchange with her husband. When she finally pulled her eyes away, she said, "Talk to him. That's all he wants."

Mu'min nodded.

"He'll blink once for yes, twice for no," she said this as she backed out of the room. "Call if you need something."

But Mu'min didn't answer her as Adam had begun a silent conversation with him as well. Adam's eyes brightened and dimmed, smiled, and then began to weep. Mu'min knew that these were happy tears. Mu'min knew that silent though he may be, his father's spirit resided strongly in the world of the living. At least for now.

Mu'min positioned the armchair that Sauda had been sitting in closer to the bed. He removed his shoes and blazer, folding it neatly at the end of his father's bed. Then he sat down, not once breaking eye contact with his father.

"All right, what shall we talk about first?"

Adam closed his eyes for several seconds, his lips weakly forming soundless words.

"Work, the business?"

Adam blinked twice.

"The trip? Well, it was long but—"

Adam blinked twice again.

"My family?"

Adam blinked once, tears forming again.

Mu'min stood and swiped away Adam's tears with his thumb. "You don't have to cry about it," he said, half joking. "I'll tell you anything you want to know." Mu'min settled back into the chair and began to tell his father about his family. He didn't leave out a single detail.

Made in the USA
Las Vegas, NV
25 April 2024

89088103R00213